WAITING FOR THE TIDE

The day the Jutland telegrams arrive in Portsea, the lives of three women change dramatically. Miriam Slattery believes that afternoon in 1916 will be the happiest day of her life. Instead, a terrible betrayal is waiting for her. Beattie Forrest, mother, grandmother and widow of sailors, faces tragedy again, and Lily Forrest, just twelve years old, will always believe that the telegram boy who brought news of her brother's death stole her birthday.

But all three have reserves of courage and hope, and as war gives way to peace, Miriam, Beattie and Lily go on to find the love and security each has been craving.

WAITING FOR THE TIDE

WAITING FOR THE TIDE

by

Julia Bryant

Magna Large Print Books
Long Preston, North Yorkshire,
BD23 4ND, England.

British Library Cataloguing in Publication Data.

Bryant, Julia
    Waiting for the tide.

A catalogue record of this book is
available from the British Library

ISBN   0-7505-1649-6

First published in Great Britain in 1999 by Hodder & Stoughton
A division of Hodder Headline PLC

Published in Large Print 2001 by arrangement with
Hodder & Stoughton Ltd

Magna Large Print is an imprint of Library Magna Books Ltd.

Printed and bound in Great Britain by
T.J. (International) Ltd., Cornwall, PL28 8RW

For

JOHN O'SULLIVAN

My husband and best friend

with love

ACKNOWLEDGEMENTS

My thanks are due to many people who very generously gave me their time and advice. Special thanks to my friend Becky Smith for rescuing my manuscript from the desk drawer and urging me on to completion. Thank you too, Hogsback Writers and Dunford Novelists.

To Margaret and Christopher Seal of Sealpoint Computing for their endless help and patience.

To Peter Rogers my local history guru and the staff of the Portsmouth Central Library and the City Record Office, also John Sadden.

Mr Robert Gieve was extremely helpful and put me in touch with several Gieves and Hawkes ex-employees who generously shared their memories with me.

Through the pages of the *News* in Portsmouth I was able to contact many ladies who had made sailors' collars and done outwork for the Marine Barracks, not forgetting badge maker Mrs Gay McGuigan.

Mr John Offord was a mine of information regarding The Theatre Royal.

Thanks are due to Margaret Collis of the Portsmouth Registry Office.

The Albertolli family, Cynthia Sherwood, Terry Swetnam and Mary Verrier also kindly shared their knowledge of Portsmouth with me.

Finally a big thank you to Carolyn Caughey my editor for saying YES!

Julia Bryant, February 1999

The extract from *Portsmouth and the Great War* by W.G. Gates is reprinted by courtesy of the *News*, Portsmouth.

Part One

JUTLAND, MAY 31 1916

'When the Jutland fog lifted and the smoke of the guns cleared, all that remained was a black, oily sea, its surface broken by a flotsam of dead fish, dead men and charred, empty hulks.'

'Some mothers received several telegrams at once, with sons and fathers serving and dying together on the same ship. All that remained were photographs on the mantelpiece. And memories.'

Keep the Home Fires Burning by John Sadden

Chapter One

June 5 1916

The telegram boy stole her birthday. He cycled past Lily Forrest taking all her thoughts of presents and tea-time pancakes, leaving her white-faced and shaken. She had refused to think about Jutland and her brother Andrew on the *Black Prince*. But now she could think of nothing else.

Everyone dreaded the telegram boy with his bag of yellow envelopes, Lily knew that. The path of that bicycle through the streets of Portsea was marked by tears and darkened windows. News of the 'Great Battle in the North Sea' – of the vast iron-clad ships sliding in minutes to the bottom had stunned the dockland community. From this close-knit warren of streets came the men who had manned and built those ships. In those straight-onto-pavement houses, women washed and scrubbed, sewed and swept with one ear alert to the sound of the doorbell or the rap of the knocker.

Twelve-year-old Lily searched for some prayer or spell to keep him away from 27 Lemon Street. 'Eternal Father Strong to save,' she gabbled as she turned into Queen Street. It looked a typical tea-time scene. The four o'clock bell had sounded and the dockyard maties cycled, like a

15

colony of ants, past the pubs and pie-shops; women pushed their prams full of outwork from the naval tailors, and sailors on shore leave, thirsty and lustful, cruised the pavements. She wrinkled her nose at the unmistakeable reek of wet fish, cooked meat and Brickwood's Beer.

For a few moments her breathing steadied, then the bicycle passed her again. Frantically she continued the hymn. 'Who bids the mighty ocean deep Its own appointed...' What was the next word? She couldn't remember. 'Oh hear us when we cry to Thee.' The words hurtled along in her head and the lump in her chest grew larger. She turned into Lemon Street and approached her home. Outside number twenty-three Mrs Vine was turning a rope with her daughter Mary, while the five-year-old twins took turns to skip.

'Come on Lil, give us a turn,' called Mary.

The three Vine girls sang a rhyme as Lily started to turn the rope. 'Charlie Chaplin went to France, To teach the nurses how to dance.' The Vines' dog tried to join in and everyone laughed at his antics. 'Salute to the King and bow to the Queen, And turn your back on the Kaiserine.'

Out of the corner of her eye, Lily saw the telegraph boy cycling up the street towards them, and ostrich-like she turned away. She bit her lip, drawing blood. Not just Andrew, but the twins' father Fred, serving on HMS *Fortune*, was in her mind. She shut her eyes and turned the rope faster. Faith and Mercy giggled and their dog barked.

The boy slowed his bicycle by putting out his foot and squeezing the brakes. The sight of him

16

snuffed out the street's fragile happiness. Mrs Vine gathered her children and ran into the house, slamming the door. Towser took the abandoned skipping-rope and ran down the street with it hanging from his mouth.

Gran opened the door and her smile vanished.

'Are you Mrs Beatrice Forrest?' asked the boy.

'Yes, I am,' she said. Holding out her hand for the telegram, she said to Lily, 'Fetch my readers, there's a good girl. Hurry, now.'

Lily tripped over the doorstep, her eyes dazzled by the sunshine. She hurtled down the passage to the kitchen. Let him be safe. Please let him be safe. She repeated the words like a spell.

Quickly she grabbed a cloth and took the frying-pan off the hob, then searched around for the reading-glasses. Her eyes flickered over the sewing-machine, the dresser and the mantel-piece, while her brain kept up a ceaseless petition for her brother's safety. Then she found the glasses on the table, and rushed back to Gran who snatched them from her hands.

Gran tore open the envelope, then put her arm around Lily before reading the form inside.

'I regret to inform you that HMS *Black Prince* was sunk 31st May 1916 and that the name of your grandson, Rating Andrew Forrest, does not appear on the list of survivors.'

Lily couldn't stop screaming. Gran pushed her down the passage to the kitchen and gave her face a stinging slap. Almost simultaneously she drew her into her arms. Lily clung to her. Heed-less of the pins and needles fastened to Gran's

17

apron, she pressed her face into the pillowy bosom and then the tears came.

Her brother couldn't be dead. As if in the pages of a photo album, pictures of him impressed themselves on her mind. Andrew taking her mudlarking. Hiding their clothes under the railway bridge, sliding over the harbour mud in their vests and drawers, calling out to the passengers making their way over the bridge above them to the waiting ferries and trains. 'Spare a penny, guv'nor. Let's dive in the mud for your penny, lady.'

She could see the commander with his armful of gold braid tossing that sixpence down. 'Go for it, Ginger,' he'd laughed. Afterwards sitting in the café eating bread pudding bought with their takings.

Gran's rage had been unforgettable. 'Begging in the street,' she'd stormed. 'Get up those stairs the pair of you, and don't think of sneaking down for any food. And,' she held out her hand to Andrew, 'I'll take those coppers jingling in your pocket, young man. They can go in the Poor Box.'

Andrew perched in the tree in Captain Seymour's garden, throwing apples down into Lily's outstretched apron. Andrew in the Sea Cadet band, his freckled cheeks puffed out, the sun shining on his brass bugle. Andrew leaning out of the carriage window at the station as she and Gran waved to him. Each image set up a fresh storm of weeping. When she finally turned her head away from the prickling needles, she became aware of another sound, dry racking sobs.

18

Gran's face was twisted in pain. Lily was terrified. She had never seen Gran cry. Still whimpering herself, she helped the old woman into the armchair by the range. She took Gran's hands in hers and frantically chafed some warmth into them. The figure in the chair was almost a stranger. The physical presence remained, yet the essence of Gran, her strength and humour, had evaporated, Lily's own grief was set aside in her anxiety. She would give up all her birthdays, all her books and ribbons, even her free place at the South Portsmouth Secondary School to have Gran back as she was used to seeing her, cheery and bustling. Moving surely from one task to the next. Gran was her rock. If she foundered, all was chaos. Lily paced about trying to remember what the lady in the bandaging class had said about the treatment of shock. Warmth and hot sweet tea was the thing. While the kettle was boiling, she raced up the stairs and dragged down a blanket from Gran's bed, and swathed it around her shoulders.

'Please Gran, oh Gran, please say something.' The cup of tea trembled in Lily's hands as she held it towards her grandmother's lips. 'You all right, Gran? Have some tea. Tell me you're all right.'

Slowly the colour came back into Gran's cheeks. 'My poor lad,' she sobbed, reaching into her apron pocket and drawing out her handkerchief. 'The cruelty, the waste.' A fresh storm of weeping overcame her.

Lily hovered, the tea going cold in the cup. She pulled the blanket up around Gran's shoulders and put the cup back in its saucer. If Gran didn't stop crying soon she would scream again. Panic fluttered in her throat. She clenched her teeth against the sound that was threatening to break loose. The clock chimed five and Gran seemed to gather herself.

'My stars, Lily! No tea laid and your father due at any minute.' She burst into fresh tears. 'Poor soul to come home to this.' Again she tried to rally herself. 'I'll go to the safe and get some milk and that plate of brawn I bought for your birthday tea.' She gave Lily a pale imitation smile. 'You set the table.'

Sick with relief, Lily laid the cloth on the table and set three plates. Gran came in from the yard with the milk jug and the plate of meat. 'Lily, you're going to have to get the tea yourself. I shall have to go along to the Vines'.'

'Gran? You can't, Dad'll be here in a minute.' Lily clutched at her grandmother's skirt. 'I can't tell him about Andrew. You must stay, you must.'

'My duck, it's the last thing I want to do,' Gran sighed. 'That telegram has knocked the stuffing out of me. But Lily, when I went out to the yard I could see those little girls crying. Mrs Vine's locked herself in the lavatory, and they're outside not knowing what to do.'

'But Gran. I can't.'

'Lily, you're twelve years old and I'm relying on you.' Gran set down the milk jug and plate of brawn. 'I'm afraid life doesn't always take account of birthdays,' she said as she walked towards the front door.

Lily tore the orange ribbon from her hair and

threw it into the fire. She wanted to smash things, to punish the room and make it as disordered and broken as she felt. How could it all remain unchanged? By the window sat Gran's treadle machine. Along the opposite wall the dresser displayed its usual odd assortment of souvenirs and everyday china: the whale's tooth scrimshawed with the story of Noah and the flood; an ivory fan from Spain; a blue jug from Weymouth and the willow pattern plates. Beside the table was the sixpenny piano stool, still waiting for its piano. Only the telegram sat treacherously between her birthday cards, marking the changing circumstances of the day.

Lily felt like the Princess and the Pea, minutely aware of everything. As she passed her hand over her hair, every strand ached. Her eyelashes felt sore and gritty and the ticking of the clock set up painful vibrations in her ears.

The sound of the key on its chain being pulled through the letter-box startled her. It was followed by the slamming of the door, and Dad's voice singing to her. 'Happy Birthday to you, Happy Birthday to you, Happy Birthday, dear Princess...' The kitchen door opened and Dad stood smiling at her, holding a parcel in his hand.

Lily tried to smile back at him as he put the parcel on the table and opened his arms to her. As she hugged him, drawing in the familiar scents of tobacco and engine oil, she fought for control. She wanted to open her present, to have at least a sliver of a birthday.

Dad took off his cap and ran his hand through his hair. 'Did you have any cards, Lily? Did they sing to you at school?' He laughed loudly. 'I can't believe you're twelve now, almost a young lady.'

She bent over the brown paper and string and tried to busy herself with the knots. Was it her fancy or was her father nervous?

'I see you've got a couple of cards,' he said, moving towards the mantelpiece and then moving away again. Had he noticed the telegram?

'Help me undo it, Dad.'

Again he laughed loudly as he came towards her. 'A sailor's daughter and she can't find her way around a reef-knot. I don't know.' Together they unwrapped the parcel to reveal a book and a wooden pencil case. 'Look, I've painted your initials on the lid. L.B.F. for Lily Beatrice Forrest.'

For a moment she forgot. 'Dad, it's lovely. The wood's like satin and the lid slides in so smoothly. Oh I like it.' She laughed up at him. 'And a book as well!' She turned the blue cover and read the title out loud. 'Palgrave's *Golden Treasury of Verse*. Thank you, thank you, thank you.' She hugged him without restraint.

'I think the princess should make her old Dad a cup of tea,' he said, settling himself at the table.

Lily took the teapot into the scullery and emptied the leaves down the sink. Dad seemed strange to her. He was loud and excitable, avoiding her eyes and almost gabbling. As she filled the kettle she heard him get up from the table and move towards the mantelpiece.

When she went back into the kitchen he was about to put the telegram back on the mantelpiece, unopened.

Lily couldn't bear it. They couldn't pretend it hadn't happened.

'Andrew's dead.' She put down the teapot and rushed into his arms. He stood unmoving.

Lily began to cry. 'Dad, say something. I was going to tell you. I just wanted...'

He looked at her as if he didn't know her. She tried to get him to sit down but he brushed her hand aside. 'I must go.'

'You can't, Dad, I haven't made your tea. Please, Dad. Don't go.'

He ran his hand distractedly through his hair. 'Tell Gran I'll be back later.' He picked up his cap and went towards the passage. She clung to him but he tore himself loose and almost flung her away from him. 'Later,' he said. 'Tell Gran I'll be back later.'

As the front door slammed behind him, Lily took the jug of pancake batter and poured it down the sink.

Chapter Two

Miriam Slattery crossed her fingers behind her back. 'Can I have the night off, Aunt Florrie? My friend's not well and she needs me to stay with her.'

Florrie raised an eyebrow, taking in Miriam's new sateen blouse. 'Looking like that, my girl, you'll be a real tonic,' she chuckled, her chins wobbling in amusement.

Standing behind the bar in the Captain Hardy, Miriam had the grace to blush. There was no sick friend. Tonight she was going to meet Alec. Tonight she would give him her answer.

Although she had known him for only a few months it seemed a lifetime. Alec was different from her other customers, their words stale and beer-laden as if passed on at the pub door from one mouth to another. Alec had a quiet sureness about him. From his first visit Miriam had been aware of the dark-haired bearded man at the table near the door. When he met her glance he smiled at her. The smile transformed him, softening the sharpness of his cheekbones and making the lines crinkle around his eyes.

She couldn't remember when he first began to stand at the bar and talk to her. Miriam looked forward to the quiet times, when there were few customers, and she and Alec could get to know each other. Slowly she began to trust him, to tell him about herself. How her sailor father had jumped ship in Australia and disappeared into the cane fields. How her mother had given up hope and taken to gin. How Aunt Florrie had offered her a job and a home at the Captain Hardy.

Alec listened to her with total attention. As she spoke, his dark eyes smiled into hers. She was drawn to his full soft mouth, watching how he shaped each word, how he licked the beer froth from his lips.

It was the night of Aunt Florrie's sixtieth birthday that drew them even closer together. After several port-and-lemons and some rousing choruses on the piano Auntie was decidedly the worse for wear. She sat slumped at the bottom of the stairs, her chins sunk on to her chest, snoring loudly.

Miriam had to enlist Alec's help in carrying her upstairs to her bedroom. She had had quite a tussle freeing obstreperous Auntie from her corsets, all the while wondering if Alec would still be waiting for her.

'She's going to have some headache tomorrow,' he said, smiling at Miriam as she re-entered the bar.

'And some temper,' Miriam laughed as she took his glass to refill it.

He shook his head. 'Any more drink and I shan't be responsible for my actions.'

Miriam came around from the back of the bar and stood beside him. 'Perhaps I don't want you to be responsible,' she whispered.

'Miriam,' he said, resting his hands on her shoulders, 'I'm out of the way of flirtation. I'm an old sailor, old enough to be your father.'

'Don't you find me attractive?' she asked, afraid to look at him.

Alec sighed. 'I'm too drunk to be cautious and not drunk enough to be careless.'

'You haven't answered my question,' she persisted.

'Do you want me as a friend or as a lover?'

Miriam flushed at the directness of his question. There was a moment when she could have turned away with a light remark, but the moment passed. 'I know what I want, Alec,' she said.

He moved his hands from her shoulders down to her wrists and turned them over, pressing his lips to where the pulse beat beneath the skin. He kissed her on the lips. Sipping and tentative, their kisses slowly became breathless and open-mouthed.

Miriam clung to him. As he stroked her face and neck she felt every part of her responding to him. 'Alec, Alec,' she breathed.

He drew away from her. 'Listen to me, Miriam. No, don't come any closer.'

She was confused by him. 'Alec, why have you…'

He shook his head. 'I want to make love with you.' He ran his hand distractedly through his hair. 'But in the right place, with both of us knowing what we're doing.'

'What do you mean, knowing what we're doing?'

'Miriam,' he pleaded. 'One thing leads to another. I can't paddle in the shallows all the time. I shall want to venture deeper. Do you want your aunt to find us on the bar-room floor?'

She was glad the room was dimly lit, so that Alec could not see her blushes.

He kissed her on the cheek. 'I'll see you. We'll talk about what comes next.'

Miriam was confused. She had wanted to be swept along by her passion and felt disappointed when Alec had drawn away from her. His last words about 'what comes next,' left her with some vestige of hope. She had to wait a whole week before he visited the pub again.

'I'm sorry I haven't been in,' he said, 'but I've

found a place for us to meet.'

'Where?' Miriam begged.

'My German friend, Eric Manheim, he's got a grocery shop in Myrtle Lane. He's been interned. I remembered he sent me the key. Asked me to look after the place.'

On the following Thursday afternoon they visited Myrtle Lane. The shop was dusty and smelt of bacon and mouse-droppings. Giggling like schoolchildren they crept up the staircase, their footsteps loud on the bare floorboards. Alec brought some matches and lit the candles in the glass holders on the dressing-table, then he closed the curtains. They lay together on the high brass bed whispering and kissing. Alec stroked her neck, his fingers flirting with the button on her collar. Smiling, he held her away from him. 'Yes?' he asked her.

She nodded.

He touched her breasts, circling them with his thumbs over the outside of her blouse. It was she who undid the buttons and drew down the shoulder straps of her camisole. He stroked her breasts with such tenderness she cried out to him.

'You're so beautiful,' he breathed against her neck. 'I want you, all of you.'

'I want you too,' she said, interlacing her fingers behind his head and pressing her body against him.

They began to undress. Alec held out his arms to her to help him off with his tight naval jersey and to untie the ribbons of his collar, his lanyard and silk scarf. Soon they were both naked.

Miriam lay on her back and Alec straddled her body, leaning back on his heels watching her as she looked up at him in the flickering candlelight. His body was lean and hard. She touched the black hair on his chest and followed its path as it narrowed like a crucifix down the centre of his belly and then withdrew her hand.

She was suddenly afraid. She had been so eager to follow his lead. She had thought she was ready. What if she said no? There was a word for women who led men on. Miriam began to cry.

Alec turned her face towards him. 'Here, let me hold you, Sh, sh,' he whispered. 'We've rushed our fences. That's all.'

'I'm sorry,' she gasped. 'I thought I was ready.'

'Are you afraid I'm going to hurt you?'

She burrowed her face into his neck.

Alec held her until her sobbing ceased. 'Miriam, I love you,' he said. 'I wouldn't have frightened you for the world.'

'I'm sorry,' she said again, her voice trembling.

Alec slid off the bed and with his back to her drew on his trousers. 'I'll make us a cup of tea,' he said, smiling gently. 'I even brought some biscuits.'

When Alec went downstairs, Miriam's thoughts seesawed between fear and desire. Images chased themselves through her mind. Shadowy figures of naked men seen through the curtains of her mother's room. The rhythmic creaking of the bed, the grunts and sniggers. Their leering faces and pawing attentions. They alternated with pictures of Alec smiling at her, holding her hand, kissing her face. She thought about Alec's kindness and patience. It was something she had not expected. From the talk among the women when she'd worked at the corset factory, men were impatient, thrusting creatures, flattering when drunk and sulky and brutish when denied their rights.

'Are we still friends?' he asked as he passed her a chipped cup on a biscuit-tin lid.

Miriam nodded.

'D'you remember I said it had to be something we both wanted?' Alec asked her.

'Yes,' said Miriam, 'and I did want to, Alec, truly I did.'

'I know.' He put down his cup and took hold of her hand. 'And I wanted you and still do. But,' he shook his head, 'if that were all, I could find a woman any day of the week. I want you, Miriam, not just your body. I want to be with you, to talk with you and listen and laugh and just do ordinary things together.'

'Like drinking tea?' she asked, smiling at him.

'Yes, like drinking tea,' he said, smiling back at her.

She held out her arms to him. They lay together some moments without speaking. When she thought he had drifted into sleep Alec turned and kissed her. Miriam felt her breath quicken as he stroked her neck. She pressed his hands against her breasts. One by one he kissed her ribs and then her belly. Slowly she felt her body responding to him. Every nerve-ending of her skin was alive to him and he sensed her need with infinite skill. She gasped as he unfolded her with his fingers and with languorous open-mouthed kisses he brought her to a quivering release. There was a sharp stabbing pain the first time he entered her but afterwards he was tender and solicitous.

Miriam laughed out loud with the joyful remembrance.

'My stars, gal,' exclaimed Florrie, jolting Miriam back to the present. 'You've been polishing that same tankard for the last half hour. You better go and meet your friend or you'll wear a hole in my glass-cloths.'

As she walked down Queen Street towards Myrtle Lane, Miriam caught her reflection in a shop window and smiled. A slim blonde girl in a Breton straw smiled back, her hair loose about her shoulders, just as Alec liked it.

As she passed by the naval barracks in Queen Street she noticed the Union Jack flying at half mast. It reminded her guiltily of all the talk in the pub about Jutland. I'll think about Jutland tomorrow, Miriam promised. I'll wear black and cry my eyes out. Just give me tonight with Alec.

She wondered if he was there already waiting for her. Had he gone upstairs and seen the clean sheets she'd put on the bed, the lilac blossoms in the vase on the dressing-table?

He'd be waiting for her answer. Yes, yes, yes! she almost shouted her response. Her thoughts had carried her to the corner of Myrtle Lane. Looking quickly to either side she turned into the back alley and searched in the recess for the key. Miriam laughed – he must be there ahead of her, as she'd imagined.

She pushed open the front door and walked down the passage. 'Alec, it's me,' she called. 'Where are you?'

Something wasn't right. There was a smell – what was it? Rum and sweat. Miriam was afraid. As she turned around to leave, the front door slammed. A man stood in front of it blocking her path.

Chapter Three

Beattie Forrest stood in the back yard of number 23 while Dolly Vine screamed from behind the bolted door of the lavatory.

Faith and Mercy took turns to squat behind the privet hedge and Mary jigged nervously from one foot to the other.

'Nip over the wall and use Mrs Pragnell's lavatory, Mary. Quick sharp now,' urged Beattie. 'Then come and tell me what this is all about.' Reaching into her apron pocket, Beattie found a halfpenny. 'You two girls go over to the shop and get yourselves a farthing bag of dusties.'

Mary returned and mumbled something about a telegram and 'Dad on the *Fortune*'. Poor mite, thought Beattie, her father killed and her mother gone to pieces. Thank God her brother Harry was safe in the naval hospital in Plymouth. Appendicitis, wasn't it? She couldn't remember. She took Mary's hand in hers. 'Go round to Hawke Street and get your Gran. Fetch her back

31

with you,' Beattie insisted. 'I'll talk to your Mum.'

Once the child had gone Beatrice changed tack. She banged on the lavatory door. 'Dolly! Come out of there at once.'

'Oh Fred, Fred!' shrieked Dolly.

'Stop that nonsense,' Beattie roared, 'or I'll get Constable Wilkes to take the door off its hinges.'

After what seemed an interminable time, Dolly drew back the bolt. She stood pale and tearful in the doorway.

Beattie put her arm around her and helped her into the house. After settling Dolly on a chair she looked around for a handkerchief or piece of clean rag. There was nothing. The range was cold, the sink was full of dishes and on the table were three bowls of stale bread afloat in cold tea. Pulling her handkerchief from her sleeve, Beattie ran it under the tap and handed it to Dolly then took off her apron to use as a towel.

She looked at the young woman and sighed. Everything about her was drab and hopeless. Her hair was scraped off her face and tied with a bootlace. Her frock was faded and dragged across her pregnant belly and her bare feet were thrust into ill-fitting boots. She needed to be sent back to the womb and restarted!

The twins came back with their bags of sweet-jar ends and their mother burst into fresh tears. They stood close together, their eyes large with fear.

'Would you two like to go and see Lily for a little while?'

They nodded.

'Can you give her a message from me?'

They nodded.

'Who will give it?'

'Bof of us,' they said in unison.

'Tell Lily, Gran says to bring along a pot of tea and some bread and butter. Now Faith, you can say that, can't you?'

Faith nodded.

'Mercy, you're to say that Gran wants her to give you something to eat and you're to stay there 'til I come and fetch you.'

Mercy grabbed her sister and they raced out of the house.

Ignoring the weeping Dolly, Beattie raked out the range and relaid it with a few sticks of wood and knobs of coke she found in the coal-box. 'Come on Dolly, dry your eyes. You'll make yourself ill carrying on like that. Lily'll be along in a minute with a cup of tea.' Beattie drew up a chair beside her and took her in her arms. 'My dear,' she said softly, 'troubles never come singly, do they?'

Dolly lay with her head on her neighbour's shoulder. How in God's name would she survive? thought Beattie. The navy would pay some sort of pension and perhaps old Mrs Pragnell, the landlady, would knock a couple of shillings off the rent. Mary could scrub doorsteps for a few coppers and there were the farthing breakfasts for poor children at the Sally Army in Queen Street. Beattie's heart sank. She couldn't see Dolly Vine as a survivor. 'We'll get through this, Dolly,' she said, with more optimism than she felt. 'Minute by minute, we'll get there.'

'Where's Mary?' Dolly asked listlessly.

'She's gone round to Hawke Street to get your mother.'

The thought of her mother struck terror into Dolly. 'Oh Lor, she'll carry on top ropes when she sees the state of the place. Oh Lor, what'll we do?'

'The best we can in the time given to us,' said Beattie. 'I'll roll up the washing and nip it along to my place and then get started on the pots.'

There was a knock on the door and Beattie opened it to Lily carrying the tray of tea. 'There's a good girl,' said Beattie, thankfully. 'Is your Dad back yet?'

'Been and gone,' said Lily shortly.

Beattie was astonished. 'What d'you mean, gone? Has he seen the telegram?'

'He took it with him.'

Beattie shook her head. She'd sort her son out later. 'Lily you've been a jewel. Look my duck, if you could just keep the twins amused for a bit longer, I would be grateful. Dolly's Mum will be here in a minute, then I'll be back to sort things.'

Poor Lily, it had been a rotten birthday, thought Beattie. Still, the twins would keep her occupied. What her Dad was up to she couldn't imagine, but by Christ she'd have words with him when he came back.

She turned to Dolly. 'Looks straighter now,' she said encouragingly as Dolly stood dazedly at the sink, dragging a dishcloth through the water. 'Sit down and have a cuppa.'

The young woman fell on the bread and butter as if she hadn't eaten for weeks. Her hand

34

trembled as she lifted the cup and hot tea spilled down her arm.

Beattie wrung out her apron in cold water and wrapped it around Dolly's arm.

It must have hurt her. There was a pink patch where the hot liquid had touched but Dolly was intent on eating. She licked the tips of her fingers and ran them across the plate to garner the last of the crumbs. Only when it was clean did she look at her arm. But she was distracted by the sound of the key-chain being drawn through the letter-box and someone hurrying down the passage.

At the sight of Mary and her mother, Dolly burst out crying.

'Now, Dorothy,' said her mother briskly, 'gather up your things. You're coming home with me.' The little bird-like woman cast a withering look at the dishevelled kitchen. 'Mary, help your mother,' she commanded.

Giving Beattie a wintry glance, she said, 'Mrs Forrest, thank you for sending for me. I can see things have gone to rack and ruin. I'll take Dorothy and Mary back with me. Perhaps the twins could stay with you until tomorrow? I only have two bedrooms.'

'Yes, well,' Beattie hesitated. That was more than she had bargained for. She was dog-tired with problems of her own to attend to.

'Then they can stay here with Mary. She's a big girl.'

Mary stood with her arms wrapped across her thin little body, as if it would break. The very idea of leaving the ten-year-old to cope on her own was monstrous to Beattie. A child who had just lost her father and brother, it didn't bear thinking about. She put an arm around her. 'You go with your Mum and Gran, my duck. I'll take care of the little ones.' She smiled resolutely.

'That's settled then,' snapped Dolly's mother dismissively.

All the while as her family was parcelled out, Dolly sat rocking and crying. She made no attempt to dry her tears. They trickled down her face and onto her dress.

'Dorothy, pull yourself together,' nagged Mrs Scovell. 'Go and get your nightdress.'

'I'll get our stuff,' said Mary, 'if you stop shouting at our Mum.'

Ada Scovell raised her hand but Beattie forestalled her.

'I don't think hitting the child will help anyone,' she said. 'It's all been a terrible shock. They need to be taken care of, not punished.'

'I'll thank you not to interfere.'

Beattie itched to give the old tartar a good shaking. But she contented herself with drawing herself up to her full height and glaring down at her. 'Least said soonest mended,' she remarked.

'That's as may be,' bridled Mrs Scovell.

Beattie went over to Dolly and took her hand. 'I'll look after the little ones and we'll see what we can do when you get back.' Dolly nodded.

'Mary.' Beattie smiled as the young girl re-entered the room with a crumpled nightdress on her arm. 'Come and see your sisters tomorrow. Have a bit of tea with us.'

Mary gave her a beseeching look. 'Yes, Mrs

Forrest,' she said.

I should have taken her as well, Beattie thought. She'll have a thin time round at Hawke Street.

Mary went to her mother and helped her to her feet.

Beattie put her cups and plates back on the tray and nodded to Mrs Scovell, not trusting herself to speak. Thankfully she let herself back into her own home.

Lily had done marvels. Faith was dressed in one of Lily's old petticoats and Mercy was sitting on the draining-board having her feet washed.

'I gave them the rest of the rice pudding you'd left in the safe, with a bit of jam,' Lily said, lifting Mercy down on to the rug.

'Lily, you've been a wonder.' Beattie hugged her granddaughter. 'Run them up to your bed and we'll sort out anything else tomorrow.'

Beattie looked at the clock. Half-past eight. What a long weary day it had been. She ached with the effort of it all. How she longed for her husband Joseph not to be dead, but here beside her. She was overwhelmed with the waste of it all. Gradually her weeping gave way to weariness and she sank into the armchair and drifted, fully dressed, into sleep.

It must have been the cold that wakened her. She opened her eyes to see her son sitting at the table with the telegram in his hand. Her resolve to berate him for leaving Lily earlier in the evening died on her lips. He was crying.

'Hello, son,' she said.

On hearing her he knuckled the tears away and

37

said, 'Why did I sign the papers, Ma? He could have been safe here with you.' He crossed the room and knelt beside her chair.

Silently Beattie drew him into her arms. She remembered pleading with him against sending her grandson to Greenwich at eleven. What was the hurry? He could join the navy when he was eighteen as a man. But what would be the value in reminding him? 'Whys will break your heart, son,' she said. 'He was a fine lad, he wanted to go.'

She held him close for the first time since he'd been a child. Rarely did he share his feelings. She thought about his impetuous marriage at eighteen and then the mystery of his young wife's disappearance, leaving Beattie to take on two grandchildren as a widow in her forties. Not that she ever regretted it. She'd been desperate for someone to fill her life. They had turned out a real credit to her.

Young Andrew was the living image of her husband Joseph with his golden hair and eyes like cornflowers. He'd tested her to the limit with his devilry. But when he stood in uniform playing his bugle she'd have forgiven him anything. That she would never see him again didn't bear thinking about.

In contrast, Lily was dark and passionate. Never the same two days together. One minute singing and the next sulking at some imagined slight. She was a bright child, the apple of her father's eye. He had encouraged her with the reading and sums and now she'd won a place at the South Portsmouth Secondary School. The Lord knew how they would afford the uniform

38

and bus fares. In return for all his attention Lily had made a god of her father and he'd gloried in it; writing her long letters, buying her books and taking her places. There'd be fireworks if ever he took up with a woman again.

'I'm sailing tomorrow,' he said, breaking into her thoughts.

'All the more reason for you to have stayed at home with Lily,' Beatrice scolded. 'What in God's name were you thinking of, rushing out like that?'

He looked away from her and brushed his hand distractedly through his hair. 'I'll write to her and explain.'

Beattie shook her head. 'By Christ, son. It's a good thing Lily has got me to rely on. Meaning well and sorry later are poor materials to cling to.'

Chapter Four

At the sound of his laugh Miriam shuddered. It was Taffy – the leering barman from the Captain Hardy. The man Alec had thrown into the street. The man who had shouted from the gutter, 'Don't think I've finished with you, Miss Butter-wouldn't-melt. I'll have you yet.'

'Got you my pretty,' he said now, clamping his hand across her mouth.

Maddened with fear Miriam bit his hand and tried to wrench herself free of him. As they fought their way down the passage she tried to kick backwards against his shins.

Taffy laughed thickly. 'I like to fight for it,' he said, his arm tightening about her waist.

In the struggle at the foot of the stairs, Miriam banged her head on the newel post and the pain made her ears ring. Where in God's name was Alec?

As Taffy released his hand from her mouth in order to catch hold of the bannister rail, Miriam screamed, 'No, no I won't. Alec'll kill you when...'

'No good screaming, girl. Your Alec has other fish to fry.'

'Liar, fat ugly liar,' she shouted. Her hat fell to the ground and Taffy crushed it under his boot.

'Wrote you a lovely letter. Off to sea he is.' Taffy laughed. 'But don't worry, I'll give you a good seeing to.'

Miriam screamed and screamed as Taffy hefted her up the stairs. 'God, let someone hear me,' she prayed.

He kicked open the bedroom door and flung her on to the bed. 'Proper little love-nest you got here,' he sniggered.

Miriam rushed towards the window and struggled with the catch. She'd jump out whatever the consequences. Taffy cleared the room in one stride and dragged her, screaming back to the bed.

Sitting astride, he pinioned her body to the bed. Manacling both wrists together with one hand, he tore open her jacket with the other. The buttons yielded as Miriam thrashed impotently beneath him. She screamed as he tore open the blouse and clutched at her breasts.

'Ooh lovely big titties you got, girl. Taffy loves big titties.' His concentration slipped as he manoeuvred her breast into his mouth with his free hand. Miriam felt his hold on her wrists slacken.

She sank her teeth into his ear and he yelled with pain. He reared up and crashed her head against the brass bedhead. Miriam felt herself sinking into darkness, dropping away from her tormentor. Then she awoke to a tearing sound as Taffy ripped her drawers in two. Terror dried her mouth. By now he had released her hands, needing both of his to prise her legs open and gain entry to her body.

Vainly she beat with her fists against his chest.

Taffy punched her in the mouth.

There was a searing pain in the pit of her belly. A burning agony drove through her, seeming to rend her apart. Some crushing force was driving her breath from her body. On and on in a relentless rhythm pushing her head repeatedly against the brass rails of the bed.

She prayed to die.

In one last heaving thrust Taffy spent himself.

Miriam's nostrils were filled with a fetid mixture of rum and sweat. Vomit poured up into her mouth and she retched violently. It slid down her face and lay in a puddle at the base of her throat.

Taffy began to snore. Warily Miriam turned her face away. Fear pulsed through her as she pressed one hand down on the bed and pushed the leaden arm off her shoulder. It fell heavily at his side. Inch by inch she slid the top half of her body from under Taffy and towards one side of the bed. The next move was fraught with danger. She pressed her hand against his knee and with infinite care managed to lever herself from beneath him. With a grunt that nearly froze her heart Taffy slid onto his back.

Whimpering and clutching at the torn edges of her clothes Miriam crept across the room. She shuddered as her hand came in contact with the vomit clinging to her hair. Although desperate to cleanse herself, escape was paramount. Her head swam as she bent to retrieve her coat from the floor. Clutching it across her chest she felt her way across the room and out to the landing. Each creak on the stairs brought her heart into her mouth. It took two attempts to draw back the bolt on the front door.

She stepped out of the shop into the darkness of the lane with no idea of the time. Still she didn't feel free and kept casting fearful glances behind her. Keeping to the side streets she forced herself to put one foot in front of the other. Her head throbbed and she ached in every joint. Her body was loathsome to her.

A cat yowled as Miriam passed an alley and she whimpered with fright. As she drew level with the back door of the pub it flew open and Miriam fell into Florrie's arms.

'Christ, Miriam, you frightened the life out of me. I came down because I heard something.' Florrie held up the candle she was carrying and cried out, 'God in Heaven, gal, what's happened to you?'

42

Miriam shrunk away from her. 'Don't, don't,' she cried, striking out and knocking the candle to the floor.

'Jesus, gal, what's up with you? D'you want to set the place alight?' Florrie cried, stamping out the candle flame, then searching in her pocket for the matches. She guided Miriam to a chair in the kitchen and lit the gas mantle. Her eyes were large with concern as she took in Miriam's split lip and torn clothing. 'Whoever did this needs horsewhipping.'

Miriam flinched. 'I've got to get washed. No, don't touch me,' she cried, clinging to the sides of the chair.

'All right, my love. It's all right, you're safe now,' said Florrie soothingly. 'I won't let no one come near you. Here, put this coat on while I heat some water.'

Miriam perched, shivering, on the edge of the chair. The evening paper lay on the table, open at the black-bordered death pages, full of messages from grieving Jutland widows. Miriam wished that she too had slipped under the sea to nothingness; had climbed out of her soiled and violated body, and been released from its pain and treachery.

She was 'damaged goods'. Alec wouldn't want her now.

Chapter Five

Lily was glad the twins had, at last, gone home. She needed to be on her own. She was sorry that Mr Vine had died, of course she was. And having the Vine family to think about had stirred Gran out of her sadness. But sharing her bed with the twins had been a nightmare. Faith and Mercy wriggled and whispered, itched and scratched, making Lily want to scream at them. Gran had had to take the nit-comb and Sassafras oil to all three of them.

Everywhere she went their eyes were on her, their fingers into her things, their bodies cramping her space. Waking yesterday with a wet nightdress was the final straw. 'When are they going home?' she'd whispered to Gran when the twins were out in the yard.

'They'll go when their mother is fit to take them, Lily,' Gran had said sharply. She stood at the table damping down the washing and rolling the clothes up ready for ironing. 'What was it I told you Matron Sankey from the orphanage used to say to us?'

'If you don't grow up to help other people, you're not worth the upbringing,' Lily answered, sullenly.

'Enough said,' Gran snapped, handing her a duster. 'I've taken all the china off the shelves and washed and dried the lot. Now you rub up the dresser with that linseed polish. I want this room spotless before your Aunt Hester passes her gimlet eyes over everything.'

Lily knew better than to argue.

'I'm going down to Liptons for some boiled ham. When you've finished dusting you can put the china back. I shan't be long.'

Uncle George and Aunt Hester were coming to lunch tomorrow and then they were all going together to the Jutland Memorial Service in the park. A visit from her sister-in-law always put Gran in a temper.

'You'd think she was the Duchess of Devonshire instead of a stoker's daughter,' Gran would snort. 'The way she looks at everything with that vinegary expression fair raises my hackles. One of these days I'll clock her one, you see if I don't.'

But Gran in a temper was a hundred times better than Gran in tears. Lily never ever wanted to see her as she had been on the day of the telegram. Before Andrew's death Lily had poured out all her sorrows to Gran who would hold her close until her tears were spent. Now she was so frightened of seeing her grandmother give way again to grief that she had kept her own feelings hidden.

She took out the book of poems Dad had given her from under the cushion in the armchair. Inside the front cover were the words: 'To my darling Lily, wishing you a very happy twelfth birthday, ever your loving Father.'

If he was so loving she reasoned, why had he rushed out and left her? Especially as he was sailing the next day. Pride had kept her from

45

going back downstairs to see him when he returned later on her birthday. In the morning he had crept into Gran's bedroom and whispered, 'Bye Lily, love,' and leaned down and kissed her face. But she had kept her eyes tightly shut and pretended to be asleep.

Trying to smother her guilty thoughts by flicking through the pages of the book, she found 'A Sea Dirge' by Shakespeare and turned the words over in her mind:

'Of his bones are coral made;
Those are pearls that were his eyes;
Nothing of him that doth fade,
But doth suffer a sea change,
Into something rich and strange.'

It was so hard to believe that Andrew was really dead; so easy to pretend that he was simply away. Lily re-read the poem. She would much rather have him home being noisy and irritating than turned into pearl and coral, however rich and strange. Quickly she flicked on through the book to Gray's 'Elegy' and stopped at one of the verses: 'Full many a flower is born to blush un-seen, And waste its sweetness on the desert air.'

Was Portsea a desert? She wondered. Surely it was up to you whether you wasted your sweet-ness, whatever that was. You had to make things happen. She had taken one step into her future last week, when she took the scholarship exam for a free place at the South Portsmouth Secondary School. Miss Lavender had said she was an intelligent girl who deserved a chance.

Gran had said they'd manage the uniform and books somehow. But Lily had felt a twinge of guilt when she saw the anxiety on her face.

Hastily she rubbed down the dresser and stood on a chair to replace Grandad's whale's tooth and all the special treasures reserved for the top shelf.

'Lily, go and get your hat. We need to put some crepe round it,' Gran called from the passage as she hung up her coat and hat.

'Why does everyone have to wear black?' Lily asked. 'When you're sad is when you need colours the most.'

'I don't know, my duck,' Beattie answered. 'It's a tradition.'

'It gives funeral people more ways of making money, I suppose,' Lily reflected, thinking about all the advertisements in the local paper for the mourning departments in the large stores.

'I know that's true, Lily,' Beatrice said as she threaded a needle with black cotton. 'But when your Grandad died, having a set of customs to go through held me together. I just put on black every day until I felt able to set it aside again.'

'But you didn't have a funeral.'

'No,' said Beatrice. 'Died of his wounds on a ship off China. No funeral, no memorial service, no nothing. Even the telegram didn't seem real. It was only when the ship came back to Portsmouth and his divisional officer gave me the Dead Man's Effects Money, and his mess-mate carried in his ditty-box that I felt it was true.'

'What's "Dead Man's Effects Money" mean?'

'An old tradition of sailors,' said Gran. 'When

47

your Grandad told me all about it I never dreamed it would ever apply to him. Seemingly, when a sailor dies on board ship, all the crew members gather before the purser and the Master-at-Arms, and his possessions are sold off. All his mess-mates bid for his knife and his uniform and such. Things are bought and thrown back and resold again. The amounts are entered in a book and the money is given to his widow or mother.'

For the first time Lily thought about Gran being left a widow. Before she and Andrew had come to live with her she had had a separate life from them with its own hopes and dreams.

'Did you want to look after us when Dad left us with you?' she asked.

Gran turned the straw boater around in her hands. 'It all happened so quickly,' she said.

'I know you didn't have any choice,' Lily said, her voice barely above a whisper. 'But...'

'Best thing that could have happened,' said Gran. 'Gave a purpose to my life. We floundered about a bit at first. Andrew missing his mother and father, and me getting into the way of babies again.' She smiled sadly. 'Now it's just you and me, my duck.'

Lily stood behind her chair and put her arm on Gran's shoulder.

'There are two decisions you've got to make, Lily. One, you can leave the flowers on your hat, if that's important to you. Two, is the service in Victoria Park. I need you there beside me. Your dad's away and we are Andrew's representatives.' Gran paused with the scissors poised over the artificial daisies.

Lily took the scissors from her hands. 'I think Andrew would want me to keep the flowers, and I'll come to the service.' She gave her Gran a hug. 'We need each other,' she said.

Chapter Six

June 11 1916

Beattie shook her head. It was no good standing in the back yard daydreaming, there was too much to do. Her sister-in-law Hester and husband George were coming to dinner before they all went, together, to the Jutland Service in the park. It was important to grieve for Andrew and for all the other lost fathers and sons in Lemon Street.

Her grandson hovered on the edge of her thoughts but still her mind recoiled. It was only a week since she and Lily had read that telegram. The hurt was still too new and raw. Soon she would let herself be overwhelmed with the pain of his loss but it couldn't be today. Lily was depending on her.

'Have you got the mint, Gran? The potatoes are boiling. I've been calling you for ages.'

Beattie jumped as her granddaughter interrupted her thoughts. 'You're a life-saver, my duck. I've been out here daydreaming.'

'Oh and Mr Pragnell's here to see you. I'm

49

going down the street to see if Uncle George is coming.'

Beattie hastily picked some sprigs of mint and followed Lily back into the kitchen. She dropped them into the saucepan and the air was filled with their fresh summer scent. Turning from the stove she smiled at her old neighbour.

'Beatrice, my dear. I'm so sorry,' he said, taking her hand in his.

It was too much. No one else called her Beatrice. No one else could fully understand her loss. Beattie managed to control herself until she heard the front door slam behind Lily, then she wept without restraint.

'My dear, dear friend,' he said, stroking her hand.

'I'm so glad you're back, Albert,' she said.

'Mother wanted to stay on at the farm with Samuel. I don't think with her weak heart she could stand to be here until after the service.' He helped her to a chair. 'But I needed to see you and know how you were faring.'

Beattie looked at Albert in his linen jacket with the rose in the buttonhole, at his panama hat with the black band. She was reminded of something Lily had said, one day, when they had been looking up the word 'wholesome' in the dictionary.

'"Conducive to health and moral well-being",' she'd read then smiled. 'I think Uncle Albert is wholesome,' she'd said.

Beattie dabbed her eyes with her apron. 'Thank you for coming,' she said.

'May I accompany you to the service this

50

afternoon?' he asked.

'Hester and George will be walking up with me, but – yes of course you can.'

'Right ho, my dear. I'll call at three o'clock. Will that suit you?'

Beattie nodded. It seemed that Albert had no sooner left than George and Hester were knocking on the door. 'George, come in and welcome,' said Beattie, accepting a whiskery kiss.

'Good morning, Beattie,' said Hester, inclining her cheek. 'How are you coping with your loss? It's a wonder you're not prostrated.'

'Prostration won't being him back, Hester.' Beattie tried not to snap but Hester's zeal for taking the heavy end of things brought out the worst in her. She took a jug of ale, fetched earlier from the pub, and handed it to George. 'You know where the glasses are. Go and help yourself. Hester, will you have some lemon barley? I made it fresh this morning.'

'George, only one glass,' Hester admonished her husband. 'We don't want you squiffy at the service this afternoon.'

'I'll have some lemon barley,' said Lily. 'I'm parched.'

'Have some ale, gal. It'll put fire in your belly,' her uncle chuckled, waving the jug at her. 'Let's you and me sit out in the yard. It's a shame to waste the sun,' he said, taking the jug with him and winking at Beattie behind his wife's back.

'The piece you put in the paper struck just the right note,' Hester said, settling herself at the kitchen table. 'Dignified, yet heartfelt. Some of the verses were embarrassing, though,' she

51

snorted. '"Do not ask us if we miss him. There is such a vacant place. Shall we e'er forget his footsteps and his dear familiar face".'

'God in Heaven,' Beattie burst out. 'If you can't give way to sentiment when you've lost a husband or a son. Striking the right note's irrelevant.'

'There's no need to be blasphemous,' sniffed Hester. 'You're obviously overwrought.' She cast a critical eye over the table. 'Perhaps I could help in some way.'

Why couldn't you have died instead of my Joseph? thought Beattie. He was such a lover of life and you suck the joy out of everything. You begrudge and carp...

'I asked if I could do something,' Hester said.

'Oh, yes.' Beattie clamped her temper. 'You can lay the table. It's just cold beef and pickles and new spuds. Lily made a junket and one of the neighbours gave us some raspberries.'

'Joseph's favourite fruit.' Hester smiled. 'I remember Mother sending him into the garden with a dish to pick some for pudding. He came back with juice all over his mouth, saying he couldn't find any.'

'You should do that more often,' Beattie chided Hester.

'Do what?' Hester asked.

'Smile of course.'

'Well, if I had anything to smile at,' whined Hester. 'There's George always down at the public house and my rheumatism...'

Beattie escaped into the yard. She was trembling with suppressed anger. 'Lily,' she called, 'help your auntie to set the table.'

'You want me to smooth her feathers,' Lily said, winking at George.

The old marine smiled fondly back at Lily as he reached into the pocket of his jacket and brought out a bag of toffees. 'That granddaughter of yours is that sharp she must be sleeping in the knife drawer,' he said, handing her the sweets. Lily kissed him on the cheek and ran laughing into the house.

George wiped the ale froth from his moustache with the back of his hand then looked up into Beattie's face. 'How are you, gal?' he asked.

Beattie saw the concern in his faded blue eyes. 'I feel angry,' she said. 'I want to rage and shout at the waste.' She stared at a drop of ale that had fallen on the old metal table. The amber liquid trembled, growing larger then shrinking through the distorting lens of her tears.

'I loved that boy, you know,' said George. 'Image of Joseph. Same devilment and laughing all the time he was. Bloody shame.'

Beattie kicked savagely at a stone on the path. 'If I could have five minutes with Admiral Jellicoe, I'd wipe the floor with him. Bloody Jonah that's what he's been to this family. He was out in China the same time as my Joseph. Why couldn't he have died instead?'

'Have you got a photo of young Andrew you could spare me?' Beattie started as George touched her arm. 'I know they must be precious to you. But if you could find one I'd treasure it.'

'Of course, I'll look one out after dinner.'

George pressed his handkerchief into her hand. 'Best foot forward, eh, gal?' he said, proffering his

53

arm, as if he were accompanying her to a ward-room dinner instead of cold meat at the kitchen table.

Beattie couldn't trust herself to speak as she gripped his arm.

'How's your garden, Auntie?' Lily was asking as they stepped back into the house.

'It's a picture, Lily. You must come up and see it for yourself,' said Hester with real warmth in her voice.

For a second Beattie could see her resemblance to Joseph, the same amazing blue eyes and full mouth. But then it was gone as Hester snatched the half-empty ale jug from George's grasp.

'I'll bring Mary Vine,' Lily said. 'She never goes anywhere and she loves flowers.'

Before Hester could protest, George said, 'Of course, gal – the more the merrier.' He and Lily chattered away during the meal and Beattie managed somehow to make the appropriate responses to Hester's mournful comments. After-wards she washed up and Lily helped George to pick a photo of Andrew out of the album.

'That's all he'll be to us now,' she said. 'A face in a photograph. We shan't never hear him laugh again or nothing.'

George put his arm around her and Lily sobbed into his shoulder.

Beattie felt panic rising in her chest. She must not give way now, she'd got the whole of the afternoon to get through. She stood twisting the tea-towel in her fingers, desperate to fling some word into the deepening pool of silence.

'I need to tidy my hair and you'll want to put

your hat on. Can we use the mirror in your bed-room?' said Hester, moving towards the stairs.

Beattie nodded and led the way. By the time she had handed Hester a hairbrush and taken her own black straw hat out of the wardrobe and skewered it on with a pearl pin she felt more in charge of herself.

Hester pulled aside the net curtain and looked down into the street. 'Looks as if the Sunday School children are going to the service. They're all forming up outside the chapel,' she said.

Beattie joined her at the window and smiled at the subdued youngsters. 'You wouldn't think they were the same nippers that plagued the life out of everyone all week, knocking on doors and running away. Look at their slicked-down hair and the girls' white dresses.'

The memory of a half-finished conversation with Hester years ago came back to her. They were out walking together and passed a chapel similar to the one in Lemon Street when Sunday School finished and the children ran by them on their way home.

'You're so innocent, at that age,' Hester had said, 'innocent and trusting. You're easy prey.'

Beattie had been startled by the fierceness of Hester's tone. 'I don't follow you,' she'd said.

'Pressed flowers from Switzerland, he said. Then he locked the door. Terrified me. Who'd take my word?' Hester was red-faced and gabbling.

'Please Hester, sit down on this bench. Tell me. I'll believe you.' But the little park had filled up with people and the conversation had never been

55

continued. Thinking about it, Beattie was ashamed of her tetchiness. Someone had broken Hester's trust and it had never been repaired.

As she turned to her sister-in-law Hester said, 'There's Lieutenant Pragnell. He's coming to your door, Beattie. Shall I let him in?' She rushed to the stairs.

'Oh Lieutenant Pragnell,' she gasped, in what Andrew used to called her 'Royal Yacht' voice. 'How naice to see yew.'

'Good afternoon, Mrs Tarrant.' Albert's voice warmed perceptibly as he noticed George behind her. 'Good to see you. How are you, old chap?'

'Not so dusty, Albert,' replied George. 'We ready for the off?'

Beattie took her time in reaching the bottom of the stairs. 'Where's Lily?' she asked.

'Right behind you, Gran. I've been in my bedroom combing my hair.' Lily looked pale and her eyes were pink-edged from crying. She had threaded fresh daisies through the band of her hat and her hair hung loose around her shoulders. There was a shy fledgling beauty hovering about her.

Beattie would like to have gathered her protectively in her arms, but this was not the moment. Quickly she ushered everyone out of the house and closed the front door.

Mary Vine, in an ill-fitting starched dress and black ribbon, waved shyly from among the Sunday School class.

'Gran, can I walk down with her?' Lily asked.

'If the superintendent says it's all right,' Beattie said.

'Come on, Duchess,' said George, grabbing his wife's arm.

Beattie allowed herself an inner gloat. Hester would have wanted to walk with Albert, 'a proper gentleman, out of the top drawer,' but George had queered her pitch. Then she felt ashamed. So much for her resolution to be kinder to Hester. It had lasted all of five minutes. She remembered another conversation when she'd asked her why she had married George, since he annoyed her so much.

'He was the only man ever to ask me,' Hester had replied.

They left the street in a neighbourly procession. Dolly Vine on her mother's arm, the twins scrubbed and silent.

Victoria Park sat between dockland Portsea and the town centre of Portsmouth. At six in the morning, dockyard maties passed through its gates on their way to work, later mothers pushed their prams and gossiped. At dusk, lovers kissed between the trees. Today it was crowded with mourners from almost every street. Soldiers in wheelchairs were placed at the ends of rows of dull-eyed women in black hats. The June sunshine glinted on the gold braid on uniforms and Sunday suits shiny with frequent pressing. Officers' wives shaded their faces with parasols and ratings' women used patched umbrellas. Beattie was glad she'd come to the service in the People's Park. Here rich and poor, prelates and prostitutes, all could come and be comforted together.

'To those who have been bereaved,' said the

57

Methodist minister, 'there is one thing I can say from the Christian faith. Your loved ones died the glorious death of heroes.'

Beattie fumed. Some bloody consolation, she thought. Our loved ones have gone, we're all here raw with grief, not knowing how to get through the next hour, let alone the next week. How did, 'the glorious death of heroes' help the woman beside her, swaying with tiredness as she nursed her baby or Dolly Vine and her little girls?

She wanted Andrew not to be dead, to be alive to all the possibilities of his young life. To be laughing and chiacking his friends, to grow and experience the warmth and excitement of a woman's body, to relish fish and chips in paper, to master the intricacies of bugle playing and to hold his child in his arms. Oh no, the glorious death of heroes was no compensation for missing out on life.

Around her between the trees and flowers were marble pillars dedicated to dead admirals and their crews. Even one with her Joseph's name on it, but she couldn't dwell on that today. Her thoughts were with the women left stranded. Their heroism was not the sudden daring act that won the medal but the daily unseen drudgery: taking in washing, sewing into the small hours for a pittance, prostitution when all else failed. Existing on tea and stale bread, sending the youngsters, late, to the market for cheap sausages and pecked fruit to keep themselves from the workhouse and their children from the orphanage. They won't be decorated with naval honours, they're the bilge-rats clinging to the wreckage that the Admiralty wants to forget.

There was a movement beside her and Lily slipped between her and Hester and took her grandmother's hand. Beattie squeezed her fingers in return. She looked down at her and Lily gave her a tremulous smile. Over the last week, her granddaughter had been like a flickering candle, one day quiet and steady and the next in floods of tears. Since she'd come downstairs this afternoon, Beattie sensed a fragile, hard-won composure in Lily. Her brother's death had been a shock to her and now she was moving towards a way of living without him. Well, she would help her all she could.

'God is our refuge and strength, a very present help in trouble. Therefore we will not fear, though the earth be removed, and though the mountains be carried into the midst of the sea.'

The sound of the words and their rhythm comforted her but their meaning eluded her. Love of God was a mystery. Her love was rooted in what she could see and touch: Lily's hand in hers, Albert's friendship, laughing and chatting with neighbours, Joseph's letters.

Slowly the service came to an end and the crowds dispersed. 'We'd better go and catch our tram,' said Hester, pecking Beattie on the cheek.

'Don't be a stranger to us, gal,' said George, pressing her hand. 'Come and see us at Eastney any time.'

Beattie smiled at George and nodded to Hester.

'I'm glad I came,' said Lily, squeezing her grandmother's hand. 'It helped to see how everyone else is sad and we all need each other.' There was a pause and then she said, 'What have we got for tea?' She blushed and put her hand to her mouth.

Beattie and Albert laughed.

'It's all right, my duck,' Beattie said, smiling at her. 'You run ahead and get the kettle on and see what you can find.' Albert took her hand and tucked it through his arm. As they passed the park-keeper's cottage with its flint walls and lace curtains, Beattie said, 'Andrew used to think this was the three bears' cottage and was always looking for Goldilocks.'

Albert smiled. They walked companionably towards Lemon Street. Ahead of them were Mrs Scovell and the Vines. Faith and Mercy skipped along with Mary behind them chewing her fingernails. As they all turned into Lemon Street they saw two ill-assorted figures perched on the Vines' windowsill. Towser was barking excitedly, jumping up and down.

The younger one was wearing the number one uniform of an Able Seaman. The older man was in a sailor's uniform with sleeves halfway up his arms.

Dolly Vine ran screaming towards them. 'Fred! Harry!'

'Dad, Dad!' shouted Mary and the twins.

Dolly was swept up into her husband's arms.

Beattie didn't know whether she was laughing or crying. She'd heard of people being mistakenly reported dead but she'd never seen the evidence at first hand before. The joy of seeing the Vine family reunited was beyond words. How Fred

60

came to be listed among the dead would be a story well worth hearing.

'Dad's blamin' well risen from the dead,' laughed Harry.

Mrs Scovell was furious. 'Trust you to come back, you wastrel,' she snapped.

Fred glared at his mother-in-law. 'Hello, poison, trust you to spoil things. You're like the bad fairy at the christening.'

'Don't you speak to me like that, Fred Vine.'

Mary and the twins were dancing around Harry, laughing and shouting.

'Mum, can't you be pleased for me?' Dolly pleaded, clutching Fred's hand as if afraid he might disappear.

Mrs Scovell shook her head. 'He's been the ruination of you, Dorothy. Left you in want while he's been swilling drink. Neglecting his children.'

Fred grabbed her by the back of the neck and turned her away from the house. 'Bugger off, you vinegary old bitch,' he roared. 'Come round here again and I'll have your drawers off and tan your scrawny backside.'

As Ada Scovell tottered away, Fred gathered his family together and swept them indoors. Dolly did not give her mother a second glance.

Lily opened the door and Beattie almost fell inside. She didn't know whether she was laughing or crying. Albert helped her into a chair and she sat with the tears rolling down her cheeks.

Chapter Seven

July 16 1916

It was almost a month since Miriam had dragged herself back from Myrtle Lane. Time enough for her bruises to fade and cuts to heal. Time enough to be back behind the bar serving up beer and backchat. Yet in her mind the shock was still fresh. Each night she woke convinced that she could smell Taffy's rum-soaked breath on her pillow. More painful than the nightmares were the dreams of Alec and the awakening desolation. If only she could shed her body like the husk of a discarded fruit. If only she could be back with Alec before... Tears leaked under the lashes and she pulled the sheet over her head.

Florrie had been a tiger in her defence. She had already sacked Taffy after Miriam's earlier complaints, now a fresh opportunity came for vengeance. A letter arrived from the army recruiting office. Florrie spoke to a friend of hers on the military tribunal and Taffy was winkled out of his lodgings and off to France. She'd been patient with Miriam's reluctance to work in the bar and set her to housework and cooking. Now Miriam knew the patience was wearing thin.

'Shift yourself, Miriam,' she said bustling into her room. 'I've parcelled up some bits and pieces for your mother. You can take them down to her.'

'I don't know,' said Miriam, doubtfully.

'What else are you going to do on a Sunday? I don't see you getting ready for church,' snapped Florrie. 'Now that reptile's been sent packing you've got to get on with your life.'

As she walked towards the tram stop in Commercial Road Miriam no longer cast admiring glances at her reflection in shop windows. She felt exposed like a snail without its shell. She felt that everyone must know of the shameful thing that had happened to her, as if she wore an indelible mark, the sight of which would make respectable people draw back from her in disgust. Clutching the parcel to her chest she walked with downcast eyes.

She had not seen her mother in over a year. Not since the row. Violet Slattery's latest conquest, 'Jumper' Cross, had begun to take an interest in Miriam, and she'd become trapped between Jumper's beer-breathed wheedling and her mother's hysterical jealousy.

Meeting Florrie at the market one Saturday she'd poured out all her troubles and her aunt had offered her a job at the Captain Hardy. It wasn't the job that appealed to Miriam – she had earned more as a machinist in the corset factory; it was the peace and privacy of a room of her own. She had delighted in its cleanliness and quiet. Over the weeks she bought little things to make it more her own: dressing-table mats that she embroidered herself, a hand mirror and hairbrush backed with sea shells, and a satin nightdress case.

Miriam fretted at her aunt's reasons for sending

her to visit her mother. Normally Florrie went herself, each week. Surely she didn't want her to go back home? The thought of sharing those two rooms with her mother and Jumper, not to mention the outside lavatory with all the residents of 60 Bevis Terrace, was unbearable. Miriam walked with dread down the back alley towards the house. She dislodged some bits of paper and cigarette packets from under the gate before pushing it open and knocking on the door.

Violet Slattery dragged a strand of hennaed hair away from her eyes and stared at Miriam without any sign of recognition. 'It's all right, Ruby – it's for me,' she called to a blowsy woman standing at the top of the stairs.

'It's me, Mum. It's Miriam.'

Her mother peered at her. As recognition slowly dawned she smiled and behind the bleached blue eyes and stained teeth was a glimmer of her past prettiness. 'Come in Babes and welcome,' she said. The air in the hallway was a frowsty mixture of stale cabbage and cheap gin. Violet slocked towards her door in an unlaced pair of men's shoes.

Jumper sat on the sofa buttoning his trousers. He was all of sixty with strands of greasy hair combed across his head. 'It's Miss Hoity-Toity,' he sneered.

'I won't stop,' said Miriam, ignoring him. 'Aunt Florrie sent me.'

'What's in the parcel, Babes?' asked her mother.

'My name's Miriam, not Babes, and it's boiled bacon and some cheese.'

64

'You always were a madam,' sighed her mother, slapping the parcel down on the table.

Jumper hovered around but Violet nudged him out the door. She handed him a jug and some coppers from a cracked cup on the mantelpiece. He slammed off swearing under his breath.

Miriam perched on a kitchen chair wondering how soon she could decently take her leave.

'How's Florrie?' asked her mother, standing at the table eating a slice of bacon out of the parcel. With a shock, Miriam noticed how her clothes hung on her and the yellowness of her skin.

'Sends her love,' Miriam mumbled. 'She's having to close the pub on Mondays 'cos she can't get the beer.'

'Like a mother to me was Florrie,' Violet said. 'Used to sleep at the bottom of her bed, I did. Florrie, I'd say, get them cheesy feet out of my face. Then she'd say, Vi, you've peed the bed again. I don't know whether I'm sleepin' down the deep end or the shallow.' Her mother laughed and for a moment something of the mother she remembered, as a little girl, showed in her eyes. Then was gone.

Miriam felt sick with disappointment. She had once loved her mother and now she didn't know what she felt. Everything in the room was as stale as her hopes. Old newspapers on the table, broken springs on the sofa and a pervasive odour of sweat and old clothes. She had to get some air. 'I won't be a minute,' she said, rushing into the yard.

Her mother eyed her knowingly when she came back and sank pale and shaking on to the chair.

'You're in trouble, aren't you?'

Miriam shook her head vehemently.

'What d'you reckon to do?'

'I'm not,' Miriam insisted, on the edge of tears.

'Say what you like, you won't get the nipper off 'is perch by talkin',' Violet sniffed. 'Go and see Ma Winters in Marsh Lane. It'll cost you but it'll be worth it to be fixed up.'

'How could you say that to me?' Miriam screamed, almost hysterical with fear. 'How could you? Is that what you want, me bleedin' to death in a back alley?' She leapt out of her chair and rushed to the door.

'Mirry, gal, don't take on so,' said her mother, reaching out to her. 'I only thought...'

'I'm leaving and I'm never coming back,' Miriam yelled, pushing her mother away. She cannoned into Jumper, knocking his jug of ale into the street.

'Clumsy cow,' he raged after her.

Miriam was too keyed-up to wait for the tram and by the time she had walked back to Queen Street the sickness had passed. But not the confirmation of her worst fears. It was three weeks since her monthly was due and now the constant nausea left her in no doubt. What was she going to do? Running away would not solve things. The source of all her secret agony and disgrace was in her growing steadily day by day – whether she wanted it or not. Aunt Florrie, she must throw herself on her mercy. Whatever happened, Aunt Florrie would think of something.

'That fresh air's done you a power of good. Put

a bit of colour in your cheeks,' said her aunt as Miriam slammed through the back door into the yard. 'How's your mother?'

'I've fallen out with her,' Miriam said, 'and I'm never going back again.'

'Never's a long time,' Florrie said, squinting into the sun.

'I'll have to tell you, sometime,' Miriam burst out. 'I'm expecting and Mum wanted me to go and have it got rid of. And, if you want me to leave, I will though I don't know where...' She burst into tears.

Florrie put down her watering-can and held Miriam firmly in her arms. 'Ssh, my pet,' she said calmly. 'Let's not rush off at half-cock. Never mind what your Mum says. What do you think? Are you sure?'

'I'm three weeks late and I feel sick all the time.'

'Well, it's early days yet,' said Florrie, 'but there's no question of you leaving here. We'll just have to make it up as we go along. We'll get you a ring from the pawnshop and find a photo of some likely lad and call you Mrs Taylor or Naylor or whatever takes your fancy.'

'Thank you, Auntie, thanks ever so.' Miriam gave her a watery smile.

'Fancy a plate of cockles?'

Miriam was surprised to find that she did. They sat in the back yard between the tubs of geraniums sipping stout and prising the cockles out of their shells.

'I wish you were my Mum,' said Miriam.

'Well I'm not,' said Florrie. 'There's things

about her you don't know.' Her aunt disappeared into the pub kitchen and came back with a yellowing photograph. It was a studio portrait of a woman with a small girl on her lap. The woman's hair was arranged in an elaborate blonde coronet. She wore a high-necked blouse with leg-of-mutton sleeves and smiled shyly at the camera. The little girl wore a starched white dress and held firmly to her mother's hand.

'She wasn't much older than you when this picture was taken,' Florrie said. 'Wanted to send it to your dad when he jumped ship in Australia. Only he never sent an address. Broke her heart he did.'

Miriam stared at the picture. Her mother had told her that her father had gone to Australia. But it had sounded like a wonderful story. 'Daddy's going to work in the cane fields and when he's saved his money, he'll send for us. We'll see kangaroos and all sorts of animals. We will Babes, I promise.'

Florrie cut into her thoughts. 'You're seventeen now, Miriam,' she said. 'Just a shade younger than your mother when she had you. How old does that make her now? Think about it.'

It was a shock. Gin and disappointment had given her mother the faded looks of a fifty-year-old. But if she had been twenty-two when Miriam was five that would mean... 'She can't be only thirty-five?'

Florrie nodded sadly. 'Just because you've had a setback, my gal – and I'm not denying as you've not been knocked sideways – you got to pick yourself up and play the hand that's been dealt

68

you. You got a pattern in your mother of what happens when you stops trying.'

'What d'you mean?' asked Miriam.

'You got to take a pride in yourself. Get back on top of things. You're a young woman with your whole life in front of you. It's up to you whether you make something of it.'

'How do I do it?' Miriam's voice was barely above a whisper.

'For a start,' said Florrie, rolling up her sleeves, 'you could do with a pastry lesson. That pie you made. The crust was like concrete. D'you want yer old Auntie to have to fork out for some of them false teeth what they're always on about?'

Miriam carried the plates and glasses into the kitchen.

Later when the pub was quiet and she was alone in bed her fears returned. She was terrified of the back-street women like Ma Winters but she longed to be rid of the unwelcome child. The thought of it growing steadily day by day in her body regardless of her wishes, made her sick with panic. During the day she was shored up by Aunt Florrie's brisk kindness but at night the terrors returned. The question she had avoided all day beat its wings in her head like an imprisoned bird. Who was the father of her baby, Alec or Taffy?

Chapter Eight

Lily re-read the uniform list for the South Portsmouth Secondary School: 2 gymslips, 3 white blouses, 1 black blazer, 1 straw hat, a lacrosse stick and so it went on. The six weeks before she could start wearing her new clothes seemed interminable. Today they were going to Handleys to get everything. Lily paced around the kitchen table waiting for Gran to get back from Goldsteins so that they could set off.

Miss Lavender had said that she was a bright, hardworking girl who deserved every chance to better herself and, in a few years, if she applied herself, she might return to Drake Street School as a teacher.

Of course the South Portsmouth would be a whole new world of Latin and Science and lacrosse sticks. A whole new set of people a world away from Lemon Street. She wondered if those girls from posh doctors' and solicitors' families would look down on her. She could just about cope with her old schoolfriends calling her a swank but if the new girls didn't like her she'd belong nowhere. It was an honour being the only girl in the school to have passed the exam but it was lonely too.

She'd had a letter from Dad saying as he would nearly burst his buttons with pride when he came home next time and saw her in her uniform. He told her that he had stopped having his rum ration which would be a saving of threepence a day which would help towards her tram fares. Dear Dad! She'd promised to write and give him every scrap of information about her first day at her new school.

Wouldn't Andrew have teased her. It was strange how he popped into her mind when she least expected it, catching her painfully un-awares. She had thought that as the weeks passed she would miss him less or that she could deceive herself into believing that he wasn't dead, just away at sea. There were stretches of time when he hardly entered her thoughts and others when she felt his presence shadowing her all day. Since that dreadful afternoon when the telegram arrived Gran had not shed another tear, at least not in front of her, but she spoke about him every day.

'We got to keep his memory in our hearts, Lily,' she said. 'That way he's never truly gone from us.'

Lily glanced at the clock. It was nearly half-past ten. Where was Gran and what was taking her so long? She put the kettle back on the range and opened the front door.

Mr Pragnell in his linen jacket and panama hat was pushing his mother in her wheel-chair towards the end of the street. As they neared the corner Gran appeared and the three of them greeted each other. Lily almost danced in impatience as they lingered, talking away as if they had all the time in the world.

She darted back into the kitchen and poured the tea. At least it could be cooling while Gran

71

gossiped. As she set the cups on their saucers the front door banged shut.

'It's hardly worth you taking your coat off, Gran. We'll be off again in a minute,' she called out.

'I've had such a nasty shock,' said Gran, sinking into the armchair. 'I'll need to gather myself awhile.'

'What's happened?' asked Lily, spooning extra sugar into Gran's cup.

'Poor Mr Goldstein's shop's been burnt to the ground, all his suits and uniforms gone up in flames.' Her grandmother stirred her tea distractedly. 'Mrs Goldstein's nearly beside herself with the worry of it all. Her husband's took bad with the shock and him with a bad heart. I shall have to whistle for my money for last week's collars and the Lord knows when they'll be able to start up again.'

'But we will still be able to get the uniform today, won't we? I mean,' Lily faltered as Gran stared at her, 'I'm sorry for Mr Goldstein but I shall be starting my new school in September and I need...'

'Uniform? What are you talking about?'

'You know, you promised today we'd go to Handleys and get my clothes.'

'Don't shout, Lily,' Gran snapped. 'Give me a moment, for pity's sake.'

'Well, could we go this afternoon, then? I'll fetch in the washing and damp it down for ironing. I'll even press it for you if we can just go and...'

'It'll be out of the question.'

'Well perhaps tomorrow, then.'

'Lily, Lily, you don't understand,' said Gran. 'The whole idea will have to be forgotten. It'll take months to get us back on an even keel. We were going to be overstretched as it was to get you to that school. Now I've lost my collar money and the rent's been put up. We'll be lucky to keep our heads above water, let alone think of luxuries like secondary schools.'

Lily stared at Gran in disbelief. 'You can't go back on your word.'

'Sit down and listen to me very carefully.'

'Only if you say I can go.'

'If you don't sit down I shall give you a good shaking, madam.' Gran glared at her.

This couldn't be happening. She had to go, she'd set her heart on it. She was bright and clever. Miss Lavender had said so.

Gran reached across the table and grabbed her arm, forcing her down into a chair.

'Your father sends me a pound a week for our food and clothing. Added to that is the navy separation allowance of six shillings. I make three dozen collars a week – that's just over a pound; then there's my widow's pension of three and sixpence. So all told we got incomings of two pounds and eleven shillings. With that we can just about manage you going to that school and a mite set aside for emergencies.'

'So that's all right then,' said Lily smiling with relief.

'Lily, Lily,' Gran sighed. 'You haven't been listening. My sewing money's gone at a stroke. The rent has gone up by half-a-crown and added

73

to that your father can't send me the money he'd hoped to for your uniform on account of having to buy himself some engine-room boots and other things.' Gran took her hands in hers. 'You know that I'd move Heaven and earth to give you your chance, but it just isn't possible.'

Lily wriggled her hands away; she couldn't just give in. 'What about asking Aunt Hester or Mr Pragnell to lend us some money?'

'Your Aunt Hester is no better placed than we are. Besides, Lily, you are not her responsibility.' Gran glared at her. 'And the very idea of going cap in hand to Mr Pragnell. His first care is his mother and some of his tenants, kept waiting for their widow's pensions and such-like.'

'I could walk to school. I could get up early and clean doorsteps. No – listen Gran,' Lily clutched at her arm. 'I needn't eat so much and I'll manage on half the uniform.'

'I know it's a bitter disappointment Lily, but you've got to face it. Going to the South Portsmouth is out of the question.'

'What about a lodger! I could share your bed like I do at Christmas.'

'And where would your father sleep when he comes home? After all the hard work he does he needs the peace and quiet of his own room. Besides, look at the fuss you make when you do have to share with me. No Lily, you've got to accept that you can't go and that's that.'

'You can't break your promise,' Lily screamed. 'I won't let you, I won't.'

'Let go of my arm, you're hurting me,' Gran cried.

'I hate you,' Lily stormed. 'You're mean and jealous! Just because you had no learning you don't want me to have it.'

With a suddenness that startled Lily, Gran leapt to her feet. She marched to the front door and held it open. 'Out of my sight until you're in a better temper. When you're ready to apologise, you can come back and not before.'

Lily stood out in the street, the sound of the front door slamming echoing in her ears. It was Saturday morning and it seemed that everyone was out there watching her. She bent her head and ran past Faith and Mercy and their hop-scotch game and into Chippy Dowell, scattering his bag of shopping all over the pavement. She couldn't stop or the tears would come. She wanted to run and run and run. A stitch in her side stopped her at Bonfire Corner and she stood kicking her feet against the dockyard wall waiting for the pain in her chest to ease.

'Hello, Lily. What's up with you?'

The voice sounded familiar. Reluctantly she looked up past the black boots and bell-bottoms into the paleface of Michael Rowan, a friend of Andrew from down the street.

'I'm on sick leave after Jutland,' he said, touching his dark glasses.

Lily nodded, not knowing what to say. Afraid to speak in case her voice shook.

'At a bit of a loose end this morning. Fancy a cup of tea at Driver's?'

Again she nodded, not really wanting tea but unable to say so.

'Mum was talking about you. Saying how

75

you're going to the South Portsmouth. Your dad must be proud of you.'

Lily took to her heels, tears rushing down her face. Heedlessly, pushing passers-by aside she ran on towards the harbour and the railway arches where she could hide herself. The shingle floor was wet and smelt powerfully of dog's pee but it couldn't be helped. It was dark and private. She'd been marched out of the house, still wearing her apron. Now she folded it up and sat on it. Clasping her arms around her knees she rocked back and forth in her distress. Once started, the tears flooded out. It wasn't fair, it wasn't fair. Miss Lavender had set her brain alight, she was burning to know everything, and now... She couldn't bear it. How could she shrink back to what she had been before? How could she get over the wanting?

Gradually she became aware of the smell of cigarette smoke. She was not alone.

'I came here when my dad died,' said Michael Rowan.

How dare he follow her? Lily wanted to give him such a mouthful.

'I didn't know how to go on living with him gone. We was always looking forward to him being with us, me and Mum and Arthur. And when he was away he wrote and told us about his ship and his mates and all what we'd do together when he got home.'

Gradually Lily stopped being angry and started listening.

'Then when I realised what a fix Mum was in, 'cos the Admiralty wouldn't give her nothing,

76

that got me going.'

'But why wouldn't they give your Mum a pension? He was lost at sea, wasn't he?'

'They said we wasn't at war so he couldn't be said to have been lost in action. Had to sell everything. My grandmother's piano, all Mum's books from her teaching days.'

'How awful.'

'Gets half-a-crown a week now from Soldiers' and Sailors' Fund and a pint of milk a day.'

'I couldn't bear losing my dad,' said Lily. 'It was bad enough losing Andrew.'

'That's what kept me afloat,' said Michael. 'When the *Invincible* went down. What it would do to Mum if I didn't come back.'

'You must have been frightened.'

'I suppose I was, but it was all happening so quickly. The noise of the guns and men shouting, it was chaos. The water was so cold and I swallowed so much of it. Someone had thrown some tightly-lashed hammocks into the sea and I managed to cling to one and use it as a lifebelt. I was being sick and shivering and my face was covered in oil. My eyes were burning. A voice yelled: "For Christ's sake swim away from the ship, she's going down." There was this horrible sucking noise and I turned away and my ship was gone. I'd lost my home and mates. I was so tired and it would have been so easy just to have let go. But I had to keep going for Mum. I could hear her talking to me. "You're the man of the house now, son. I'm relying on you."'

Lily shivered. She hoped that everything had happened too quickly for Andrew to be lonely and afraid. They sat in the darkness neither saying a word until Michael got to his feet.

'Why don't we go and have that tea,' he said. 'Sittin' here's not doing neither of us any good.'

Lily scrambled to her feet. 'I must look like the wreck of the *Hesperus*,' she said, blinking in the sun and smoothing her hair off her face with her fingers.

'I've got a comb and a handkerchief,' Michael said, drawing them out of his pocket. 'They're not toffee-nosed in Driver's and we can choose a dark corner.' While he brushed the shingle from his trousers Lily dried her face and tidied away some straggly ends of hair. They crossed the road and went into the café.

Noise, heat and a rich mixture of smells engulfed Lily as she opened the café door. Hot gravy, spicy puddings, sweat and cigarette smoke swirled around her. Lily sat in a corner away from the door while Michael got their tea. Her tears were spent; the first fierce pain of her disappointment had passed leaving her with a dull ache. She knew, in comparison to Michael's losses, her misfortune was small but still it stung. Her place at the school had been won on merit and then snatched away without any hope of restitution.

'D'you take sugar? I put some in the spoon on your saucer. Hope the tea's not slocked all over it.'

Lily smiled her thanks and Michael took off his glasses.

For the first time Lily looked at him. He was pale and sharp-featured but his eyes were a curious greeny-brown and fringed with thick sooty lashes. She didn't realise she was staring at him until he blushed and looked away.

'I never asked you what you were crying for,' he said stirring his tea. 'I was too caught up in me own troubles.'

'Gran can't afford for me to take up my scholarship. I was really horrible to her.'

'I know what that's like,' said Michael. 'I wanted to finish my Dockyard Apprenticeship. I knew Mum couldn't afford for me to stay on so I had to leave and join the navy instead. The hardest thing was pretending I didn't mind.' He smiled shyly at her. 'I didn't think I'd ever get over the disappointment but I did in the end.'

'How did you do it?'

'I don't know really,' he said. 'I found something else to turn my mind to. I learned a new trade. I'm a torpedo man,' he said proudly. 'There's a lot of maths involved, and I'm good at that and I can still read what I like in my free time. After all,' he smiled again, 'you still got the same brain, you just haven't got the money.'

'What d'you mean?'

'Well I s'pose you've got to turn it in another direction. It doesn't stop you reading and finding out things.'

'S'pose not,' said Lily, trying to sound convinced.

'Look,' said Michael standing up, 'I'd better get back and give Mum a hand. Wants me to whitewash the kitchen. D'you want to walk back with me?'

'I'll have to face Gran sometime,' said Lily

resignedly. It was strange. Michael Rowan had often been to the house and sat chatting with Andrew. Why had she never noticed before how easy it was to talk to him? He didn't swagger or show off and yet there was a determination beneath his quiet manner. In a curious way he was quite handsome if you took the time to look at him. As they turned the corner into Lemon Street and said goodbye, Lily's courage faltered.

Her fingers trembled as she turned the key in the lock. Gran was standing at the sink with her back to her as Lily opened the kitchen door.

'You're back, then,' she said without turning round.

'Yes,' said Lily.

'I'll dish up the dinner.'

Lily couldn't bear it. She wanted to run to Gran's arms and for her to say that everything was all right but she knew, for that to happen, she had first to say sorry. Lily put her hand on Gran's shoulder. 'I'm really, really sorry, Gran. Truly I am.'

Her words hovered in the silence then Gran reached up and took her hand and squeezed it. 'Least said soonest mended,' she said, turning around and hugging Lily fiercely.

Chapter Nine

Miriam began to settle into her new life. She could not say that she felt happy but with Taffy posted to France, at least she was safe. If she had no interest in her coming baby Aunt Florrie more than made up for it. She insisted on Miriam having a rest in the afternoon and drinking half a pint of milk stout every morning to put iron in her blood. The sour malty taste made Miriam's stomach heave but Auntie was adamant. She stood over her and posted a square of dried bread into her mouth after every gulp of liquid. She reminded her of a vigilant sparrow perched on the nest with a beakful of worms. Florrie had helped her to concoct a story about her hasty marriage to Private Norman Naylor of the 3rd Hampshires and an even hastier widowhood when he perished on the Somme. Miriam herself had chosen her wedding ring.

'Fourteen-carat gold that is,' said the pawnbroker. She took it reluctantly from his hand, encased in a grubby fingerless glove. 'Won't leave a black mark like the brass ones.' His eyes had flickered over Miriam's loose overcoat, making her blush.

'How much is this?' she said, picking up a tarnished frame containing a picture of a dark-haired, mustachioed young soldier.

'A tanner,' the pawnbroker said. 'That and the

81

ring half-a-crown the two.'

Later, as she sat at the kitchen table congratulating herself on having downed her morning stout without a tremor, Auntie dropped her bombshell.

'I've had enough of the pub game,' she said, pulling a crumpled envelope out of her pocket. 'I'm fed up with the argie-bargie with the brewery and having no fit men to help me. This letter from Maude's decided me. Time to sell up and ship out.'

'Who's Maude?' Miriam asked, her heart thumping in alarm.

'She and her husband used to be the licensees of a pub in Gosport. Then they moved down to Dawlish, in Devon, to run a small hotel. George died six months ago and she'd like me to be her new business partner.' Florrie's boot-brown eyes shone with excitement. 'There'd be room for you as well.'

Miriam couldn't go. Alec would never find her in Dawlish.

'What's to keep you here?' Florrie asked. 'Your mother'd be no support and this Alec of yours is a very shaky bet.'

'What choice have I got?' asked Miriam sulkily.

'A bloody sight more than your mother had when your Dad slung his hook in Australia,' Auntie snapped, her jowls trembling.

'I'm sorry,' Miriam had been quickly contrite. 'It's all been a bit of a shock.'

'So am I, duck,' said Florrie. 'Course, if you're dead set against coming there is another option.'

'Does it mean I can stay in Portsmouth?'

82

Florrie shook her head. 'It's over in Gosport. Blimey, Miriam,' she chuckled, 'it's only across the harbour, not the bleedin' North Pole.'

They both laughed and the painful knot of anxiety in Miriam's stomach eased.

'Maude's daughter, Daisy Spurgeon, has a little place over there. Her husband's away and she'd like a bit of company. Got herself a job on the trams and wants someone to lodge with her and do the cooking and such like.' Florrie laughed. 'If I know Daisy the place will have gone to pot.'

Miriam thought quickly. Gosport was only a halfpenny ferry ride away and there was still a chance of bumping into Alec. She tried to smile with some conviction. 'I might as well get settled in as soon as possible. Then you can be off to your new life.'

'That's the style,' said Florrie heartily. 'You've relieved me of a deal of anxiety.'

The style lasted as long as it took for Miriam to reach her bedroom. She flung herself on the bed and gave way to a storm of weeping. All her carefully constructed optimism collapsed. What if Daisy didn't like her? What if she became ill and Daisy turned her out into the street? Not for the first time she thought of the laudanum bottle Auntie kept in her bedroom for when her rheumatics were really bad and she needed a good night's rest. It would be so easy to finish off the bottle and drift away from everything. She lay on her back, her hands resting on her stomach, wondering if she had the courage to take that step. Would it be courage, though? What of poor Auntie finding her gone? But then she was off to

83

a new life anyway. It would make things simpler.

She lay alone in the darkness intensely aware of her body and its life continuing whether she willed it or not. Her chest rose and fell with each breath she took. As she pressed her hands against her ears she heard the strange shushing sound like the sea and then the beat of her heart. Replacing her hands on her stomach she sensed a feathery, fluttering movement too faint to be felt with her fingers. No, it was nothing – and then another flicker. Miriam could not stop a glimmer of excited curiosity. Could those tiny tentative sensations be her child quickening within her? What if it were truly Alec's child that had clung to life in spite of Taffy's brutal invasion? Didn't that persistence deserve more than to be snuffed out at the first difficulty? Miriam wept at the poor welcome she'd given her baby so far, then got shakily to her feet. She splashed her face and hands with cold water from the wash-basin. Combing her hair in the mirror she gave herself a weak smile. Perhaps this Daisy girl would be as nice as Auntie said. Perhaps everything would be all right after all.

By October a new licensee had taken over the Captain Hardy and letters had been exchanged between Daisy and Miriam. On a Sunday morning, late in the month, she and Aunt Florrie walked down to the harbour and on to the ferry pontoon.

Auntie pressed a gold bracelet into Miriam's hand. 'It belonged to your Grandma and it'd fetch a tidy sum if ever you needed it,' she said. 'And here's a fiver, put it away for emergencies.'

She gave Miriam a fierce hug. 'If it doesn't work out with Daisy, you've got my address. Remember, you've got your old Auntie behind you.'

'Thanks for everything,' Miriam said. 'I'll never forget you.'

'I should bloody well hope not,' said Auntie, her eyes bright with tears.

As the ferry loosed its moorings and ploughed out into the harbour, Miriam turned to wave at the diminishing figure on the quay. Aunt Florrie with her hectic rouged cheeks and velvet cloche became a speck in the distance. Tears blinded Miriam's eyes.

The ferry passed HMS *Victory* anchored off Gosport, still dressed overall in flags for Trafalgar Day celebrations. The sailors on the ferry raised their hats and the passengers cheered. The little boat churned to a halt at the jetty and Miriam stepped ashore. She turned for a last look across the harbour to Portsmouth. 'I'll be back,' she promised a passing seagull.

Gosport seemed to have the same flavour of a naval town as Portsmouth but on a smaller scale. She walked past the Isle of Wight Hoy, the public house that had once belonged to Daisy's parents, then along the High Street until she reached the library where she turned left according to Daisy's instructions. Yes, there was Frobisher Row, a group of tiny terraced houses. Miriam knocked on the door of number 7.

The door was bounced back on its hinges and Daisy, fat and freckled, stood there in her green tram overcoat and trousers, beaming at her. 'Come in,' she said, grabbing Miriam's bags and

85

throwing them into the tiny passage. 'I'll have to be off in a minute. I'm due at the terminus at two.'

Miriam was overwhelmed by the chaos. One armchair was full of washing and the other with books. On the table was a confusion of flower-pots, a greasy plate and a heap of flower bulbs.

Daisy laughed. 'I'm a messy mare but you'll get used to me. I'll be back about half ten. You're in the front bedroom. I've made the bed.' The door slammed shut.

Miriam found the teapot and poured herself a cup of stewed tea. Wrinkling her nose she tried to identify the mixture of smells pervading the little house: certainly burnt lard from Daisy's recent fry-up, damp earth from her re-potting and scorched cloth from some recent ironing. She wrestled with the catch on the window and managed to pull up the bottom half, drawing in some cold autumn air. Leaving the clearing up for later she clutched the rope bannister and climbed the narrow stairs to the front bedroom. Breathless from carrying her bags, she lay on the bed studying her room. There was a cheerful rag rug on the floor and an armchair in faded velvet. Opposite the brass bed was an oak chest of drawers with a candle stub in a saucer on top. Hanging above it was a picture.

Miriam found matches and lit the candle for a closer look. She stood on the chair and spat on her hankie to clean the glass. The scene that emerged was of a farmhouse kitchen at dinner-time. Gathered around the table were an old grandmother, her daughter and three children. A

86

horse poked his head above the half door and the mother leant towards him with a crust in her hand. It was called 'One of the Family'. Miriam was enchanted by the domestic details. She loved the hump-backed pastry on the meat pie, the rounded arm of the toddler leaning on the creases of the tablecloth and the little girl at the opposite end of the table with her coppery hair and blue ribbon. She lost herself in the scene, imagining family life in the security of the farmhouse until the chill of late afternoon sent her downstairs.

She closed the window and banked up the fire from the scuttle beside the hearth. After tidying the living-room she investigated the larder. There were jars of pickles and a box of vegetables with earth still clinging to their roots. Miriam smiled to herself as she set about the mammoth task of washing up. 'Messy Mare,' or not, she had taken to Daisy. By the time she returned at ten-thirty Miriam had a stew simmering on the range and a plate of bread-and-butter and a pot of tea at the ready.

'Knew we'd hit it off the minute I saw you. It's wonderful to come in to the smell of cooking. Can't stand to be on my own,' Daisy said, in her rapid-fire way of talking. She took off her cap and undid her tie. 'Henry'll be pleased to know I've got myself some company.'

Life settled into a rhythm of sorts, as Miriam fitted her days around Daisy's tram shifts. She got used to eating their cooked dinner at midday one week and six o'clock in the evening the next. Often she walked down to the terminus to snatch a few words with Daisy and to watch her turning her trolley around; climbing downstairs with the rope and swinging the great arm on the roof across from one wire to the other. When she'd waved her off on her next journey Miriam would look across the harbour at the ships in the distance at Portsmouth. She wondered if Alec was one of the doll-like sailors climbing up the sides of the great grey Dreadnoughts. In the evenings she sewed baby clothes from market remnants. She made friends with the tram girls who often called in for a cup of cocoa on their way back from their shifts.

'D'you think you could take up the hem of this skirt for me? My chap's comin' home on leave next week,' one of them asked her.

'Here, Miriam, could you let out this blouse for our Mum?' another pleaded.

'You want to charge for the sewing. They're all on good money, now,' said Daisy. 'That Violet got two pounds last week, what with her overtime and all.'

The girls were happy to pay the odd shilling and Miriam got a Post Office book and saved towards a sewing-machine.

Most nights she slept soundly but, now and then, she'd awaken sweating and terrified. The fear that she was carrying Taffy's baby was unbearable. Her survival depended on the child belonging to Alec. She nourished the belief by resting her hands on her belly and telling her baby all about him. Sometimes there would be a fluttering response beneath her fingers as if it could hear. She confided everything to her silent, listening child.

Daisy immersed herself in plans for her garden, sending tiny hand-painted diagrams to Henry with lists of flowers and vegetables. 'He's set his heart on us having a smallholding,' she said. 'It's what keeps him going.'

From the start Miriam had been truthful with Daisy and Private Naylor's photo was shut in a drawer. She told her about Alec and their hopes for the future, how there'd been some confusion and they'd lost track of each other. She couldn't bring herself to talk about the nature of the confusion. No mention of Taffy must enter her refuge with Daisy.

'Don't give up,' her friend said. 'Hope's like food. You can't live without it.'

On Christmas Day Daisy produced a crib made from a banana crate with coat-hanger rockers. 'It's very important for the baby to have its own bed so you don't lie on it in the night.'

The local doctor confirmed that her baby would be due late in February. She paid ten shillings to the midwife and was given a list of things to get for herself and the coming child. She watched her body with a mixture of dread and fascination. Her nipples changed from pink to brown and tiny silvery lines criss-crossed her belly like the rivers on a map. Once she saw a ripple of movement crossing her body as the baby turned in her womb. She was filled with wonder and impatience.

Unbidden thoughts of her mother came into her head as the birth drew near, thoughts of early childhood before her father had gone away.

There had been happy times but she had submerged them under a cloak of bitterness. Times when they had all snuggled up in bed together, on winter mornings when Daddy was home on leave. Moments in the yard with her mother teaching Miriam to skip. Poppy, the beautiful rag doll in the velvet dress that her mother had made for her fifth birthday. Yes, she admitted to herself, it hadn't all been bad, not all of it.

Early one morning she awoke to a grinding pain in her back. As she got out of bed liquid trickled down her leg onto her bare feet. Miriam was panic-stricken. Was the baby on its way? She wished she knew more about how it would arrive. If only she and her mother had been more settled instead of flitting from place to place. She might have got to know someone who was carrying and would have told her what to expect. If there had been brothers and sisters she would be more in the way of things.

The clock downstairs chimed eight. Daisy was on the early shift and wouldn't be home until after two. Why did it have to happen when she was away? Daisy always gave her such confidence.

Hastily she dressed and wrote a note to Nurse Boyden. She opened the front door and called to a man across the road. He cycled quickly away with the note, once he knew its destination.

Miriam wanted to go to the lavatory but was fearful in case the baby came and fell into the pan. She took a bucket with her and squatted on it, just in case. On the way back up the path she had a sudden pain that made her cry out. As she was dithering between staying downstairs or going to bed there was a knock at the door.

'Mrs Naylor, how are you feeling?' the midwife asked, carrying her bag into the house.

'I don't know,' said Miriam, feeling foolish. 'When I got up all this water trickled down and I've had some bad pains.'

'Well, my dear,' Nurse Boyden said, smiling at her, 'it sounds as if your baby is on its way. Now, fetch me some hot water and I'll wash my hands before I examine you.'

Miriam felt an immediate trust in the quiet, grey-haired woman.

'Take off your drawers and roll up your skirt, my dear,' she said, examining her gently. 'Ah yes, you've begun to dilate but there's a long way to go yet. First babies are in no rush to leave their snug little billets.' She took what looked like a silver trumpet out of her bag and placed the wide end on Miriam's stomach and bent her head to listen at the other. 'The little one has a steady heartbeat,' she said approvingly. 'We'll have a cup of tea and check what we need.'

'I've got a mackintosh sheet, binders for me and the baby, safetypins, and newspaper for the floor. A clean nightie for me and of course the baby clothes,' Miriam said, ticking the items off on her fingers.

'You've done well, Mrs Naylor,' said the midwife stirring her tea. 'We'll go and prepare your bed.'

As Miriam climbed the stairs another pain wrenched her belly.

91

'Good, now that was at ten-fifteen, we'll see what time the next contraction is and I'll fit another visit in between.'

Miriam sat up fearfully in bed. The mackintosh felt bulky under the sheet and she couldn't get comfortable. 'You're not going to leave me, are you?' she gasped.

'I must check a young woman round the corner. I shan't be more than half an hour. You've got heaps of time before things start in earnest. There's no need to lie in bed if you're happier walking about. Note the time of the next pain. I'll be back soon.'

Directly the midwife had left another pain flared up. Miriam looked at the clock, five past eleven. She paced the room wishing Daisy were with her. Then thirst drove her downstairs. She drank half a jug of lemon barley and had to go again to the lavatory. Uncertainty tautened her nerves. Midday came without even the slightest twinge.

Nurse Boyden returned and listened again with her silver trumpet. 'When is Mrs Spurgeon due back from the trams?' she asked.

'Not 'til after two. You won't leave me again, will you?'

'Why don't you get your dinner underway for you and your friend. It'll give you something to do. I have a new mother with twins to check on. Once I've seen to her I'll be back for the duration.'

It was half-past twelve, as Miriam spooned mashed potato on top of the mince for a cottage pie, that the pain returned. She willed herself to finish what she was doing. After peeling some carrots she sat and waited for the midwife. Just as she thought the pain had subsided it flared again making her sob with fright. By the time Nurse Boyden returned she was almost hysterical with fear.

'Every thirty minutes,' the midwife said with satisfaction. 'Pop upstairs on the bed and I'll bring us both a drink.'

Miriam dozed uneasily between the pains. Gradually the distance between them grew shorter. She felt hot and sweaty. It seemed that no sooner was she gasping after one contraction than she was caught up in the next. If only she could unbutton her body and slip out of it like a discarded dress and reclaim it once the baby was lying clean and snug in its cradle. 'Oh please make it stop,' she begged the midwife. 'I'm so frightened.'

'You're safe, Mrs Naylor, trust me. When you get the next pain, pull on the towel tied to the bottom of the bed.'

Miriam heard Daisy's key in the door.

'Ah good,' said the midwife. 'Mrs Spurgeon can sit with you a while.'

'I didn't think it would hurt so much or take so long,' she whispered when her friend trundled into the room carrying a tray with a plate of cottage pie.

Daisy laughed. 'You've only been in labour seven hours. Our Mum said she was all day with me and thirty-six hours with our Ethel. Thought you might like some dinner.'

'Well, you thought wrong,' snapped Miriam,

'and if all you can do is witter on about your bloody family you can bugger off downstairs.'

'Might as well eat it myself,' said Daisy impassively. Miriam wanted to hit her.

'Would you like some lemon barley water? It'd cool you down,' offered Daisy. 'And I'll bring some water for you to have a wash and I'll sort your hair out. That'll make you feel brighter.'

Miriam burst into tears. 'I'm sorry I was horrible to you,' she sobbed.

'You have a good blubber and I'll be back in two ticks.'

Miriam felt soothed and comforted as Daisy washed her back and brushed her hair up from her face and tied it back with a ribbon. As the afternoon became the evening the pain intensified. 'Aah! Aah!' Miriam screamed, driving her nails into Daisy's wrist.

It was almost midnight when Nurse Boyden said, 'No more pushing now. The head is coming. Steady, yes, we have your baby now. It's here, a little girl. Rest now while I cut the cord and we wait for the afterbirth to come.'

The room was filled with an urgent wailing.

'You have a Monday's child born 11.45 p.m. the fifteenth of February 1917. Six pounds two ounces, congratulations!'

Miriam lay in an exhausted fog of happiness with her baby on her breast. She was besotted. When Daisy and Nurse Boyden had gone downstairs she examined her child minutely. She had a mass of black hair and thick dark lashes. Long fingers curled around hers. Miriam smiled delightedly at the neat little ears flat against her head and her mouth already seeking sustenance. 'You are your Daddy's girl,' she laughed, seeing no trace of Taffy's squat hands and colourless lashes. But when her daughter opened her eyes they were blue. The fear returned.

'I thought she'd have brown eyes, like her father,' she said to Nurse Boyden.

The midwife smiled. 'All babies' eyes are blue to begin with.'

Daisy was thrilled. 'She's like a rosebud. I must write and tell Henry all about her.'

Miriam felt a rush of affection for her friend. They had become as close as sisters in the last few months. 'You choose her name,' she said, holding the baby out to her.

Daisy blushed. 'I think Rosemary, for remembrance,' she said, stroking the baby's cheek. 'Wherever she goes I'll remember her and love her.'

'Rosie, to begin with,' said Miriam. 'And can I have something to eat, I'm starving.'

It was a magical time as her baby grew and changed. She delighted in the intimacy of feeding her. Watching her mouth searching frantically for her breast, seeing her eyes begin to focus on her face, feeling her fingers tightening their hold on her.

Daisy was equally besotted. As the days brightened she liked to have Rosie out in the garden so that she could call to her as she set out her plants. On her days off she would walk over to Elson Village, with Rosie in the pram, to visit her mother.

The war went remorselessly on. The queues at the shops became longer and for less food. Daisy swapped some of her home-grown fruit for honey from a local beekeeper and they gorged themselves on stewed apple and blackcurrant jelly. In August the news from France was terrible; the obituary columns from Passchendaele rivalled Jutland.

Between tram shifts, Daisy worked in the garden weeding and hoeing. 'I know it's daft,' she said, 'but I feel as long as I keep the garden up to scratch, Henry will be all right and'll be back to see it.'

Another Christmas passed, with Rosie a chubby and chuckling baby. Her eyes had now turned to hazel, the exact shade of the little girl in Miriam's picture. Miriam splashed out and had a photograph taken of herself and her daughter and sent it to Aunt Florrie. A hamper arrived from Dawlish with a weighty fruitcake, a slab of Cheddar cheese, some Devon honey and two bottles of milk stout. There was a brief note commanding her to 'Get yourself down here and show me my great-niece'.

On New Year's Eve Daisy opened a bottle of parsnip wine and they raised their glasses, 'To Henry and Alec's safe return.'

'Nineteen-eighteen – you don't think we'll be making this same toast in a year's time,' said Daisy with a sigh. Her eyes filled with tears and she brushed them impatiently away. 'What frightens me is that I can hardly remember what Henry looks like.'

'Hold Rosie for a tick and I'll make us both a

cup of tea,' said Miriam. 'That parsnip wine is making you mournful.' When she came back from the kitchen her daughter and her friend were both sound asleep. Would she and Alec be together this time next year? she wondered. Would he be holding Rosie in his arms?

The war continued but the year, for Miriam, was marked by Rosie's first steps in March as she wobbled along the garden path towards her outstretched arms. In October she said her first word, 'Daisy.' Then everything changed. Miriam returned from an afternoon walk to find a soldier standing outside the house. It was Henry.

Part Two

'In a few minutes all of Portsmouth seemed to be in the streets, cheering, laughing, crying. Every voice was raised, every flag was waved and the sound of a great multitude of joyous men, women and children swept over the town; while high overhead rang out the Pompey Chimes after a silence of years.'

Portsmouth and the Great War
by W.G. Gates, the *News*

Chapter Ten

November 11 1918

A monkey, his tiny face ghostly in the swirling November fog, peered at her through the kitchen window. Lily couldn't believe it. A monkey in a nightdress waving a Union Jack. Where could he have come from? She put her hand to her head. Perhaps the flu had affected her brain – but if it had, why would she see a monkey and why the Union Jack?

She dared not hope. The papers were full of victories and surrenders. Last Friday the German High Command had been given seventy-two hours to consider the terms of the Armistice. The deadline was today, Monday the eleventh of November at eleven a.m. The clock on the mantelpiece struck twelve.

At her feet two-year-old Blyth Vine sat playing with a heap of empty cotton-reels. He gurgled delightedly at the monkey as it tapped impatiently at the window.

Pulling a blanket around her shoulders, Lily went over to the window and lifted the child into her arms. 'It's a monkey,' she said.

The two-year-old studied her face intently, his blue eyes following the movement of her lips. 'Key, key,' he offered, looking back at the monkey.

101

Gran had called him a magical child. Named after the place on the Northumbrian coast where his shipwrecked father had been rescued, Blyth seemed to have turned the Vine fortunes around. Fred had gone back to the fleet very little the worse for wear and even Mrs Vine now had a job in the dockyard painting lifebelts.

'Seems fated,' she'd said, 'me paintin' them things after my Fred'd been saved from the sea.'

Gran came up from the cellar, her face flushed with her exertions. She set down the bath of wet washing and tidied some wisps of hair under the man's cap she always wore on Mondays. 'This fog gives me the pip. We'll have to have the washing hanging about indoors like a Chinese laundry.'

'Look at the window, Gran,' said Lily.

'What's that?' she shrieked.

'It's a monkey.'

Gran shuddered. 'Merciful Heavens! Where can it have come from?'

'Why is it waving a flag? Oh Gran, d'you think the Peace has been signed?'

Tears filled her grandmother's eyes. 'Please God let it be true.'

There was a loud knocking on the door.

Lily, carrying Blyth, followed Gran along the passage. As she opened the door they heard ships' sirens from the dockyard and from the Town Hall the chiming of bells.

'The Peace, the Peace, oh Glory hallelujah.' Gran clasped her caller around the neck and kissed him soundly. Chippy Dowell, their shy, pixie-faced neighbour, blushed to the roots of his hair.

The street was alive with sounds. Doors banged; dogs barked and people spilled on to the pavement; women, their hands soapy from the week's washing stood at their doorsteps calling to each other, 'The Peace, thank God!' Grandad Onslow blew his bosun's whistle and Ma Abrahams from the corner shop handed out toffees to the passing children.

Gran waved and called to everyone. She took Blyth over to Mrs Abrahams and he dipped his hand into the sweet-jar.

Lily stood on the doorstep with Chippy who fidgeted from one foot to the other.

'Oh Chippy lad,' said Gran, re-crossing the street. 'I'd forgotten all about you. What is it you want?'

'Ma sent me to ask you have you seen her monkey?'

Gran burst out laughing, 'Since when has your mother had a monkey?'

'Mr Carlucci's been took to the workhouse,' Chippy mumbled. 'He gave him to her. She calls him Lloyd George.'

'Your mother's named her monkey after the Prime Minister?'

'Key, key,' called Blyth, wriggling out of Gran's arms.

'Come in,' said Gran, holding back the door. 'Lloyd's in the garden right as rain.'

Blyth tottered into the yard where the monkey sat shivering on the windowsill. Chippy tucked him inside his jacket and gave the paper flag to Blyth.

'We'll all have something to celebrate,' Gran

103

said, taking the rum bottle off the top of the dresser.

Lily felt weightless with relief. No more telegrams, no more black-edged pages in the paper. No more worrying about Dad. Any day now he could come whistling down the street. But not Andrew – he would never come home. No Armistice could bring him back nor hundreds of other girls' dads and brothers. She thought of Arthur Rowan at number 17 who'd been invalided out of the 3rd Hampshires. On summer mornings he'd be lifted in his chair on to the pavement and sit shivering even on the hottest day.

'Poor devil,' Gran had said. 'He's neither dead nor alive. At least our Andrew's suffering was short.'

Thank goodness Mrs Rowan still had Michael. Lily had not seen him again to speak to since Black Saturday, as she called it. Gradually she had settled back into Drake Street School and Miss Lavender had been ever so kind. She'd even lent her some of her own books. The disappointment, although not so painfully acute as it had been, was not fully healed. Whenever she saw a girl in the South Portsmouth uniform she burned with the injustice of things.

After blowing her nose she looked again at the monkey who stared back at her, his liquid eyes watchful. Lily listened to the comforting sounds of the kitchen. The clatter of cups, the gurgle of the tea being poured, and the cork being pulled from the rum bottle.

Blyth climbed on to Chippy's knees and poked

a curious finger at the monkey. In response, Lloyd began to examine the toddler's blond curls.

Lily laughed. 'He reminds me of the Nit Nurse,' she said. 'Why is he wearing a night-dress?'

'Ma hasn't got him dressed this morning,' Chippy said, matter-of-factly. 'He's got a sailor suit and lots of other stuff. She got me to knock him up a little cot to sleep in, but he spends most of his time running along the picture-rail. Only thing is he knocks things over and when he gets the squitters the smell fair turns me stomach.'

'You don't say,' said Gran. 'Best keep him where he is. I got this little boy in my charge and I don't want him bitten or squittered on.' She took hold of Blyth and carried him out to the scullery to wash his hands.

'This tea in't 'alf good, Mrs Forrest,' said Chippy, sipping appreciatively.

'Yes lad,' chuckled Gran, 'that rum has pepped it up a treat.'

It seemed strange that Gran should call Chippy a lad when he was really a man. 'Hasn't got all his buttons shanked, but there's not an ounce of harm in him,' she'd said. Mrs Dowell had been fifty when Chippy was born and her son had grown into a gentle lanky changeling.

'Here Chippy,' said Gran, pouring some rum into an empty medicine bottle, 'take this to your mother, and tell her to drink to the Peace.' She began to slice some thick doorsteps of bread. 'We'd better make haste. Mary and the twins will be here in a couple of shakes.'

Blyth banged his spoon on the table. 'Mary,

Mary,' he cried excitedly.

The key rattled through the letter-box and the Vine girls burst into the room all talking together. 'It's the Peace! Miss Lavender says we can have the afternoon off to celebrate.'

'Hello my babes, bin a good boy 'ave ya?' As Mary smiled at her brother her pinched face softened and she looked almost pretty.

'Sit up everyone and get this down you,' Gran said, serving up steaming bowls of bacon and split pea soup.

'Can we go to town this afternoon?' asked Mary between mouthfuls. 'Miss Lavender said there'll be flags on the Town Hall and everybody cheering.'

'The Armistice is a landmark in 'istry,' chimed in Faith.

'You're right,' said Gran smiling at her. 'The Armistice is a day you'll never forget. Something you'll tell your grandchildren about when you're all old ladies like me.'

'You're coming aren't you, my babes?' said Mary, sweeping Blyth up into her arms.

'Comin' too, Lil?' asked Mercy.

'It's your first day downstairs, Lily. I'm not having you with bronchitis, Peace or no Peace,' Gran said firmly. 'You girls do the dishes and I'll put the washing out now the fog's cleared.'

'P'raps we won't never 'ave to go to school again,' said Faith flinging half-dried spoons into the drawer. 'I'm goin' to be like Elsie Marly, in the story,' she said. 'Elsie Marly's grown so fine she won't get up to feed the swine but stays in bed 'till half-past nine.'

'I'm going to be Curly Locks, what eats strawberries and cream all the time,' said Mercy, handing a plate to Lily to put away.

'Off you go,' Gran said, bustling in from the garden. 'Here's sixpence. Get me a newspaper and you can keep the change.' She held up a warning finger. 'Stay together and be back by four o'clock.'

They collided with their mother who burst into the kitchen, her cap askew and her face hectic with rouge. 'I feels all lit up,' she cried, flinging her coat on to a chair. 'I wants to kick up me legs and dance and never stop.'

Blyth shrank away from his mother under the pram blankets and the twins looked to Mary for direction. Their sister looked at Gran who signalled them to continue on their way.

'Dolly, sit down. You're making me dizzy,' she said. 'Lily, go and freshen the pot. I expect Mrs Vine would like a cup.'

Lily was glad to escape. Dolly's fits of excitement made her uneasy. She was like a bolting horse. She didn't want to meet her eyes and see the wildness in them.

'Da, dee-dee, dee-dee, da-da,' Dolly cried, careering around the room, lurching into Lily as she came back into the room with a loaded tray. The sugar basin slid off the edge and emptied itself into Lily's shoes.

'Dolly, for the Lord's sake, anchor yourself,' snapped Gran, forcing her into a chair.

Lily poured the milk into the cups. As she passed one to Mrs Vine the sugar grated between her shoes and stockinged feet.

107

'Drink it yourself, Miss Brainbox,' jeered Dolly, leaping to her feet. 'I'm off up town to catch my girls.' The front door slammed behind her.

'I'm glad she's not my mother,' Lily burst out. 'Poor Mary never knows where she is and Blyth's afraid of her.'

'You get no choice with your parents,' sighed Gran as she swept up the sugar.

'She's awful.'

'What she is now, Lily, is what life has made her,' Gran said, moving over to the sewing-machine.

'What d'you mean?' asked Lily.

'When Dolly first moved here, as a young bride, she was a pretty, dreamy little thing. She had no idea how to run a home. Her mother didn't like Fred so she left Dolly to stew in her own juice, so to speak.'

Lily was astonished. 'I can't believe she was ever pretty,' she said.

'It seemed,' Gran continued, 'she was no sooner married than Fred was back at sea leaving her in the family way.'

'Poor Dolly,' said Lily, feeling the first inklings of sympathy for her friend's mother. She liked it when Gran spoke to her as if she were a grown woman. It was happening more often lately. She wondered if it was because she would soon be taking up her apprenticeship at the naval tailors.

''Course, as her neighbours, we tried to give her a hand but she got into debt with the tally-man and Fred was no help. Just gave her more children to worry over.' Gran sighed. 'She was just beginning to get on top of things when she

108

fell for Blyth and then the telegram about Fred being lost at Jutland set her off.'

'But he was safe and sound in the end,' protested Lily. 'And then everything came right for her. Blyth was such a beautiful baby. And she loves the job in the dockyard.'

'I think that telegram snapped something in Dolly. She daren't trust things any more. Got no stability. Either she's soaring high in the sky or she's stranded. Puts me in mind of a kite.'

'Perhaps there's no one holding her string to keep her safe,' said Lily, emptying the sugar from her shoe into the coal scuttle.

'You've got the beginnings of wisdom there,' said Gran, smiling at her.

'Is wisdom better than cleverness?' Lily asked as she settled herself in the armchair and pulled a blanket around her.

Gran picked up a collar before answering. 'Cleverness to my way of thinking is quickness. Some people when you put a problem before them they can see in a flash what's needed and they act accordingly. I think cleverness can be something you're born with like blue eyes or freckles.' She fed a collar under the needle and machined a seam. Breaking the thread with her teeth she continued, 'Wisdom comes over time as you watch and listen and weigh up things. It's hard won through making mistakes.'

'Do you think you ever get so wise that you see the mistake coming?'

Gran laughed. 'You're wanting the short cuts and wisdom doesn't come that way.'

With the warmth of the fire, the whirring of the

sewing-machine, and the ticking of the clock Lily felt her eyes growing heavy. She didn't know how long she had been dozing before she became aware of voices. Through half-closed eyes she made out Gran and Mr Pragnell standing in the doorway.

'You must be out of your mind, Albert, to think of such a thing,' Gran whispered fiercely.

'I think it's a practical solution to my dilemma,' said Mr Pragnell, quietly. 'Now that Mother has passed on, I need no longer concern myself with the housekeeping. Not that it wasn't a pleasure to repay her for all the care she showed me all my life.' His voice trailed away.

'Nobody could have looked after her as lovingly as you did, Albert,' said Gran, patting his arm. 'But to take in a complete stranger and possibly a child.'

'Beatrice, what choice do I have? I want to spend more time at my painting, to be able to go out for a whole day without having to rush home for anything.'

'You know you could have your meals with us. I'd be happy to clean for you. There's never been any question...'

'Beatrice, Beatrice,' said Mr Pragnell, taking her hand, 'we've been over this a thousand times. I don't want you to clean for me. I want us to be on an entirely different footing. You know very well what I proposed for us.'

Instinct warned Lily to remain apparently asleep. What were the conditions Mr Pragnell had proposed? Proposed – the word leapt about in Lily's brain like a live coal.

'But, Albert,' said Gran, still holding his hand, 'you could get one of the neighbours' girls to clean for you and give them a shilling. A stranger in your house is a big risk.'

'You don't understand. I feel that here I am, an old bachelor rattling around on his own, when there are people with nowhere to lay their heads.'

Lily peered at Gran from under her lashes.

'Oh Albert,' she said crossly, letting go of his hand. 'You're too trusting. Some of these young girls would rob you blind. What about your reputation, having a woman in your house?'

'Why are you so concerned for my reputation, Beatrice?' Uncle Albert sounded angry. 'You are being very contrary. You know who I want to share my home with. If I didn't know you better I'd feel that you were being dog-in-the-manger over this.'

Gran fidgeted with the fringe of the tablecloth. Her face was flushed and she wouldn't look at Mr Pragnell. The silence lengthened to snapping-point. Then she seemed to take a decision. 'Perhaps I'm getting mistrustful in my old age,' she said.

Albert made to protest but she overrode him. 'But it's your business, you must do as you see fit.'

'I had hoped for your blessing,' said Mr Pragnell quietly. 'However, as you say, it is my business entirely.' He walked out of the room and Gran did not accompany him.

'Thought I heard someone in here,' Lily said when the treadle was busy again.

'You were dreaming,' snapped Gran. 'I'm just going to fetch in the washing. You clear the table.

111

We'll have some toast and dripping later.'

Lily tried to puzzle out the meaning of what she had overheard. Gran had blushed when she questioned her. They couldn't be sweethearts, surely? They were old. Gran was sixty-two and Mr Pragnell was even older. It was something she'd never thought of. Spooning was for people in the pictures like Mary Pickford or young people like herself. She'd wondered when someone would want to kiss her and whether she would let them. Most of the men she would like to spoon with only existed in books, like Mr Darcy or Sidney Carton.

Her thoughts changed tack. Was Gran really jealous of Mr Pragnell's housekeeper before she'd even arrived? What would she be like? She might have a face like an old boot and run off with all his money. Or she might be so beautiful that he would cast Gran aside and marry her instead. Lily shrugged. She wouldn't make any difference to her, of that she was certain.

Chapter Eleven

It was a week since the Armistice and still Beattie couldn't believe that the war was really over. After the first flurry of excitement, when they'd danced in the street to someone's gramophone and Dolly had been brought home from the Town Hall after midnight by two American soldiers, life had settled into something that was neither peace nor war.

Lily went to school for her last few weeks of the Christmas term. Beattie churned out the collars at her old treadle and Ma Abrahams, after her rush of generosity in handing out toffees, reverted to her normal penny-pinching habits, shaving the mould off the cheese and leaning her finger on the scales. Much to Dolly Vine's fury the dockyard started laying off the women workers and she took over the care of Blyth.

Beattie missed the little lad. He was coming on a treat with her and Lily singing to him and teaching him new words each day. She had felt like giving Dolly a good shaking when she saw Blyth the previous day in wet drawers, all grubby and snotty-nosed. But having the child to look after had put her behind with her collars and tempted as she was to keep him under her care, she couldn't afford it.

There were signs that the Peace was taking hold. The blackout was over and housewives had been promised double-ration meat coupons for Christmas. Newspapers said that priority would be given to the demobilisation of married men and those running their own businesses. Beattie thought of May Gooding, the young woman who lived in the next street. When her husband was away at sea, she ran a little shop from her front room, displaying plates of tired-looking cakes, crocheted table-mats, spill-holders and such. The neighbours bought things more from pity than need. Directly her sailor husband came home on leave the merchandise disappeared, only to re-emerge when he was safely back on board. Since

113

the raid on Zeebrugge, seven months ago, in which May's husband had been killed, the little shop was rarely closed.

Beattie reached in her apron for a handkerchief. Hearing the letter-box rattle she hurried to the front door. It was a letter postmarked Scapa Flow. Quickly, she made herself a cup of tea, put on her glasses and settled in the armchair before opening the envelope.

Dear Ma,

Peace at last! You can imagine the cheer that went round the ship at the news. Last night the whole fleet was lit up in celebration. Suddenly along thirty miles of ships at anchor, lights erupted from one mast to another piercing the darkness. It was a marvellous sight. And the noise! There was the deep bellow of the Dreadnoughts' sirens, the woof, woof of the little torpedo boats and the Starshell rockets exploding overhead. Then promptly at nine o'clock we were once more plunged into darkness and silence.

I don't know what peace means to anyone else but to me it's coming home to you and Lily. Fourteen days' leave at Christmas. Sitting by the fire with a pint of ale, no throbbing engines, no saluting and jumping to it. After four years these last few days will seem endless.

Holed up in Scapa Flow these last few months the boredom and cold has been deadly. Fortunately on a big warship such as ours there is some space for entertaining ourselves. The young lads have had roller-skating races along the deck. One of the seamen broke his ankle. None other than Michael Rowan, Arthur's brother from number 17. About the last thing

114

his mother will want to hear with all her trouble. Still, he should be able to hobble on to the train and get down to Pompey for his leave.

My main anxiety is keeping free of this flu that's raging through the ships so that I'll be fit enough to tackle all those little jobs you'll have lined up for me.

Of course all our celebrations and looking forward is shadowed by thoughts of family and comrades that can't be with us. Andrew will always be a scar on my heart. By God Ma, this war has got to have been for some purpose and the Peace lead us to better times, or what was all that bloody sacrifice for? My love to my two best girls. I should be with you sometime on Christmas Eve. Have the fire banked up high and tell Lily to have the draughtsboard ready.

Your loving son Alec.

Home for Christmas. Beattie's spirits soared. She vowed to make it a Christmas they'd never forget. She could contain herself indoors no longer but must get some little thing to celebrate for when Lily came home at dinner-time.

Normally she would have rushed along to Albert with her news. He had been distraught at his mother's death a month ago. But since he and Beattie had disagreed over the question of a housekeeper there'd been a coolness between them. She knew it was her place to go and apologise. After all, how he ran his household was his own affair. Joseph would have called her a bitch. But then if Joseph were alive it wouldn't have mattered. Beattie shrugged. She'd get Albert something from the baker's too – he never could resist gingerbread men.

115

As she stood in front of the mirror tidying her hair her thoughts went back to when, as a kitchen-maid, she'd first worked for the Pragnell family. Her heart pounded at the memory.

She was fourteen and straight out of the naval orphanage, standing shivering on the doorstep with Matron's letter of recommendation. 'I've come about the position of scullery-maid,' she'd whispered to the tall woman who opened the door.

'Come inside, my dear. Dr Pragnell did say to expect you.' She smiled. 'Follow me. I have just to label some medicine and then we can have a talk.'

Mrs Pragnell turned to go up the stairs and Beattie was fascinated by her hair which hung down her back in a thick golden plait.

It was all so different from the orphanage. No smell of cabbage and soda, no feeling of being dwarfed by the high ceilings, no stale tired air. There were black-and-white tiles on the floor and a rich red stair-carpet. The curly wooden bannisters reminded Beattie of barley-sugar. She looked around the dispensary at the huge blue and green bottles with their gold titles: Arnica, Belladonna, Tincture of Benzoin. She had been famished for colour and difference.

Mrs Pragnell stood at a high desk and, dipping her pen into some blue ink, wrote on a label in a swirling script. When the writing was dry she wrapped the bottle in white paper and took a stick of sealing-wax and held it under a little burner, then fixed the ends of the paper with a round red blob.

'Now, Beatrice, tell me what you can do,' Mrs Pragnell said, turning to face her.

Encouraged by the kindness in her employer's voice Beattie detailed her rudimentary household skills.

'That all sounds satisfactory to me. Now we'll go down to the kitchen and Mrs Frostick will give us some lemonade. Then you shall go back to the orphanage and collect your things.'

Beattie was in a daze. Even Mrs Frostick's apparent coolness failed to dampen her spirits. She'd fallen on her feet at last. When she hurried back again with her things tied together in a bolster-case she met the rest of the family. Dr Pragnell was as tall as his wife with a thin tired face and black hair streaked with grey. Samuel, the big, boisterous, brown-eyed elder son, was going away to farm in Canada. Albert, the blond grey-eyed younger boy, would soon be sent to Osborne House in the Isle of Wight as a naval cadet.

Life had a quiet ordered routine. Her cooking and sewing skills flourished under Mrs Frostick's guidance. On his leaves at home, Albert helped her with her reading and showed her his stamp collection. When he went to sea as a midshipman he sent her long letters with pen-and-ink drawings of sea-birds and Chinese junks.

Beattie moved up the rungs from scullery-maid to cook. Samuel came home from Canada and married a farmer's daughter and settled in Romsey. Albert kissed Beattie and gave her a forget-me-not brooch for her eighteenth birthday.

Beattie had blushed. 'Thank you, Albert. It's

117

ever so kind of you,' she'd said, kissing him on the cheek.

Mrs Pragnell had seemed less than pleased at their friendship. Beattie sensed that she had somehow overstepped the mark. Or had the mark been invisible up until that moment?

Mrs Pragnell need not have worried. A few weeks later Beattie had met Joseph and he turned her world upside down. Albert faded obligingly into the background and poor Dr Pragnell died of typhoid six weeks after giving Beattie away at her wedding to Leading Seaman Joseph Forrest.

Beattie shook herself. She was dwelling far too much in the past lately If she intended to get to Queen Street and back by dinner-time she'd better look lively.

'No, the gingerbread men all went an hour ago,' the assistant at the bakery said. 'What with the sugar rationing still being on, we don't do that many. There's some crumpets.'

Beattie shook her head then walked out of the shop. She still had a few ounces of suet left from her meat ration, she'd make a jam roly-poly for tea and knock up a drop of custard. Albert could share it with them. As she turned back into Lemon Street Beattie decided to call on him and issue the invitation, before going indoors. She could not afford to lose a friend of such long standing over something that was clearly her fault.

As she approached his house she noticed a young woman with a pram standing outside. She was studying her reflection in the window and tidying away wisps of blonde hair under her

118

woolly hat. Hearing someone behind her she turned and smiled.

Beattie was struck by her fresh country-girl colouring. She was what Joseph would have called comely. Her face was flushed by the cold wintry air and her blue eyes had an open clarity. She held a scrap of newspaper in her hand. 'I've knocked on Lieutenant Pragnell's door, but there's no reply.'

'I expect he's out and if you've come about the housekeeping job I think he's suited,' Beattie said shortly.

'I can't be too late.' The young woman's eyes filled with tears. She wiped them away with the back of her hand. 'I don't know what I can do.' She stood staring at the front door.

A little bonneted head poked over the top of the pram apron. 'Mumma, Mumma,' cried a baby girl, her face flushed with sleep. She had toffee-coloured curls and large dark eyes. Must favour the father, Beattie thought, seeing no resemblance to her mother.

'Rosie, sweetheart, Mummy will take you in a minute.' The young woman turned to Beattie. 'Well, I'll be off now. Thank you, Mrs–?'

'It's Mrs Forrest, my neighbour,' said Albert from behind her. How long he'd been standing there, Beattie dared not think. He must have followed her up the street.

The young woman stared at her. 'Mrs Forrest,' she said, her face flushing. 'Pleased to have met you.' She held out her hand and Beattie was forced to take it.

'My name is Mrs Naylor,' she said, turning to

Albert. 'I've come about the housekeeping position.'

'Perhaps you would like to come inside,' said Albert, opening his front door as wide as it would go. 'Bring your pram. It's too cold to leave the little mite outside. Good-day to you, Mrs Forrest.' Albert closed the door behind himself and his visitors.

Beattie burned with shame. Why had she told such a barefaced lie? Well, she'd been found out. And it served her right. Joseph would have said, 'Beattie, that was unworthy of you.' But if Joseph had been there she would never have said it. What was it about the young woman, stepping into Arthur's house, that provoked such un-kindness in her?

Chapter Twelve

'Mrs Forrest, pleased to have met you.' Her heart was beating so frantically, Miriam didn't know how she managed to get the words out. Mrs Forrest, the name she'd dreamed of owning herself. The woman whose name it was stared at her through fierce dark eyes. Screwing up her courage Miriam offered her hand. The woman took it reluctantly. There was no friendly squeeze, no smile of welcome. Her hand was released almost as soon as it had been taken up.

'My name is Mrs Naylor, I've come about the housekeeping position,' she said to the elderly man who had made the introductions and to Mrs Forrest's departing back.

Could that be Alec's mother? Of course, she reasoned, there could be other Forrest families in Portsea. But her heart had turned over when she saw the woman. It was as if Alec were looking at her through those dark eyes. How had this happened? Something connected their meeting to the advertisement in the newspaper. Frantically she tried to puzzle out what it was. Alec must have said something to her that linked everything together. What was it? Nothing came.

It was unbelievable. She had been standing next to Alec's mother, little Rosie's grandmother. Who knew but Alec might not walk down the street at any minute.

'I said, come in Mrs Naylor. Mrs Naylor, are you with me?'

Miriam was jolted back to the purpose of her visit. 'Oh. I'm sorry, Mr Pragnell, I didn't hear you.' She bumped the pram over the doorstep and down the narrow passage. The heat from the kitchen range wafted over her. Gratefully she sank into the seat offered to her.

'I'll make us some tea and get a biscuit for your little one.'

Miriam closed her eyes and tried to calm herself. Breathing deeply she tried to take stock of the situation. She was without a job or a home with a child dependent on her. She'd not the luxury of time to think about Alec or his family.

'Mummy, Mummy,' Rosie grizzled.

'Here you are.' Mr Pragnell opened the biscuit barrel and was about to hand it to her daughter.

'No – please,' she protested. 'She'll have the lot all over the place. Thank you. One will be quite enough.'

'What is her name?' he asked.

'Rosie,' Miriam whispered.

As Mr Pragnell gathered the tea things together Miriam began to take in her surroundings. The room was what Florrie would have called 'shabby-genteel'. There was a faded Turkish rug by the hearth and two well-worn leather arm-chairs. A large desk stacked with ledgers filled one wall and over the mantelpiece was a portrait. A young married couple stared out at her. The husband wore a grey frock coat and his wife was decked out in a high-necked gown, complete with bustle.

'Obadiah and Augusta, my parents,' said Mr Pragnell following her gaze. 'Don't they look a steely pair?'

Miriam nodded her thanks as she took a cup of tea from her host.

He laughed, 'My father couldn't knock the skin off a rice pudding. Mother could be a tiger in his defence but she was a woman with a great heart.' Mr Pragnell sighed and turned away from her, hiding his face in his hands. There was a long silence.

Miriam, terrified he was going to cry, cast about for something to say. 'What happened to your parents?' she asked.

Mr Pragnell took a handkerchief from his pocket and blew his nose loudly, startling Rosie who held out her arms to be taken out of the pram.

'Typhoid took my father some years since, but Mother passed on last month.' He spread his hands out in a gesture of helplessness. 'Hence my advertisement for a housekeeper. I can cook and clean quite adequately but my painting takes precedence. As you can see things are not exactly ship-shape.'

Miriam smiled, wondering what Mr Pragnell would have made of Daisy's house.

'What I require is someone to do the cooking and housework in exchange for their accommodation and food.' He stirred his tea before adding, 'What are your skills, Mrs Naylor?'

'I'm a good hand with pastry and stews and roasts but nothing high faluting.'

'I think we can manage without faluting,' he laughed.

Miriam began to feel at ease.

'I'm assuming, Mrs Naylor,' he said, still smiling at her, 'that you are a widow and receive a pension.'

Miriam gulped. So what was he saying? It was all payment in kind, no cash in hand? She felt as if she were clinging to a ledge. Every time her fingers gained an inch of security something levered them off. Could she manage with just her bed and board and keep up the war widow story? Well, pretence wouldn't put any coppers in her purse, that she did know. Looking up into Mr Pragnell's face she took a decision.

'I was deserted before my child was born,' she said. 'I lived with my cousin but now her husband's come back I've got to find some work.' Miriam let out her breath in a shaky sigh. There, she had done it. She'd burnt her boats.

Mr Pragnell put down his cup and sat for some moments without speaking.

Miriam covered her anxiety by taking Rosie out of the pram and sitting her on her lap. 'I've some money in the post office towards getting a sewing-machine.' Then, trying to fill the silence, 'I might be able to get some out-work from a tailoring shop.'

'Mrs Naylor,' he said patting her hand, 'thank you for being honest with me. I shall, of course, respect your confidence. I will give you five shillings a week for yourself in addition to your board and lodging. Is a month's trial agreeable to you?'

'Yes, Mr Pragnell. I would be happy with that.' Miriam hugged her daughter tightly. A month's grace. So much could happen.

'When could you begin your employment?'

'Today,' Miriam hesitated. 'I mean I need to start today or I'll have to get somewhere to stay for the night.'

'Wee wee,' Rosie cried.

Miriam felt a warm trickle run down her leg as Rosie jumped off her lap.

She was mortified. 'I'm so sorry, Mr Pragnell,' she gasped, feeling herself with shame. 'It's been a long day and I haven't had a chance to change her. Is there somewhere I can take her?'

'Please don't distress yourself,' said Mr Pragnell kindly. 'I come from a medical family. In children nature takes precedence.' He directed her back down the passage to a small front room. 'This will be for you and Rosemary.' He looked around him, smiling to himself. 'This was my mother's bedroom. Since her death, I have, of course, replaced the mattress and bed linen.'

Miriam blushed, realising that he must have seen her look of dismay.

'I think the pram will have to live in the kitchen pro-tem. We'll find a spot for it later. Take your time, Mrs Naylor. I shall be in the living-room, when you're ready.'

Miriam sat with Rosie on a chair beside a high brass bed. She didn't quite know what to make of Lieutenant Pragnell. He didn't seem at all used to employing people. She was sure his mother would have demanded references and sent Miriam away until they were satisfactorily taken up. He looked like pictures she'd seen of Admiral Beresford, from the election posters for the Conservative Candidate on buildings she'd passed on the way to Lemon Street. But Mr Pragnell lacked the Admiral's commanding stare. There was a slight military look about him but there was a bit of the actor too. Like old Claude who used to come into the Captain Hardy. Only a bit though, because Claude didn't really know whether he was Albert or Victoria whereas Mr Pragnell liked women. Miriam was sure of it. She knew that he thought her pretty, was charmed by her rather as he might have been by a favourite granddaughter. She felt safe with him. It was another resident of Lemon Street she was not so sure of.

There was a tap on the door. 'I've brought you some hot water,' said Mr Pragnell handing her a jug.

125

'Thank you,' she said taking it from him. 'I'll be out directly.'

Miriam washed and changed Rosie who looked curiously around the room. She was nervous of letting the child toddle about as she was so quickly into everything. Hastily she dropped the wet nappy and petticoat into the bucket under the washstand and carried Rosie in her arms for a tour around her new bedroom. They looked at themselves in the oval mirror above the little fireplace. It was framed in green metal with a gilt strip inset like a ribbon that finished at the bottom edge in an ornate bow.

'Mummy, Mummy.' Rosie pointed at the glass.

Miriam smiled and pointed to her daughter. 'Rosie,' she said.

Her daughter stared at the mirror in silence. It was difficult to know whether she saw herself as a separate individual or whether the word Rosie was hard to say.

She struggled to get down. Holding tightly to her hand, Miriam let her slide down to the floor. 'Mummy and Rosie's room,' she told her daughter as they looked at their new surroundings.

The high brass bed was just big enough for both of them. She'd have to tuck her daughter in firmly and put her on the side next to the wall so that she didn't fall out. Perhaps later she could manage to get a proper cot. There was a warm rug on the floor and a well-filled coal scuttle. They would be cosy in here, Miriam thought approvingly.

Sitting Rosie on the rug with an old necklace to

play with, Miriam took off her hat and combed her hair. She let out a sigh. Had she really met Alec's mother or was the name just a coincidence? If she had, a lot could be gained by the situation. She could find out where he was and when he would be likely to return. And even if Mrs Forrest didn't take to her, she'd be certain to love Rosie. After all, she chuckled, she was her grandchild.

Feeling calm and purposeful, Miriam took hold of Rosie's hand and they walked down the passage to the kitchen.

Mr Pragnell stood up as she came into the room. 'Mrs Naylor,' he said, 'let me show you around your new quarters.'

The three of them climbed the stairs. There were two rooms; one in the front of the house had been turned into a studio. It smelt of turps and linseed oil. It seemed, to Miriam, amazingly full of light until she noticed the panes of glass set into the roof. Canvases were stacked around the walls and in the centre of the room was a rough kitchen table crowded with jars of brushes, a strange wooden plate thing spattered with different colours and silver tubes of paint. By the window was a painting on an easel of a galleon with its sails billowing against the wind. But what took Miriam's attention was a large brass telescope. The sight of it took her back to a May afternoon with Alec.

They were standing outside a shop in Castle Road filled with seafaring objects.

Alec pointed to an old telescope in the back of the window. 'There's a Bring-'em-near,' he said, 'just like Albert Pragnell's.' He'd squeezed her hand. 'He's got one just like that. I practically lived at Albert's when were in Lemon Street.'

It must have been that half-forgotten incident that prompted her to keep Daisy's newspaper and make her way to Lemon Street. If only she could have sealed that afternoon like a ship in a bottle. She and Alec hand in hand. Before Jutland or Taffy or Rosie. Miriam bit her lip. No, she wouldn't have missed her daughter, not for the world.

'Are you interested in paintings, Mrs Naylor?' said Mr Pragnell, startling her back to the present.

'I like this one,' she said, turning to a framed canvas leant against a chair.

'What is it that you like?' he asked.

'It tells a story. "The Midshipman". The young boy in the coach is on his way to join his first ship and his mother over there is trying not to cry.' Miriam pointed to the other occupant of the coach. 'Perhaps the naval officer watching them is remembering his first trip away from home.'

'Ah yes,' said Mr Pragnell. 'You may well be right.'

'Is this your work, Mr Pragnell?' she asked.

'It is my passion, certainly,' he said, then shook his head ruefully. 'But as to my livelihood?' he shrugged. 'Were I to rely on the sale of my pictures in order to eat, we'd be on short commons indeed. No. My mother bought several houses in Lemon Street when my father died, and I live on the rents and my naval pension.' He frowned with mock severity. 'I am the wicked landlord.'

128

Miriam laughed, feeling more and more at ease.

'I shall keep this room locked – then there will be no accidents,' he said, standing back to let her out into the tiny space between the rooms. 'I know with children that curiosity overcomes all else. This is my bedroom, which I like to clean myself. Now, what I shall require is that you bring me up a cup of tea and shaving-water, promptly at eight o'clock each morning and then I shall come down and breakfast with you at eight-thirty. You will have the run of the house, downstairs,' he said, 'except for when I join you for my meals.'

They went downstairs and Mr Pragnell showed Miriam the kitchen. He laughed apologetically as he pointed at the scanty goods in the larder. 'I've been existing on bread and cheese and fried bacon over the last few days. You will have to make a comprehensive list of requirements and go shopping tomorrow.' He scanned the shelves. 'There's some cold meat, bread and butter and plenty of milk. Olive, my sister-in-law, sent me down some cake so we shan't starve 'til morning.'

Miriam smiled. The kitchen looked clean enough and there were no pots or crocks in the sink but the tablecloth could have done with an iron and the floor needed sweeping. It felt unlived-in, as if meals were hastily thrown together and hurried through. There were no smells of recent stews or evidence of baking. She itched to take it under her care, to shake the mats, to polish the fender and blacklead the grate.

'Now,' said Mr Pragnell, 'I have some things to attend to in my studio. Perhaps you could unpack your things and lay out some supper for us at six o'clock. We can discuss anything else then.'

Miriam laid out their meagre clothing in the two dressing-table drawers and slid a parcel under the bed. It was the painting of 'One of the Family' that Daisy had given her. It had taken her all her courage to leave the little house in Gosport and her dear friend. She couldn't have done it without the painting that had become so much a part of her life. All her hopes and dreams of a settled future had been confided in to the family behind the glass. Even so, it would be a long time before she felt sufficiently settled to hang the painting on the wall. Going back into the kitchen she sat Rosie back in the pram with an egg-poacher and some clothes-pegs to amuse her while she washed the tea things. Later she searched out an iron and put it to heat on the range. They would have to make do with a cold supper but at least they'd set it on a freshly ironed cloth.

Someone knocked loudly on the front door. Miriam hesitated to answer it and heard footsteps coming down the stairs.

She wondered fearfully if the caller was Mrs Forrest.

Mr Pragnell was laughing and the caller sounded like a young girl.

The door from the passage opened as she said, 'Isn't that the best news you've heard in ages, Uncle Albert?'

He turned to the girl and said, 'Lily, meet my

130

new housekeeper, Mrs Naylor, and her daughter Rosie.'

Lily had long black hair caught back with a pink ribbon and large dark eyes. She reminded Miriam of a young gypsy. 'Hello little Rosie,' she said, taking the baby's hand in hers and kissing it.

Rosie chuckled.

'My name is Lily, can you say that? Lily.'

Rosie studied her intently.

'Hello Lily,' said Miriam, smiling at her.

'Pleased to meet you,' she said, shaking her firmly by the hand. 'I'm Lily Forrest, from next-door. I think you've already met my grand-mother.'

Miriam stared at her in disbelief. No, she couldn't be. He would have told her. No, she wouldn't believe it. There must have been a brother that he had not told her about. That was it.

'Of course,' laughed Mr Pragnell. 'You have met her grandmother already. Well, Lily tells me her father will be home for Christmas. Then the family will be complete.'

'What is your father's name?' asked Miriam, trying to keep her voice steady.

'Alexander Joseph. But mostly he's called Alec. Mrs Naylor, are you all right? Here, sit down a minute. Uncle Albert – fetch some water.'

Miriam clutched the glass as if it were a lifebelt.

Lily was Alec's daughter? Why had he never said? And more frightening still, what else had he failed to say?

Chapter Thirteen

Lily had taken to Miriam from the start. She was only six years older than herself and as eager as she to make friends. Miriam had eyes the colour of ultramarine, exactly the shade that Mr Pragnell mixed for his paintings of the sea. When Lily was talking to her they would widen with astonishment or crinkle at the edges with laughter and sometimes fill with tears. Of course she had called her Mrs Naylor to begin with, but soon they were on first name terms.

'If you don't call me Miriam, there'll be nobody to say it. My Auntie's down in Devon and my husband's gone,' her friend said.

Then there was Rosie her chubby, chuckling daughter. Her hazel eyes studied Lily closely when she spoke to her and each day it seemed she had mastered a new word. ''illy,' she called, holding out her arms to be picked up.

Lily would sit with Rosie on her lap while Miriam did the ironing or mending. One thing especially drew them together: their love of storytelling.

'My father could fill the room with magic,' Miriam said. 'All the Irish tales of the brave Oisin and Niave of the golden hair. She came from Tir nan-Og, the Land of Forever Young.' Miriam stood holding one of Mr Pragnell's shirts gazing into the fire.

'Beyond all dreams my land delights
Fairer than any eyes have seen,
All year round the fruits hang bright
As the flowers bloom in the meadows green.'

'Where is your father now?' asked Lily, captivated by Miriam's stories.

'Went to Australia when I was eight years old and never a word since.' Miriam paused from making bread soldiers for Rosie's tea. 'When he didn't come back everything went to pot. There was no money and we had to keep flitting before the rent was due.'

'You'll have to share my Dad,' said Lily.

Miriam brushed a strand of hair from her face. 'Tell me all about him,' she said.

'He looks a bit like me,' Lily said, 'with black hair and dark eyes, only he's tall and has a beard. He tells me stories and poems, mostly about the sea. His great-grandfather was a topman with Nelson at Trafalgar.'

'What did they do?' asked Miriam resuming her ironing.

'They worked high up on the main mast in charge of dropping or raising the sails. Isaac Forrest, he was called and he lived to be ninety-five.'

'A bit of a hero, your brother must have loved to hear about him.'

'That's what made him want to join the navy. Poor Dad, he blames himself for Andrew's death.'

'Your dad couldn't have stopped him,' said

133

Miriam, taking another shirt off the clothes-horse. 'Now the war's over he should be home to see you, don't you think?'

'Gran had a letter. He'll be home on Christmas Eve.'

'You must be excited.' Miriam's face was flushed with the ironing.

'Oh yes,' said Lily, 'and you'll get to meet him, too, and Rosie.'

It was to Miriam she went the day her monthlies started. 'Gran told me it would happen one day but–' her voice trailed off uncertainly.

'You're the lucky one, being told what to expect,' said Miriam. 'I was terrified. Thought I was bleeding to death. My mother told me off 'cos my dress was stained and said I wasn't to tell any boys.'

'Poor you,' said Lily,' I don't understand about telling boys. Why in the world would you want to tell them and why would they want to know?'

'Because once you have your monthlies your body's ready to make babies.' Miriam shrugged. 'My Mum was always one for jumping ahead meeting trouble halfway. You sit there with Rosie for five minutes. I'll go in my bedroom and find you a couple of squares and some safety-pins to tide you over 'till your Gran gets back.'

Lily sat turning the pages of the toddler's book. She felt very mixed about this new event in her life. She was impatient to grow up: to leave school, to put her hair up and be treated as a young woman instead of a schoolgirl but the changes in her body were confusing. They happened whether she wanted them to or not and they had consequences she didn't fully understand. It felt, sometimes, as if she were trapped in a stranger's skin. Her budding breasts were both an embarrassment and a source of pride but the hair under her arms and on her body was a shameful secret. She had pretty days and plain ones when her hair was lank and greasy and spots covered her chin. It was a seesaw of alternating confidence and gloom.

Miriam gave her shoulder a squeeze as she came back into the room. 'You won't be fourteen forever,' she said.

Lily smiled. Miriam always seemed to know what to say to put things right.

'You're ever so lucky to have a Gran to talk to and a Dad that loves you. Just knowing there's people that care about you doesn't half make a difference.' Her friend handed her the squares in a paper bag.

'I know Gran's good to me,' said Lily, 'but she's an old lady. Now I've got someone young to talk to.' She gave her friend a hug before picking up her school books.

'Lovely for me too,' said Miriam. 'But don't make your Gran feel left out, will you?'

Lily shook her head.

Late in the afternoon of Christmas Eve Gran gave her seven shillings to get all the food shopping at Charlotte Market. 'You know the drill, ducks. Get the fruit and veg first and leave the meat 'til last. It's four o'clock now so you can take your time. Big Arthur won't drop his prices 'til after five. I'm

135

expecting your Dad about seven.'

Lily knocked on Mr Pragnell's door and Miriam opened it. Her long blonde hair was loose about her shoulders, not tied back as normal. She seemed distracted.

'No, there's nothing I want from the market. I'll see you later, maybe Christmas Day. Don't bother knocking when you get back. I might be out.'

As she passed the Vines' house Mary opened the door. 'You goin' up the market?'

'Want to come with us?' Lily asked.

'I should take Blyth with me,' Mary said, 'but he and Ma are asleep by the fire.'

'Mary, take your chance. It's Christmas Eve. Let's go and have some fun.'

The two girls linked arms and ran laughing down the street.

'I loves the market, don't you?' said Mary. 'Specially when it's dark, like now. All the fruit shining under them lights and all the chiacking what goes on.'

Lily squeezed her friend's arm in agreement. They loaded up the bottom of their bags with potatoes, sprouts and carrots. Mary bent under the fruit stalls for pecked apples lying loose among the cabbage leaves. The next stop was the baker's stall for yesterday's bread and broken biscuits. Lily got some Paregoric cough-sweets for Gran. Mary bought a pennyworth of suet and some loose cigarettes for her mother.

'Let's get some crack-jaw. My treat,' said Lily expansively, handing a halfpenny to Mrs Jack on the sweet stall. She broke up the slab of toffee

136

with a silver hammer and the two girls resumed their shopping, cheeks bulging.

There was a crush of sailors' and soldiers' wives and daughters pressed anxiously around the meat stall. Pinched faces watched the butcher intently. After six he let the meat go at half price. 'Who'll give me three bob for this chicken? Five pound if he's an ounce.' Big Arthur's eyes raked the crowd.

'Here,' said Lily waving her purse.

'Lady with the red hat,' said the butcher, pointing to Lily's tam-o'-shanter. 'What do we say about gals in red hats?'

'All hats and no drawers,' the crowd roared.

Lily blushed as she took the blood-stained parcel. She was about to hand over her money when instinct told her to examine the goods.

'Hey, mister – this chicken's only got one leg,' she yelled.

'What d'you want me to do about it – throw in a pair of crutches?' Big Arthur shouted. 'D'you want to take him for a walk or eat him?'

'I want a proper chicken,' Lily insisted.

'Cor look at them pleadin' faces. Enough to make old Scrooge melt,' Big Arthur said, as he snatched up a two-legged fowl and a string of sausages.

The crowd roared their approval.

'Three bob to you darlin' now clear off before I end up in the poor-house.'

Lily drew fresh applause as she planted a kiss on the butcher's whiskery cheek.

'Wah!' gasped Mary. 'You aren't 'alf darin', our Lil.'

137

'Well,' said Lily, 'it's Christmas and you and me are out to enjoy ourselves.'

'Lovely hot taters, two a penny. Warm yer belly and yer 'ands both together.'

Lily and Mary stumped up a halfpenny each and handed them over to the hot potato man. The potatoes were steaming, so they tossed them from hand to hand impatient to bite into their wrinkled jackets.

The two girls stood with their bags of shopping between their feet well satisfied with their afternoon's work. At last the potatoes were cool enough to eat and they munched away in companionable silence.

'Spare a penny for a wounded soldier, girls. Buy a bit of elastic.' The man leant against the wall of the pub, his crutches beside him.

The raw misery in his face made Lily suddenly afraid. 'Sorry, mister, I'm all spent up, but you can have this half a spud.' She put it on the tray hanging from the man's neck, among the matches and bootlaces. He reminded her of the war. She gritted her teeth trying to swallow down the memories. Waving to Andrew at the station, then the telegram and seeing Gran cry. Hurriedly she and Mary picked up their bags and walked out of the market through the darkened streets.

Dad was coming home. The thought quickened her steps. Only a couple more hours and he would throw his kit-bag into the hall and the quiet pace of their lives would vanish. There would be hugs and presents; long walks by the sea; games of draughts and life would hurtle along full of jokes and stories.

She knew that Mary, too, was looking forward to seeing her Dad and brother. Harry always pitched in with the washing-up and stuck up for his sister when Dolly nagged her. Often she wished she were one of a large family but a visit to the Vines' usually cured her discontents.

At last they arrived in Lemon Street. The two girls hugged and wished each other a 'Happy Christmas' before they walked towards their own front doors.

'Hey, Lily. I thought I was the one needing glasses.'

She turned and smiled at Michael Rowan, hobbling towards her on crutches. 'Blimey! Dad wrote and said you'd hurt your ankle; didn't realise you was one of the walking wounded.'

Michael laughed. 'Ma nearly broke the other leg when I told her I'd been skating on the deck. Anyway how are you? Did you get to the school you wanted in the end?'

Lily shook her head. 'I'm starting my tailoring apprenticeship at Denby and Shanks after Christmas.'

'They're the real top-notchers when it comes to uniforms and stuff. You've done well.'

Lily glowed. She really liked Michael and was flattered that he should bother with a fourteen-year-old when he must be almost twenty.

'Tell you what. If you fancy a game of draughts over the Christmas, come and knock on our door. It would cheer Ma up no end to have someone fresh to talk to. Arthur doesn't say much and what he does you can't always understand.'

'I'd like that. Yes I would,' Lily said, not wanting their meeting to end but not knowing how to prolong it.

'You taken root on that pavement, Lily?' Gran called from the doorway. 'I'm getting shrammed to the bone here waiting for you.'

'See you soon,' Michael said as he turned towards his house.

'I hope so,' Lily breathed. The day was getting better and better.

'My God, child,' Gran gasped as she took the bags from Lily's frozen hands. 'You're like ice. Sit down and let me unbutton those boots. Your Dad'll have to put new soles on these, they're just about done for.' Gran's brown eyes were alive with curiosity. 'I bet it was packed down there. How did you get on?'

Lily regaled her with the pantomime over the chicken.

'Fancy a slip of a thing like you standing up to Big Arthur,' Gran chuckled, handing her the toasting-fork and a slice of bread.

Lily rested her feet on the fender in front of the black-leaded range. The heat seeped through her stockings and she revelled in the warmth, then her chilblains began to itch and she regretted her impulsiveness.

They sat by the fire eating their toast and dripping. Lily stabbed a lump of coal with the poker and a shower of spark fairies blew up the chimney. 'I wish Dad would hurry up,' she sighed.

'It's a long journey from Scapa Flow,' said Gran. She looked at the bag of vegetables and the

140

plump chicken. 'It would be neighbourly of us to invite Mrs Naylor and Rosie to share their dinner with us tomorrow. It's lonely for a widow at Christmas-time.'

'That would be lovely, Gran. I'll nip over and ask her now,' said Lily, thrilled to have Miriam included in their celebrations.

'Let's make a proper job of it,' said Gran, breaking into Lily's thoughts. 'I'll write out an invitation.' She got her pen and ink from the dresser. 'Don't stay over there jabbering. I need you here to get things ship-shape.'

Lily raced across the yard, eager to tell Miriam about her triumphant shopping spree. She leant across the laurel bush to tap on the kitchen window and then stopped. Miriam was not alone.

Chapter Fourteen

Miriam had shut the door behind Lily and watched the young girl walk down towards the market, then stood at the widow, sick with hope. The years of waiting for Alec now concertinaed into minutes. At any moment he would pass by. She could waylay him – there was nothing to stop her.

Mr Pragnell was visiting his brother and Rosie was fast asleep. Even Lily was out and Mrs Forrest would be too busy in the kitchen to be watching at the window.

141

Two years and seven months it was, since last they'd met. She'd walked away from that little house in Myrtle Lane, her heart singing. He had asked her to marry him. And then she'd returned with her answer. Swift as a hand snatching a fly from the air her happiness had gone, crushed under Taffy's fingers.

Miriam turned to look at her sleeping child. In spite of Taffy's violence and her near despair, Rosie had survived. What would Alec think of his new daughter, she wondered? It had been a bitter disappointment to find that Rosie was not his first and only child. She had wanted to run away from Lily and Lemon Street. So much of Alec's life remained a mystery, especially the circumstances of his marriage. But she had stayed. And in the last five weeks had settled into her position as Mr Pragnell's housekeeper, treated with respect.

After their first awkward meeting, Mrs Forrest had gone out of her way to be helpful. She'd promised to show her how to do the collars, once Miriam had got her own machine. It had been strange to sit in Alec's home, seeing his photograph on the mantelpiece, pretending polite interest, watching Mrs Forrest dandle her grandchild on her lap. Often she wanted to be done with false pretences, to make a clean breast of things. Pride always stepped in and halted her tongue. She wanted Alec to claim her and Rosie because he loved them, not out of shame and obligation.

As for his other daughter, Lily was a gem. Rosie loved her. She was helpful too, entertaining the child when Miriam was busy. It was she who had told her what time Alec's train was due in Portsmouth.

Miriam cast another reassuring glance in the mirror. Her hair shone after a hundred brush strokes and her new lace collar sat neatly around her neck. She smoothed her hands approvingly over her flat stomach.

In spite of all her preparations she was assailed by doubts. Everything hung on this meeting. Alec might be distant and aloof, he might bring a young woman with him, laughing and clinging to his arm, he might be wonderfully surprised and cover her face with kisses. She was like a gambler risking everything on the flip of a coin. Biting her finger she looked out of the window. Please, please come, she begged. Anything would be better than this agony of suspense.

And then Miriam saw him walking towards her. She opened the front door and called to him. 'Hello, Alec,' she said, her voice sounding strained and unnatural.

He stared at her in disbelief. 'My God, Miriam, where'd you spring from?' he said as he walked towards her.

Miriam took him by the hand. 'We're neighbours now,' she said, closing the door behind him. 'Come in. I'm all alone.'

Alec took off his cap and set down his kit-bag before following her into the kitchen. 'I can't believe it, after all this time. It's like a dream.'

'You can pinch me if you like,' she said, smiling at his stunned expression.

Instead, Alec took her hand and gently kissed

143

her fingers. His tenderness was painful to her as it drew out all her regrets and longings. 'Why didn't you write to me?' he asked. 'Not a day's gone by without me thinking of you, wanting you.' He held her away from him and said again, 'Why?'

Miriam couldn't bear for him to look at her with such misery in his eyes. 'I'll make us some tea,' she said. 'Sit down, you must be tired.' She turned away to fill the kettle. So often she'd rehearsed what she would say to him yet now her practised words stuck in her throat.

'How did you know where to find me?' he asked.

'D'you remember the Bring-'em-near, of Mr Pragnell's?'

Alec was smiling but puzzled. 'What, old Albert's telescope?'

Quickly she told him about the newspaper and the vacancy for a housekeeper and how she'd made the connection.

'So you're old Albert's housekeeper. Where is the old buffer?'

'Gone visiting to his brother's.' She was busy with the cups and saucers when he spoke again.

'Are you married now, Mirry?' he asked. 'Did you desert me for a younger, richer man?'

She was stung by his words. 'I was the one deserted, Alec,' she said.

He leant across the table appearing not to have heard her. Taking her hands in his, 'Mirry,' he said. 'Oh God it's good to see you.' He smiled at her and laughed delightedly. 'You know, I'd given up hope.'

She drew a long shuddering breath. 'Alec, I waited and waited for you. Why didn't you come?'

'It was all taken out of my hands.'

'But how?'

'It was the telegram, saying my Andrew'd been killed at Jutland. It was my Lily's twelfth birthday. I'd gone home to have tea with her before coming on to meet you. When I got there and saw the telegram and the state that Lily was in I wrote you a note and slipped it with the key behind the brick. I told you I was sailing the next day and asked you to call on my mother.'

'I never got any letter,' she cried.

He carried on speaking. 'My son dead. I couldn't believe it.'

'Alec – you knew where I was!' Miriam said, fighting back the tears. 'Why didn't you leave a message at the pub?'

'Miriam, I expected you to find the note at Myrtle Street. I was sick with worry. I was sailing the next morning. I wrote to you at the pub and called round there the next time I came home. They said Florrie'd sold up and they'd never heard of Miriam Slattery.' He shook his head helplessly. 'I thought you'd changed your mind.'

Suddenly she was angry. What was the good of all his efforts? They had been futile. 'He took the letter and tore it up in front of me,' she shouted.

'Who did? Mirry, what are you talking about?'

'Something happened,' said Miriam, avoiding his eyes, 'something, I can't...'

Alec gripped her hands tightly. 'What happened, Mirry?'

She stared down at the tablecloth. The stripes around the edge merged into each other as her eyes filled up with tears. 'I was so excited. I couldn't wait to see you. I almost ran up the lane and then,' she swallowed nervously, 'when I got there, the key was gone. I thought you – Alec, you're hurting me. Let go of my hands.'

He sat down with his back to the window, his eyes full of concern.

She remembered the sickly smell of rum. Then, oh God, how could she tell him? Sweat trickled down her back and her heart seemed to leap in her throat.

Alec's eyes pleaded with her.

'Taffy, he–' She covered her mouth with her hand as if to stifle the words.

'What did Taffy do?'

The tears spilled on to her hand. Miriam cast about for a handkerchief then dabbed her eyes on a tea-towel drying by the fire.

'What did he do?' Alec repeated.

'He was hiding behind the door.' Her voice shook. 'I ran to the window. He – he dragged me away.'

Alec gripped her shoulders. 'Tell me he didn't, Miriam. Not that, I couldn't bear it.'

Vomit, acid and bitter, rushed up into her mouth. She ran into the scullery. The retching tore at her stomach. Hastily she sipped some water from the tap.

Alec was slumped in his chair, his face in his hands.

Miriam stood shivering by the fire. The memory of Taffy pawing at her, tearing her

146

blouse, scraping her flesh with his fingernails maddened her. What was Alec's distress compared to hers?

She pulled his hands away from his face. 'He hurt me.' She said it again more loudly. 'Tore at my clothes and dragged me down with him on to our bed.'

Alec stared at his plate.

'He banged my head against the wall and then–' she almost spat the words at him. 'He used me as if I were a street whore.'

Alec recoiled from her words as if she had struck him.

'I wanted to die, I was in such pain. I felt soiled and worthless like a bit of rag in the gutter.'

The clock in Mr Pragnell's room chimed six. She sat in the armchair staring into the fire, her fingers picking at the hole in the chintz-covered arm. The anger had seeped away and she was left empty and exhausted.

'Christ!' Alec smashed his fist on the table making the milk leap from the jug. 'I'll kill him.' The cups and saucers rattle.

Miriam jumped. She looked at Alec. His eyes were dark with pain. She got up from her chair and sat herself opposite him at the table. 'I love you Alec,' she said. 'Nothing that's happened can change that. And nothing that's happened can be changed.' Very slowly she turned his hand over and kissed the palm. Then she folded his fingers over the kiss as if it were a present. There was a pink sore-looking patch of skin around his wrist. She pulled up his sleeve and saw a new tattoo in the shape of a butterfly.

Shamefacedly he tried to cover it again. 'Had it done just before we left from Scotland. To mark the Peace and coming home on leave.'

She traced the shape with her fingers, then pressed her lips against the butterfly before lowering his sleeve. All the while her eyes anxiously besought him to look at her. 'I didn't think I'd ever get home,' she said, her voice barely above a whisper. 'I crawled from one park bench to the next and then along the street from one garden wall to another.'

'Mirry,' he said, reaching out to her, smothering her hands with kisses. 'I'd give anything for this not to have happened.' He fought to gain control of his voice. 'And for us to be as we were.'

She studied his face, noting the sprinkling of grey hairs in his beard, how the skin was stretched tight over his cheekbones, and bruise-like shadows under his eyes. She longed to kiss him, to soothe him into forgetfulness.

They sat in silence, holding hands across the table, amid the jumble of spilt sugar and over-turned cups.

'Why did you never tell me about your children?' she asked. 'It was a shock to find out that Lily is almost a grown woman. She's only six years younger than me.'

'I was all set to, that evening,' he said. 'I was waiting to see if you were going to say yes. It was Lily's twelfth birthday. I was eager to take you home. Then when I went home and saw the telegram everything fell to pieces.' He shuddered. When he spoke his voice was full of tears. 'I don't know.' He held out his hands in a despairing gesture. 'I feel angry, and sad, and terribly ashamed.'

'How can you feel ashamed?' she whispered. 'How could either of us have known what was to happen?' She sighed. It was all said now. All that remained was for her to tell him about his little daughter. 'There's something else, Alec. I didn't know, that evening when I went to see you and give you my answer.'

'What was it you didn't know?' The sharpness in his tone made her falter.

'Alec,' Miriam's eyes pleaded with him. 'I was just going to tell you. That before ever Taffy touched me, I was carrying your child.'

He passed a hand over his eyes. 'I can't, it's too much. I can't believe it.'

'You have a little daughter, Alec. Her name is Rosemary, though I call her Rose. Please Alec, let me show her to—' She was interrupted by the sound of the bedroom door opening and feet running down the passage.

'Mummy!' The door opened and Rosie stood there rubbing the sleep from her eyes.

'Alec, please look at her,' Miriam begged. 'She's you daughter.'

'Mirry.' It was Alec's turn to plead. 'It's been a shock. Give me some time to take it in. For God's sake, give me time.' As if in a daze he got up from the table and walked past the little girl staring up at him and gathered up his cap and kit-bag.

'Alec, please, at least say hello.'

'Mirry, you've sprung this on me. I wasn't prepared.' He turned towards the passage. 'I'm so bloody tired, I don't know what I'm saying.

Just let me have some time with my family. I can't cope with it now.' The front door closed behind him.

Rosie held out her arms. 'Kissie, kissie.' Her arms tightened around her mother's neck.

Miriam rested her cheek against Rosie's damp curls. Tears leaked under her closed eyelids, down her face and on to her best blouse. Miriam held her daughter tightly, her mind in an agony of disappointment. She had hoped for too much.

Chapter Fifteen

Beyond the leaves of the bush and the net curtain at the window Lily could just make out the dark shape of a man, sitting at the table with his back to her.

Opposite him was Miriam. She was facing Lily. Under the glow of the lamplight she seemed magically transformed. Her thin anxious face was smoothed and softened. Her hair hung loose and golden about her shoulders.

She watched Miriam lean forward and draw the man's arm towards her, across the table. She took his hand and very slowly turned it over and kissed the palm. Then she folded his fingers over the kiss as if it were a present. Lily saw her push up the man's sleeve and trace the shape of something just above his wrist. She stood on tiptoe and leant closer to the window. Under the lamplight she could just make out a pink patch of skin with something etched on it – a scar perhaps or a new tattoo. Miriam pressed her lips to the mark before covering it up again.

Lily had never seen a man and woman behave towards each other with such tenderness. It was like nothing within her experience. She had no memory of her mother or knowledge of her parents' feelings for each other, beyond knowing that her father would never speak of his wife. There was no warmth or understanding between Aunt Hester and Uncle George, certainly none that she'd witnessed. And as for Gran and Grandad – well, he'd been lost years ago in China.

She'd seen the painted women of Queen Street who traded the sailors' coin for kisses; there was no tenderness in that. The fragile delight between Miriam and the man behind the curtain was new to her. It pierced her tenuous understanding of love, leaving her wounded and exposed. Tears pricked behind her lashes.

Then the silence was broken by the sound of a child crying.

Miriam moved away from the table and as the man got to his feet, Lily ducked down below the windowsill. Her face flushed at the thought of being caught spying on her friend. She heard the front door slam as the man left the house then she crept into the scullery and left Gran's note on a pile of washing.

She needed to be alone, to make sense of her feelings. The only private place was the outside lavatory; dark and cold and smelling of ammonia. Lily's hands shook as she tried to light the candle.

All the little excitements of her day seemed paltry compared to the tender scene she'd just witnessed. Lily hungered for someone to love her, to think her worthy of such attention.

Between Miriam and the man behind the window was such a power of understanding, such a valuing of each other. Why, when she and Miriam had become such friends, had he never been mentioned? Had she imagined their closeness? Was it only she who confided things and Miriam merely listened?

Lily began to shiver. The candle flickered and went out. Drawing her sleeve across her wet face she clicked the latch and opened the door.

Across the yard outside the lighted kitchen stood her father. 'Dad! Oh Dad,' she cried rushing into his arms, nuzzling into his black beard and drawing in the smell of tobacco and engine-oil. A whole year without sight of him and four of anxiety lest he be killed. Years of friends losing their fathers and coming white-faced to school.

She hugged him fiercely. 'Oh Dad,' she cried again, 'I'm so glad to see you.'

'Lily you'll crack my ribs, child,' he said smiling down at her.

She and Gran fussed over him, pouring his beer and fetching his slippers.

'Alec, you look all in,' Gran said. 'I can see you've missed my cooking, you're thin as a lath.' As he got up to clear the table, she said, 'Put the crocks in the sink, we'll deal with them tomorrow.'

Now that the first excitement was over, Lily

152

looked at her father more closely. He was, as Gran had said, much thinner than she remembered. There were dark smudges of fatigue under his eyes and his cough was worse than last time.

He smiled at them. 'It's the journey, such a trek from Scapa.' Then he beamed. 'But Christmas at home with my two best girls. Who could ask for anything more?'

Lily tossed and turned in bed beside Gran, trying to ignore her gusty snores. Her brain was racing. The excitement at the market had been eclipsed by the events of the evening. Poor Dad, he looked so tired. Still, a few days of Gran's fussing would soon put him right.

But what of Miriam and the mysterious man behind the curtain? Thinking about them made her feel hungry, but not in the sense she was used to. There were tingling sensations in her breasts. Lily turned on to her stomach and pressed her body into the mattress. She pushed her hand down between her thighs and began to stroke herself. Ripples of feeling spread from her fingers up inside herself making her gasp. She arched her back and continued the delicious probing until she reached a taut aching peak of fulfilment.

When at last she fell asleep the mysterious stranger in Miriam's kitchen glided in and out of her dreams. Instead of Miriam it was she who sat under the lamplight, her hair gleaming, satin-black. But every time she reached out to touch him something held her back. Something she couldn't understand.

On Christmas morning, Lily stared at her

reflection in the dressing-table mirror. How large and dark her eyes seemed now that her hair was drawn up from her face. She fingered the necklace that Gran had let her wear, just for Christmas Day. The beads caught the light from the candle, rose, azure and gold flashed from the crystal facets. It had been a twenty-first birthday present to Gran from Mrs Pragnell.

'Like a mother, she was to me,' Gran said as she pinned up loose ends of Lily's hair.

Lily wished that her own mother were here beside her now which was strange since she had never known her. Mary Forrest had drowned off Portsmouth Point when Lily was just a baby. But lately she'd felt the need of someone nearer her age than Gran. Would her mother be proud of her? she wondered. Would she think her pretty? There were no pictures of her around the house and Lily had only a sketchy history of her life. Mary Kenny had met Alec Forrest when she was in service for a naval family in Lion Terrace. He had called at the house with a message from the dockyard. Mary had opened the door and been instructed to let the young sailor wait in the kitchen for a letter in reply. Six months later they were married.

This much had been gleaned, reluctantly, from Gran. Dad would never speak of her. Lily had even sneaked a look in the wooden ditty-box which Dad took with him when he went to sea. The photos inside the lid were of Lily and Andrew and Gran. It was as if her mother had never existed.

'Come on Madam Pompadour – that's enough

admiration for one day,' said Gran, tapping her head with a brush. 'You take your Dad a cup of tea while I put myself together decently.'

'Gran you look lovely,' gasped Lily when she emerged from the bedroom. Her cream blouse encased her pulpit-like bosom and around her waist was a belt fastened with a swirly silver buckle.

Dad gave her a mock salute.

Gran snatched up her gloves. 'Alec, you get that bird in the oven by ten o'clock then set a match to the front room fire,' she said, as she and Lily set off for the Christmas morning service.

St George's Church was icy and the congregation huddled for warmth in the front pews. All the window sills were crammed with holly and beside the brass lectern was a vase of bronze chrysanthemums. Lily tried to separate the mixture of smells rising from the worshippers. Mothballs from little-used clothes, wintergreen rubbed on wheezy chests, the grapefruit tang of the flowers and the occasional whiff of pipe tobacco. Many people wore black armbands in memory of a soldier killed on the battlefields of France or a sailor drowned in the waters off Jutland.

The Reverend Merchison climbed the stairs to the carved wooden pulpit and after a vigorous clearing of his throat announced his text. 'And they shall beat their swords into ploughshares, and their spears into pruning hooks; nation shall not lift up the sword against nation, nor shall they learn war any more.' Tears stung Lily's eyes as she listened to the vicar's words. Could that really

155

ever be true?

'My dear people,' he said, 'we are, on this first Christmas of the Peace, the remnant of God's flock. It is our bounden duty now to walk in the paths of peace. Neighbour must shake the hand of neighbour; enmities must be forgotten.' He drew a crumpled handkerchief out of his surplice and blew his nose resoundingly. The vicar looked like a remnant, himself. His once auburn hair was now sparse and scattered across his head in rusty wisps. He held out his hand to Gran and Lily as they left the church. 'Happy Christmas Mrs Forrest and to you, Lily,' he said.

'More like a scarecrow every day,' Gran muttered. 'If his poor dead wife could see him now.' She tutted. 'I'd invite him to dinner today only he'd be sure to put a damper on things. Oh yes, Miss, that reminds me. Is Mrs Naylor coming to have dinner with us or not? What did she say?'

Lily blushed. 'She was seeing to Rosie, so I left the note on the table. I forgot to go back and ask her,' she said lamely.

Gran gave her a searching look. 'Best do it myself, now.' She knocked on Miriam's door. 'You go on indoors and get the sprouts ready.'

A burst of heat struck Lily as she opened the kitchen door and the smell of roast chicken wafted from the range.

'Give your old Dad a Christmas kiss,' said her father. Lily hugged him eagerly.

'I've got a special present to thank you for the letters you sent me,' he said, sitting on the arm of her chair. 'They used to be almost as good as photographs. I'd open the envelope, and there

156

you'd be. I could picture Gran treadling away on the old machine and you doing your school-work at the table.'

It took Lily ages to untie the string and pull away the paper. Inside was a book bound in red leather with its title picked out in gold letters: *Great Expectations* by Charles Dickens.

Enchanted, Lily ran her fingers over the letters and held the book up to her nose to sniff the newness of the leather. 'I've written inside for you,' said Dad, anxious for her approval.

Lily turned the page; there in his beautiful copperplate were the words: 'To my Darling Lily, of whom I have Great Expectations, Your Loving Dad, Christmas 1918.'

'Oh, Dad, it's beautiful. The best present I've ever had,' she said, hugging him tightly.

'You know, Lily,' said Dad, holding her hands in his. 'I wanted you to have proper schooling for you to train up to be a teacher but...' There were tears in his eyes.

Lily swallowed hard, not wanting him to know the strength of her own disappointment. She'd taken such joy in helping the five-year-olds learn their letters. Miss Lavender said she had a real aptitude. 'I'll still be able to read at night and have your letters to look forward to,' she reassured him.

'When d'you start at Denby and Shanks?'

'Straight after Christmas. I've bought my tailoring shears and seen the forewoman, Miss Pearson.' Lily tried to sound eager, although, in truth, she was dreading her first day as a tailoring apprentice.

Further discussion ended as Gran bustled into the room. 'What are you thinking of, Alec, opening presents at this time? If we're to get the dinner on the table in time it's all hands to the pump.' She put on her apron and Dad and Lily flew about, laying the table, peeling sprouts, sharpening knives at her barked commands.

At one o'clock there was a knock on the front door.

'That'll be Mrs Naylor. Go and let her in, Lily,' said Gran, as she stirred the gravy in the roasting-tin.

Lily felt anxious about seeing Miriam after spying on her the night before but any awkwardness was dispelled by Rosie. She chuckled and smiled at her. ''illy, 'illy,' she cried.

Gran bustled in from the kitchen and smiled warmly at Miriam. 'Mrs Naylor, you're heartily welcome, my dear,' she said kissing her on the cheek. 'Let me introduce you to my son, Alec. Alec this is our new neighbour, Mrs Naylor and her little one, Rosie.'

'Happy Christmas, Mrs Naylor,' said Dad. 'I'll take your coat. Warm yourself by the fire.'

Miriam blushed at his attention. She handed Lily a small paper package. 'Happy Christmas,' she said.

Lily kissed her and took Rosie in her arms. 'I'll put it with the others in the front room and we'll open them after dinner. I've got some things for you and Rosie, too.'

'I'll take it,' said Dad, hurrying out of the room.

'Let's get you settled for your din-dins,' said Lily, pulling out a chair with a cushion on top.

158

She tied her securely in place with a long scarf.

Dad came back into the room and Rosie stared up at him.

'That's my Daddy,' Lily said. Rosie gave him a tentative smile.

Miriam had not moved from her place by the fire.

Dad knelt down beside Rosie and began to talk to her. 'That's a big spoon for a little girl,' he said. 'I'll go and fetch you another one.'

'Come on Miriam, have a seat beside her,' called Lily.

Her friend seemed flustered and didn't immediately sit down. She busied herself with tying a bib around her daughter's chin.

'Take your seats everyone it'll be on the table in two ticks,' called Gran. 'Alec, come and carry the vegetables in.'

Dad settled the dishes on the table then seated himself opposite Miriam. He seemed ill-at-ease and fidgeted with his knife and fork.

Lily was surprised at the silence between them. Dad was normally so friendly and eager to put people at their ease.

'Make way, make way,' Gran cried, carrying the chicken to the table. From its breast hung sausages like a mayoral chain, and forming a guard of honour around the edge of the plate were a batallion of roast potatoes. Steam rose from the dishes of carrots and sprouts.

Dad carved and Gran spooned vegetables on to the plates. Lily was kept busy eating her own dinner and attending to Rosie.

'It all tastes delicious,' said Miriam shyly. 'I

never expected to have such a feast. Mrs Forrest, thank you ever so much for asking me.'

'You're more than welcome, my dear,' said Gran patting her hand. 'It's lovely to have a little child in the house again. Isn't it, Alec?'

There was a pause as if Dad had not heard and then he seemed to rouse himself and smiled at his new neighbour. 'Of course it is,' he said. 'Mrs Naylor, more chicken and stuffing too? It's Mother's secret recipe.'

Lily felt a surge of happiness. She bit into a roast potato's crispy golden skin and watched Rosie licking gravy from her lips. It was perfect, all of it, from the home-made blackberry wine winking in the glass to the starched tablecloth and willow-pattern plates. The dresser was almost bare having been stripped of plates and serving-dishes for this so long-awaited Christmas feast.

'You look so pretty with your hair done like that,' said Miriam. 'Makes you look ever so grown-up.'

'A proper young lady,' Dad said, smiling at his daughter.

Lily blushed with pleasure.

'Pass your plates everyone.' Gran stood up and carried them into the kitchen. There was great excitement when she returned carrying the Christmas pudding ablaze with a generous helping of rum.

Rosie's eyes were round with astonishment. She clapped her hands and everyone laughed.

'The little darling,' smiled Gran. 'She's a credit to you, Mrs Naylor.'

Miriam blushed with pleasure.

'Ooh, I'm full up fit to burst,' sighed Dad as he filled everyone's glass. 'Now, I should like us all to drink to my mother in thanks for this handsome meal.'

'To Gran,' Lily cried.

'Mrs Forrest,' said Miriam.

'Thank you son,' said Gran, her eyes shining. 'I'd like to toast all those men that gave their lives for us, especially our Andrew and of course, Mrs Naylor – your husband.'

She rushed into the scullery, noisily blowing her nose.

Miriam stared at her plate and Dad coughed.

After a tense silence Gran called out, 'Alec, you go in the front room and entertain Mrs Naylor and Rosie. Lily and me will clear the dishes.'

Later, when she carried a tray of tea into the front room the atmosphere had eased. Rosie had fallen asleep on Miriam's lap and she and Dad were talking together. Lily poured out the tea and handed round the cups. Gran joined them and they opened the presents.

'Fit for a duchess,' she exclaimed at the embroidered tray-cloth Lily had laboured over at school. 'The back's as neat as the front. A real professional piece of work.'

Lily glowed with pride. She opened the package that Miriam had brought. Nestling in a bed of tissue-paper was a handbag mirror framed with lace and with green satin. 'It's so dainty,' she exclaimed and got up to kiss her friend.

'What have you got Mr Forrest?' asked Miriam as Alec unwrapped his present from Lily.

Dad laughed. 'I think this is a big hint about my letter-writing,' he said, showing them all the paper wallet Lily had made with separate pockets for pens, stamps and blotting-paper. On the front she had written. 'The pen is mightier than the sword.'

'This is from me and Gran,' said Lily, handing Miriam a strawberry punnet that they had lined and decorated with an oddment of pink-and-white gingham and filled with different-coloured cotton-reels, a paper of pins, a thimble, some sewing-needles and a peg doll for Rosie.

'I don't know what to say.' Miriam looked as if she would burst into tears. She leant across the table and squeezed Gran's hand. 'Thank you,' she whispered.

'Who's for a bit of fortune-telling to liven up the party?' said Dad taking a red apple from the fruit bowl. He smiled at Lily. 'If I can peel this apple in one strip we'll drop it on the floor and it'll fall into the shape of the first letter of your true love's name.'

Lily watched her father's fingers deftly turning the apple. At any moment the skin could break and the spell would lose its power. She noted every detail. The sprinkling of dark hair between his knuckles, the traces of engine-oil under his fingernails, and the mother-of-pearl handle to his penknife. She held her breath as the peel curled back on itself, like a long rosy ringlet, and the apple lay naked on the dish.

'Hey presto!' cried Dad, ready to drop the peel at Lily's feet. She laughed and Miriam clapped her hands.

'Drop it on the floor, Dad, quick,' Lily pleaded.

All eyes were focused on him. As he raised his hand in front of her his sleeve slid down his arm and Lily saw the pink patch of skin and the new butterfly tattoo.

For a moment she sat there in a state of sickening disbelief as the connection was made in her head between the scene she'd witnessed last night in Miriam's kitchen and the mark on her father's arm.

'Look pet, what is it, d'you think? Is it an M or an N?'

She didn't wait to see but rushed blindly from the room and out of the front door.

Her feet clattered across the deserted pavements and her breath streamed out in front of her in the frosty air of late afternoon. The man she had seen kissing Miriam, the man she had dreamed about, was her father. She tried to outrun the knowledge but it kept pace with her. 'Dad and Miriam,' the words drummed in her head and her heart seemed to beat to their rhythm.

Her flight took her along the dockyard wall to the harbour with its shingle beach. Lily flung handfuls of stones in to the sea, until shivering and exhausted she sank down against a rowing-boat and wept. Everything, everything had been snatched away from her. Before she'd had a chance to know her mother she'd been taken, then Andrew. She still couldn't believe he was really dead, that she would never ever see him again. Not hear his shrill whistle or watch him drag a comb through his wiry curls. She rubbed

163

a sleeve across her eyes. Hot on the heels of Andrew's death had been her loss of the scholarship and then even that wasn't enough. There was this secret between Dad and Miriam. Miriam – her new best friend.

How had that happened? Miriam had only been their neighbour for a few weeks and all that time Dad had been in Scotland. Surely they wouldn't have behaved as they did at a first meeting. And if they had known each other before why, why had Miriam pretended they were strangers?

Could she be mistaken? After all, tattoos were common enough among sailors. No. The awkwardness between them earlier in the day now made sense. There was a secret power between Miriam and her father that Lily couldn't compete with. She was frightened by her anger and powerlessness.

And now she'd lost Miriam as well. She hadn't realised until that moment how important her friendship had become to her. In a matter of weeks, they had become almost sisters. Lily clasped her hands around her knees and wept afresh.

Gradually the sound of footsteps crunching over the shingle followed by drunken laughter broke into her thoughts. Two sailors staggered around the boat towards her. 'It's a Christmas fairy,' one of them slurred. 'Here my sweetheart, won't you give me a kiss?'

'Leave 'er, Nobby. She's only a kid,' protested his friend.

'Come to your Uncle Nobby, 'e'll teach ya a

thing or two.'

She took to her heels, easily outdistancing his fuddled footsteps.

'Silly little bitch,' he called after her.

Lily didn't know what to do. She was cold and the seawater had seeped through the soles of her shoes. Where could she go? If she went home they'd want to know why she had dashed out like that. What could she say? She had so looked forward to Christmas, had been so certain that Dad's arrival would make everything right. Now her head was throbbing with a mass of confused feelings. Stealthily, like a maggot in a piece of fruit, the discovery of Dad's involvement with Miriam had eaten away at her joy. She had been so secure in her place in his affections, and now she was not so sure.

Chapter Sixteen

Christmas morning. Miriam yearned to pull the covers over her head and blot it out entirely. She had gambled everything on Alec's return and now it had come to nothing. Only the crumpled blouse on the floor and her swollen eyelids were proof of his fleeting visit. There were no more tears, plans or wishes. She was empty.

If only she could stop his words from going round and round in her head. 'It's been a shock. For God's sake give me time. I can't cope with it now.'

When would he be able to look at his little daughter, tomorrow, next week, never?

Rosie stirred and Miriam reluctantly got out of bed and fetched the chamber-pot. However much she wanted to sleep the day away she couldn't do it on a wet mattress. 'Quick, wee-wee for Mummy,' she whispered, pulling up Rosie's nightie and lifting her on to the pot. The child shuddered as her body came into contact with the cold china and kept her eyes tightly shut, pressing her hands into her armpits for warmth. 'Good girl,' Miriam cooed as she lifted her off the pot and put it on the floor. Rosie burrowed back under the bedclothes.

Dragging on her coat and shoes Miriam went down the yard to the lavatory and emptied the pot. She sat on the wooden seat trying to pull the day into some sort of shape. There were two choices: either she crawled back under the covers or she dressed herself and Rosie and made them some sort of celebration.

The memory of a childhood Christmas came back to Miriam with the heart-stopping force of a nightmare. Even now, she could still smell the stale mixture of sweat, urine and cheap gin wafting from her mother's body as she had lain snoring beside her on that Christmas morning. Afraid of her mother's uncertain temper she had crept across the room and felt about for the candle and matches. She'd held the candleholder up to the clock on the mantelpiece and seen the big hand on the twelve and the little one on the seven. Too early to dare to wake Mummy.

The pain of that memory had been relieved

when she had spoken of it one day to Alec. He had drawn her into his arms and held her until her tears were spent. 'Tell it to me, all of it. Once it's told it won't have the power to hurt you any more,' he'd said.

She'd told him of her father's pride in the clock, how he had made a wooden case for it and entrusted her with the job of winding it every night with a brass key. 'He went off to Australia to the cane fields and promised to send for us. I knew that when he did I would pack that clock in my suitcase.'

'You must have loved your Dad very much,' Alec said, pulling the covers around them. 'Now we're back in that room with your mother and it's all cold and shadowy. Tell me, what time did you wake her up?'

'It was half-past eight. She swore at me and said I'd have to wait until twelve.'

'I want to get into your story and get your mother by the scruff of the neck and shake her. However did you pass the time?'

'Oh, I sang carols and counted everything in the room beginning with A, then B, then C. I watched those hands snailing around that clock face for minutes and minutes and minutes. Twice I held it up to my ear convinced that it had stopped. Everything in me was waiting,' she'd told him. 'The hair on my head, my teeth, even my toenails. And then the two hands met at twelve.'

'It's all right, my love, I've got you. You're safe, you can tell me,' he'd said, drying her tears with the sheet.

'Before waking her,' Miriam dragged out the words, 'I went into the kitchen and found a biscuit and two raw sausages wrapped in newspaper. I put the biscuit on a plate and carried it to the bed with a cup of water. "Happy Christmas, Mummy," I said.'

'What's bloody happy about it?' her mother had whined, flinging the plate on the floor then drawing the covers back over her head.

Hot tears had gushed down Miriam's face as she remembered standing shivering in that kitchen. 'I tried to eat one of those sausages,' she wailed to Alec. 'It was cold and greasy and gritty. And then I went back into the bedroom and snapped the hands off the clock.'

She had cried out her pain against his shoulder and beaten her rage against his chest. And then he had stroked her and kissed her, been mother, father and lover in his tender and passionate attention. 'I love you,' he'd whispered into the spaces between her ribs, 'I love you,' on the soles of her feet, 'I love you,' against the entrance to her sex.

Her body quivered in remembrance of that afternoon. Of being held and nurtured by him. Of beginning to trust. But Miriam shook her head trying to dispel the hopes raised by those seductive memories. Alec or no Alec she must make a Christmas for Rosie.

In the pantry there was half a cold chicken left from yesterday's dinner, a pork pie and some fruitcake sent from Devon by Aunt Florrie. The bread-bin yielded almost a full loaf and there was butter, milk and cheese, even a sack of vegetables on the floor. More than enough food until Mr Pragnell came back on Boxing Day.

The fix she was in was of her own making, she reminded herself. Mr Pragnell had invited them to stay with him and his brother in Romsey. 'My sister-in-law Olive would be delighted,' he'd said. 'She misses her own family since they've emigrated to Rhodesia.'

Miriam had declined, saying that she was visiting her friend Daisy in Gosport. It would have been quite possible. When she had written to Daisy giving her their new address and thanking her again for the picture, she had received a very affectionate reply. Daisy would have been only too pleased to see them. Resolving to make the best of the day, Miriam picked up her clothes and crept from the room. Quickly she relaid the fire, scooping the ashes into a bucket and criss-crossing some sticks with twists of paper and crowning the top with lumps of coal. She knelt by the hearth and set a match to the fire then held a newspaper across the mouth of the grate until with satisfying crackles it caught alight.

Rosie called from the bedroom and Miriam took her up into her arms. She glanced at her reflection in the mirror, dismayed at her eyes, still puffy from last night's tears.

'Mum, Mum, Mum,' Rosie cried rubbing her nose against hers in an Eskimo kiss.

After washing and dressing herself and Rosie, Miriam made some sugar toast and they ate it sitting together in the armchair by the fire. When she'd cleared the plates she said, 'Let's see what

169

Aunty Florrie has sent us,' getting a large paper parcel out of the sideboard. Inside were two presents. For Rosie there was a pink winceyette frock and for Miriam a blue crepe blouse with a V neck.

Dear Girls,

Happy Christmas from Devon. Maude and me are rubbing along nicely. The business is doing well and Maude asked me to say that you are both welcome to come down and stay for a little holiday when the weather is better.

Let me know nearer the time and I'll send the fares and meet you at the other end.

Do send us a snap of the pair of you. I'm starved for a look at you both.

Love in haste, Florrie.

'We're going to be two pretty Christmas fairies,' Miriam cried, dancing her daughter round the room. She sat Rosie in the pram to play with the wrapping-paper and string whilst she ironed their new finery.

She was startled later by a loud rapping on the front door.

'Hello my dear, Happy Christmas,' said Mrs Forrest. 'I forgot to say in the note it's one o'clock sharp.'

'I'm sorry – I don't understand,' Miriam said. 'Won't you come in?'

'No, I've the dinner to see to. You are coming, aren't you? I'm so looking forward to having a baby in the house again and you've my son to meet as well. Mustn't stop. One o'clock then.'

Miriam nodded to Mrs Forrest's departing back. There'd been some sort of mix-up. She was expected to have dinner with Alec and his family. How could she face him again after last night? How could she refuse? They were neighbours. If she didn't go Mrs Forrest would probably send Lily in after her.

It was a sick charade. They would be there as the needy neighbours when in reality they were – what? Rosie was Lily's sister and Mrs Forrest's grandchild, but what was she? Certainly not Alec's wife and if they were not married that made her child a... No, she wouldn't say it.

I don't suppose Alec will like it any better than I do, she thought. And then, why shouldn't I go? Why should I hide away in here with a bit of cold chicken when I could have a proper Christmas next-door?

Hastily she bathed her eyes in cold water then put on her best black skirt and new blue blouse. She rummaged in the dressing-table drawer and found an embroidered handkerchief and a little mirror which she wrapped up to take as presents. Her courage almost failed her at the Forrest front door but Lily eagerly welcomed them inside.

''illy, 'illy,' Rose cried.

Miriam was enveloped in the scents of Christmas wafting towards her from the polished chairs and table, the roasting meat, tobacco smoke and crackling wood in the grate. Before she had a chance to see whether Alec was in the room, Mrs Forrest hurried over to her, kissing her cheek.

'You're heartily welcome,' she said. 'Let me

171

introduce you to my son. Alec, this is Mrs Naylor and her little one, Rosie.'

Miriam sensed rather than saw Alec put down a bundle of cutlery and turn towards her. She could hear the tremor in his voice as he said something to her about her coat. Her fingers were clumsy as she tried to undo the buttons. She gave it to him, their hands scarcely touching in the exchange.

Rosie ran to Lily who swept her up in her arms.

Miriam was aware of Alec talking to Rosie and watched them covertly. They were so alike, especially as they were now smiling at each other. Rosie had the same dark lashes as her father, the same short space between nose and mouth, the same full lips. Miriam felt a stab of anger. Here she was accepting a charity dinner when she was entitled to so much more. The anger carried her through the meal. She sat opposite Alec and heard herself praising Mrs Forrest's cooking and complimenting Lily on her appearance. She could not have said what she was eating, the mere act of swallowing took all her concentration.

Rosie clapped her hands in delight when Alec poured rum over the Christmas pudding and set it ablaze with a match. When the meal was at an end Mrs Forrest gave a toast to 'All the brave men who gave their lives for us in that dreadful war. Especially our Andrew and your husband, Mrs Naylor.' Then she rushed into the scullery in tears.

The sincerity of her neighbour's concern for the bogus Mr Naylor shamed Miriam. She wanted to leave but somehow let herself be hustled into the front room with Alec.

'You two have a chat together,' his mother urged. 'Lily and me will clear the pots. Bring you in a cup of tea in two shakes.'

Miriam sat with Rosie on the horsehair sofa while he busied himself with the fire.

She willed him to speak to her, to make some recognition of her presence. Alec fiddled with the fire-irons and straightened the ornaments on the mantelpiece.

'Am I stranger to you?' she snapped. 'Is this how we're to carry on?'

'I need time to think,' he muttered.

'I gave you that time,' she ground out the words. 'I could have told your family but I thought, when Alec sees his child he'll be only too glad to claim her.'

'I thought you were dead,' he said turning towards her. 'Suddenly you're there, alive in front of me.' He ran his hand distractedly through his hair, his words tumbling over each other. 'I didn't know what I felt, joy, then rage and grief.'

'Why grief?' she asked, her mind in chaos.

'Not being there to save you from that bastard,' he said.

'Then why did you leave me last night? Why wouldn't you even look at Rosie?' She prayed that they wouldn't be interrupted before Alec gave her his answer.

He gripped her hands. 'Panic,' he said. 'Then, when I'd had time to think, I was ashamed of letting you down.'

'I don't know where I am with you,' she cried.

'Do you still love me? Do you believe that Rosie is your child? Do you want to make a life with us?'

'Yes to all three,' he said. 'Mirry, we'll talk about everything, I promise,' he said. 'But first let's just enjoy Christmas.'

They had one brief kiss before Lily came in with a loaded tray.

Alec took Rosie while Miriam drank her tea. The afternoon was transformed. They were now a family, laughing, joking and exchanging gifts.

He took an apple from the fruit bowl and did some fortune-telling nonsense for Lily. But as he dropped the peel on the floor she leapt from her chair and ran out of the house. The three of them were bewildered by the sudden turn of events.

'What was that all about?' Alec shrugged his shoulders.

'The Lord knows,' said his mother, picking up the peel and throwing it in the fire where it hissed and sizzled before shrivelling away to nothing. 'She's got so pettish lately. I never know from one day to the next. She's either up in the bows or down in the hold.'

'Bow wow, doggie, doggie,' crowed Rosie, holding out her hands to Alec.

'No, my little sweetheart,' he laughed as he swung her up in the air. 'Not bow-wow. Up in the bows.'

'She's bright as a button,' said Mrs Forrest. 'More cake anyone?'

'I'm full to bursting,' Miriam said shaking her head.

It grew dark and still Lily had not returned. All

their efforts at jollity were now exhausted. The clock struck six.

'Alec, take her coat and go and look for her,' his mother said anxiously. 'She'll catch her death out in this cold. Mrs Naylor, don't feel you have to go,' she said distractedly.

'I need to get Rosie to bed,' said Miriam smiling at both of them. 'Thank you for a lovely day and please, let me know when Lily gets back.' She ignored Rosie's 'sleepy-blanket', lying on the floor by the fire.

Later, as she knew he would, Alec called to return it.

'All safe and sound,' he said. 'Lily's all riled up with me. Says I know what I've done but won't admit it.' He shrugged.

'All's well that ends well,' said Miriam, anxious to be done with the subject when there were so many other things she wanted to talk about. 'Put the blanket beside her,' she whispered, opening the door to her room. 'I'll go and make some tea.' After watching Alec smiling down at her daughter she crept away.

She pulled the kitchen curtains and stood staring into the fire. Only last night Alec had rushed from the room as if he never wanted to see her again. And now? Her happiness had the fragility of a butterfly, like the one tattooed on his wrist.

At the sound of Alec's footsteps she turned towards the door. Ignoring the cups of tea he went to the armchair and pulled her down onto his lap. 'I thought I'd never see you again,' she breathed, nestling against his shoulder.

175

'Sh, sh,' he whispered, turning her face towards him and cupping it between his hands. He began to kiss her, his beard grazing her cheek.

She returned his kisses, wanting to be swept away, wanting to lie with him pressed against her. Yet, when he kissed the hollow in the base of her throat she drew away. 'We must talk, or we'll get ahead of ourselves,' she said, standing up and smoothing down her skirt.

'I'm too roused up to think straight,' Alec laughed.

'It's not just us,' Miriam said. 'There's Rosie and Lily and your mother to think of.'

'I want to be with my new family but I'm still tied to the old one,' he said. 'If you'll trust me a little longer–' His dark eyes pleaded with her. 'When I come home on summer leave I'll tell Ma and Lily and we'll go on from there.'

Miriam picked at a thread in the tablecloth. It was something and nothing. 'As long as you tell them you're Rosie's father,' she said. 'Not that we only met at Christmas.'

'It looks like I'm not facing up to things, I know,' he said, 'but Ma has brought up my children mostly on her own. I owe her a lot,' he sighed. 'And there's Lily.'

'That's the heart of it,' Miriam flushed with anger. 'Your princess mustn't know that Daddy's not perfect.' She bit her lip. They were quarrelling and she couldn't draw back.

'Mirry,' he put his hands on her shoulders. 'It's been one hell of a shock. I want to take care of you, I want to find that Taffy and hurt him.' He clenched his fist. 'Really hurt him. I need to talk

176

to Ma and Lily and I don't feel up to doing any of it.' He was almost crying. 'Just let me have this one Christmas. It's the first we've shared without our Andrew. In the summer I'll tell them. There's no question of my not accepting Rosie.'

'What choice do I have?' she asked, tears welling in her eyes. 'I've had to bear all the pain and loneliness on my own. Now, when you're back in my life, I've to behave as if I'm a guilty secret.'

'You can tell them now,' he said quietly, 'and I'll not deny it. But it should come from me, taking my responsibilities, not being shamed into it.'

And with that she had to be content.

When he left she wandered restlessly around the kitchen. She dragged a creased nightdress out of the washing basket. As she did so a piece of paper fluttered to the floor. Idly she turned it over and read the unfamiliar writing. *'Dear Mrs Naylor, We should like you to share Christmas Dinner with us. Please send Lily back with your reply. Sincerely Yours, Beatrice Forrest.*

So the invitation had been made last night. Lily had brought it. Why had she not tapped on the window or come in through the scullery, as she usually did? Because ... Miriam's stomach churned in alarm. Lily must have seen them. But she was so friendly today until that nonsense with the apple. Was that the cause of her rift with her father? Miriam wondered. If Lily knew about her and Alec, what would she do? Perhaps the decision to tell Mrs Forrest was already out of their hands.

Miriam bit her lip. In the last few weeks she had worked so hard to gain Mrs Forrest's respect and liking. Today she felt as if she'd succeeded. But what would happen when she found out about her deception?

Lily had a secure place in her father's affections and she was the apple of her grandmother's eye. What chance had Miriam and Rosie against such family solidarity?

It was like being on a see-saw; no sooner were you riding high than something tipped the balance and you were back again scraping along the bottom.

Chapter Seventeen

Beattie had always hated that last morning when the leave was drawing to an end. Today was no exception. At ten o'clock Alec would be boarding the *'Jellicoe* Special' on the first leg of his journey back to Scapa Flow. Less than two hours away.

While he stood in his vest and bell-bottoms, shaving at the sink, she made a start on his breakfast. Dropping a knob of lard into the old black pan she watched it slowly melt in the heat from the hob. She would miss her son. In the two weeks since his arrival on Christmas Eve Beattie had grown used to having him at home. She liked seeing his razor on the sink, hearing him whistle, having a man about the house again.

Lily would miss him too. Although one would never think it from her behaviour. What had got into the child she couldn't fathom. Everything

178

had been going swimmingly until Christmas afternoon when, for no reason at all, she went off like a rocket. Beattie and Alec and Mrs Naylor were left staring at each other, like a parcel of fools. Eventually, Alec had gone looking for Lily and Mrs Naylor had taken herself home. Her granddaughter had come back wet, sulky and cold. Beattie had lost her temper and sent her to bed. After which, Alec had gone next door to return Rosie's blanket and by the time he returned the day was over.

She shrugged as she turned the rashers and dropped two eggs into the pan. If Lily wanted to stew in bed on a Saturday morning that was her lookout. There were other calls on her grandmother's time. For instance, that cough of Alec's was getting no better. He'd spent half his leave asleep in the chair. 'You fit to go back?' she asked.

'When I've finished off my breakfast, I'll let you know,' he said, standing behind her with his arms round her waist.

'Alec, you'll squeeze the life out of me,' she chuckled. 'Pour us a cup of tea, son. I'll just nip across to Ma Abrahams and get you some bronchial mixture.'

'Poison, more like,' he protested. 'Stay and have some breakfast with me, it's your last chance.' He pulled out the chair for her and took his loaded plate from her hands.

Although very different in appearance and temperament from his father, Alec had the same easy grace. A way of drawing people to him. She sat like a favoured child while he buttered her toast.

'Crisped to a turn just as I like it,' he said as he bit into the bacon. 'I hope Lily wakes up in time to say goodbye. She was dead to the world when I looked in on her just now. What d'you think's upset her? She was so happy and excited Christmas Eve and then...'

Beattie shrugged. 'Leave her son. I'll get to the bottom of her pettishness. She reminds me of the little girl with the curl in the nursery rhyme.'

'When she was good, she was very, very good,' Alec joined in.

'And when she was bad she was horrid,' they said together.

Alec put his plate in the sink and began to finish dressing. 'Put me straight, Ma,' he asked, bending down so that she could reach up and pull his collar down over his jersey. It was a movement she'd made time and again for his father and then for Andrew.

As if reading her thoughts Alec said, 'I think about him, Ma, all the time. You picture your children going to your funeral, not you going to–' he stopped and Beattie waited for him to end the sentence. Still with his back to her he stood fidgeting with his shaving gear.

'You have to say it, Alec,' Beattie urged. 'It's so easy to pretend he's not dead when there's no body to touch or funeral to go to.'

'I say it, Ma, over and over.' Alec's voice was barely a whisper. 'But then I see a lad just like him and I forget. And when he gets close the disappointment's so – so hard to bear.'

'I know, son.' Beattie put her hand on his shoulders. 'You and me and hundreds of others.

180

There's no magic road to recovery. Just minute by minute, one step in front of the other.'

'I always did want the quick answer,' he said, reaching up and holding her hand.

'I'll go and get your cough mixture,' Beattie said, knowing he wanted a moment to himself. They were distracted by a tap on the kitchen window. Beattie drew back the curtain to find Mrs Naylor standing there.

'Come in, my dear,' she said, opening the back door. 'Have a cup of tea, there's plenty in the pot.'

'I've just tacked those collars, like you showed me,' said the young woman, stepping into the scullery. 'Only I didn't want to go any further till you'd checked them.' She saw Alec and flushed in confusion. 'Sorry, I'm interrupting.'

'Sit down, Mrs Naylor,' said Alec, turning eagerly towards her. 'I'll pour you some tea. Ma, d'you want another cup or shall I pour it for you when you get back?'

'Cripes, son, I'll forget my head next.' She picked up her purse. 'Back in a tick, Mrs Naylor,' she called back over her shoulder as she stepped into the street, leaving the front door on the latch.

The shop bell jingled and Beattie was greeted with a gale of laughter.

'Well, don't that beat all,' cried Ma Abrahams as she spooned some jam into a cup for a boy in a moth-eaten jumper. 'A farthing, Charlie.' She put the coin in a fringed bag tied around her waist, before turning to her new customer. 'Have

181

you heard about Tiptoe Turner's latest carryings-on?' she asked.

Beattie shook her head.

'Go on, tell her, Mrs Onslow.'

Granny Onslow settled her ample frame in the chair at the end of the counter and launched into her tale. 'Seemingly this Officer was in the George having his gin and when he went to pay for it 'is wallet's been took. The landlord sends for Constable Wilkes and he goes hot-foot round to Tiptoe's house in Hawke Street.'

'Bottle of bronchial mixture, please,' whispered Beattie while Granny Onslow drew breath.

'Knocks on the door and Mrs Turner opens it, tears running down her face. "What you doing intrudin' on my grief?" she says. "Whatever you come sniffin' round here for, 'tweren't my Tiptoe. He's lying in his coffin waiting for the lid to be screwed down."'

'Wilkes must have felt a real fool,' said another customer who'd slipped in while the tale was in progress.

The narration continued. '"Sorry to have troubled you," he says. "Perhaps I might pay my respects."'

Ma Abrahams chuckled as she took Beattie's money.

'Well,' said Granny, drawing out the climax. 'She takes him into the front room and there right enough is Tiptoe lying stretched out on a trestle in his shroud and tucked up neatly in a sheet. At the head and foot is two brass candlesticks with the candles all lit proper like. Wilkes shakes his missis's hand and goes down to the end of the road. But he's not happy. Leaves it another five minutes then sneaks back and hides under the windowsill. Gradual-like he pokes his nose up over the ledge.' Her great bosom heaved with mirth. 'There was Tiptoe sat up, large as life and smoking a fag as he's lit from one of they candles.'

The four women laughed heartily.

Beattie chuckled to herself as she slipped back into the house. It would be a good tale to tell Alec. But the story died on her lips. The atmosphere in the kitchen was charged. Mrs Naylor and Alec were standing together in the doorway leading out to the scullery. Her face was totally unguarded. She was looking up at him, smiling, her hand on his arm. Alec was looking down at her. His face wore such a look of hunger that Beattie had to turn away. It was as if he needed to memorise every detail of her face before it was lost to him. Beattie felt an intruder in her own home. She closed the kitchen door sharply behind her and stood as if she had just come into the room. Like water thrown on to a fire her appearance quenched the look between them.

'I must get back to Rosie,' Mrs Naylor said. 'Safe journey, Mr Forrest,' she called as she turned into the yard.

'I'll bring down my kit-bag,' said Alec making for the stairs.

'Alec, what were you and...'

He brushed past her, and the sound of Lily calling from the bedroom put paid to further questions.

Beattie was exasperated.

'Dad, are you still there?' Lily cried. 'Oh Dad, I'm sorry.' She rushed down the stairs and into his arms.

'Love, of course I wouldn't go without saying goodbye to my princess,' Alec said, whirling his daughter round the kitchen.

Beattie, desperate to make sense of what she'd seen, was caught up in getting Alec ready for leaving. 'There's a bread pudding wrapped up nice and firm in greaseproof and brown paper. Put it in the top of your bag,' she called as she went into the passage to get her coat. 'Lily, you clear up the kitchen and make yourself some toast. Say goodbye to your Dad, now. We've got to get going.'

'I want to come with you,' Lily insisted. 'I can get some toast up and eat it while I get dressed.'

'Why couldn't you have decided this last night?' snapped Beattie. 'You're getting us all flummoxed, now.'

'Oh, go on, Ma,' pleaded Alec. 'She'll tidy the galley when she gets home.'

'I will, I will, if you'll just say yes.'

Beattie sighed. 'What chance do I have with the pair of you ganging up on me?'

In no time they were on their way. Alec strode ahead with Lily running beside him. Beattie trotted behind, questions drumming in her head. Once at the station he had to have his travel warrant checked and get himself on the train.

'This place gives me the pip,' Beattie said, stamping some warmth back into her feet. 'It's so full of sadness. Even the pigeons are downhearted. Look at them up on the roof girders,

184

can't raise a coo between them.'

Alec's laugh turned to a cough. It was a while before he had the breath to speak. 'Cheer up, Ma,' he said, leaning out of the carriage window and kissing her cheek. 'I'll be back on summer leave soon.'

''Bye, Dad. I'll write and let you know how my first day at work goes.' Lily stood on tiptoe and Alec kissed the top of her head.

'Look after yourselves,' he shouted, as the train started to move away.

'You too, son,' Beattie mouthed, watching his face disappear behind a cloud of steam. Pulling her coat collar high around her neck she pushed her way through the crush of waving women and marched out of the station.

'Right, young lady,' she said to Lily. 'You can wipe that mournful look off your face, quick sharp. Straight back home. I want everything spotless.'

'Where you going, Gran? I thought we'd walk back together.'

'Well you thought wrong,' said Beattie, not ready yet to be appeased.

Lily slouched away.

Beattie sighed. She must go and talk things over with Joseph. Crossing the road into Victoria Park she settled herself on the bench opposite the Pagoda. She focused her eyes on the plaque under the Chinese Bell knowing the inscription by heart.

'This bell was taken at the capture of the North-West Fort, Taku, June 1900 and brought home by HMS *Orlando*. This monument was erected by the officers and men in memory of their comrades who lost their lives during the commission.' A list of names followed, including that of PO J. Forrest bracketed with those killed at Tientsin.

'Sorry it's been so long, Joseph,' she said, as if he were sitting across the path from her. 'You know what it's like at Christmas. So much to do. Still, it passed off quite well, considering. Something's going on with Alec, though. Hasn't been himself, this leave, not by a long chalk. Goes out and comes in no word to anyone. What d'you reckon he's up to? S'pose if you'd been around he'd have been off boozing with you.'

What would Joseph look like now, she wondered, nearly nineteen years on? Would his red hair be flecked with white, the way hers was now steel-grey? Would he still want her with the same passion? Would she abandon herself to him with the same zest and impatience?

A gust of wind stirred memories of standing on Farewell Jetty, that last time. Hearing the marine band playing 'Anchors Aweigh' and the wives and sweethearts waving and calling. For months she'd slept with his old shirt in her arms drawing in the very last smell of him. Couldn't bear to wash it, specially after the telegram came.

'Christ! I miss you Joe,' she said, 'and now young Andrew gone as well. Please God it's me goes next.' Angrily she blew her nose. 'And that Lily's driving me to distraction. She's either up in the bows or down in the hold. Hopefully starting work will calm her down.'

Beattie got up and walked over to the Pagoda

and traced her husband's name with her gloved finger. She tried to still her fears. The lie that she had swallowed all those years ago was coming back to haunt her. What was it really that had brought it to the surface? Was it the hunger in Alec's face or something behind that Miriam Naylor's blue eyes? Something that spelled disaster for all of them.

She liked the young woman. She was a tidy hard-working little body. The way she kept that baby fed and clothed was a credit to her. Beattie felt a flicker of shame as she remembered her earlier hostility to Albert having a housekeeper. But then when she'd come in for Christmas dinner with her hair all gauzy round her shoulders, she'd have stirred the senses in any man – let alone, Alec.

'Joseph,' she suddenly burst out. 'He can't take up with another woman. Not when Mary's still alive.'

Chapter Eighteen

Lily's heart was thumping in fright as she carried her shears and thimble to the workroom in Half Moon Street. She was dressed all in black. Only the white blouse belied her funereal appearance. Taking a deep steadying breath she knocked on the door.

'Miss Forrest? Go through to the cloakroom, please. Hang up your coat and wash your hands.

I'll see you in five minutes,' said Miss Pearson, the tall steel-haired forewoman.

The room was empty. Lily hung up her coat on a brass hook and washed her hands at a chipped basin with a minute square of carbolic soap. Between the splash marks on the mirror she could see her face fever-pink with nerves. Anxiously she looked around for a towel. Not finding one she lifted her skirt and dried her hands on her petticoat.

'Miss Forrest, hurry up, there's much to be done before eight-thirty when the other staff arrive,' said Miss Pearson standing at the door, startling Lily with her noiseless entrance.

'Now your first task every morning will be to sweep the workroom. The pieces of cloth are to be put in that sack and the cotton threads and such can be thrown into the dustbin.' Noting Lily's puzzlement, Miss Pearson said, 'A firm from London collects the scraps of cloth and pays good money for them. Apparently they use it for underfelting carpets.'

In the centre of the workroom were two long tables, and beyond them by the tall windows were six treadle sewing-machines. Miss Pearson directed Lily's attention to a strange oblong gas jet on which several irons were heating. Beside them were ironing tables and underneath two buckets of water.

'You must make sure they are kept full of water, so that the cloths can be damped for pressing,' she said. 'At about ten minutes to eleven you will fill the kettle, there beside the gas jet, and make us all a cup of tea.'

Lily's head was spinning as she took up a broom and began sweeping the floor. The cotton dust made her cough and when she had finished filling the sacks Miss Pearson sent her to wash her hands again and fetch her scissors.

Two girls were chattering over the basins as Lily shut the door behind her. Their conversation continued as if she wasn't there.

'Ruby, that blouse is beautiful. Where'd you get it?' The speaker was small and bird-like with darting brown eyes.

'I got this sailor to give me two of his silk scarves and made up the pattern myself.'

Lily was startled when the girl called Ruby turned around. Her hair seemed to scorch her head in a red halo of curls and her green eyes burned fiercely in her pale face.

'What d'you give him?' asked the other girl.

'I let him hold my hand and promised to write to him.'

'Will you?'

Ruby gave a throaty chuckle. 'Catch me wasting my time on a blue-jacket, Dora – I got bigger fish to fry. Threw the paper away the minute he was out of sight.'

'Did you give him your address?'

'In a manner of speaking.' Ruby sighed at her reflection in the mirror. 'Told him my name was Ethel Pearson and I lived in Curzon-Howe Road.'

The two girls collapsed over the basins in hysterical giggles.

Lily decided that she didn't like Ruby. There was a glinting cruelty about her like the blades of the pair of a scissors she was holding.

The door opened and their laughter was smothered instantly.

'Miss Froggat and Miss Somers, have you introduced yourselves?' Miss Pearson turned to Lily.

'This is Miss Forrest, our new apprentice. She will be working with me this week and then I will decide which of you will take her under your wing.'

Ruby Froggat glared at Lily. 'You'd better be quick if I'm to take you on. I don't want no greener holding me back.'

'We'll have to wait and see, won't we?' Lily was amazed at her own daring, but she wasn't going to toady to the likes of Ruby Froggat, even if it meant getting the sack on her first morning.

'Miss Forrest, I hope your needle is as swift as your tongue,' Miss Pearson remarked dryly. 'Have you got your thimble and shears with you?'

Lily nodded as she followed her back into the workroom.

She was given two pieces of navy serge, a needle and some tacking-thread.

'Now, Miss Forrest, hold the material on top so that it is slightly fuller than the cloth underneath. That's it. Don't have the thread too long or you'll be forever undoing the knots.'

Lily's fingers trembled and the needle was slippery with sweat.

'That's right, firm light stitches. Relax, Miss Forrest. Don't grip the material like a lifebelt.'

While she'd been bent over her sewing the rest of the staff had come in and taken their places.

Two grey-haired men sat cross-legged on one of the tables, sewing, while another cut out lengths of cloth with a huge pair of scissors. A tiny woman with thick-lensed glasses was sewing gold epaulettes onto an overcoat. There was the thump of an iron on the pressing-table as another man set to work. By the window two girls were sitting at sewing-machines guiding trouser seams with their hands as their feet pressed the treadles. Suddenly there was a scream of pain.

'Oh, Ivy not again,' sighed Miss Pearson. 'Mr Savours, get the tweezers and the iodine. Unscrew the needle from the machine, quickly, before you get any blood on the trousers.'

Ivy was deathly pale as Mr Savours, the ironing-board man, bent over her and pulled the needle out of her fingernail. She winced as he dabbed the iodine onto the wound and wrapped a bandage tightly round her finger.

'You'd better go home for the rest of the day Ivy. That'll be a shilling docked from your wages unless you stay late on Friday and make up the time.'

As Lily looked up, Dora caught her eye and gave her a friendly wink. She and Ruby were busy making buttonholes. Their needles flashed in and out of the uniform jackets at lightning speed.

Mr Savours watched Ivy leave before turning to Lily. 'My mouth's as dry as the bottom of a bird's cage. It must be time for tea.'

She rushed over to the gas jets and filled the kettle from a tap in the wall. There was no space to put the kettle and Lily tried to lift one of the irons but it was immovable.

191

'Fourteen pounds they weigh. Do yourself an injury trying to move one of them,' said Mr Savours winking at her.

The iron was red-hot and the old tailor lifted it effortlessly with a woollen holder and plunged it into one of the buckets of water. Lily was enveloped in a cloud of steam and the acrid smell of hot metal.

Miss Pearson moved quietly from one worker to another making adjustments here, a word of praise there, all in the same measured tone.

Everyone thanked Lily for the tea except for Ruby who was deep in conversation with Miss Markham, the gold lace woman.

'Did you read that bit in the paper about the admiral's daughter what married an ordinary Tommy what she'd nursed in France?'

'Fancy that,' said Miss Markham, rubbing the stitching-thread against a ball of bees wax.

'Must be soft in the head,' Ruby snorted.

'That'll never be your trouble,' Miss Markham laughed as she heated her bees wax stick gently with an iron. 'You'd need a blowlamp to melt your heart.' Everyone laughed but Ruby.

At last, half-twelve struck on the dockyard clock.

'Before you go home for lunch, you can accompany Miss Somers to the shop and deliver these uniforms to Mr Syme,' Miss Pearson told Lily.

With two jackets, stiff with gold braid, hung over her arm, Lily hurried to catch up with Dora.

'No, don't go in the front, Admiral Shanks'd have a fit,' Dora said, pulling Lily away from the

192

revolving glass door. 'We're the tradesmen's entrance. That's for the nobs and the gentry.'

Lily blushed. 'Don't worry,' Dora said, smiling up at her. 'You'll soon pick up the ropes. I hated it when I first started.'

'But you look as if you were born with a needle in your hand,' gasped Lily. 'I was watching you doing the buttonholes.'

'Just practice really. Tell you what, Lily, I'll ask Miss Pearson if I can have you to teach next week. How's that?'

'I'd like that, Miss Somers.'

'Name's Dora, out here. Now ring the bell.' Lily shifted the jackets from one arm to the other. 'They weigh a ton, don't they,' said Dora. 'It's all that gold braid. Sixpence an inch that costs.'

'Cripes,' Lily gasped. 'At five shillings a week, he's wearing my wages just on two rings. Four rings to each sleeve, then the epaulettes.' She whistled in disbelief.

Dora laughed. 'And all you gets is a rupture through carrying it. Course that's not counting the embroidery on his cap.'

A tall fair-haired man in an immaculate dark suit opened the door. While he was speaking he looked appraisingly at Lily. She could feel herself blushing but was determined not to be the first to look away.

'This is Miss Lily Forrest,' said Dora, performing the introductions as if they were at a society gathering instead of the back door of the tailor's shop. 'Miss Forrest, Mr Bernard Syme.'

'Delighted to make your acquaintance,' drawled Bernard.

Lily had never seen a man with such clean hands. She was fascinated as he took the jackets from her. His fingernails looked as if they had been polished and at the base of each was a perfect half-moon cuticle.

He took her hand, smiling at her confusion. Although his grey eyes seemed to look right into her, there was a mask-like secrecy about his face. Even his smile was applied from the outside. Whatever he read from his observation of Lily she could detect nothing from his pale impenetrable features. A bell rang in the shop and he disappeared as quickly as he'd come.

'You want to be careful with Bernard,' said Dora. 'He's Ruby's feller, or so she thinks. She'd scratch your eyes out if she thought you was trying to muscle in.'

'But he's old! He must be thirty,' said Lily still flustered by Bernard's attentions.

'You better get off home to your dinner,' Dora said, 'and when you come back be careful of Ruby. You can't afford to make an enemy of her on your first day.'

'I know,' sighed Lily. 'Ruby made me wild when she was talking about cadging those silks off a sailor.'

'Never mind that,' Dora butted in. 'You just remember to call her Miss Froggat or she'll make you really sorry.'

'But, Dora, it's not fair. That poor sailor's spent half his pay on her. She's treated him really...'

'There's not much in life that is fair, Lily,' Dora said calmly.

'But, Dora –' Lily protested.

194

'You get your dinner and give your tongue a rest. Be back by quarter to two or Miss Pearson will be docking your wages before you gets any.'

Lily walked home through Queen Street, stepping into the road to avoid two sailors carrying their drunken friend face down between them.

As she turned into Lemon Street she saw Gran at the doorway scanning the road.

'How did you get on?' asked Gran, following her indoors.

'Well,' said Lily cautiously, 'it wasn't a bit like I expected. I didn't do much sewing. I was sweeping up and making tea but I made a friend.'

'You can't have too many of them, Lily. What's Miss Pearson like? Is she a bit of a tartar?'

'Not really. She's quiet and calm and seems to know what everyone should be doing.'

'One of the old professionals,' said Gran approvingly, ladling out some Irish stew. She handed Lily a steaming bowl then stood with the bread clasped against her chest, slicing towards herself. She reminded Lily of Mrs Gargery in *Great Expectations*. The resemblance was a fleeting one. Mrs Gargery was thin and full of suppressed fury; Gran was plump and placid, slow to anger and quick to forgive any wrongs against her.

Thinking about *Great Expectations* reminded Lily of Dad and her excitement when he had given her the book at Christmas. She'd been mean and distant to him all over something she had imagined that she'd seen through Miriam's widow. Thank goodness she and Dad had parted

195

friends at the station.

'What are the other apprentices like?' asked Gran, breaking into her thoughts.

'There's this girl, Ruby Frogatt. She's beautiful to look at Gran, but she knows it and sort of trades on it. She made me wild.' Lily related the incident of the sailor's scarf.

'You want to watch your step with her. Thinks she's got a free ticket for life. You got to beat her at her own game.'

'How d'you mean?' asked Lily, mopping up the remains of the stew with a second slice of bread.

'Strategy,' said Gran. 'Don't let her goad you into losing your temper. Bide your time and keep your powder dry.'

Lily laughed. Gran sometimes appeared to talk in riddles but when she took time to puzzle out the meaning there was always a solid kernel of commonsense.

The clock on the mantelpiece struck half-past one. 'My stars above the crows!' exclaimed. Gran. 'You'd better get yourself back to work.'

Lily kissed her and hurried out of the house. 'Remember,' Gran called after her, 'you catch more flies with honey than vinegar.'

'At the end of the road she nearly bumped into Miriam and Rosie.

''illy, 'illy,' shouted the little girl, delightedly.

'Sorry, Rosie,' said Lily flushing with embarrassment. She hadn't been to see Miriam since Christmas. 'I've got to rush. I'm going back to work.'

'Good luck,' said Miriam. She looked tired and pale.

196

Lily felt guiltily relieved there was no time to talk. Miriam deserved an apology but something held her back from making it. A sliver of suspicion that wouldn't go away. Of course, the man in Miriam's kitchen on Christmas Eve could have been anyone. Dad's new tattoo also proved nothing. Hundreds of sailors must have chosen to celebrate their first leave since the war by getting a fresh tattoo. What nagged at her was the time Dad spent with Miriam on Christmas night and the fact that Miriam had not asked her why she was being so unfriendly towards her. Almost as if she felt guilty or something. Her see-sawing thoughts brought her to the workroom door. Once through there she knew there'd be no time for such trivialities. This was the world of work.

The afternoon settled down into a steady rhythm of thumping irons and whirring treadles. Miss Pearson smiled: 'You've acquitted yourself very well, Miss Forrest.'

Lily was startled at the compliment and blushed with pleasure.

'Now, see if you can fell this lining on your own.' As Miss Pearson turned towards the pressing-table, Dora licked her finger and drew a giant tick in the air.

Lily saw Ruby glare at her but she didn't care – she'd found a friend.

Remembering Gran's words, she gave Ruby a smile of honeyed sweetness.

Chapter Nineteen

Miriam stood shivering at the doorstep. If only wishing could bring a letter, she thought, as the postman passed her door and disappeared into the February fog.

Her rushed goodbye to Alec seemed a lifetime ago – certainly longer than the five weeks it had been in reality. On the morning he was due to leave she had knocked on the Forrests' back door with the excuse of borrowing a reel of cotton. At the sight of her, Alec had sent his mother over to the shop for an unwanted bottle of cough mixture. And then they were alone. He had taken her into his arms, moulding her to his body pressing his fingers against her spine. He'd kissed her hair, her eyelids and her mouth. There had been such an urgency between them. Were it not for his mother's imminent return they would have lain together on the kitchen floor.

'I'll be back in the summer,' he'd promised. 'As soon as I get to Scotland I'll write to you.'

His promises had crumbled like pie-crust in the long intervening weeks. Angrily Miriam rubbed her tears away with her apron as she crept down the passage past Rosie asleep in her pram. Again she shivered. No, she could not be ill, there was too much to do. Miriam swallowed down her fear. There was no possibility of taking to her bed with Rosie to care for.

Awaiting her on the sideboard was a stack of sailors' collars she was part-making for Mrs Forrest. The thought of tacking on those white tapes, mitring the corners and hand finishing them to the regulation sixteen stitches to the inch made her head spin. But before that there was Mr Pragnell's dinner to get by one o'clock, less than half an hour away. She must lay the table with the damask cloth, the bone-handled knives and the silver cruet. Miriam sighed. Her life stretched endlessly before her, measured out in soap and needles.

The sound of Mr Pragnell's key in the door had Rosie awake and bouncing with excitement. 'Paggy, Paggy,' she cried.

'Mr Pragnell, I'm sorry. I'm all behind today.'

'No matter, Mrs Naylor.' He smiled cheerily at Rosie and tickled her under the chin. 'I'll scan my paper while you catch up with things.'

Hastily Miriam unharnessed Rosie from her pram and tied her into a kitchen chair, giving her a soldier of bread to tide her over until she'd served the dinner.

The pages of Mr Pragnell's newspaper seemed to crackle more loudly than usual and his voice boomed in her head as he read out snippets to her from President Wilson's speech at the Paris Peace Conference.

Steam rose from the saucepan as Miriam spooned the mutton stew into three bowls. It enveloped her in a sweet fatty odour making her stomach heave. Gritting her teeth she mashed up Rosie's dinner and set it aside to cool. 'Ready now, Mr Pragnell,' she said.

'Capital! I'm as hungry as a hunter,' he declared, reaching for her serviette and tucking it into his waistcoat.

Miriam tried to eat, but the mouthful of potato rasped against the sides of her throat like sandpaper. She handed Rosie her spoon and the child splashed it excitedly into the bowl, making puddles on the tablecloth.

'It says that the influenza appears to have been brought here from Scapa Flow at Christmas, by the sailors coming on leave.'

Mr Pragnell's words distracted Miriam and as she turned towards him, Rosie flung her dish on the floor where it shattered into pieces.

A wave of heat washed over Miriam. She must get the child out of her sight before she struck her. With fumbling fingers she untied Rosie from the chair and thrust her out into the yard and shut the door. She sank into the armchair holding her head as the pain skewered behind her temples. Rosie banged on the window screaming hysterically. Behind her Mr Pragnell was saying something that made no sense.

'Mrs Naylor ... the child ... you're ill ... fetch Mrs Forrest ... I will.'

If she could just get herself an empty space where nothing was required of her. If she could only get Rosie to stop screaming. Dragging herself out of the chair Miriam stepped over the broken bowl and out into the yard.

The sudden rush of cool air made her giddy. Rosie had by this time run down the yard towards the sound of voices next door but catching sight of her mother she changed direction, running with open arms. Between them was a backless kitchen chair. Miriam willed herself towards it. Within inches of her goal she tripped over the ash bucket cutting her shin on the ridged handle.

The ground seemed to rise up and strike her. All of her body was raw and jangling with pain. Something warm and wet was seeping into her shoe. She lay whimpering on the path while Rosie sobbed and clutched at her.

Gradually she became aware of Mrs Forrest talking slowly and calmly. She was being lifted into the chair. Rosie had stopped crying.

'Just rest there while I bind up that cut on your leg. That's it. Mr Pragnell's taken charge of Rosie so you've nothing to worry about.'

'I feel dizzy. I'm going to be–' Her throat burned as the vomit rushed up from her stomach and down her dress.

'Lean on me, Mrs Naylor, that's it, slow and steady. You've got flu, my dear. You'll have to go horizontal for a good few days.'

Miriam had come to the end of coping. She sat in her room like a helpless child while Mrs Forrest brought hot water and sponged her face and hands and helped her into a clean nightdress. She sprinkled a cloth with lavender water and bound it around Miriam's head before folding back the sheets and helping her into bed.

'You just lose yourself for a few hours. Rosie can come in with me. I'll make you some toast water and when it's cooled I'll fetch it in.'

Miriam sank down beneath the covers, the bandage cool against her burning forehead. She slept and slept with one day running into another. It seemed whenever she awoke Mrs Forrest was there with her, easing her throat with her honey and vinegar syrup or renewing the lavender cloth or simply sitting beside her bed. She felt like a child in the care of its mother. Quietly, calmly, Mrs Forrest took charge.

At first she was anxious all the time about Rosie. She would start up in the night terrified that her child had died, but as the fever receded she remembered that she was sleeping with Lily. Occasionally Lily herself would call in with Rosie to visit her.

Miriam would hug her daughter close and fret at how she went back to the Forrests' house each time with barely a wave in her direction. Each visit she seemed to have learnt new words and to have become less of a baby and more a little girl. Lily herself was coolly polite.

Miriam looked forward to Mrs Forrest's visits, to the beautifully laid trays. The marmalade in a tiny glass dish and the snowdrops in a blue egg-cup. She would keep her informed about her neighbours and all the day-to-day happenings in the street.

'I won't stop long my dear,' she would say, 'it's a good blowing day and I must see to the wash and get back to Rosie so that Lily can get to work.' Or, 'Mr Pragnell's like a dog with two tails. He's just got a letter from the Society of Marine Artists to say that the painting that he took to London has been highly recommended.'

'Thank you Mrs Naylor, that's awfully kind of you,' he said, beaming from ear to ear when

Miriam congratulated him. 'Fancy you remembering it was HMS *Leviathan* leaving harbour.'

'Well, it was one of the paintings I saw when I first came here,' she said, smiling at her employer as he hovered in the doorway of her room. 'I loved the billowing sails and all the little details with the rigging that you pointed out to me.'

'It took me an age to complete it,' he said, 'but I feel justly proud of the accuracy.'

'Well, you will be able to spend more time in your studio next week. I shall be up and about by the weekend and ready to look after the house again.'

'*Festina lente,* my dear. Hurry slowly. I'm sure Mrs Forrest will put up with me for a few more days.' Miriam smiled to herself. Mr Pragnell's affection for Mrs Forrest was a secret he was very bad at keeping.

Slowly she recovered and Rosie returned to her.

'I shall miss the little scrap,' Mrs Forrest said. 'I love them when they're just changing from toddlers to children, watching them develop their own characteristics. But Rosie has been special. She's made a place for herself in my heart. She held up her hands out to me so trustingly that day you were took badly.' She kissed the child and sat her on Miriam's bed. 'Still, I must get on. Mr Goldstein will think I've left the country if I don't get some collars round to him today.'

'Thank you for all you've done, Mrs Forrest,' said Miriam, feeling acutely ashamed of how she was deceiving Alec's mother in spite of all her kindness.

'Not at all, my dear,' her neighbour smiled at

her. 'It's the least you would do for me if the boot were on the other foot. Now Mr Pragnell's going to Romsey for the weekend and I've got in all your shopping so you'll have a couple of days to find your feet again.'

Early on the Saturday morning as she lay in a drowsy half sleep Miriam heard the rattle of the letter-box and the soft thud of something hitting the mat. She slid out of bed and tiptoed down the passage. Hopefully she picked up the letter and turned it over. It was addressed to her with a 'Rosyth' postmark.

Miriam knelt by the window letting the light from a gap in the curtains fall on the envelope. Fearfully she unfolded the letter.

My Own True Love,

How sad it makes me to think of you waiting for a letter and me not able to write. I have been in hospital with flu which later turned to pneumonia. January has been a complete blank. Tomorrow I go back on board so I am taking this opportunity to write sending my fondest love. Tears gathered in her eyes as she thought of him lying sick all those miles away.

Scapa Flow is dismally grey and cold. There are many German ships here and the sailors have a wretched time cooped up in foreign waters, not able to go ashore or speak to anyone.

I am saving every last penny towards my summer leave to spend on my new little family. I have not forgotten my promise to you and will talk to Ma and Lily as soon as I'm home. For now I have enclosed a ten-shilling note for you to buy yourself a treat of some sort.

Miriam unfolded the note and sat looking at it. A dozen ways of spending it came to mind, from hat trimmings to petticoat lace. A whole ten shillings she didn't have to account for! Smiling to herself she returned to the letter.

I long to see you again and hold you close, also Rosie. I have made her a little Jumping Jack the Sailor toy and I'm impatient to show it to her.
With Deepest Love,
Ever and Ever,
Your Alec.

'He loves us,' she whispered to the sleeping Rosie. 'He loves us, he loves us.' She laughed softly to herself as she read and re-read Alec's letter.

For the first time in weeks she felt hungry. Leaving Rosie well tucked up she went out into the kitchen and took stock of the larder. Instead of looking at the two bottom shelves with their usual run of flour, bread, suet and split peas she let her gaze wander over the items on Mr Pragnell's shelf.

There, like the ward-room of the larder, were the quality goods essential to any genteel household: Gentleman's Relish, Oxford Marmalade, black caddies of Orange Pekoe and Earl Grey tea and a blue-and-white jar of preserved ginger.

Miriam quickly laid and lit the fire, placed the kettle on the trivet then set herself a tray complete with a napkin in a silver ring. She cut some bread very thin and spread it with butter then spooned on to it some of Mr Pragnell's apricot conserve. 'Earl Grey, I think,' she said in

205

her best 'Palmerston Road' voice as she opened the lacquered caddy. She sipped the tea, holding the cup with her little finger crooked in the approved manner. She closed her eyes and breathed in the delicate scent of orange and bergamot. The apricot jam was richly satisfying. Her tongue quested the last sticky morsel from her lips. 'He loves us,' she said to herself like a magic charm.

In a whirl of energy and celebration at getting Alec's letter, she tidied the house and caught up on Mr Pragnell's ironing. On the Sunday afternoon she took Rosie walking in Victoria Park. By the time they returned in the wintry gloom of early evening she was exhausted with barely enough energy to wash and feed Rosie and get her into bed.

She lay down beside her daughter and tried not to drop off to sleep as Rosie prattled on about the events of the day.

'Yes, darling, we went to the park and saw the trees and the doggie and the little girl with her dollie's pram.'

'Horsie, cop, cop,' insisted Rosie trying to prolong their talk.

'Clip-clop, clip-clop,' Miriam murmured.

Gradually Rosie's talking stopped and her eyes closed.

Miriam took Alec's letter from beneath her pillow and read it again. He would be back in the summer. Soon she might become Mrs Miriam Forrest. The name had a well set-up ring to it.

A tap on the window abruptly interrupted her thoughts. Standing shivering at the front door was Mercy Vine. She handed Miriam a grubby envelope. 'Lady give it me for ya,' she said.

'Thank you, Mercy. Hadn't you better nip back home? It's too cold to be hanging about.'

'Ma's tight, she don't care where I goes,' said Mercy calmly. 'And I got sommink to arst yer.'

'Come into the kitchen and I'll stir up the fire,' said Miriam puzzling over the envelope. It had the one word 'Miriam' printed in pencil. She felt sick. It was from her mother, she knew it. How had she found her?

Mercy tugged at her skirt. 'What do you want?' she asked impatiently.

'It's 'ankie trill tomorrer an' I ain't got one.'

'Tell me again slowly,' Miriam sighed.

'Miss will 'it me wiv a ruler.'

Miriam knelt down beside the seven-year-old, her impatience gone as quickly as it came. She smiled into her eyes, brown as boot-buttons and seeming too large for her face. Her nose was encrusted with snot and her nails were bitten to the quick. 'Why will she hit you?'

''Cos it's 'ankie trill an' I ain't got one.'

'Ah, handkerchief drill,' said Miriam understanding at last.

'Our Mary give me a bit of rag last time an' I put it up me knicker leg. Then it fell out at playtime an' I lost it. Didn't 'alf whack me, she did.'

'Sit there a minute and I'll get you one.'

Miriam crept into the bedroom past the flickering night light and eased open the top drawer of the dressing-table and felt for the pile of clean hankies. She remembered hankie drill.

Going to school in creased frocks with hems half hanging down and never a clean hankie to be found. All her classmates waving their handkerchiefs, all except her. The teacher, in her crisply ironed pin-tucked blouse and polished shoes had looked at her class of back-street children with immaculate disdain. Well that wouldn't happen to Rosie, of that she was determined.

She handed the handkerchief to Mercy who stood by the kitchen door dancing from one foot to the other.

'Ta, Mrs Naylor,' Mercy's face split into an impish grin. 'Can I go to the lav, nearly wettin' myself?'

'Off you go, quick smart,' said Miriam, opening the back door. Reluctantly she opened the envelope.

Dear Miriam,

I saw you talking to Big Arthur down the market but you went off for I could say nothin he told me you was living in Lemon Street. Jumper has gone and left me potless. I am at the workhowse this lady what visits say she will pass this on for me. Come and see your old ma for it too late. Violet Slattery.

Mercy came back into the kitchen hitching up her knickers. 'Hurry up, now,' snapped Miriam, impatient to be on her own. The child scuttled out of the front door.

Miriam took the note and tore it into pieces, flinging them on the fire. Never, never would she see her mother again. She was done with her past.

208

Chapter Twenty

The early summer sunshine struggled through the window making everything look faded and fagged out. Beattie sighed; she was sick of being indoors and famished for the sight and sound of the sea. A visit to Hester along at Eastney was well overdue. Albert would be nearby, at the Royal Marine Barracks, painting a portrait of the Major General; she might even walk back with him. Leaving the dinner-time dishes to drain she went upstairs, dragged off her working clothes and put on the navy coat-dress she'd bought in the January sales. She topped it off with her straw boater, veteran of many seasons. 'Hello old faithful,' she said as she secured it firmly on her head with a pearl pin.

She passed down the street greeting Granny Dowell who sat in her doorway knitting while Lloyd George her monkey scuttled up and down the passage. Dolly Vine, in a world of her own, perched on her doorstep singing while Blyth rolled a marble down the gutter.

Beattie turned thankfully towards Queen Street and The Hard. She'd seen more than enough of her neighbours. Ever since Christmas the flu had been knocking them down like ninepins. She'd been hard-pressed to cope with all the pleas for help: child-minding, taking in their washing, making extra bowls of soup, lending half-crowns for the doctor's visit. Not to mention Miriam and her child.

A closeness had grown up between them all during the young woman's illness, almost as if they were family. The times when she took in her meals and sat with Miriam had become precious to both of them. Beattie took pride in Miriam's recovery. Each day she was stronger, hungrier and more talkative. She spoke with affection of her Aunt Florrie and with some bitterness about her mother. Then there was Daisy in Gosport who sounded a real treasure. 'You must write to her and have her over for tea. Mr Pragnell would like you to see this as your home.'

'I'm beginning to – see this as home, I mean,' Miriam had said shyly.

Beattie had sat with Rosie on her lap singing to her as she had with Andrew and Lily. The little girl had repeated the tunes, each day seeming to remember more of the words. All children responded to singing and stories, Beattie told herself, but there was something about Rosie she couldn't fathom. It was as if she had known the child before. Her little fads and foibles did not surprise her. Even before Rosie waved her hands in distress Beattie knew that she hated sticky fingers. The way she turned her head, her habit of bunching up her frock in excitement and rubbing her ears when she was tired were all familiar. But how?

A loud toot from a paddle steamer coming into Clarence Pier startled her back to the present. She'd walked from the harbour to the beginning of the sea-front without even noticing. Now she

210

watched the day trippers strolling along the pier, waiting to board the steamer to the Isle of Wight and optimistically carrying parasols. Across the Solent the Island was clearly visible with its patchwork of fields, the spire of St John's Church in Ryde and a fringe of sandy beaches. Such clarity usually meant bad weather.

Beattie loved being out on the 'prom', strolling between the two piers seeing all the hurly burly of the seaside, whelk stalls, jellied eels and candy floss. A group of sailors walked by whistling at a threesome of giggling girls ahead.

Beattie chuckled. Of course, it was the first of May, White Cap Cover Day. She felt a surge of optimism at this sign of early summer. Traditionally on May the first all the sailors topped their navy caps with white covers then, on the first of October they removed them again for the drabness of the winter uniform. The cotton covers had to be kept white by applying a wet cloth to a block of blanco. If it rained, streaks of blanco ran down the sailor's face and onto his uniform.

As Alec used to say, 'The "uniform microbes" who make the regulations have no idea of practicalities.'

Beattie smiled: in Joseph's day they had worn straw hats.

She left the western end of the sea-front and stuck out along the prom towards the South Parade Pier. This was Southsea, Portsmouth's more elegant sister. Here were the posh hotels where elderly guests could be seen snoozing in the lounges whilst on the promenade nursemaids pushed perambulators and young children bowled their hoops.

Beattie squinted up at the seagulls. Joseph had said that old Chief Stokers came back as seabirds. With their clashing beaks and grating voices he was probably right but if she couldn't have him back as a man, she'd be buggered if she'd make do with a seagull. Laughing to herself she made her way to the water's edge. She breathed deeply, relishing the clean cold air. Her anxieties floated away from her as she gazed at the sea. Never the same mood and never the same colour, that was its lure and satisfaction. Sometimes an angry pewter tide lashed the shore, flinging stones and seaweed across the road and then having exhausted itself, lay barely moving in a green torpor. How often had she gazed out at it, trying to draw Joseph's ship back over the horizon. Today the sea was playful. Waves flirted with the shingle: kiss and retreat, kiss and retreat. Beattie threw a last stone into the water then crossed from the promenade towards Hester's home in Cromwell Road, opposite the Marine Barracks.

As Beattie approached, women were passing in and out of the Clock Tower to return their weekly sewing of Marine's khaki shirts, cholera belts and canvas bread-bags. Some struggled with parcels, others suitcases or loaded prams.

'It's our Beattie,' shouted George, as he opened the door. 'What a turn-up.'

She followed him out into the garden and smiled at Hester who was kneeling on the garden path surrounded by seed boxes. How different she seemed in her own setting. Tendrils of faded auburn hair escaped their pins and freckles dusted her nose. Beattie felt a sudden rush of affection as she watched Hester set the plants into their borders. Her large hands with their broken fingernails had such sensitivity. She wanted to take them in her own and brush away the earth and kiss their swollen arthritic knuckles. Instead she bent and patted her arm saying, 'You've got it beautiful out here, Hester. You're the monarch of all you survey.'

Hester laughed. 'You're right, Beattie. This is my little bit of Heaven. When I'm dibbing about in the soil, I'm at peace.' Then as George settled himself and Beattie on a wooden bench she showed a flash of her old asperity.

'Get up, George. Put the kettle on and get some of that seed cake out of the pantry.'

The rich scent of wallflowers hung in the air, their purple petals contrasting with the border of creamy primroses.

'What you got in these boxes?' Beattie asked.

Hester glowed. 'They're pansies, all different colours. I brought them on in the front bedroom. It gets the sun first thing, like a little greenhouse.'

'They always reminds me of cats' faces, do pansies,' said Beattie.

'Yes,' said Hester. 'They seem to smile at you.'

George set a tea tray beside them and attempted to seat himself next to Beattie but Hester once again forestalled him.

'Go down the Three Marines,' she said, giving him a shilling from her apron pocket. Unabashed, George gave Beattie a whiskery kiss and set off to his local.

213

The two women sat in companionable silence with eyes closed feeling the sun warming their faces.

'How's Lily?'

'Growing fast,' sighed Beattie. 'At Denby and Shanks doing her apprenticeship. She'll be fifteen next month.'

'Good Heavens!' exclaimed Hester stirring her tea. 'It only seems like yesterday that you came up here with the pair of them in a pram saying Mary'd died and Alec was off to China.'

'Fifteen years ago,' said Beattie, watering the plants as Hester set them in the trough. 'Mary going turned my life upside down. I'd just got myself settled into a routine of sorts. Coping without Joseph and taking on the sewing. Then in the space of three weeks or so Mary's dead, Alec's off to the China station and I'm looking after two motherless babes.'

'All credit to you, Beattie,' said Hester. 'Lily has turned into a fine young woman. After all these years, it's a wonder your Alec hasn't married again. It's a long time for a handsome well set-up man like him to be on his own.'

Beattie picked up a piece of garden twine left on the grass sand began fiddling with it. 'He seems in no hurry,' she said, trying to ignore the picture in her head of Alec and Miriam looking at each other, that last day of his leave when she'd surprised them by coming back too soon from the shop.

'If he marries and Lily settles to her apprenticeship your worries will all be over.' Hester picked up their empty cups and set them back on the tray. Then as if suddenly remembering she added, 'I was on the tram the other day. A few seats ahead of me was this woman. There was something familiar about her but I couldn't place what it was. Then when she turned and passed me on the way to get off, well I nearly had a fit. She was the image of Alec's Mary. You know, those great dark eyes and thin pale face. I thought I was seeing things.'

Beattie twisted the twine tighter and tighter around her finger. Hester's voice seemed to advance and recede from her, one minute soft and blurred and the next booming in her ear.

'I even got off at the same stop so that I could speak with her but she disappeared into Handleys. I must have been mistaken, unless she had a twin.'

Beattie looked at her finger turning blue and slowly unravelled the string. The fears and doubts she had swallowed down, all those years ago, when Alec had come back from identifying Mary's water-logged body, were painfully revived. Unknowingly Hester was bringing them back to the surface.

'What's the matter, Beattie? You've gone pale. Are you all right?'

She had to get away or she'd be done for. Be on her own to try and regain control.

'She is dead, isn't she, Bea?' Hester said. 'There couldn't have been a mistake? Alec identified the body didn't he?'

'Hester, for God's sake! It was bad enough when it happened,' Beattie cried, springing to her feet and pacing up and down the path. 'You know

215

it's something I can't bear to talk about.'

'Oh Beattie, please don't rush off. Have another cup of tea.' Hester took her arm and led her back to her chair. 'I wish I'd never mentioned it. You know I'd rather cut out my tongue than upset you.' Hester was almost in tears.

Beattie was desperate to leave. Somehow she forced herself to sit still. 'Don't worry, Hester,' she said, dredging up a smile. 'You just caught me off guard. I'll be right as ninepence in a few minutes.'

'You drink that while it's hot and I'll pot you up some pansies to take home with you.'

Hester rattled on about the garden and Beattie swallowed down the tea as fast as she could. Once the flowers were in a pot and settled in her shopping bag she got to her feet. 'It's been good to see you and George. I'll nip along again one Sunday with Lily, now the weather's brightened. No, you stay there in the sunshine. I'll see myself out.' Beattie kissed Hester hastily on the cheek, then made her escape.

She almost ran down the road, her heart banging against her ribs. Someone, perhaps it was Albert, called to her as she passed the Marine Barracks but she pretended not to hear. If she could just get down on to the beach and be by herself. Thankfully there were few people about to see her distress, a couple of Marines and a man in the distance with a dog. With tears pouring down her face Beattie scrabbled over the pebbles to the water's edge. Oh God, oh God, what if it were true and Hester really had seen Mary? She couldn't come back now. Just as Lily was settled, just as Alec was on the brink of something.

All those years ago when Alec had come back, white-faced, from the mortuary, he'd said, 'It was her and that's an end to it. Never, ever say her name to me again.'

'Alec.' She'd grabbed his arm and he'd pulled it free, almost knocking her over. 'How do you know it's her? The police said she'd been in the water for a long time and her face was bruised.'

'You don't have to remind me,' he said, going to the dresser and reaching down the rum bottle. 'That face and what the sea did to it will haunt me. I had to go outside and be sick before I could go back in and sign the papers. And the cold,' he shivered, 'it's got right into my bones. Never, never do I want to talk about her again. She's out of my life, forever. Do you understand?'

He was angry but beneath the shouting he was frightened.

'Alec, I know you're lying,' she'd said. 'I know you were unhappy with Mary. But this is not the way out of it.' Pleadingly she'd said, 'It could be Mary, of course it could. But what if that poor woman lying there is someone else's wife or mother? Someone dearly loved and missed.' She sat opposite him at the kitchen table and took his hand. This time he did not resist but wouldn't face her. 'I could go and see her. I could say you were too upset to be sure.'

And then it happened – the thing she couldn't forget. Alec had taken his father's Bible from the shelf and placed it between them on the table. 'I swear on my children's lives and on this Bible

217

that the woman I saw was Mary.'

Still, she could have overridden him. Still, she could have gone to the mortuary, but she hadn't, and in not going she had become part of the shameful secret.

Frantically she searched for her hankie. Oh, where the hell was it? Losing control terrified her. But the consequences if Mary Kenny were still alive would be overwhelming.

The sound of footsteps crunching over the pebbles added to her panic. She kept her face turned resolutely towards the sea. Couldn't let anyone see her in this state.

'Beatrice, my dear.'

No, not even Albert could help her now. She ignored him while she scrabbled in her pockets for the elusive handkerchief.

He gave her his own and stood beside her, tossing stones into the sea until her crying stopped. 'Let me unfold my painting-stool for you. I'll just anchor it on the stones. That's it, my dear.'

'Oh Albert,' she gasped. 'I've got myself into such a state.'

'So I see,' he said, kneeling beside her, holding her hands. 'You're not alone, Beatrice. Whatever is distressing you I am here with you.' He took a newspaper from his pocket and spread it on the stones before sitting down beside her.

'I don't know where to start,' she said.

'You need tell me nothing,' he said. 'We can sit here watching the waves rise and fall. And when you are ready we can stroll home at our own pace.'

'I think Alec's wife, Mary, is still alive,' Beattie blurted out suddenly. 'Hester thought she saw her on a tram the other day.' She clutched Albert's hand. 'And even though Alec identified her as drowned, all those years ago, I have never felt certain, in my heart, that it was her.'

'But, have you seen her with your own eyes?' said Albert, lobbing another stone into the water.

Beattie shook her head.

'There must be many young women like Mary of medium height with blue eyes and black hair. Of course it may be grey by now.'

'I've been expecting it all these years,' said Beattie.

'I was in Singapore when all this happened, Beatrice. By the time I got home you and your grandchildren had settled to your new life with each other.'

'It was all a mistake, the whole marriage,' said Beattie as if he hadn't spoken. 'Alec was barely eighteen and Mary was pregnant. I was still grieving for Joseph. They'd hardly any money and I think having Lily was the last straw. Mary was ill all through the time she was carrying and when Lily was born she couldn't seem to take any interest in her. The house went to pot and there was never a meal ready for Alec. He just got impatient with her. One day she brought the babies round to me. She hadn't bothered to comb her hair, it was all anyhow. She said she was going to the shops and that was it.' Beattie sighed. 'I never took much notice at the time but when I look back I can see she was saying good-bye. She kissed both of them before leaving. Of

219

course Andrew was nearly four then and he was crying. She said, "Ma, you've been good to me," and she kissed me, too. Something she'd never done. Later by the side of the chair I found a bag with a photo of Mary in it and a pair of silver earrings.'

'Did Alec not have any idea where she might have gone?'

'Each night he walked the streets looking for her. We told the police and then after three weeks or so, Constable Wilkes came around to say this body had been found washed ashore at the Point. It was two days before Alec was due to go on a draft to the Far East. Alec seemed certain it was her even before he'd seen the body. Constable Wilkes said there had been a collision with a boat and it would be difficult to identify the woman; the face was very badly bruised and swollen.'

'A husband would recognise his wife by other signs,' said Albert. 'We all have little distinctive imperfections.'

'Alec wanted it all to be over and to get away as soon as possible. Once he knew the children would be cared for he wanted the body to be her, true or false.'

'It must have been an enormous ordeal for him. A young man barely in his twenties with two young children. Mary was an orphan, wasn't she?'

'Yes, like me.'

'Did you attend the funeral?'

Beattie shook her head. 'I was so caught up with Lily and Andrew, adapting to having babies around again, making them feel safe and cared for. And I was never convinced that it really was Mary in that coffin. I thought about some mother or husband missing their daughter or wife. Still searching for her, and there she was down in the mortuary. Every knock on the door had my heart in my mouth thinking it was Mary come back again.'

'Do you still feel that she is alive, Beatrice? Not just because of what Hester has said.'

Beattie shook her head. 'I don't know what to think, Albert and that's the truth. The fact that she's never been seen or heard of and has never contacted her children would point to her being dead. But I suppose there's a bit of guilt in me that I, perhaps, wanted her dead. I was needed by those children and given a fresh purpose in life. And for Alec of course it was his escape from an unhappy marriage.'

'What frightens you about her being alive?'

'It would prove that my son had lied to me. That we both had lied to Lily. I'd be frightened of losing her.'

Albert squeezed her hand. 'You don't think that all the love and care you have given her over the years would be so lightly discarded?'

'What about Alec? That's what really frightens me. He may be looking to marry again. What if Mary turned up at the wedding? She could destroy us all.'

'So a chance remark from Hester has stirred up a hornet's nest?'

'Not altogether.' Beattie sighed. 'Albert, if only I was certain.'

'Ah certainty,' he nodded. 'Wasn't that what

poor doubting Thomas wanted?'

Beattie patted Albert's hand. 'I don't know what I'd do without you,' she said.

'I wish you knew what to do *with* me. My heart will grow barnacles waiting for you to decide.'

'You know I love you as a friend,' said Beattie smiling into his dear familiar face. 'But I still feel married to Joseph even after all these years.'

'Friend it shall be,' he said.

'Thank you for being here,' Beattie said. 'You saved me from going to pieces.'

'My privilege. Is there anything concrete I can do?'

'Like what? Albert, what are you suggesting?'

'Putting something in the paper, asking Mary to contact you. Talking with Constable Wilkes.'

'No.' Beattie shook her head, vigorously. 'I'll just have to live with my doubts. Now I've shared them I'm not so frightened.'

Albert took her arm and they started the long walk back to Lemon Street.

Beattie had lied. Albert had been a comfort, of course he had. But she was still afraid. If only he had taken charge of her as Joseph would have done.

There was a quotation Lily's teacher had written in her autograph book.

There is a tide in the affairs of men,
Which, taken at the flood, leads on to fortune,
Omitted, all the voyage of their life
Is bound in shallows and in miseries.

Poor Albert, she thought, too timid to strike out

222

for what he wants. Contenting himself with half a loaf.

She felt exhausted, what with all the walking and the tears and now there was a strange hollowness where the secret had lain.

Chapter Twenty-One

Like a blowsy old barmaid on her last fling, Queen Street threw caution to the winds. Flags were flung across the road from one shop to another. Thirty-five pubs competed in patriotic bombast. The Royal Oak declared, 'God Bless Our Boys in Blue' whilst the Bear retorted, 'Britons never shall be slaves', and from the Cock and Bottle came the assertion, 'We've had our fill of Kaiser Bill.'

It was the morning of the Peace Pageant, Saturday July the nineteenth, and the rain showed no sign of letting up. Lily noticed that the colours on some of the garlands were running into each other. What if the Union Jack ribbons around the straw hats she and Dora were wearing got wet? They'd end up with striped faces.

Since starting work at Denby and Shanks Lily and Dora had become firm friends. Miss Pearson allowed Dora to take Lily under her wing. She had shown her how to baste the padding and linings into the uniform jackets with rows and rows of tacking stitches. While Lily laboured over her basting, Dora worked attaching the linings to the collars and lapels so that they would sit neatly around the wearer's neck. This required padding stitches which had to be almost invisible from the front of the garment. They were tricky, and the seamstress had to have the top layer of material fuller than the one underneath.

'Don't think I'll ever get to sew like that,' sighed Lily. 'My fingers are like bunches of sausages.'

'Blimey, Lil,' laughed Dora. 'Don't be in such a hurry. I been workin' here for nearly three years. It's all about gettin' your hands and eyes and brain working together.'

Best of all were the times when Dora invited her home to her noisy family in Unicorn Street. The Somers family ran a large bicycle shop and lived over the premises. Next to the shop were sheds where dockyard maties paid sixpence a week to store their bikes before passing through Unicorn Gate to their work. In the evenings Mr Somers would have all the bikes ready and waiting for their owners' return.

'Clever is our Dad,' Dora said proudly. 'There's hundreds of bikes, but he never makes a mistake, always knows which is which.'

Mrs Somers was equally busy. She would be up at five making up fourpenny bags of sandwiches for the men.

Today Lily was going to have her dinner with the family before setting off with Dora to see the Pageant. As she approached Somers and Sons Bicycle Sales, Repairs and Storage, Dora's Dad, his brown shop coat straining over his stomach, was locking up.

'Good morning, young Lily,' he said breezily,

stepping back and letting her go ahead of him up the stairs. At the top she met Mrs Somers coming along the passage carrying a plate of sliced meat. She gave Lily a tired smile. 'You look pretty, dear. Go in and sit down. You know everyone, don't you?'

'Shall I take that for you?' Lily offered to carry the dish.

'That's kind,' Mrs Somers breathed.

Everyone squeezed around the bulbous-legged oak table that dominated the little upstairs room. Lily was wedged between Mark and Barney, Dora's brothers. Opposite were Dora and Mr Somers. There was a chair at the end of the table for Mrs Somers but she seemed to take her meals standing up in snatched mouthfuls between fetching and carrying for everyone.

All the talk was of the Pageant. 'It'll be a day to remember and no mistake,' said Mr Somers. 'There'll be the Royal Marine Band in their red coats, all the navy top brass, all the floats with their flowers.' As he spooned mashed potato on to his plate he said, 'You two boys behave yourselves. No coming home the worse for wear and crashing into your grandma's bedroom like you did last time, giving her the fright of her life.'

'Certainly not, Pater,' said Mark, winking at Lily. He was sharp-faced and brown-eyed like Dora. Having his eighteenth birthday on Armistice Day he'd narrowly missed the war. 'I 'spose you'll be mooning over Mabel, from the paper shop,' he teased his younger brother. Barney blushed furiously.

Lily liked Barney, often the butt of his larky

225

brother's jokes. Once she'd met him in the Carnegie library and found they shared an enthusiasm for Sherlock Holmes stories. When Dora discovered that Lily and Barney also shared the same birthday she dubbed them The Terrible Twins.

The meal was interrupted by a thumping on the floor above and shrieks of, 'Myrtle, Myrtle!'

Mrs Somers' hands flew to her face. 'I've forgotten Ma's dinner.'

'Give it me,' said Dora, slamming a plate on a tray. 'I'll take it up to the old shrew.'

'Myrtle, sit down and eat your dinner,' said Mr Somers. 'Mark, you can go out to the kitchen and get the apple pie and custard.'

'Seeing as I'm bringing it in, I get to eat the biggest piece,' Mark said, winking again at Lily as he got up out of his chair.

Mrs Somers smiled at her son when he returned and cut him a generous portion which he immediately swamped with custard before passing the jug to anyone else.

'The sun's out,' said Dora returning to her place. 'We'll have to be at the Town Hall by half-past one if we want a good view of everything.'

Once the pudding was finished Mr Somers rubbed his hands together and said, 'Now if we're to see the sights, it's all hands to the pump. Dora and Lily, you clear the table and wash up. Barney, you get Gran's bath-chair out of the shed. Myrtle, you get her dressed and ready and Mark and me will carry her downstairs.'

Lily was curious to meet Dora's Grandma. So far she'd only ever heard her screeching or tapping her stick. The two girls washed and dried the dishes with great speed, eager to be at the Pageant. They were adjusting their hats in the hall mirror when Grandma appeared.

Bonneted and shawled, she looked like a large angry baby. She was lowered into an armchair while Mark and his father caught their breath. 'Myrtle,' she snapped, 'I'm covered in bruises. These two clumsy lummoxes'll be the death of me.' Peering around the room she spotted Lily. 'Dressed up Doll! Who are you?' she demanded.

'I'm Lily Forrest, Mrs Bargent. I'm Dora's friend.'

'That froward young maid,' snorted Grandma, slapping the hand that Lily held out to her.

Dora stood behind her chair poking out her tongue.

'You two girls go off and enjoy yourselves,' whispered Mrs Somers. 'Thanks for your help,' she said, as she swathed Granny Bargent in a blanket before the sweating Mark and Mr Somers carried her down to her bath-chair on the pavement.

The sun had struggled through the clouds and the streets were thick with sightseers waving and cheering. Festoons of flags hung from the signal masts in the Royal Naval Barracks, and the officers' quarters across the road displayed a huge portrait of Nelson.

Lily fizzed with excitement. 'Ooh Dora,' she shouted, 'look at that policeman's horse! Isn't he beautiful? And look at those paper lanterns in the park.'

Together they forced their way through the

227

crowds. 'Cripes, we shan't see a thing if we're not nippy and get up one of them,' Dora said, making for the huge stone lions mounted one either side of the Town Hall. 'Blimey, how we going to get on?' she said, looking around at the sea of people packed around the steps leading up to the animal statues.

'There's Charlie Onslow, he lives near me. I'll ask him to give us a bunk up,' said Lily, pushing past a stout man in a top hat.

Twelve-year-old Charlie obligingly made a foothold with his laced fingers and Dora clasped her arms around the lion's neck. Within seconds Lily was sitting behind her and between them they hauled Charlie on to the lion's rump.

Lily feasted her eyes on the spectacle below. There was a mass of hats and caps. Every available window had faces pressed to it, every lamppost had a figure clinging to it and every mouth was cheering. Massed bands trumpeted and uniformed figures marched with glinting rifles.

Space had been made on the edge of the pavement for the wounded. One-legged men on crutches, men with one sleeve pinned to their jacket along with the medals. Haunted faces with dull eyes and ears deaf to the fevered celebrations.

A girl dressed in white, representing Peace, rode past on a float covered with palms and flowers. Lily caught her breath. Silence settled on the crowd. Handkerchiefs fluttered and tears fell. Then they recovered their spirits.

'Here Lil! That's the girls from the Mikado

Café. Ooh i'n't that lovely?' Dora shouted in her ear.

The café tableau was covered with orange flowers, gladioli, marigolds and tiger lilies. The Mikado dressed all in black with gold studs on his boots waved regally to the crowd. Each side of the throne sat three girls in gold kimonos carrying flowered parasols.

'Wish we'd been old enough,' said Lily, as the procession ended with contingents of Wrens, land girls, tram drivers and female dockyard workers. 'I'd like to have been a crane driver.'

Six o'clock boomed out from the Town Hall tower. 'Nearly bust me bloomin' ear-drums,' bellowed Charlie.

'Let's go down The Hard now there's going to be a bonfire and fireworks,' yelled Lily above the noise of a brass band.

The steps beneath them were crowded with people. 'How're we going to get down?' Lily shouted into Dora's ear.

'I don't know Lil, but I tell ya I'm bursting to go to the lav,' Dora shouted back.

'We'll have to stand up on the lion's bum then catch hold of that old toff's shoulder,' advised Charlie. Full of patriotic zeal, the elderly gentleman beside the lion's rump failed to notice Charlie clutching at his shoulder. When the full weight of the twelve-year-old commanded his attention he pushed him violently away. Charlie floundered and found himself clutching the ample bosom of the old toff's wife. She screamed in outrage as he slithered down her satin frontage.

'You young guttersnipe,' shouted her husband,

229

raising his walking-stick, his eyes popping with rage.

Lily and Dora followed Charlie's example, first glancing backwards, then making use of the shoulders of a man cheering so wildly he seemed impervious to their clutches.

They linked arms and careered towards Queen Street drunk with laughter. Outside the Royal Oak a group of women were haranguing the sailors, their faces painted with rouge and powder.

'What'll I get for a tanner?' yelled Charlie, rushing up to one of them and lifting her skirts.

'Bugger off you cheeky young sod,' snapped the woman, lunging at Charlie with her fists raised. She cracked him across the nose and he began howling with rage.

'Had your eyeful, you silly little tart?'

Lily looked into the face of the woman. Her lips were painted in an exaggerated cupid's bow and her eyes ringed with mascara seemed full of hate. There was a distinct blue shadow on her chin. Dora hustled her away.

'Here,' said Charlie, catching up with them. 'It weren't a woman at all. When I lifted up 'er skirt you could see his...'

Lily was frightened by the sudden violence and the hatred in the man's face. The grotesque caricature of a woman sickened her. 'Shut up, shut up,' she screamed, tearing down the pavement, heedless of the people she cannoned into. A painful stitch in her side halted her at the dockyard gate.

'What's the matter, Lily?' asked Dora, equally

230

out of breath. 'It was Charlie what got a nose-bleed not you.'

'Sorry, Charlie,' mumbled Lily not knowing what to say. 'Here – dip my hankie in the sea and hold it on your nose.'

As Charlie scampered over the stones Dora put her arm around Lily's shoulders. 'You must've seen old Stella before?'

'I suppose so,' she said doubtfully.

'He was always in the panto. My Dad used to take us on Boxing Night. Stella was Widow Twankey in *Aladdin*. We used to laugh our heads off at him. Lovely signing voice too. Then he took to drink and got the sack.'

'But why does he want to dress up as a woman in the street?'

'I dunno – 'spose our clothes are a bit more colourful. She knocks around with lots of old actors and such.'

Lily felt foolish rushing off like that. Why did she always want things to be different from what they were? She wished she was like Dora, always cheerful and matter-of-fact.

'My guts is rumbling,' said the irrepressible Charlie. 'Let's go up Driver's caff and get some bread pudding.' With his face smeared with blood and hair falling over his eyes Charlie was reassuringly familiar.

Dora spat on her hankie and cleaned his face and Lily combed his hair.

''Ere you two,' he yelled. 'You're not my bleedin' mother.'

They had a shilling between them. It bought three pieces of pudding and a cup of tea. The

231

food seemed to restore the easy comradeship of the day. Afterwards they wandered down to the water's edge to look at the ships out in the harbour dressed overall with flags.

Lily wished that Dad was home. Now she'd had time to think about it she regretted her sulks at Christmas. There had been a silence between them ever since. Gran had got a letter from Scapa Flow but there had been none for Lily. She regretted falling out with Miriam too and missed their talks. Often when she'd been sent in to her house while she was ill, Lily had been on the point of making it up but somehow the right moment never came. When she looked back on what she had seen through the window on Christmas Eve it all seemed very shadowy and inconclusive. And now, strangely, the thought of Dad getting fond of someone didn't matter quite so much. Since leaving school and starting work her life was more than Gran and Dad. She resolved to write to him the next day. Perhaps she'd make something for Rosie as a way of smoothing things over with Miriam, too.

Lily, Dora and Charlie stood throwing stones into the water until a shout from the mud flats attracted their attention. 'The bonfire, they're lighting the bonfire!'

All at once the beach was filled with people. Fish boxes, fruit cartons, driftwood, everything possible was piled high in the air. Sitting on top, his head at a rakish angle, was an effigy of Kaiser Bill.

'Stick a rocket up his arse,' yelled Charlie.

'You watch your mouth, sonny,' said a

232

constable, cuffing his ear.

'I'm off,' said Charlie, diving into the crowd.

'It's been the best day in ages,' said Dora, linking arms with her friend. Lily was suddenly happy.

The sky darkened and from the Dockyard Gate hundreds of light-bulbs blazed into life with the message, 'Peace Our Reward'. Ships' hooters sounded and one by one each vessel was illuminated. Fireworks burst into life.

Someone started singing and soon the whole crowd joined in. Mums and Dads, kids, wives and sweethearts, drunken sailors all swaying together.

From the other side of the bonfire Lily saw Bernard Syme. His face flickered in the firelight. At one moment he looked handsome, his blond hair gleaming, and then in the shadows his features seemed sharp and wolflike. Lily couldn't look away. It was like a fairground mirror.

She leapt in terror as a firework exploded behind her. Bernard had disappeared and so had Dora. Lily was afraid. Today everything had been shaken loose and she needed time for it all to fall back in place. She must find Dora.

A familiar voice called to her from the shadows between two upturned rowing-boats. 'Hello, Lily. How's my little diamond in the rough?' Bernard was laughing at her.

He caught her upraised hand with practised ease and pulled her down beside him. 'Let me give you something to remember.' Quickly he bent his head forward and kissed Lily on the mouth. Before she could think what to do he

233

kissed her again, his lips soft and insistent. Lily trembled. She began to kiss him back. His arms tightened around her. Slowly he pressed his lips against hers. Gently his tongue sought hers as one kiss fed on another. She wanted more.

Someone laughed. It was a harsh mocking sound. 'Cradle-snatching again, Bernard?' Ruby Frogatt tapped him on the shoulder with her parasol. 'What was you doin'? Warmin' up for the real performance?'

Quickly Bernard released Lily. 'I was just being sociable to our young apprentice.' He linked arms with Ruby and they walked away laughing together.

Lily got out her handkerchief and scrubbed her mouth until her lips burned. Scalding tears spilled down her face. Beside her on the shingle lay her hat, the ribbon on it soaked with water and the colours seeping into the straw. She carried it down over the stones and tossed it into the sea before turning back up the beach to find Dora. If only she could leave herself behind and emerge later on another shore, not as the Lily she was now but someone new and different and certain.

Chapter Twenty-Two

It had seemed weeks and weeks to wait and now it was here, Saturday August the twenty-third. In a couple of hours she would meet Alec at the railway station in Cosham. Miriam could hardly contain her excitement. She had asked Mrs Forrest to look after Rosie, saying that she was going to visit her mother in the workhouse. Alec had asked her not to say anything about their friendship until he'd had a chance to speak to his mother himself. It was easier said than done.

'Give your mother my kindest regards,' Beattie said. 'Take her these jam tarts, they're freshly made.'

Miriam looked into Mrs Forrest's open smiling face and felt suddenly shabby in her deception of her neighbour. Tarts for a tart, she thought savagely. Wouldn't that be the older woman's opinion when she found out how Miriam had deceived her? 'That's very good of you, Mrs Forrest. I'll be back as soon as I can,' she murmured.

'Rosie likes tarts,' said her daughter, hopefully.

'Auntie Forrest has saved you a couple, my pet,' said her neighbour, smiling at the little girl. 'Let's just say goodbye to Mummy and then we'll have our tea party.'

They both stood waving to her until she turned the corner.

Miriam caught sight of herself in a shop window in Queen Street. The outfit was a triumph of the imagination over the meagre contents of her purse. The white piqué blouse she'd bought from the dockyard-wall market was transformed with a refashioned Prussian collar and new buttons. It lent new life to the navy hobble skirt made the year before. But the real snip was the court shoes snatched from the dustbin in Lion Terrace, when the maid's back

235

was turned. A bottle of dye and a good steaming over the kettle had brought them up good as new. Settling her straw hat at a jaunty angle she set off to catch her tram. Would Alec be as delighted with her appearance as she was herself? she wondered.

Cosham was a village just over the bridge from Portsea Island. Miriam had not been there since she was a child, when her father had taken her to the Easter Fair on the slopes of the hill. The sun was warm on her back as Miriam alighted from the tram with a real sense of being on holiday. She was at the station by 1.15 p.m. giving her time to go into the Ladies Waiting Room to tidy her hair. The train lumbered into the station behind a cloud of smoke. Doors slammed, passengers alighted and were borne away. Miriam was all attention. Her eyes searched the carriage windows. Her jaw was thrust forward and her feet were poised to run towards him. After the next blink of an eye he would be with her, after the next swallow. With a loud hiss of steam and slamming of doors the train left the platform.

She was frozen with disappointment. A farmer with a basket of hens stepped back onto her foot. What with his apologies and the squawking of the birds she was completely taken by surprise when Alec tapped her on the shoulder.

'Hello, Mirry,' he said, bending to kiss her. 'I'll just stow my kit-bag in the left-luggage, then we'll find a place for tea.'

He looked old and tired, not at all as she remembered him. His uniform was crumpled and his fingernails grimy with engine oil. Miriam watched him walking away from her. She bit her lip and pretended to study a theatre poster. Maria Minette was appearing in a Parisian Music Hall Farce entitled *Gay Bohemia* at the King's Theatre. She had read the poster three times before Alec reappeared.

'Feels strange, doesn't it?' he said, smiling at her as he took her arm and guided her out of the station.

Miriam felt her breathing slow down. Perhaps it was going to be all right. She'd been living with an Alec of her imagination, the reality was bound to be a let-down.

'Sitting on the train all those hours I felt as nervous as a young lad just started courting. Then when I saw you I couldn't believe my luck.' He threaded his fingers through hers. 'Mirry, I'm so glad to see you.'

She smiled up at him. The touch of his hand, the pressure of his thumb on the pulse in her wrist and she responded with all her remembered delight.

The High Street was full of Saturday bustle: children with hoops, dogs, perambulators, old men with walking-sticks. Miriam and Alec crossed the railway track and made for the stop for the green-and-cream trams of the Portsdown and Horndean Light Railway. They went up the curving staircase and sat on the open top deck. The tram climbed up the side of the hill, past fields of corn golden in the sun.

They got off at the top of the hill and turned to look at the view spread out below. Far in the distance was the Isle of Wight, a narrow curving wedge of greeny-blue hills behind an inch or two of sea studded with grey ships.

Alec laughed. 'They look as if you could fit them in your pocket, don't they?'

Miriam nodded.

'And yet,' he said, 'inside are hundreds of men, living their lives, between those grey bulkheads.'

Like pilchards in a tin, she thought.

'Funny seeing ships like that from the outside,' he said.

'There you go, backwards and forwards across the world and here we stay, the women waving and waiting.'

They stood hand-in-hand in silence. Below them lay Portsmouth, its buildings like dolls' houses with a sprinkling of trams and cars scurrying about. Alec turned her towards him and kissed her gently on the mouth.

'I couldn't wait a minute longer,' he breathed.

Miriam squeezed his hand. It was going to be all right.

They followed a path that led to the Bellevue Tea Gardens and went in through the gate. 'Tea for two and bread, butter and jam, please,' said Alec to a waitress in a starched apron and black dress.

At a table opposite a family of six shared four cups of tea. The husband, in the blue uniform of a patient from the military hospital nearby, stared unseeingly into the distance.

Miriam took he beaded cover from the milk jug. 'I've dreamed about us taking tea together,' she said.

'Feels like make-believe,' Alec said, splashing a sugar lump into his tea. 'Like we're sat on the stage. Any minute someone will pull the curtains and the show'll be over.'

'Don't say that, Alec,' she said, tears welling in her eyes.

'I'm only teasing. It's years since an old widower like me took tea with a pretty lady.'

Miriam's brain was teeming with questions. When was he going to ask about Rosie? What tale would he tell his mother? Did he still love her?

Alec cleared his throat. 'Last Christmas I came home dog-tired and looking forward to some time at home with Ma and Lily.' He took her hand and squeezed her fingers. 'Then you opened the door and everything changed.'

'Weren't you pleased?' Miriam asked in a whisper.

'Of course,' he said, 'but I had to try and make sense of so much all at once.' He ran his hand through his hair as he always did when uncertain. 'I'd battened down my feelings because I thought I'd lost you for ever.' His eyes pleaded with hers for understanding.

'Each fresh thing you told me was another hammer-blow. One after another. First what that bastard did to you, then you having the baby. I thought, Christ, Mirry – I thought our baby had died. My head felt as if it would burst.'

He was speaking so softly Miriam had to lean forward to catch his words.

'I was angry and sickened by it all. Mostly I was ashamed. When you told me our baby was alive, I couldn't take it in.'

Miriam picked at an embroidered daisy on the cloth. Why had she thought it would be so simple, that they could just take up their lives where they'd left off?

'When I saw Rosie for the first time, she had such a look of my Andrew: those lovely copper curls. Well, I was lost.' Alec covered her hand with his.

Miriam took a trembling breath and dared to look at him.

'I want us to be married, all legal and above board.' He held her gaze unwaveringly. 'But first, Mirry, you've got to give me time to talk to Ma.' He must have seen the anxiety in her eyes almost before she felt it herself.

'It's about respect. Ma's brought me up mostly on her own and she's been mother and father to Andrew and Lily since Mary's been gone. I need to tell her what's in my mind and what's happened between us. All of it.'

Miriam felt a sharp resentment. She was going to have her life exposed to the judgment of another woman. Then there was Lily. 'So I shall be put on trial and if your mother doesn't think I'm good enough, what then? And Princess Lily, is she to have her say too?'

'Mirry, don't be so silly. It won't be like that at all.'

'Silly am I?' snapped Miriam, near to tears.

'Calm down,' said Alec, leaning across the table and taking hold of her arm. 'You're getting all this out of proportion. Besides, people are looking.'

If she stayed a minute longer she'd either burst into tears or hit him. Abruptly she stood up, knocking over the sugar basin and rushed out of the room and through the gardens, slamming the gate behind her.

Crossing the road she ran down the hill until she was out of breath. Her eyes filled with tears. Why had the talk of telling his mother everything so angered her? Or was it fright that she was feeling? In the last few months she'd come to love Mrs Forrest and she knew her feelings were returned. Her good opinion had given her confidence. Under her guidance she had started making collars, had even been taken on by Mr Goldstein. Due to her neighbour she was managing to put by a little money each week. How would Gran feel about Miriam when she found out how she had deceived her? Since moving to Lemon Street Miriam had acquired a family. If everything came to nothing she would have lost far more than Alec.

Of course she still had Aunt Florrie and Daisy. But she would be received in Devon as the poor relation and in any case the news in Auntie's last letter had been far from encouraging. She'd had pneumonia and was more of an invalid than a partner in the hotel. As for Daisy, she had her hands full with the smallholding she and Norman had taken on.

It seemed that the whole of her future would be decided in the next few hours. Tears ran down her face as she tore angrily at the grass, winding the stalks around her fingers to get a firmer grip. She dragged out the roots, chalky soil fell on her dress.

'Hey, what's all this about?' said Alec.

241

Startled at his approach, Miriam burst out, 'Your Ma will know as I've lied. That I'm not Mrs Naylor, just Miriam Slattery with a drunken mother in the workhouse and a bastard child.'

He shook her fiercely. 'Don't ever say that. Rosie is my child and I shall give her my name.' His face was grim. 'One thing I can't abide is lying. Had enough of that last time.'

Miriam could not stop shaking. Alec held her until her sobbing began to subside, then took out a handkerchief from his pocket and brushed the earth from her dress.

'I'll have a talk with Ma tonight, then it'll all be over bar the shouting.'

'What about Lily?' asked Miriam, anxiety gnawing at her stomach.

'Well,' he said guardedly, 'I can't say as what she'll do. You were both the greatest of chums a while ago. Once she's got used to things...'

'But what about you?' she asked.

Alec took off his cap and rumpled his hair. 'I know I've been a hero to my daughter and I can't deny as I enjoyed being one. But Mirry, she'll have to accept that things have changed between us. They were bound to sooner or later, anyway.'

'Can I ask you something, Alec,' she said hesitantly, 'and if you answer me I'll never bring it up again.'

He nodded, his face telling her nothing.

'Why did you say that you'd had enough of lies with your first wife?'

'We were both of us too young and too different ever to have married,' he said, looking straight ahead. 'She was full of life and fun and not ready

242

for children. Mary had never lived in a family and never had much of anything. She was greedy for life and things. Being at home all the time and me being away drove her crazy. She comforted herself with buying things at the door from the tally man.' He frowned. 'So we were always in debt. She was pretty and men noticed her. I didn't know how to cope, so we spent all our time rowing. When Lily was born she took no notice of her, then one day she walked off on her own and never came back. The police found her body washed up on the beach. Ma took charge of Andrew and Lily and I went back to sea.'

'Did you never miss her, Alec, or feel sad at how things had turned out?'

'I try never to think of her,' he said, still staring into the distance. 'When I do, I have to remember myself as a young, hot-headed, thoughtless lad. It wasn't all Mary's fault, not by a long chalk.' He shrugged as if casting off the subject. 'Still, we live longer to do better.' He turned and smiled at her. 'Do you know what I'm really looking forward to? Seeing little Rosie.'

Miriam smiled. Alec put a finger to her lips as she was about to speak and pointed to a group of butterflies on a clump of yellow vetch. 'Chalk Hill Blues,' he said. At his words the butterflies rose up above them in a quivering cloud, disappearing as quickly as they came.

Alec drew her towards him, cupping her face in his hands. 'Your eyes are as blue as the wings of those butterflies,' he whispered, kissing her face and neck.

She touched his beard, smoothing the black

243

wiry hair away from his mouth, and tracing the shape of his soft full lips. Returning his kisses she tasted the familiar mixture of salt and tobacco. Alec was often a mystery to Miriam, his thoughts and feelings hidden from her; then magically he would reveal himself and she would be moved to tears by his tenderness and vulnerability. It seemed that they had both been hurt and unhappy in the past; perhaps they were being given a second chance if only she was brave enough to take it.

She took off her hat and leaned across him. They were hidden behind the golden canopy of her hair.

'I could eat every last bit of you,' he sighed, kissing her fingertips then placing her hand against his chest. The warmth of him and the steady throbbing of his heart excited her.

They moved until they were under the shelter of a hawthorn bush. Alec pressed his lips against her throat, then gently eased her dress away from her shoulder. Miriam stroked his hair.

He undid the buttons on her blouse and slid his hand under the strap of her chemise, curling his fingers over her breast. The excited cries of children coming towards them interrupted their idyll. Miriam hastily tidied her clothes.

'Paradise postponed,' Alec murmured, pulling her to her feet and holding her against him. His kiss was long and searching, leaving her breathless.

Miriam smiled as they walked hand-in-hand down the hill to Cosham. She just had to get through the next couple of days and it would all be plain sailing.

'I'll leave you here,' Alec said, as they reached the tram stop. 'I want to get my thoughts organised before I see Ma. I'll try and drop in later and let you know how I fared.'

They kissed briefly and Miriam watched him walk slowly towards the station. A few minutes later she had boarded her tram. 'A single to St Mary's Road,' she said to the conductor.

The last time she had seen Violet was that terrible day, when she'd called on her and Jumper at Bevis Terrace. The day she discovered she was carrying and Violet wanted to send her to that dreadful Ma Winters to be rid of it. Then there was the letter asking her to visit her in the workhouse. Eight months ago that was. Would she still be there and what state would she be in?

As she walked up the road to the workhouse, Miriam felt her spirits plummet. She clutched the little bag of jam tarts that Mrs Forrest had given her and sighed. At least she had brought her something. The long corridor to the Guardian's Office reeked of disinfectant, making her nostrils sting.

'Who are you looking for?' asked a tall, elderly clerk.

'Mrs Violet Slattery,' she muttered. 'I'm her daughter.'

'I'll ask Miss Penfold,' he said, and shuffled out.

Miriam looked at the huge desk, her eyes sliding away from the ledger marked Register of Deaths. She felt dwarfed by the high ceiling and

245

the imposing plaque on the wall opposite. It announced that the Portsmouth Union had been formed in 1835. Through the window she saw two inmates carrying a basket of laundry between them, their hands reddened from workhouse soap. They clumped along in ill-fitting boots and shapeless striped dresses reaching to their ankles. Neither of them was her mother. Guilt and resentment see-sawed in her stomach.

Behind her a woman in nurse's uniform entered the room. She was needle-thin and her head craned over the top of a high starched collar. 'Miss Slattery, I believe,' she said briskly.

'Yes,' answered Miriam turning to face her.

She suffered the nurse's frosty appraisal. Miss Penfold obviously thought her too overdressed by half. 'Well, Miss Slattery,' she said, 'you have certainly taken your time.'

Flushing under her scrutiny, Miriam burst out, 'Do I get to see my mother or not?'

Miss Penfold gave a wintry smile. 'You have had a wasted journey. Your mother died last week.'

Her words had the force of a slap. Miriam caught her bottom lip in her teeth to stop it trembling.

'What d'you mean – died?' She gripped her hands together, the nails biting into her palms. 'What did she die of?'

'Alcoholic poisoning.'

Tears started up behind Miriam's lashes. 'I, I want to see the entry in the book,' she stuttered, her breathing ragged with distress.

The clerk pointed to the page: Mrs Violet

246

Slattery, cause of death, cirrhosis of the liver. Age thirty-eight years. No relatives. Thirty-eight! Her mother had looked nearer sixty when she'd seen her three years ago. Black roots showing through her hennaed curls, her face the colour of a window-leather.

The nurse moved towards the door. 'Mr Myers,' she said, 'if this woman wishes to claim any property make sure she provides proof of her identity.' Then she added, 'By rights she should make some contribution to the funeral expenses.'

The words ignited Miriam's rage. 'What expenses?' she screamed, rushing at Miss Penfold. She poked her narrow chest with an angry finger. 'A matchwood coffin and no priest at the graveside.'

Miss Penfold turned away but still she was harried.

'Treated like so much rubbish,' Miriam continued, making fierce jabs at the nurse's back. With a sudden twist of her body, Miss Penfold thrust Miriam away, strode to the door and slammed it behind her.

'Old bitch,' Miriam shouted.

The clerk, pink-faced with embarrassment, moved a chair towards her. 'Sit down a minute, Miss, while I finds your mother's name in the property book.'

Tears rained down her face as she gulped some water from the glass the clerk handed to her. At last he found the page. Mrs Slattery: one handbag containing photographs, a tube of cachous and a broken rosary. The pitiful list stung Miriam to fresh tears.

247

'What about identification?' said the clerk.

'All I want is the snaps and the beads,' sniffed Miriam.

The clerk shuffled his feet uncertainly.

'I'll sign for them. I'm housekeeper to a Warrant Officer Pragnell, twenty-five Lemon Street.'

'Well, don't you say as I gave them to you,' he said as he unlocked the cupboard, opened a battered handbag and thrust an envelope and a rosary into her hands.

'You might as well have these,' she said, giving him the bag of jam tarts.

'That's kind of you, Miss,' he said. 'I'm sorry for your trouble.'

Miriam nodded, unable to speak. She couldn't remember getting on the tram or asking for a single to Commerical Road but she was there, crammed between two old ladies, with a ticket in her hand. In spite of the August heat, she shivered. One thing she felt certain of: her mother had not died last week of cirrhosis. She had died of disappointment years ago.

Chapter Twenty-Three

Rosie was running her ragged.

As soon as the jam tarts were eaten and her fingers washed, she was off her chair and rummaging in the laundry basket.

'I'll need eyes in the back of my head with you,

I can see,' said Beattie as she damped down the ironing.

'Rosie do it,' the child demanded. Giving her a saucer of water and a pile of handkerchiefs, Beattie settled her on a chair beside her.

The child watched intently, trying to imitate the scooping-up movement of the hand and the shaking of the loosely-closed fist which released drops of water onto the washing. Soon there was a puddle on the table and the saucer was empty. 'All gone, Rosie get more water.' The child jumped down and ran to the sink but was unable to reach the tap.

Beattie took a jug from the dresser and filled it with water. She opened the back door and gave it to Rosie. 'Now, you give those daisies a drink and let Auntie Forrest get on with her work.'

'One daisy have a jink, den annuder daisy have a jink.' The child's voice faded away as she went further down the yard. Beattie attacked the ironing. Soon there was a stack of folded blouses and handkerchiefs ready to take upstairs. As she took the ironing blanket off the table it occurred to her that Rosie was very quiet.

'My stars, child, what are you up to now?'

Using the jug as a spade, Rosie had made a satisfying mud pie. 'Rosie makin' a gardin. Look, Auntie Fowist, Rosie makin' gardin.' There was mud on her shoes and dress, and spattered on her hair.

Beattie sat her up on the draining-board in the kitchen and gave her a good wash. Rosie smiled up at her as she ran a comb through her curls. Yet again the child reminded her of her grandson.

249

The same colouring and restless energy. Andrew would have been nineteen now.

'Now, madam, don't you move a muscle. Auntie Forrest is going to take you out, but first I've got to set myself to rights.'

Holding the parcelled-up collars by the string in one hand and Rosie in the other, Beattie made her way to Goldstein's in Queen Street. The bell tinkled over the door and she blinked, accustoming herself to the gloomy interior.

Isaac Goldstein ran his tape measure over the collars, grunting in satisfaction. He counted fifteen shillings into her hand. 'From you, Mrs Forrest, always good work and never you keep me waiting.'

'Needs must,' Beattie replied. 'If the navy paid its widows their dues, I'd not be here.' They laughed at the well-worn complaint.

'We're lucky to be alive,' he said quietly. 'I never thought I'd get over that fire in my shop. Then when I look at some of those poor devils, limping around the streets on crutches, I say, Isaac, what you got to complain about.'

'I see in the paper as the dockyard maties are coming out on strike,' she sighed. 'That'll be just the opportunity the Admiralty's been looking for to weed out the troublemakers. No good coming out when there's not enough work to go round. Should have come out during the war when they was worth their weight in gold.'

'That would have been considered treason, sabotaging the war effort. Might have been shot like those poor young soldiers out in France, that ran away,' said Mr Goldstein. 'Happened to my

250

poor sister Rachel's boy. They might as well have shot his mother at the same time for the good her life is worth to her now. All the family branding him a coward, nobody helping her to mourn.'

'Oh, Isaac, I am sorry.' Beattie patted his arm at a loss for anything to say.

'The world has gone mad, Mrs Forrest. The government sending the soldiers home in cheap shoddy suits. Poor wrecked young men. How are we going to mend our lives?'

'I don't know, Isaac,' she said, 'I really don't know. All I can think of is time and kindness.' He nodded his thanks for her sympathy and Beattie took Rosie firmly by the hand and left the shop, the bell tinkling behind her.

They crossed the road to the bridge leading to the harbour station. It was swarming with sailors making their way to the Gosport Ferry and visitors down from London for the day. Beattie found herself a space at the railings and lifted Rosie up in front of her. She searched in her pocket for the bag of farthings. Below them in the harbour mud were several skinny children diving for pennies. She doled out the farthings to Rosie, to throw one at a time. The mudlarks slithered about to the amusement of the passers-by. Beattie watched the young rogues with affection, remembering Andrew and Lily's antics.

Seeing a midshipman amongst the crowd, a scrawny youngster yelled, 'Throw a copper in the mud, officer. I'll stick me head in for a tanner.'

After diving for the supposed sixpence, the lad yelled, ''Ere! you cheapskate, that weren't a tanner what you chucked in, it was a bleeding

251

farving covered in silver paper.'

'Oh sorry, my mistake, old man.'

Beattie glared at the swaggering youth. What a stingy trick! A tanner was nothing to him, but a fortune to the nipper slithering in the mud. Before he could think of another rejoinder she took his cap and threw it in the sea. 'My mistake, old man,' she mimicked. 'I reckon you'll have to pay this young shaver here a real sixpence to get your titfer back.' Satisfied to see the midshipman's confidence severely dented, she laughed with the rest of the crowd. Obviously the thought of facing his commanding officer without his full uniform unnerved him. Bloody good job too. It made a change for the mudlark to be on the winning side. She chortled to herself as the red-faced middy handed over a silver shilling in exchange for his slime-soaked cap.

'All gone,' said Rosie sadly, as she threw the last farthing into the water.

'Well young lady, I don't know about you, but I'm nearly done for,' said Beattie when they returned to Lemon Street. 'Let's anchor your bottom and get you some biscuits, then Auntie Forrest had better get this place into shape.' She went to the wire wall-safe in the kitchen to fetch some milk and sniffed suspiciously. 'That's nearly on the turn. I'd best use some condensed and save that to knock up some scones tomorrow.'

As she poured the water over the tea she heard a tentative knock on the back door. It was Miriam.

'I'm really ever so sorry to have taken so long, Mrs Forrest, only it was bad news.'

'Sit yourself down my dear, you look all in. Here have a cup of tea, gather yourself together, there's no rush. The child is well content.'

Miriam perched on her chair looking distractedly around the room. 'My mother took bad last week and they buried her on the parish.' She put her hand to her mouth as if to stop the words being true. 'Just gave me this packet of photos and such... Not much to show for her life.' Her voice trailed away.

Beattie set the cup on the table in front of her young neighbour. 'What a shock for you. Well, poor soul's out of her suffering now,' she said. 'No more tears or heartache.' How young she was to be a widow and to have lost her mother too. Beattie's heart quickened in sympathy. They sat in silence, drinking their tea and watching Rosie playing with the button box.

As the clock chimed five there were footsteps in the passage. The door was swung back and there stood Alec.

The sight of him had Miriam leaping to her feet, the tea half-drunk, and hustling Rosie out of the room. 'I'd better be getting indoors, you'll have things to talk about.' She was flushed and ill-at-ease. 'Thank you very much for having Rosie, it was very kind. Goodbye, Mrs Forrest.' Neither she nor Alec acknowledged each other's presence.

'You're welcome to share a meal with us, Miriam. Well, just as you like my dear,' Beattie said to her neighbour's departing back. 'I'll pop across and see you later when you've settled the child. Poor soul,' she said to Alec, 'she's just gone to visit her mother in the workhouse, only to find that she was dead and buried last week.'

'I'll go after her and offer my sympathy,' said Alec, making for the back door.

'And why would you do that?' said Beattie looking at him sharply. 'What is she to you that she needs your good wishes? Cripes, Alec, you've only just set foot in the house. Besides, if she'd wanted company she'd have stayed to tea. Aside from anything else you haven't given your old mother a kiss. Away nine months, I'm starved for the sight of you.'

'Keep your hair on, Ma,' he said, kissing her cheek, then hugging her tightly.

When she'd had her fill of hugging, Beattie held him away from her at arms' length. 'Let's have a look at you. My God!' she exclaimed. 'That pneumonia's taken its toll.' Reaching for the frying-pan, she commanded, 'Now sit you down while I get your tea together.'

'Where's Lily?' Alec asked as he settled himself at the table.

'Oh she's off out with Dora, her pal from work.'

'That's good. It'll give us a chance to have a good natter.'

Beattie eyed Alec thoughtfully. His usual routine when coming home was to tuck into his meal then disappear behind the paper. Any exchange of information had to wait upon his readiness. As if he needed time to loose the bonds of the navy before he could settle back into the life of his family. There was a nervousness about him as he pretended to read, flicking through the pages and watching her when he

254

thought her attention was elsewhere.

She set the bacon and eggs on the plate and carried it to the table. As she poured the tea her mind flitted back to his last letter. He had written that he wanted to have a long talk with her about his future. How he was trying to make up his mind about 'taking a step that will change all our lives, for the better.'

She took a deep breath. 'Let's be having it, son. All that talk in your letter about the future. Out with it now. You know I can't abide mystification.'

'I'm going to get married.'

She was stunned by the baldness of the statement. 'So that's the way of it,' she said.

'Yes, that's the way of it, Ma.' There was a hint of defiance in Alec's look.

Oh God, all the panic the other week that Mary might truly be alive, that her vague misgivings were well-founded, and now this. 'It takes a bit of digesting, son,' she said, gripping her hands tightly together. 'There was no mention of anyone at Christmas. I – I never dreamt–' Her words drained away.

Alec leant across the table and took her hands in his. 'Ma, I want you to listen and say nothing 'til I've finished. I've nerved myself up to tell you and you'll have to bear with me.'

'Just tell me, son,' she said, holding tightly to his fingers.

'A few months before Jutland I met this girl and we started talking. I never thought anything would come of it, she being so much younger than me. But it did and I asked her to marry me. On the day of Lily's birthday, when we got the

255

telegram, I was all set to bring her home to meet you both and then–'

Beattie cast her mind back to the horror and confusion of that afternoon: Alec rushing off and leaving Lily with no explanation. She'd been too hard-pressed with her own grief and that of her granddaughter, apart from the crisis in the Vine family, to look for a reason for Alec's disappearance.

He ran his hand distractedly through his hair. 'I went ahead of the time I was due to see her to our usual meeting-place and left a letter. Then I came home to you and Lily.' His face twisted as if in pain and he covered his face with his hands.

All these years when I thought we were getting through our grief, she thought, and all the while there's been this secret agony eating away at him.

'She went to the meeting-place and when she got there...' Alec continued, his voice ragged with distress. 'When she got there. Oh Christ, Ma.'

Beattie stood in silence, her hand on her son's shoulder, waiting for him to master his pain. All the while she could feel him trembling.

'Thought as how I'd let her down,' Alec continued. 'She was having our child and I never turned up. Ma, I never turned up. I'd rushed around and left her a letter but that bastard tore it up. Nothing, nothing I could do. I had to sail without seeing her.'

Beattie went to the dresser and got a bottle and two glasses. 'Here, son, take this down; it'll steady you.'

Alec took a gulping draught of brandy then set

256

the glass down on the table. 'When I went round to the pub where she worked, on my next leave, it was all new people. Didn't know anything about her.' His voice was steadier and the colour was seeping back into his face. 'I had to go back to Scotland and I never saw her again until last Christmas. I didn't even know I had another daughter.'

Now it was Beattie's turn to have a drink. She closed her eyes and let the brandy burn its way down her throat. Something was nagging at her, a sense deeper than words, as if in some part of herself she knew what he was going to tell her.

'It was when I came home on leave,' he said, 'that I got to hear the full story of that night when she went to meet me.' Alec held his face in his hands.

Beattie waited in dread. Something had happened, too terrible for Alec to speak of. In the wake of that night when the news of Jutland had spread through the streets breaking people's hearts, there was another wounding.

'She went to meet me, to say yes, she would marry me. And he was there and he – he – he...' Alec banged his fist on the table, his teeth clenched, the tendons in his neck taut with rage.

'Son, stop it,' Beattie commanded. 'It's gone and done with. Have the rest of the brandy.' She took his fist and held it until he uncurled his fingers. 'You've met up with the young woman again and been given a second chance. With all the poor devils lying on the ocean floor you're bloody lucky to get it.'

He got up and went out into the scullery. She

257

could hear him running the tap. He came back into the room his face dripping water, reaching out for a towel from the clothes-horse.

'When do I get to meet this woman and her child?'

'You have already, Ma,' he said watching her closely.

Everything was snapping together in her head. The meeting last Christmas, the little daughter, the look, the look when she came back from the shops, the look between them. 'It's Miriam,' she cried. And then the anger came. 'Christmas,' Beattie exclaimed. 'You knew about that little girl then and you've done nothing all this time?'

'I couldn't take it in at first. As I said we lost track of one another then I had to go back off leave and I got ill. I needed time to make sense of it all.'

'Well,' Beattie snorted, 'time's a luxury Mrs Naylor's not had. If that is her name.'

'Slattery, her name's Slattery,' Alec mumbled, avoiding the accusation in his mother's eyes.

'While you've been making up your mind, that young woman has had to work her fingers to the bone to keep her child decently clothed and fed. My grandchild, I might add.' Beattie slammed the kettle back on the stove. 'I'll say this for her. She's got some pride. Many another would have come crying to the mother of the man as shamed her.'

'I did not shame her,' Alec said, glaring at her.

'Well,' snapped Beattie, refusing to be intimidated, 'you've not been in a rush to take up your responsibilities, have you?'

258

She attempted to absorb all that he had told her. No wonder she was drawn to that little child next-door, and no wonder she so reminded her of Andrew. In spite of what Beattie had said to her son there was hurt that Miriam had not trusted her. She poured the water into the teapot. Well, well, mother-in-law and grandmother all in one day. One thing was sure, it would all need very careful handling.

'What do you say, Ma, to inviting Miriam and Rosie round to tea tomorrow? To get things onto a proper footing between us?' called Alec from the scullery where he had taken the dishes.

'Aren't you forgetting something?' she demanded. 'What about your other daughter? Doesn't she deserve to be told properly before we have this family tea-party?'

'I thought perhaps you could tell her for me,' Alec said, handing her a wet plate.

She rubbed it furiously with the tea-towel. 'You've always got to be the bloody Prince Charming to Lily and leave me to tell her she can't take up her scholarship or any other bloody thing that puts you in a bad light.'

'I only thought as how it'd come better from you,' he pleaded.

'Don't soft-soap me, Alec, I won't stand for it. Either you tell Lily properly or Miriam's not coming into this house. It's my name on the rent-book when all's said and done,' she snapped, abandoning the washing-up and storming upstairs to her bedroom. She paced about picking up her hairbrush, putting it down again, and then fiddling with some hairpins. God, he made her angry. Just as she'd got things running sweet he was back creating complications and leaving her to carry the can. But that was sailors all over. They came ashore in their tiddly suits, charmed the drawers off the women, then buggered off across the sea. 'All cock and no conscience,' as Joseph would say. But what did she really feel beyond her first exasperation?

Miriam was such a needy young woman, so young to have coped with so much. Then there was little Rosie, she smiled to herself, no wonder she'd taken to the child. If only it could all pan out as it did in the *Girl's Mirror* or *Peg's Paper*. If only she could be certain that Mary was really dead. But even then there was Lily to take into account. Young girls could be so judging and intolerant. She'd been such pals with Miriam early on. It wouldn't be only Miriam's deception that would rankle with Lily, but her father's. He had loved someone in secret, had given her a child and pretended she was a stranger. Unknowingly, Lily had played with and grown fond of her own sister. Beattie sighed – what a tangled web it was.

The sound of someone coming up the stairs broke into her thoughts. Slowly the door opened and a stick with a white handkerchief tied to the end was waved in front of her.

'What are the conditions of the truce?' Alec said, smiling at her.

Beattie was not amused. 'I want you to take Lily out tomorrow morning and talk to her. Give her some of your time. Listen to what she's got to say. This is your last chance, Alec. Don't start off

260

on the wrong foot for lack of a bit of thought.'

He gave her a hug. 'Thanks Ma. You always put me straight.'

'Oh bugger off,' she said, pushing him out of the door. 'Go and tell Miriam as she's welcome to a cup of tea tomorrow afternoon and leave me in peace.'

Beattie picked up the wedding photograph of her and Joseph. 'Oh Joe, I wish to Christ you were here beside me. I'm so weary of it all,' she sighed. 'The patching and scratching about to keep going.'

After unlacing her boots she lay on top of the bed. She'd just have five minutes then go downstairs and think about what to get for tomorrow's tea. But she couldn't rest. In all their talk neither she nor Alec had spoken of Mary.

Chapter Twenty-Four

Mechanically Miriam set about getting Rosie's tea. She wanted nothing for herself. It had been hard enough swallowing that cup of tea with Mrs Forrest. Thank goodness Mr Pragnell was away at that naval dinner and not expected home until the morning.

From the moment when the news of her mother's death had been flung at her, a hard lump had lodged itself in her throat. It was like a tight ball of tangled string, the threads made up of fear and anger and regret.

As she poured some milk into a cup and made a potted-meat sandwich, her daughter prattled on about her day.

'Fardins, Rosie frow fardins in the water. All gone, fardins, all gone.'

Miriam smiled absently as she took off her shoes. They had been pinching for hours. Her feet had been sweating in the summer heat and now her toes were covered in navy dye. The whole outfit was crumpled and stale-looking. Once she'd got Rosie into bed she would strip off and freshen herself. Coolness and quiet, she craved them. After washing Rosie and settling her in the armchair with a book of nursery rhymes she tidied the kitchen. She swallowed nervously, the lump still in her throat.

Turning on the tap she cupped her hands, gathering a little pool of water, managing to sip a few drops. Next-door, at this very moment, Alec could be telling his mother all about her. Oh God! What would he say? Please let it be that he loved her. Where would he start? How they had met; their afternoons in the house in Myrtle Lane? The terrible night with Taffy? All their waiting and hoping? Surely the news that Rosie was her grandchild would reconcile Beattie to everything, wouldn't it?

She left the scullery and went into the kitchen to find Rosie fast asleep in the armchair. Covering her with a blanket she crept down the passage to their bedroom, bringing back her nightdress and a clean towel. Miriam opened the kitchen window and drew the curtains, creating a cooling breeze. She undressed in the shadows,

262

poured some water into a bowl and rubbed herself all over with a soapy flannel. Perching naked on the edge of a kitchen chair, she dipped her feet in the bowl washing away the navy dye before rubbing them dry. After emptying the bowl she held the flannel under the tap drizzling water over her skin, feeling it tighten in response to the icy droplets. She stood savouring the feeling for a moment or two before putting on her nightdress.

Miriam sat in the armchair opposite Rosie, nerving herself to open the handbag. The smell from the grubby lining of face-powder and cachous summoned up her mother in all her rackety being. Threading the blue glass beads of the rosary through her fingers brought images of her parents flickering through her mind. She could hear her father's soft Dublin brogue whispering the prayers. Hail Mary full of grace, blessed art thou among women, And blessed be the fruit of thy womb, Jesus.

As a child she had heard the words saying, Blessed be the fruit in the room with Jesus. She had a picture in her mind of a woman, as pretty as Mummy, sitting in a room full of fruit, feeding jewel-red apples to a chubby Baby Jesus. Yes, Violet Slattery had been pretty with hair as blonde as her own, slim and tall with blue eyes and long delicate fingers. They seemed so quick and nimble, cutting out paper dolls, making shadow birds against the wall or shucking peas into a basin. Those blue eyes lighting up as soon as Miriam's father walked into the room.

At bedtime she and her mother had been held

263

in thrall by the magic of her father's stories and the lilting sadness of his voice. They were all yearning to escape, if only for a moment, from the drabness of their lives. And when Miriam was eight years old Jack Slattery did just that. He went to the other side of the world and took their dreams with him. She felt a sudden flicker of anger. How easy it was for men to run off when things turned sour, to cast themselves up on a different shore and take on a new, more interesting life.

Gradually she became aware of the sound of someone tapping at the back door. It was Alec. At the sight of him she burst into tears. Full of concern, he stepped into the kitchen and drew her towards a chair and sat with her on his lap.

Miriam clung to him. 'She's dead, Alec. My mother's dead and I never went to see her.'

'Ma told me. I'm so sorry, love,' he said holding her more tightly. 'Poor Mirry, what a shock. There my love, you cry it all out. I've got you, darling, sh, my love, sh, sh, it's all right.'

She buried her face in his neck, soaking his shirt with her tears. 'Stay with me,' she pleaded.

He held her close until with a last gasping sob her crying stopped. 'Mirry, you're cold,' he said as she began to shiver. 'Let me close the window, then I'll make us a cup of tea.'

She felt a stab of disappointment as he released her and began moving around the kitchen. She wanted him to hold her close, to comfort her. Tea she could have at any time.

He went over to Rosie and kissed her sleeping face. Then he picked up the kettle and filled it at the sink. 'Ma sent me over to invite you to tea tomorrow,' he said.

'What else did she say?' Miriam asked, suddenly anxious.

Alec grinned. 'As I expected she gave me a good rollocking. Said she could cope with anything but deceit.'

'Oh God, what must she think of me!' Miriam cried.

'Well,' Alec laughed, 'you've come out of it better than me. She reckons you've got a lot of pride. Just said she was disappointed you didn't feel you could trust her. It was me as got the roasting for not telling her at Christmas.'

Miriam frowned. 'Your mother's been so good to me, Alec. Now I shall get off on the wrong foot.' She bit her lip then asked, 'What exactly did you tell her?'

Alec handed her a cup of tea. 'I said I'd met you a long time ago, we'd planned to be married then we lost track of each other on account of Jutland.'

'You didn't tell her about Taffy?' Miriam gasped.

'Christ, no, Mirry I wouldn't breathe that to a soul.' Alec smiled at her. 'Tell you what, Ma's tickled pink about Rosie being her grandchild.'

'Tell her Rosie and me will be pleased to have tea with her,' said Miriam as she glanced across at her daughter.

'Knock on the door about three o'clock,' Alec said.

'Knock on the door?' she flared. 'You've got to call for us. Do it proper or not at all.'

'You and your pride, Mirry,' he laughed.

'Pride is all I've had to cling to,' she said as she picked up the yellowing envelope from the table.

Inside were two photographs and a postcard. The first one was of herself with her mother. It must have been taken on the same day as the snapshot only in this picture Miriam was giggling as if she had just been tickled. Two images of a happy childhood that was painful to remember.

'Your mother was a real beauty,' Alec said.

'A lifetime ago,' Miriam sighed. She kissed the picture of Jack, her handsome father. 'He could tell such stories, Alec,' she sobbed. 'Then, he just went away.'

The postcard was of Sydney Harbour, Australia. It was addressed to Miriam's mother.

Dear Violet

Have jumped ship and can make more money in the cane fields.

Will send for you both as soon as I can. Here's to our new life Down Under,

Love Jack.

P.S. Kiss Miriam for me.

Alec looked at the faded sepia view. 'So Jack the sailor went off to be a jackaroo,' he said.

Miriam nodded. 'And he took my heart with him. Everything went wrong. I never felt safe again. My mother changed from being pretty and happy to crying and screaming and letting everything go to pot. There was the drinking and the men and never being settled anywhere. But,' her voice trembled, 'I would have tried to forgive her if I'd known she was dying.'

266

'I know, I know,' he said. 'But she's at peace now and she'll never again be disappointed.' He took a hankie out of his pocket and dried her tears. 'Shall I have to go to Australia to steal it back?

'Steal what?' she said, her thoughts still with Violet.

'Your heart, of course,' as he stood up to light the kitchen lamp.

Miriam stepped up on to Alec's feet bringing herself level with his face. 'It was only a corner that he took. I saved the rest for you,' she said twining her arms around his neck.

All the while that he had sat with her, Miriam had been aware of the pulse beating in his neck and the soft fullness of his mouth.

They moved around the room in a shuffling waltz. Alec sang to her, 'I'll be your sweetheart, if you will be mine.'

'All my life, I'll be your Valentine,' she murmured.

He brushed her lips with his. They stood in the bedroom doorway, sipping and tasting each other.

'Stay with me,' she murmured.

'Where's Albert?' Alec asked.

'Away 'til morning,' she whispered against his neck.

'Are you sure you're ready, after what happened with Ta–?'

'Alec,' she cut in. 'I don't want ever to talk about it again. Everything about that night – even the smell of the lime flowers on the way to the meeting-place – it's all vile to me. He stole from

267

me.' She shuddered. 'He broke in and stole.'

Alec stroked her hair.

'This is you and me, Alec. It's me inviting you. I'm making you a present.'

He sat down on the bed and Miriam stood facing him. Slowly she slid her fingers under the ribbon straps on her shoulders and pulled her nightdress down over her shoulders letting it fall to the floor. 'Don't you want me?' she asked.

Her skin quivered as Alec gazed at her.

His eyes lingered over her breasts then followed the curve of her belly. 'Want you, Mirry?' he said. 'I've never stopped wanting you.' Alec began to undress, struggling with his jumper until she helped him pull it over his head. His body was lean and hard, the hair on his chest startlingly black against his white skin. He shed the rest of his clothes and lay down beside her.

Miriam sighed as he began to kiss her. With each caress of his lips against her skin, with each breath against her neck she felt herself made new, emerging from the imprisonment of the past. His mouth was tenderly insistent, drawing her to him, reaching into the quick of her being. 'Yes oh yes,' she breathed. His fingers unfolded her to the delicate probing of his tongue. Then she became aware of his desire stirring against her thighs so the kisses intensified.

'Mirry,' he whispered, 'I need to love you, now.'

'Wait,' she commanded, taking his penis in her hand and feeling it tense and throbbing under her fingers. Alec moved astride her and she wound her legs around his waist. She opened herself to him with her free hand then slid his penis inside herself.

'Oh,' Alec sighed, 'oh, that feels so good. Like I've come home.'

As he thrust himself into her so she drew him deeper. They were an urgent striving unity. She dug her fingers into his shoulders and his breath was hot on her face. Miriam cried out as Alec brought her to a sobbing dizzying fulfilment. He lay with his head on her breasts as she drew her fingers through his hair. The light stole from the room. A draught of air from the open window ruffled the curtains, cooling their skin. Miriam pulled the sheet up over their shoulders. She felt as if she were suspended in time. Not fretting about the past or dreading the future but caught up in the perfect present. Held between breathing out and breathing in.

'I love you,' Alec whispered. 'It's more than wanting. You heal something in me.'

Miriam's voice was choked with tears. 'I do so love you, Alec,' she whispered back.

He sighed. 'Mirry, I don't want to leave you but I've got to make the right start with Rosie. I don't want her to find me here and be frightened. Besides, Ma's probably waiting for me.'

Miriam wondered what would it be like to fall asleep in Alec's arms, instead of feeling the warmth steal from the bed. She waited for the back door to click shut behind him. Instead she heard his footsteps returning to the bedroom.

'I've brought someone to keep you warm,' he whispered, laying their daughter on the bed.

Miriam smiled as she tucked Rosie in beside her. Sleep eluded her as her mind drifted

269

between the past with its broken promises and the future with its uncertainties. How fleeting had been that perfect moment when they were one flesh, one pulse, one heart. How soon they were caught up again in the web of other lives, other needs.

Again she had given herself to him with no thought of tomorrow. Clasping Rosie's hand in hers she prayed she would not live to regret her impulsiveness.

Chapter Twenty-Five

'Ooh, do it quick Dora, before I change my mind.' Lily clenched her teeth as her friend stabbed the threaded needle through her right ear-lobe. 'Cripes,' she gasped, 'that didn't half hurt.'

'Well, there's the other one to go, unless you wants to look like a pirate,' said Dora as she knotted the thread for the second time.

'They feel like they're on fire,' Lily moaned as she dabbed at them with a wet rag. Her face, damp and ghostly white floated towards her from the mottled glass on Dora's dressing-table. All this pain to please Bernard, and in the end would he really notice?

Yesterday, when she delivered the uniform jackets to the shop, he had stepped out of the doorway towards her.

'What pretty ears you've got, Lily,' he'd said,

270

touching them with his pale fingers. 'Like little shells, just made for whispers. Why haven't I noticed them before?'

''Cos I've never had me hair up before,' Lily snapped, thrusting the uniform jackets into his arms and running back to the workroom. She was hungry for his attention but what he fed her was dazzling and insubstantial. He pierced her fragile façade with practised flattery. Bernard was like the handsome sailor doll her father had given her with its winning smile and sawdust heart.

'A real trashy piece of goods,' sniffed Dora. 'Not worth baiting your line for. Leave him to the sharks like Ruby.'

When she was away from him she agreed with Dora's valuation. But, when she was in the presence of his cool blond arrogance, she was lost to the sharp appraising side of herself and became giddy with desire. Knowing that his fleeting attentions made Ruby jealous added spice to each encounter.

Dora gave her a hankie. 'Blow your nose, then comb your hair around them ears,' she advised. 'They looks like overtime at the slaughterhouse. What are you going to do for earrings?'

'I don't know,' said Lily feeling foolish. 'I only made my mind up to have them done on the way round here.'

'You don't 'alf rush into things half-cock,' said Dora.

'Well, I had to do it while me courage was up.'

Dora laughed and her sharp-featured little face shone with good-humour. 'Tell you what,' she said, picking up her handbag. 'I got a shilling. I'll

271

treat you to the pictures. Lilian Gish is on at the Picture House.'

'What's it about?' asked Lily as she combed her hair gingerly over her throbbing ears.

'Ooh, Auntie, you know the one that works up the Picture House? She reckons it's heart-rendering. The first night she couldn't hardly play the piano for crying.'

'I want my heart mending not rending,' laughed Lily as she followed her friend down the stairs and out of the house.

It wasn't only Bernard who she wanted to think of her as grown-up, now. There was Dad who would be home at any minute. Lily didn't know quite what she felt about him and Miriam. She had been so certain that he was the shadowy stranger kissing her friend in the kitchen on Christmas Eve and now she was not so sure. After all, tattoos were two a penny in the navy. It could have been anyone. And then there was the uncomfortable thought that if it wasn't Dad why was she being so horrible to Miriam? Her mind skittered away from the question of what business it was of hers anyway. It was always followed by another even more disturbing thought. What right had she to be unfriendly to Miriam, whatever the circumstances?

'Here Lily, put a spurt on. We'll miss the beginning,' Dora called over her shoulder as they turned the corner into Commerical Road. They just managed to tag onto the end of the queue outside the Victoria Picture House as it began to move rapidly towards the entrance.

They were hardly sat down inside before the

272

lights dimmed and the title *Broken Blossoms* flashed onto the screen. The coughing and rustling of sweet-papers ceased. Dora's auntie played tinkling bell-like notes on the piano as a young Chinese man set out on his travels to England. Lily forgot her pain as she became involved in the film. The scene shifted to the home of Battling Burrows the East-End boxer and Lucy, his pathetic daughter. Battler moved threateningly towards Lucy and the audience booed in outrage. Then the cinema came alive with more boos and hisses when Battler dragged Lucy home from the Chinaman's shop and killed her. There was a crescendo of cheering as the Chinaman shot Battler and cries of 'Shame!' when he killed himself.

Lily and Dora dabbed their eyes then, linking arms, hurried back to Queen Street to top off their evening with a penn'orth of chips.

'Ooh isn't that Lilian Gish pretty?' said Dora, blowing on her chips.

'Mmm,' agreed Lily. 'I felt sorry for the Chinaman. He was so kind. But what about Battler?'

'Blimey, I'll never complain about my Dad any more.'

'He doesn't hit you, does he?'

''Course not,' snorted Dora. 'But he can't half shout. How are your ear'oles?'

'Still on fire. Still, I've only got to get through the next few days and I'll be able to get some earrings down the market.'

'Cripes, I'd better get a move on,' said Dora as the Guildhall clock chimed ten. 'Dad will really shout if I'm much later.'

'Bye Dora,' said Lily smiling at her friend. 'I'd better get going too or Gran will tell me off. See you Monday.'

As she turned into Cross Street she passed Michael Rowan and a young girl laughing in a doorway. She hurried past, feeling suddenly lonely.

Nobody greeted her as she turned the key and stepped into the passage. The house was silent. The light was on in the kitchen but there was no sign of Gran. There was a jug of barley-water on the dresser; she poured herself a glass. The chips had made her thirsty. She was too restless to go to bed yet so she picked up her library book, *The Hunchback of Notre Dame,* and settled into the armchair, becoming absorbed in the fate of the beautiful Esmerelda. How well she understood the gypsy's love for the handsome Captain Phoebus. Gradually the words began to swim before her eyes. Eleven o'clock struck on the mantelpiece clock. Lily got up and stretched herself. She was about to go through to the outside lavatory when she heard someone moving about out in the scullery.

Reaching for the poker, she crept behind Gran's chair. It was Dad. Smiling to herself she prepared to jump out on him. Then as his voice floated towards her singing, 'I'll be your sweetheart, If you will be mine' her stomach churned. He must have been over to see Miriam. It was her he was singing about. The image of them together kissing each other sickened her. Once more she had been cast in the role of a Peeping Tom but this time there was no escape.

She watched him hugging his happiness, drifting around the room with a foolish grin on his face. Her skin crawled with embarrassment as if she were seeing him naked. He must reclothe himself as her father before they faced each other again. Taking a biscuit from the barrel, he wandered around the room dropping crumbs. Her cramped muscles screamed for a change of position. Still Dad wandered about, picking up her book then putting it down. Then as swiftly as he'd entered the room he turned out the lamp and left.

Lily picked her way around the furniture, in the dark, her head a mass of confused thoughts. It was as if her father had left something of his excitement in the room like a cobweb trailing across her face. Taking off her shoes she crept up the stairs to bed. As she slid between the sheets, Gran's snores were comfortingly familiar.

The sun was hot on her face the next morning and the throbbing in her ears reminded her of yesterday's impulsiveness. Gran's voice floated up through the open door. 'Lily, come on, chop, chop. There's a cup of tea waiting.'

Half asleep she wandered over to the mirror and drew her hair away from her neck. She stared in horror at her swollen ears. The cotton was stuck fast. As she dragged on her petticoat Gran's voice sharpened to irritation. 'Put a spurt on, Lily or your toast will be cold.'

As she opened the kitchen door Dad leapt forward and give her a ferocious hug.

'How's my girl?' he cried. She screamed with pain. 'Whatever's the matter, Lily?' he asked, loosening his grasp.

'It's my ears,' she sobbed. 'I got Dora to pierce them.'

'Merciful Heavens,' gasped Gran when she saw them.

'We'll have to cut that cotton out and bathe them with salt and water,' said Dad. 'You get on with tidying the front room, Ma, I'll see to this.'

Lily had intended to be distant with Dad but events had overtaken her. She sat in Gran's chair while he fussed about her, full of sympathy. Gradually the stinging stopped and she felt calmer.

'D'you feel up to a stroll along the front?' Dad asked as he handed her some toast.

Lily nodded. Everything was back to normal. Gran bustling about and Dad making her breakfast. She gave him a kiss on the cheek before going upstairs to finish dressing. As she buttoned her blouse, Gran came in with a small box in her hand.

'Your mother left these for you,' she said, 'that last morning when she left you and Andrew with me. Book about ships for him and these for you.'

'Do you think she did that because she knew she was never coming back?' asked Lily, her heart thumping at the sudden unexpected mention of her mother.

'I've puzzled over that for many a year,' said Gran sadly.

'But she couldn't have known she was going to get drowned, unless...?'

'Don't you want to look inside the box?' Gran asked, interrupting Lily's disturbing thoughts.

Lily opened the white cardboard lid. Inside, nestling in tissue paper, lay a pair of earrings. They were made of thin strands of gold twisted together like the pattern on a stick of barley-sugar.

'Oh Gran.' Lily flung her arms around her. 'They're so dainty, can I put them on now?'

'Let's just give them a wipe over with a bit of methylated spirit, just to make sure they're clean. I'm warning you, Lily, they'll hurt like blazes.'

Lily gritted her teeth and shuddered as Gran threaded them through her ears. Tears ran down her cheeks as she held a damp cloth to her burning lobes.

'You've got all the pain over in one day, better than letting them heal and have to go through it all again,' said Gran. 'They're gold so there's not much chance of them festering.'

Lily peered into the mirror as soon as the bleeding had stopped. 'Ooh I do like them Gran,' she sighed, 'they're ever so pretty.'

'And you're a pretty girl just like your mother,' said Gran, smiling at her.

'Tell me about her, please, Gran.'

'Well, she was dark-haired and daintily made. A Dolly Daydream,' Gran smiled, 'just like someone else I know.' Lily blushed.

'I have a picture of her I've been keeping for you that she left with the earrings.' Gran bent down and pulled Grandad's ditty-box out from under the bed and unlocked it with the key she wore around her neck.

Lily waited impatiently while Gran lifted back the lid and rummaged inside, eventually handing her a tarnished silver frame. Wonderingly, Lily turned it over and looked at the photograph inside. She was startled at the resemblance to herself: the same black hair, the same straight brows, dark eyes and thick lashes. Her mother was smiling out of the picture at her. Lily had such a longing to know all about her.

'Our natures were totally different,' said Gran. 'I was all for getting the work done and out of the way, and Mary,' she smiled sadly, 'well, next week was soon enough. We had many a set-to over it. But the thing I remember best was her singing. It was lovely, pure and...' Gran's voice trailed away and they both started up guiltily as they became aware of Dad standing in the doorway. How long had he been there?

'All that about your mother's in the past. It's the future we got to settle,' he said, taking Lily's arm and leading her downstairs.

'Alec,' Gran's voice had a warning note, 'be careful.'

'This is my business, Ma, and I'll settle it how I see fit.'

Lily bridled at Dad's roughness with Gran but at the same time she was afraid. She had the sense of crossing an invisible threshold. The front room was hot and dusty from lack of use. Gran had been polishing the mantelpiece and all the ornaments lay jumbled together on the sofa. It was as chaotic as Lily's thoughts.

Dad cleared his throat. 'As I said, Lily, it's about our future.'

'What future?'

'Yours and mine,' he said, pushing his hair

impatiently away from his eyes. 'Your Gran's, Miriam's and your sister Rosie.'

'What d'you mean, my sister?' gasped Lily. 'She's Mr Naylor's child.'

'No,' said Dad, avoiding her eyes, 'she's my little girl.'

She leapt at her father striking him with her fists. 'Liar, liar,' she screamed at him.

'Lily, stop it. You stop this carry-on or I'll slap you so hard.'

'Liar, liar, liar.' She couldn't stop. 'Liar, liar!' she cried, wrenching herself from his grasp. She was his girl, not Rosie.

Suddenly the door burst open and juddered back on its hinges. Gran stood bristling in the doorway. 'Stop that noise at once, Lily. I will not have it.'

The words died in Lily's throat.

'Ma, I'm sorry,' her father said quietly. 'It wasn't Lily's fault.'

'You will be sorry, Alec. Of that I'm certain,' said Gran fiercely. Lily gave a shaky sob.

'Now, Lily,' said Gran, 'you go and wash your face and make a pot of tea. We'll sit ourselves down and talk like sensible women.'

Lily rushed from the room, only too glad to get away. She filled the kettle with trembling hands then paced about the kitchen. Her tears kept breaking out afresh as other worrisome thoughts struck her. She felt enmeshed in a web of lies. Rosie was her sister, she was three years old. So Dad had known Miriam before, long before she became their neighbour. And Miriam, Lily twisted her handkerchief in agitation, pretending that Dad was a stranger to her when all the time he'd been in her bed. All those times when she'd shown her Dad's letters and told her her deepest secrets, Miriam had lied behind those smiling eyes. What of the Christmas present, last year, when Dad had written and said she was his darling Lily? About having 'Great Expectations' of her. A fresh outburst of crying halted her as she went to fetch the milk from the wall-safe in the yard. She kept her head firmly down just in case Miriam should see her. She stirred the sugar savagely in Gran's cup and slopped it in the saucer. Resolutely, she splashed her face with cold water then carried the tray along the passage.

The door of the front room was open and she heard Gran say, 'By Christ, Alec, I'm glad your father's not here today.'

'But Ma,' Dad protested.

'No wonder Mary pushed off out of it.'

'Don't you—'

'Don't I what?' Gran challenged. 'You whored around with a young girl barely sixteen, left me to look after your kids and now when you're ready to get your life back on the rails you can't even tell your own daughter properly.'

'I was going to take her along the front and break it to her gently,' said Dad. 'It was you telling Lily things about Mary that set me off.'

'Lily has every right to know about her mother. Why the hell you had to blurt it out all arse-about-face, is beyond me.'

'She'll calm down, Ma, you can always get round her.'

280

Lily stood outside the door, the cups rattling on the tray.

'I've more respect for my granddaughter than to get round her.'

'You know what I mean. Don't get on your high horse, Ma.'

'Get out of my sight,' Gran shouted. 'You come back with Miriam at three o'clock. In the meantime, I'll try and repair your handiwork.'

Dad rushed past Lily and out into the street, slamming the door behind him. Gran's face was flushed with anger as she turned to take the tea-tray from Lily and set it on the table. But her voice was warm with understanding as she said, 'Are you too old to sit on your Gran's lap now you're wearing those fancy earrings?'

Lily hurtled into her arms. 'That's it, your old Gran has got you safe. Cry it all out then we'll set about repairs.'

Lily clung to her, oblivious of the stinging in her ears, pressing her face into Gran's apron, drawing in the familiar smell of lavender soap. 'I didn't think Dad would ever lie to me,' she said when all her tears were exhausted and she'd settled herself in the armchair opposite Gran. 'And Miriam – she was my best friend.'

'It was bound to happen one day,' said Gran as she poured the milk into the cups. 'We make such heroes of our fathers, especially when they're not around enough for us to see the chinks in their armour. We're bound to be disappointed.'

'But he lied to both of us. Why, Gran?'

'Well, seemingly,' said Gran as she blew on the hot tea, 'he was all set up to marry Miriam before

Rosie was born and then there was some dreadful mix-up around the time that Andrew was killed and he and Miriam lost track of each other.'

'But why didn't Miriam tell us she knew Dad when she arrived here?' Lily persisted.

'Well, there you got to admire that young woman.'

'Why?' Lily was genuinely puzzled.

'She had to struggle along, an unmarried woman with a young child. She'd called herself Mrs Naylor, the war widow, and got herself employment and a place to live.'

'But you would have taken her in and made her welcome.'

'Ah, but she had more pride than that,' said Gran. 'She wanted to see how the land lay between her and your dad after all that time. She wanted him to marry her out of love, not obligation.'

'And is Dad going to marry her?'

'It's what they both want,' said Gran quietly.

'But what about my mother? When I was bringing in the tea you said as how she'd cleared off, not that she'd died like you told me.'

Gran looked steadily at Lily for some time before she said, 'Your mother disappeared when you were a baby, Lily. Then an accident was reported in the paper of a young woman's body being washed up on the beach. Your father identified her as Mary Forrest your mother.' She got to her feet and put her cup back on the tray. 'Whatever you want to know about your mother that's in my power to tell you I will, but today

282

we've got other calls on our time.'

'What d'you mean, Gran?' asked Lily curiously.

'I've invited Miriam and Rosie to tea.'

Lily leapt to her feet. 'How could you do that?' she shouted.

'Because,' said Gran, taking Lily firmly by the arm and pushing her back into her chair, 'this is my home and whatever your father has done, Miriam will be my daughter-in-law and Rosie is my granddaughter.'

'Well, I shan't be here,' said Lily sulkily.

'You'll help me get the tea and make them welcome.'

Lily tossed her head. 'I don't want them to be welcome.'

Gran fixed Lily with one of her steely looks. 'Your wants have nothing to do with it,' said Gran firmly. 'Miriam and Rosie are coming to tea and will be made welcome.'

Lily stood trying to outface Gran. She thought about rushing out of the house in a temper but decided against it. If she fell out with Gran she'd have nobody on her side.

Chapter Twenty-Six

It's like a painting, thought Beattie, standing at the kerb with her pudding-basin. Drawn up beside her was the rickety cart belonging to Charlie Madgewick, the one-legged watercress seller, with its buckets slopping over with water.

Charlie in his shiny old suit was holding out some lumps of sugar to Rosie. The little girl in a pink puffed-sleeved dress and frilly white apron held out her chubby hand.

''Is name's Blazer,' said Charlie, referring to his shuffling old black pony, 'on account of the white blaze on his forehead. Get your mum to hold out your hand to him – that's it – hold your palm out flat.'

Miriam was glowing. Her blonde hair was loose about her shoulders and her blue eyes shone. The glow came from some very recent loving, if Beattie's memory served her right. Alec stood tall and proud behind her.

What would be the centre of interest in the painting? Beattie asked herself. The plump old woman holding out her basin to receive the glistening green cress from the gnarled hand of the seller? Perhaps it would be the proud bearded sailor with his beautiful woman? Or the child holding out her hand to the nimbling muzzle of the old pony? And then she saw Lily standing at the doorstep staining the scene with her bitter glances.

Beattie reached into her apron pocket and gave Charlie his halfpenny. It's going to be a long hot afternoon, she thought. Fixing a smile firmly on her face she turned to Miriam and Rosie. 'Welcome, both of you,' she said. 'Come in and settle yourself in the front room.'

Lily, pale and sullen, stepped aside, and Miriam, flushed and defensive, went past her into the house. Rosie, sensing the charged atmosphere, refused to sit with her mother and plumped herself on Lily's lap. Alec, caught between three fires, perched uneasily on his seat.

Beattie was thankful for the breathing-space in the kitchen making the watercress sandwiches. There was enough hostility in her front room to power a battleship. One of Joseph's salty sayings came to mind: 'A bugger-up in a pudding-basin.' That just about captured it. As she assembled the sandwiches, questions teemed in her head. How would Alec afford to keep two families? How would they all get on squeezed together in one house? Three women in one kitchen? And what about Albert? Slow down, she admonished herself, getting het up will solve nothing. Taking a deep breath she took hold of the laden tray and carried it down the passage.

Rosie was still squinnying. 'It biting my neck,' she said, tugging at the collar of her dress.

'Let Mummy undo it,' coaxed Miriam as Beattie set the tray down on the table.

'Lily do it,' Rosie insisted, flouncing away from her mother.

'Please do it for her,' begged Miriam close to tears. Lily stared fixedly at the floor.

Rosie rushed over to Lily and climbed onto her lap again. Once the button was undone she leapt down, kicking over the tray and the pot of scalding tea. It narrowly missed her as it smashed against the tiles in the grate.

'You naughty girl,' cried Miriam, smacking her hand. Rosie howled with rage and scuffed the spilled sugar into the rug.

Lily glared at Miriam. 'It wasn't her fault,' she snapped. 'That collar's rubbed her neck red-raw.

Pretending to be all lah-di-dah when...'

Alec moved towards her with his hand raised. Beattie thrust Lily quickly towards the door. 'Brush and dustpan and a damp cloth, Lily, at once,' she commanded. Somehow she had to calm things down.

'Miriam, sit down, my dear. Least said soonest mended. The important thing is that the child isn't scalded.' Taking a paper bag from the table drawer Beattie gathered the sandwiches from the tray on the floor and put them inside. She got another bag and did the same with the scones.

Rosie had stopped howling and was watching her from the safety of Alec's lap.

'Do you know what I'm going to do?' Beattie asked, when she was sure of her granddaughter's attention. 'Have a picnic in the park.'

'Rosie likes the park.'

'Would you like to come?' The child nodded vigorously. 'You say sorry to Mummy, and you can come with me.'

Rosie rushed over to Miriam. 'Sorry,' she mumbled into the folds of her dress.

'I don't know what's got into her,' she said as Lily came back into the room.

'Here, give that to me,' said Alec, taking the brush out of Lily's hand. 'You have a breath of air with Rosie and Gran, it might improve your manners.'

Beattie could see that he hoped to have Miriam to himself. Well, that was not going to be the way of it. She and that young woman needed to have a talk. Besides, her son had a lot of ground to make up with her after that fiasco with Lily.

286

'Miriam is coming with us, Alec,' she said. 'You get this place shipshape and have the kettle on for five o'clock. Lily, take Rosie out to the lavatory and then set off for the park. We'll catch you up later.' As she went upstairs for her hat she felt the threads being drawn back under her control.

Miriam and Alec hastily drew apart when she returned. Handing a parasol to Miriam, she said, 'Take this my dear, it'll keep the sun off your head.' She looked at Alec and he held her gaze, his brown eyes unfathomable. Why were they so often at odds with each other – he rushing into things and she like the dung-cart after the Lord Mayor's Show always having to clear up after him.

They passed the Vine children, the twins on the doorstep and Mary out on the pavement, sitting on a kitchen chair with Blyth on her lap. The little boy was snotty-nosed as usual and there was a listlessness about the little group. From inside the house Dolly seemed to be crashing the furniture about and singing loudly.

It occurred to Beattie to ask the kids to join their picnic. But she didn't have the energy to take on the Vines today. Besides, she wanted to talk to Miriam.

As they walked towards the park in silence Beattie saw that it was not going to be an easy task. The young woman's face was turned resolutely away. 'Miriam,' she floundered when she could bear the silence no longer, 'I thought that we'd become friends, over the last few months. Now, we've got even more reason to get on together if we're to be a family.'

Ignoring her, Miriam set up a furious pace. Beattie struggled to catch up. The handles of the string-bag cut into her fingers and the lemonade bottle banged against her leg. By the time she drew level again she'd developed a painful stitch.

'I'm that wild with your Lily,' Miriam burst out, 'treating me as if I was dirt.'

'It's bound to be a bit awkward at first,' Beattie gasped.

Miriam glared at her. 'I am not dirt and will not be treated as if I was.' She almost spat the words at her and was off down the road before Beattie could open her mouth.

When they reached the park she flung down the parasol and began pulling leaves from the hedge, savagely stripping them from their stems. 'I know what you and Lily think of me,' she said in a fierce whisper.

'What do we think?'

'That I'm a scheming whore that's trapped your son and Lily's precious Daddy.'

'I'm sorry you think that of us,' said Beattie knowing the young woman's words were born out of anger and hurt pride.

'Well, what do you think?' asked Miriam, scarlet-faced.

'You're a woman of great courage and dignity,' Beattie said, trying to keep her voice from shaking. 'I admire the way you've coped, supporting yourself and Rosie.'

Although she appeared to ignore her, Beattie knew that Miriam was listening. In the distance she could see Rosie riding on Lily's back. She was anxious to clear the air between herself and

Miriam before the girls rejoined them. 'Alec has told me that Rosie is his child,' she said, 'and that makes her my grandchild. It's strange, but I had taken to her straight away and wondered why we had such a bond between us. I'm sorry things didn't go right for you both with the war and everything. But now all's well that...'

'I wanted to die,' Miriam cut in, 'it would have been so easy. If I could have just swallowed down a whole bottle of laudanum I'd have drifted away from it all.'

Beattie was shocked.

'But Rosie quickened in me and somehow I had to draggle things together for the pair of us.'

Beattie took her hand and guided her to an empty bench. Miriam's fingers were icy cold in spite of the August heat.

'I was living with Aunt Florrie.'

'Oh, yes. You've spoken of her before,' said Beattie. 'She moved down to Devon?'

'That's right,' Miriam continued. 'Then I had a stroke of luck. My Auntie's friend had a daughter in Gosport who wanted company while her husband was away in the war, so I moved in with Daisy.' She smiled. 'That was our first home, Rosie and me. Daisy was a treasure, but when her husband came back it was only fair we should find somewhere else.'

'So that's how you came to be our neighbour.' Beattie could feel the tension between them beginning to ebb. Miriam nodded.

'It was a lucky day for Albert.' Beattie was rewarded with a smile.

'It was a gamble. I knew Alec had spoken of his

289

family in Lemon Street. I wanted to test the waters.'

'You've got spirit,' said Beattie admiringly. After all, the girl could have come crying and tried to shame Alec into marrying her. Just like the first time.

The unwelcome memory of Mary Kenny intruded into her afternoon. What a knowing little piece she'd been and how she'd got them all dancing to her tune. Who knew whether Andrew was really Alec's child. Until you looked at him, Beattie chided herself. Image of his grandfather he was, Joseph in miniature. What could she tell Lily about her mother? Really nothing much more than she'd said already. Mary had certainly been a beauty and Lily was looking to be the image of her. Please God, she implored, let Mary be dead. Let me be mistaken in thinking that Alec lied to me about the body washed from the sea. But there was Hester, she'd sworn it was Mary she'd seen on the bus. Jesus, she could appear at any minute and ruin their lives, all of them.

'Are you all right, Mrs Forrest?'

'I was lost in my memories,' she said. 'This park does that to me.'

They looked across the lawns to where Lily and Rosie were standing near the Orlando Memorial. The little girl, secure in her new sister's arms, was reaching up to touch the Chinese bell within its stone arch.

'Alec told me that his father's name is written there,' said Miriam.

'Yes,' Beattie said, 'I feel closest to Joseph in

this park but not just because of the memorial. You see, it was here that I first met him.'

Rosie caught sight of her mother and rushed over to her. Lily dawdled behind her, looking at the ground. The reminiscences were halted while Beattie passed around the sandwiches. No one said anything. Rosie settled herself beside Lily and handed her the watercress out of her sandwich. Miriam smoothed a strand of hair from her face and looked into the distance.

Beattie could hardly swallow. She racked her brains for something to say as she poured the lemonade into cups and handed it around. Refusing a drink, Lily began to make a daisy chain and Rosie rolled over on to her stomach and watched her.

'And how did you and your husband meet?' asked Miriam, pulling up a daisy and giving it to her daughter.

Beattie smiled gratefully. 'It was the day the park was first opened – May the twenty-fourth, Queen Victoria's birthday. There were bands and bunting and when the Mayor turned on the fountain everyone went wild. I was a young maid in service to a doctor and his family. I was taking their dog Bijou for a walk.' Beattie laughed. 'What with all the clapping and cheering I let go of his lead and he ran off.'

It was scorching hot and the sun had glittered on the bugles of the Marine bandsmen. Beattie had rushed after Bijou and ran smack into Joseph.

'I looked up into the eyes of this bearded, red-haired giant and was dazzled. His face seemed to

291

be surrounded by a fiery halo.'

'Like Phoebus, the Sun God,' murmured Lily, setting a daisy chain around Rosie's neck.

'Doggie, where Doggie?' asked Rosie.

Beattie laughed. 'Bijou had got his lead wrapped round Joseph's legs. By the time we had got him unravelled the die was cast.'

'Ice-cream, have ice-cream, Mummy?' asked Rosie, her attention captured by the cart near the fountain.

'I'll get her one,' said Lily reaching into the pocket of her skirt. 'And a cornet for you, Gran?' She walked past Miriam jiggling the coins in her pocket.

'Don't forget Miriam,' Beattie called. If Lily wanted to keep up her childish vendetta, she'd get no help from her.

'That's kind of you,' said Miriam, coolly. 'I'll have a cornet, too.'

Rosie caught up with Lily and they sped off to join the queue.

While Beattie gathered up the remains of the picnic, she studied her future daughter-in-law. She could see why Alec was besotted. There was a drowsy lushness that hovered over her thickly-lashed eyes and full lips, an indefinable essence that was wholly her own. As she put the cork back in the lemonade bottle Miriam said, 'Mrs Forrest, what happened next?'

'Where?' asked Beattie, startled by the question.

'In the park with you and your Joseph.'

'Oh, he walked me back to the doctor's house where I lived, and we saw each other every

292

minute I could get away.' Beattie laughed. 'Poor Bijou nearly had his legs walked off him.' Miriam smiled. 'On the last evening, before his ship sailed, he proposed and I said yes, although,' Beattie blushed, 'I was at the time engaged to someone else.'

'It wouldn't have been Mr...?'

'I had to write and tell him it was all over between us,' cut in Beattie. Whatever Miriam guessed she did not want her to voice her suspicions. Better his name was not spoken. 'He took it very well in the circumstances.'

Miriam smiled innocently. 'Did you ever see him again?' she asked mischievously.

'Ah! Here are the girls,' cried Beattie, thankful for the diversion. 'Rosie, you've more ice-cream on your face than ever went into your tummy.'

Lily handed Miriam her cornet and was thanked by a nod of the head.

Long experience of picnics had caused Beattie to pack a damp flannel. She put it to good use on Rosie's face and hands before eating her own cornet. The spikey atmosphere between Lily and Miriam persisted. Beattie would have liked to have given her granddaughter a good shaking, but she knew that the young women would have to sort it out themselves and would not appreciate her interference. 'You girls can make your own way home,' she said, squinting up at the Town Hall clock towering over the park. 'It's almost five o'clock. Your dad should have the kettle on by now.'

'Couldn't we all go together?' said Lily.

'You've to make your peace sometime,' said

293

Beattie quietly, guessing at Lily's reluctance to face her father after the recent dust-up.

Lily flounced off with Rosie dragging at her hand.

'Have you had much chance to talk about when you're getting married?' Beattie asked as the new-found sisters disappeared into Queen Street.

'No time at all,' said Miriam, getting to her feet and brushing crumbs from her skirt. 'What with the shock of my mother dying and one thing and another,' she shrugged her shoulders. 'Perhaps tonight.'

'Well, he's got the whole of his leave before him. You'll have to fix up banns and all sorts.'

It was as she turned the corner into Lemon Street that Beattie heard the screaming. Her stomach clenched in fear. Wild cries, like those of an animal caught in a trap. The neighbours were standing in their doorways looking up the street towards a man struggling with a woman. An ambulance was parked with the back doors open.

'Alec, it's Alec,' cried Miriam, running towards them.

'Stand back, let him get her up the steps. Stand back I say,' commanded Constable Wilkes.

'Christ, she's got a knife,' shouted Beattie. 'Dolly, don't! Oh, Dolly.'

Locked in a ghastly dance Alec and Dolly lurched back and forth. A nurse stood on the steps of the ambulance leaning towards them. Dolly waved the knife above her head narrowly missing Alec's face and slapped him with her other hand.

He held her tightly around the waist and kept

reaching up for the knife. Still she screamed. Constable Wilkes pushed Miriam into Beattie's open door where Lily, Rosie and the Vine children cowered in terror. As the constable turned towards Beattie, she grabbed the whistle, hanging from his jacket, and blew it fiercely. Dolly was distracted and Alec grasped her wrist, forcing her to lower her arm. The knife clattered to the ground.

There was a confused rush of sound and movement. The doors of the ambulance slammed shut quickly followed by the revving of the engine. Everyone stepped back into the pavement.

'Mrs Forrest, are you all right?'

Beattie found herself sitting on the window-ledge with Constable Wilkes bending over her. 'You saved the day,' he said. 'I don't mind telling you, it was touch and go.'

'Alec, where's Alec?' She reared up in alarm.

'He's just pacifying the kids. You get indoors now and have a sit down. I'll send someone round later for them.'

'Alec, what in God's name's been going on?'

'Hero, your son is a bloomin' hero.'

'Went after him with a knife she did.'

'Off her head completely.'

'Wants locking up.'

'You 'orrible cow. Shut yer bleedin' mouth.' Mary Vine erupted from behind Alec her fists flying.

'And they wants puttin' away at the same time.'

'Mrs Perks, I'll thank you to be quiet,' said Constable Wilkes. 'And the rest of you in to your homes.'

'Go with the others, love,' said Beattie to Mary, getting slowly to her feet. 'I expect your Blyth is crying for you.'

'I'm fine Ma,' Alec said, kissing her on the cheek. 'Full story later. I've to go with the constable, make a statement or something and I'll call in the barracks and see if they can get Mary's brother home for a while. Something needs sorting.'

Beattie sighed. Would this day never end? Looking pale and tired Miriam came towards her with Rosie and Blyth. 'I must get Mr Pragnell's tea soon. Shall I take him in with Rosie and me? If the worst comes to the worst he can bed down with us until things are sorted.'

'That's good of you,' Beattie smiled gratefully. 'You sure you're all right?' Miriam nodded. 'That's halved the problem at a stroke.' She turned into her house and was immediately swallowed up in tea-making and settling the twins and Mary with something to eat. Faith and Mercy were tearful, dirty and ravenous. Thirteen-year-old Mary was chalk-faced and silent. After their meal Beattie sent Lily upstairs with Faith and Mercy and closed the door behind them. 'Can you tell me what happened?' she asked, taking the empty cup out of Mary's hand.

'She wouldn't stop screaming.' The girl began to shake. 'The noise went right through me head. She was wild she was, and we was all scared of her. Last night we was all in bed and she kept waking us up and wantin' us to dance with her. Then she was asleep all day. We was hungry and there was nothin' in the kitchen. Blyth took her purse and was lookin' inside and she woke up and went mental she did. She got the carvin' knife and chased him into the street. I got 'old of 'im and she was goin' to stick it in me and Mr Forrest comes out and gets 'old of her.'

'You must have been very frightened,' said Beattie, taking her hand.

'Then she went all quiet and she looked as if she didn't know what's happened or nothin', like she was broken.' Mary sat dry-eyed and silent. It was Beattie who had to control her tears. The poor burdened little girl, she thought, the cruelty and unfairness of life.

'Where's your gran?'

'That old bitch.'

Beattie didn't know whether to laugh or scold Mary for the ripeness of her language. At least she still had a spark of fight in her. 'So you don't think your gran will come around and take care of things?'

'Gone off to Auntie Betty's in Yorkshire. Don't want to know about our mum.'

'I see,' said Beattie, wishing she felt equal to the task in front of her.

'Mrs Perks, her in number six, reckons Mum's gone off her head and we'll be put in the workhouse.'

'Stuff and nonsense. You got a good dad and a brother and you got the Forrest family behind you.'

'Harry, could Harry come home?' asked Mary. 'Dad don't matter but if we could get Harry...'

Beattie smiled at the change in the child at the mention of her brother. 'Yes,' she said. 'Mr

Forrest has gone to find him.'

'If he comes back we don't need no one else.'

'Well, you've always got us behind you. Hasn't she, Lily?' Beattie appealed to her granddaughter as she poked her head around the door.

Lily nodded. 'Twins are asleep in Dad's bed. D'you want a game of draughts, Mary?'

Beattie smiled her approval. There was nothing like involvement with the Vine family to make you count your blessings. 'That'll be Mr Forrest back from the barracks,' she said, getting up to answer the knock on the front door. 'He'll be able to tell you when your brother's coming home.' But it was Albert.

'Beatrice, I've just seen Mrs Naylor. I believe there's been something of a crisis.'

'You could say that,' she said smiling at him. 'But I think it's been a bugger-up in a pudding-basin.'

Chapter Twenty-Seven

Miriam was on the verge of tears as she climbed into bed between Blyth and Rosie. The day had been such a disappointment. So different from her dreams of being welcomed into the Forrest family. Lily had seen to that, flouncing about the room treating her as if she were little better than a whore. Her heart pounded with anger. What had she been going to say when her Gran interrupted her?

298

'Pretending to be all lah-di-dah when...' she'd shouted.

What would she have said had she not been interrupted? That Miriam was a loose woman who had got her claws into her saintly father? What right had she to judge her? And, as if that were not enough, there'd been Dolly Vine flashing that knife around. Alec could have been killed. He'd looked so pale and tired when he'd gone off with the constable to the police station. Why, why hadn't he come back and told her what had gone on down there?

She shivered, in spite of the September heat, and tucked the sheet more firmly around the three of them. Blyth lay on his back, his thumb jammed into his mouth. Poor little nipper, she thought. Even after a good wash there was still a neglected stale-milk smell about him. Miriam turned onto her side and drew Rosie into her arms.

Why had she got involved with the Vines? Almost without noticing she had become part of Lemon Street with all its joys and woes. For the first time in her life she belonged somewhere and was accepted. Impulsively she had offered to help and been rewarded by the gratitude in Mrs Forrest's eyes. But much as she valued being part of things she resented having to share Alec with his mother and half the neighbours.

So much had happened in the last two days: her engagement, the death of her mother, Alec's love-making; the tea-party and then the street fight. After oceans of humdrum waiting she seemed to be hurtling along from one crisis to the next. Her

299

thoughts swung between anger at Lily and anxiety over Alec.

After drifting into a restless sleep she awoke not knowing whether it was night or early morning. As she lay between the two children, images of her mother came to her, as she had been when Miriam was a little girl before the false dreams of Australia.

Mummy waiting at the school gate, bending her laughing face to her and swinging her round and round in her arms. Folding newspaper and cutting out rows of paper dolls, twisting her fingers and making shadow dogs and rabbits on the wall beside her bed; finding dandelion clocks and holding them out to her while Miriam puffed out her cheeks, blowing the seeds away. But all that was in the golden days before Jack Slattery went off with his wife's dreams and left her to grow drink-sodden and resentful.

What had happened to her father? Miriam wondered, not for the first time. Why had he never sent the money? Had he been killed in a fight or died of some illness before he could send for them? The suspicion that he might have met another woman, might even have other children was something she shied away from. It couldn't be Daddy's fault.

She sank back into sleep. It was either the wet clammy feeling of her nightdress sticking to her back or the daylight streaming in through a gap in the curtains that awakened her some hours later. It was morning and Blyth had wet the bed. 'Quick, quick,' she said shaking the two children, impatient to strip the bed before the

300

mattress got a soaking.

They stumbled half asleep and Miriam stripped them off and wrapped them in dry towels before rushing into the kitchen and steeping the sheet in cold water. Hurriedly she bent to light the copper. After getting herself and the children washed, dressed and seated at the table with some bread and sugar she went upstairs.

'Oh, Mr Pragnell,' she said as she stood outside his bedroom door with his jug of hot water. 'Things are a bit topsy-turvy. I had to take little Blyth in with us for the night; his mother's taken badly.'

Her employer frowned. 'That's unfortunate. I had hoped to be breakfasted early today and to be downstairs doing the accounts by nine.'

'I could bring you up a tray and the paper while I set things straight.'

'You've obviously got your hands full this morning. Yes, well that will have to do. I will settle to the accounts this afternoon,' he said doubtfully.

'Oh thank you,' Miriam said before dashing back to the kitchen. Why did he have to work downstairs today when she was so frantic with washing and cleaning and children?

After clearing the table, she settled Blyth and Rosie in the back yard with a bowl of bubbles and a couple of clay pipes. Miriam found the blue-bag for the rinsing water and was busy stirring the starch she'd made the night before when she got the distinct feeling that she was not alone. Someone was watching her. The back door was open into the garden and she became aware of someone blocking out the sun. As she turned towards the door Alec sprang forward and wrapped his arms around her. She shrieked with fright.

'How's my sweetheart?' he said, kissing her on the cheek.

'Nearly scared out of my skin,' she snapped. 'And why didn't you let me know you were back safe last night?' she burst out, pushing him away. 'I couldn't sleep for worrying about you.'

'Didn't Albert tell you? I gave him a message for you, to say that I was back safe.'

'But it was your place to come and tell me, not Mr Pragnell's. You were gone hours.'

'Sorry, my love. We had to wait for two doctors to certify Dolly and take her off to the asylum, then there was Harry to find. Well – they tracked him down to Whale Island. I borrowed a bike and took a message for him.'

'That's miles away over the causeway, nearly out of Portsmouth.'

He laughed. 'Don't I know it. That bike was a real boneshaker, I was fit to drop by the time I got back here.'

'I was so worried,' she chided. 'And that Lily of yours was so rotten to me. What had got into her?'

Alec scratched his head. 'To tell you the truth, Mirry, I made a right pig's ear of telling Lily about you and Rosie. I had it in my mind to take her along the sea-front and break the news gently, but it all got out of hand.'

'How did it?'

302

He shrugged helplessly. 'She was upstairs talking to her Gran and I went up to tell her to get a move on. They didn't hear me calling and the door was open so I went in. Talking about Mary, they were. You know, my wife that was.' She nodded. 'I don't like to speak of her. It just muddles things.'

'But Alec, whatever you feel, she was Lily's mother. The girl must wonder about her sometimes.' Miriam surprised herself at her defence of Lily, but knew from their talks when they'd been friends that she hungered for someone to tell her about her mother.

He shrugged defensively. 'I just got angry with Ma, she seemed to be taking things out of my hands. I dragged Lily downstairs and then told her all in a rush. Not as I wanted to at all.'

'Not as she did either, I bet.'

'No, poor kid. She flew at me like a tiger, then Ma calmed her down and sent her into the kitchen before giving me a tongue-lashing.'

'I thought it was me that set you all off,' said Miriam. 'When I walked into that front room yesterday, you could have set a match to the atmosphere. Even Rosie was off hooks.'

'Well, it's all out in the open now,' he smiled down at her. 'We've just got to get the Vine tribe out of our hair and have some time on our own. Although I've promised Ma I'll take Blyth and the twins down to Clarence Beach to get them off her hands.'

'But Alec,' she protested, 'couldn't Mary do that? She's old enough, isn't she?'

'Ma says she wants her at home with her today.

Something about her needing a bit of mothering. Listen, Mirry.' His dark eyes pleaded with her. 'I got some fence mending to do with Ma, after yesterday's fiasco. But I could take Rosie as well. Then you could join us later on.'

Miriam sighed. It was tempting to have the morning free of children and it would certainly speed up the washing.

'Come on, sweetheart. When did you last go to the seaside? Buy you a stick of rock,' he wheedled.

She pushed him aside and lifted some boiling clothes out of the copper into the tin bath. Alec carried the bath to the sink and hooked the steaming clothes with a rolling pin into the cold water. When the bath was empty he turned and drew her into his arms. 'My queen of the soap suds,' he said smiling down at her.

The sun shone through the scullery window warmly on her back. She reached up and kissed him on the mouth. He moulded her to his body and kissed her until she was breathless. Miriam wanted to linger with him, to have him make love to her amid the soap, the steam and the sunshine.

It was a while before either of them became aware of the wailing cries of Blyth and Rosie and the hammering on the back door. 'It broken,' Rosie cried, holding up two jagged pieces of the bowl that had held the soap suds.

'Quick, give it to Uncle Forrest,' Alec said taking them from her. 'Blyth, don't touch – you'll cut your fingers.'

Miriam flushed guiltily as she searched out some newspaper to wrap the broken china.

'You'd better go,' she said. 'I'm way behind here and you're not helping.'

'Sorry,' he said. 'Look, you get the nippers ready and I'll be back in half an hour to take them off your hands. Shall we go down to the seaside?' he asked them. Rosie and Blyth squealed with excitement.

'You'll be careful with her, Alec. Make her keep on her sunbonnet and hold her hand if she goes near the water,' Miriam cautioned later, as she stood at the door with both children changed and eager to be off.

'I'm an experienced Dad,' he laughed, slinging a string bag over his shoulder and taking a child in each hand.

The twins followed behind, their long brown hair for once neatly plaited and tied with red ribbons. 'We do like to be beside the seaside,' they sang, their freckled faces pink with excitement.

'See you later,' Alec said, turning and winking at her.

Miriam had the last of the washing blued and out on the line in no time. The sunshine made her restless and eager to be out of doors.

Mr Pragnell came into the kitchen as she was mashing the potatoes for lunch.

'I believe I should offer you my congratulations,' he said, beaming at her. 'The Vines' misfortune drove the news out of my head. Congratulations, my dear.'

'Oh, yes, Mr Pragnell, thank you,' Miriam blushed.

'Young Alec had a grin from ear to ear when he told me the good news last night.' He put his hand to his head. 'I had a message to give you last night and I completely forgot. I do apologise, my dear. Mrs Forrest was at sixes and sevens with the Vine family and it completely slipped my mind.'

'It's not important, now that I've seen him again.' Miriam set a plate of sliced mutton and mashed potatoes down in front of him.

'Well, I'm delighted,' he said, jumping to his feet and getting a bottle of sherry and two glasses from the sideboard. 'To you and Alec. I wish you good health and good fortune,' he said, handing her a brimming glass.

Miriam sipped her sherry, savouring its rich raisiny taste. She held the glass up to the light. 'It's such a lovely colour, like a polished table or my little Rosie's eyes.'

'Your engagement is a happy outcome to your coming here,' he said, dipping his fork into the mashed potato.

Miriam said, smiling shyly at him. 'This has been my first proper home – and Rosie's.' She found she was unexpectedly hungry and cut into the meat with relish.

'It may be that you will want to move in with Mrs Forrest, now, since you will be part of her family. Or perhaps Alec will want a place of his own.'

Miriam swallowed a large mouthful of potato whole before speaking. 'I – I doubt there'd be room next door,' she said, horrified at the thought of sharing a house with Alec's mother,

306

let alone Lily. 'We've barely had time to discuss anything as yet.'

'Of course,' he said, pulling a plate towards him and cutting himself a generous slice of his brother's farmhouse cheese. 'There's plenty of time for things to fall into place. Now, I must finish my accounts. I shall not be in to supper, so the rest of the day is yours.'

'I'll just do the pots and then I'm off to the beach to join Alec and Rosie,' said Miriam, wiping the last of the piccallili from her plate with a piece of bread.

'Enjoy yourself,' he said, seating himself at his desk and opening a ledger.

Putting on her straw hat she called over to Ma Abrahams' for a penny bag of stale cakes and a bottle of barley water. As she left the shop she ran full tilt into Lily making her way back to work. 'I want a word with you, Lily,' she snapped.

With a toss of her head Lily flounced past. Miriam fizzed with anger. She wanted to slap her smug little face and might have done so if Mrs Forrest had not opened her door and called to her. 'Here's an old sunshade for the beach. And just tell that son of mine to make tracks by four o'clock. I want those kids spruced up before their brother comes for them.'

'See you later, Mrs Forrest,' she said, taking the sunshade and hurrying away. Fury with Lily fuelled her footsteps and she was crossing Southsea Common before she'd calmed down. Late-season holidaymakers milled around her. Children were laughing and calling as they queued for rides in brightly-coloured wooden carts pulled by frisky young goats. Nursemaids gossiped to each other as they pushed their prams and young men doffed panama hats to blushing girls.

She crossed the road onto the esplanade and scanned the beach for Alec and Rosie. It was crowded. Market traders had their stalls on the edge of the sea. Jellied eels, meat pies, and Southsea Rock vied to satisfy the holidaymakers' appetites, sharpened by the sun and salt air. A blast from a ship's hooter made her jump and she shaded her eyes against the sun as she watched one of the Isle of Wight steamers cast off from Clarence Pier. A few moments later there were shrieks of excitement as the wash from the departing craft sent waves rushing up the beach. Amongst the crowd scurrying from the advancing sea were Alec, with Rosie and Blyth holding on to his hands and the twins following behind giggling helplessly.

She had never seen him looking so carefree. His bell-bottom trousers were rolled up to the knees and on his head was a straw hat worn by sailors from the days of sail. 'Alec, Alec,' she called. It was a while before he heard her above the hubbub.

'Mummy,' Rosie cried, rushing into her arms. 'Water chasin' us, Mummy. Come see water.' She joggled excitedly.

'You look like Neptune,' Miriam said, smiling at Alec as he reached forward to kiss her.

'This is my prince,' he pointed to Blyth whose face was flushed and neck wreathed with a garland of seaweed. 'These are my princesses.

308

Ah! Champion, barley water!' he cried, leading her to an old blanket littered with shoes and stockings. 'The queen's throne,' he declared, pointing to a deckchair fat-bellied with summer breeze.

Happiness bubbled up inside her. 'Alec, you're so silly,' she said, handing around the bottle and the bag of cakes.

'Don't you like being silly, Mrs Forrest?' he teased.

'Don't call me that yet,' she protested, looking carefully around her, as if the other people on the beach were about to rise up in protest. 'We mustn't tempt fate. A lot could go wrong between now and...'

'Between now and when, Mirry? Let's name the day. I think whatever was going to go wrong has been righted now. Let's put a bit of faith in our future, just you and me. How about a Christmas wedding?'

Miriam was aware of Blyth and the twins listening with rapt attention. She searched out a couple of coppers from her pocket. 'Here, you three. There's twopence, go and get a stick of rock between you. And save a bit for Rosie.'

'How about getting married on January the third? It'll be a double celebration,' she suggested as the Vines scampered away.

'January the third?' he raised his eyebrows. Furiously Miriam flicked his leg with the wet towel. 'Help, help!' Alec cried in mock protest. 'No, I haven't forgotten it'll be your twenty-first birthday. That would be champion.'

Rosie sat in front of the deckchair playing with

the stones. Miriam pulled the brim of her sunbonnet down to shade her eyes. 'It's lovely being down by the sea,' she said, 'just the three of us. Like we were a real family.'

'We will be soon,' he said, taking her hand and kissing her fingers one by one.

'Mr Pragnell gave me a glass of sherry and toasted our engagement. Seemed to think I'd be moving next door with your mum and Lily.' It was a while before Alec said anything and Miriam waited tensely for his reply.

'I think three women in one kitchen would be asking for trouble, don't you?' he said, picking up a stone and lobbing it into the sea. She nodded thankfully.

'If we could just let things stay as they are until Christmas, I might have got my Petty Officer's rate by then and that would mean another pound a week. Might even be able to rent a little place of our own. Or Albert might let me move in with you for a few months till we've got a bit put by.'

'I wouldn't mind that,' said Miriam. 'If Mr Pragnell agreed. After all he spends most of his time upstairs or with his painting friends so we'd be mostly on our own.'

'See – there's the money I give Ma, for her and Lily. If I was living with you she wouldn't have to buy food for me when I'm on leave and Lily will be earning a bit extra when she's done her first year at tailoring. I might be able to cut down what I give her soon. Here,' he said, leaning forward and undoing the buckles on her shoes. 'Fancy a paddle?'

'Alec, I've got my stockings on,' she protested.

'Well,' he said, 'if you lean back in the deckchair and push them down from the top I'll pull them off your feet. Come on, quick. Nobody's looking at us.'

Miriam looked around her at the people on the beach, each intent on their own activities, snoozing behind newspapers, picnicking or gazing out to sea. She looked down at the water's edge at the little waves washing the stones leaving them shiny like sucked toffees.

Alec eased her feet out of her shoes and held them in his hands. He gave her a slow lazy smile and she was giddy with desire. She leant back in the deckchair and put her hands in her skirt pockets and wriggled and pushed her stockings and garters down her legs. She guided the stockings down towards Alec's waiting fingers.

'Hey presto!' he cried, pulling them off her feet and folding them with the garters into her shoes. 'Shall we go paddling with Mummy?' he asked Rosie.

'Yes,' said the little girl, looking up at him and squinting against the sun. He swung her up onto his shoulders and turned to Miriam, taking her hand.

The stones were warm from the sun. She hobbled over their hard uneven surfaces. Holding her skirt up to her knees she stood at the water's edge waiting for the next wave to lap her feet. 'Oooh!' she shrieked as the icy water covered her ankles. 'You didn't tell me it was so cold.'

'You'll soon warm up,' he laughed, setting Rosie down on the stones. She held her frock up like her mother and hopped up and down in the water soaking the legs of her drawers. 'Mummy do it.' She urged Miriam back into the water.

'Here comes a big one,' said Alec as mounds of green water surged up the shore and broke against their legs. Linking hands and laughing they ran back up the beach to the deckchair. Miriam got a dry pair of drawers out of her bag and Alec held a towel around Rosie while she was dried and changed. 'It's been the best time for ages,' she said, 'just being together.'

Alec squeezed her hand. 'And for me,' he nodded.

Blyth and the twins trudged back over the stones their cheeks bulging and their faces pink and sticky with rock.

'Did you save a bit for Rosie?' Alec asked Mercy.

'Well, we bashed it on the stones and it broke in three bits an' we couldn't get it no smaller,' said Faith looking at Mercy to back her up.

''Onest,' her sister said. 'Wouldn't break into four.'

'Cripes,' Miriam exclaimed. 'Your ma said to have them back by four as she wants to spring-clean them before Harry gets home.'

'You kids, bring back this bucket with water and wash your faces and hands,' Alec said before turning towards an old man in a deckchair opposite. 'Excuse me, sir,' he asked. 'Could you tell me the time?'

Fussily the man folded his paper before drawing his watch out of his waistcoat pocket. 'A quarter to four,' he pronounced.

'Right everyone,' Alec said, 'gather up the towels. Miriam, you get up and I'll fold the chair. I'll carry Rosie while you take the bag.'

'No, the girls can take the bags. I'll give Blyth a bit of a carry; he looks half asleep.'

The little boy was hoisted on to her back by his sisters and they were soon all straggling back towards Lemon Street.

'Come on you kids, I want you spruced up for your brother,' called Mrs Forrest from her doorway. She smiled at them all. 'Don't you look better for a drop of sun, the lot of you. Miriam, go and have a breather for five minutes. Rosie's dead to the world. Alec will bring the little one in when she wakes up.'

Miriam resented Mrs Forrest always taking charge. Why couldn't Alec bring Rosie in now and spend some time with her? Then, looking at her neighbour ushering the Vine family into her house, she felt a stab of guilt. 'See you later,' she called to Alec, and turned to open her front door. The house felt stuffy and enclosed; she opened all the windows and took off her hat. It had been an ordinary afternoon on the beach such as any family in Portsea might spend. Would life with Alec ever be routine and ordinary? she wondered. In a few years he would be leaving the navy. Hopefully he would find other work – might even be home every night. How would that feel?

Remembering the washing still on the line she went out into the yard. As she dropped the pegs back into the bag and folded the pillowcases over her arm, Lily stepped into the yard next door with Alec close behind. They were hanging out the beach towels.

'Hello Lily, had a good afternoon at work?' Miriam asked, trying to keep her voice steady. Lily tossed her head dismissively.

Miriam felt herself shaking with rage. 'Lily, come over here please. I have something to tell you,' she called.

'Go on Lily,' said Alec. 'Step over and see what Miriam wants.' Mulishly his daughter turned and walked towards her.

Directly Alec went back indoors Miriam grabbed Lily by the arm and dragged her into the kitchen, thrusting her roughly into a chair.

'Now, Miss High-and-mighty. You and I have some talking to do.'

Chapter Twenty-Eight

Lily struggled to get to her feet, her face flushed. 'You can't keep me here,' she gasped, her voice shaking. 'I'm not your prisoner.'

'No, you're not,' Miriam said, her voice dangerously calm. 'And I am not a slut and won't be treated as such by you or anyone else.'

Lily tried to get out of the chair but Miriam thrust her back again. 'Before you leave this house,' she hissed, 'you and me are going to get a few things straight between us.'

Lily could feel her heart banging in her chest but she was determined not to show her fear.

'You don't have to like me,' Miriam told her, 'but by God, you're going to treat me with respect.'

'You lied,' Lily burst out. 'Pretending to be my friend and all the time–'

'I've always been a friend. And when did I lie to you, when?'

'Pretended you didn't know my dad when all the time you were...' Something in Miriam's face made Lily hesitate.

'Don't hold back now you've got your chance to condemn me.'

Lily swallowed hard. This was not as she'd played out the scene in her bedroom, with Miriam humbly begging her forgiveness.

'P'raps I can find the word you're looking for. Whore, was it? Like them that drop their drawers in Paradise Alley?'

Lily squirmed. She put her hands up to her ears but Miriam pulled them away.

'You thought that was the sort of woman your dad would take up with? Sixpence standing up and a shilling lying down?'

Lily reared up, shoved Miriam aside and rushed for the door. She never reached it.

'Let me go,' she screamed as Miriam beat her to it. They gasped and grunted, their cheeks flushed and hair falling about their faces. Backwards and forwards they went between the chair and the door. Just as Lily tried to gasp the latch of the door Miriam would wrench her away and when Lily was in danger of being thrust in the chair she would summon up her last ounce of energy and break free of Miriam's grasp. But slowly, steadily Lily lost ground.

'You'll hear all I've got to say even if I have to tie you to that chair,' Miriam snarled as she stood over her defeated opponent. Lily flinched. 'I've loved your father for three years and more. He was all set to take me home to meet you the day the Jutland telegram arrived. Then everything changed.'

Lily gulped. The pain and confusion of her twelfth birthday struck her afresh, with Gran's tears and her bewilderment at Dad rushing suddenly away. It was the day, she now realised, that had ended the warm security of her childhood.

'Think you've been very hard done by, don't you?' Lily stared mutinously at the floor. 'Your mother gone before you got a chance to know her and then your Andrew lost at sea.' Lily shrugged. 'You don't know the half of it,' Miriam snapped.

'What d'you mean?' Lily asked, resenting her tone.

'You've had your Gran behind you all the time, protecting you, and your Dad bringing you presents and treating you like a princess. Haven't you?' Unwillingly Lily nodded.

'Did you never think that your Dad might be lonely? That one day he'd want to get married again? Or did you think he was waiting for his princess to grow up so he could marry *her*?'

'That's ridiculous. I'm not a child,' Lily shouted. 'I was angry because you tricked me and lied about things. And Dad did too.'

'So we should have asked your permission?'

'No, it's just– You're making me sound like a selfish little kid,' she stormed. 'And I'm not, I'm

316

not.' Tears of rage and frustration brimmed over, spilling down her cheeks.

Miriam handed her a tea-towel from the laundry basket. 'Look, Lily,' her tone was softer, less abrasive. 'I know it's all been a horrible shock and your Dad could have done it better. But flouncing about glaring at all of us won't make it go away. And it certainly won't get rid of me.' She leaned forward and touched her arm. 'We were really good pals once.'

Lily didn't want to like Miriam again. But she couldn't seem to hold out against her. 'It was when he peeled the apple on Christmas Day,' she muttered. 'I saw his new tattoo and it connected up with the man I'd seen you kissing through the window the night before. You'd pretended to me and Gran that you'd never seen him before.'

'I could try and explain, Lily. But first you'd have to promise to listen till I'm done,' said Miriam, sitting down opposite her in the other chair. Lily nodded, too tired to do anything else.

'The day of the telegram I went to meet your Dad to tell him I'd marry him like he'd asked me. But when I went to our secret place he wasn't there and there was no note from him either. Instead–' Miriam covered her face with her hands. There was a long silence. Lily waited, unable to imagine what would come next.

Miriam shook her head. 'No, I can't tell you. Just thinking about it brings it all back. The shock and the fear. I was only a couple of years older than you. Didn't stand a chance. Leapt out of the darkness at me, he did.' Miriam began to cry, shuddering sobs that made her body shake.

Lily sat helplessly by, not knowing what to do. She had fought to get away from Miriam but now, with her so upset, she couldn't leave.

'Somehow or other, after dark, I managed to get back to my Auntie's pub and she took care of me,' Miriam continued. 'I waited and waited for Alec to come and make everything all right, but he never did. There wasn't going to be a happy ending.'

Lily stared at Miriam hunched over the table. It was all so awful. Awful because she couldn't understand what had happened to Miriam. Something that Dad would have protected her from. She remembered the day of the telegram, about Andrew, how strange Dad had been, how he had rushed away in spite of it being her birthday. He must have gone to meet Miriam or left a letter and she didn't find it. Like when Tess d'Urberville, in her favourite Hardy novel, put the letter under the door for Angel Clare and it slipped under the carpet and was never found. Only this was real life with real consequences.

'What I didn't know when I went to meet Alec that day was that I was expecting his child. So then, at seventeen I was going to have a baby whose father was lost to me, might even be dead.' Lily could feel the pain behind the words. 'My Auntie wanted to leave the pub and move away. I wanted to stay. I just had this splinter of hope that your Dad and me would meet up again and have some chance to put things right between us. Besides,' she said, uncovering her face and pulling at a thread in the wrist of her blouse, 'going all that way to Devon frightened me. It

318

seemed like flying to the moon.'

'What did you do?' asked Lily, relieved that Miriam seemed calmer now.

'Auntie fixed up with me to go and stay with her friend's daughter Daisy in a little house in Gosport. I had to invent a husband and call myself Mrs Naylor. Buy a wedding ring from a pawnshop and a photo of this soldier who was supposed to be Rosie's Dad.' Miriam bit her lip. 'I packed up my things and set off. I remember waving to my Auntie as the ferry drew away. It was the loneliest, most frightening day of my life.'

'What about your mother?' Lily asked. 'She would have helped surely?'

'My mother,' snorted Miriam. 'She was tucked up with her pal Jumper and too puddled in gin to help anyone. Her only advice was to fix myself up at...' She tugged savagely at her sleeve. 'Well, we won't go into that.' After straightening her blouse, she brushed her hair away from her face and tucked a stray tendril behind her ear. It was as if she were tidying her mother away. Looking up, she smiled at Lily and said, 'Funny, isn't it? You're desperate to know your mother and weave all sorts of dreams around her. Yet, I knew mine too well and could have wished her gone. And now?' Miriam bit her lip and her eyes filled with tears. 'You always think,' she gasped, 'that things'll come right in the end. There'll be time to set them straight. In spite of all the disappointments and fallings-out, that you'll part from each other with a few loving words. But she's gone now and I can't feel sorry.'

Lily was desperate to do anything to ward off

Miriam's tears. On the draining-board was a basket filled with washing brought in from the line. Lily took a clean handkerchief and threaded it between Miriam's hands. 'I'll make some tea. That'll buck you up,' she said hopefully, using Gran's sterling recipe against tribulation. Her words hung in the air between them.

Miriam sniffed and dabbed at her eyes, not appearing to have heard what she had said.

Desperately Lily changed tack. 'What was she like, this Daisy that you went to?'

'Daisy!' To Lily's intense relief Miriam smiled to herself. She blew her nose vigorously, then said, 'Daisy was a lifesaver. A big roly-poly pudding of a girl. Took me in and we looked after each other. She chose littlin's name for her. Rosemary for remembrance. I think I would have stayed with Daisy forever if her husband hadn't come home from France. Then it wasn't fair to be cluttering up their lives.'

'That's when you came to Uncle Albert's?'

Miriam nodded. 'I came over to Portsmouth with Rosie packed in the pram like a little pilchard surrounded by all my worldly goods.' Lily laughed. 'I went into Driver's café down on the Hard and sat there over a cup of tea and read the paper that someone else had left. And there was your Uncle Albert's advert asking for a housekeeper, along with a dozen or so more.'

'What made you choose his over the others?' Lily asked.

'His name, Albert Pragnell, was familiar to me. It rang a bell in my mind. Besides Lemon Street was in walking distance of the Hard.'

'So you didn't know we lived next door?'

Miriam shook her head. 'What a shock that was. I almost took to my heels when I met you but where could I have gone? It was half-past four on a winter's night with a young baby and only half-a-crown in my pocket.'

'Why didn't you tell Gran about you and Dad? After all, Rosie is her grandchild and my sister,' Lily demanded as she poured the water into the teapot.

'I had to be sure there wasn't another Alec Forrest in the neighbourhood. But first, I needed a place of safety for myself and Rosie. Sorting out anything else was a luxury to be thought of later.'

'I'd have burst out with it, straightaway.'

'What if your Gran had said that Alec was married and that I was a liar trying to blacken his name. He could very easily have got married. I didn't know. Besides...'

'Besides, what?'

'I didn't want to risk my safety. Mr Pragnell's been really good to me, almost like a grandad. I knew I wouldn't get another job that easily and certainly not another governor like him. And I wanted to meet your Dad on my own. To tell my story and to have him choose to be with me, not be shamed into it by his mother.'

'So why didn't he say anything that first Christmas?'

'He had his own reasons, the same as I'd had mine. It was a shock that was sprung on him, he needed time to...'

Lily jumped as the back door sprang open and her father stepped into the kitchen with Rosie in

321

his arms. 'Wants to see her sister,' he said, setting the little girl down in front of her.

Miriam was equally flustered. 'Alec, d'you want to stay and have a cup of tea with us?'

'If I'm made welcome,' he said, looking questioningly between the two of them.

'Story, story,' said Rosie, holding up a book of fairy tales.

Lily was desperate to be on her own to have time to make sense of things. She felt uncomfortable. With her there they couldn't be as they would like with each other. And yet they couldn't ask her to go and in staying she felt more and more of an intruder.

'Story, story,' insisted Rosie, tugging at her skirt.

'Uncle Forrest read to you,' said Dad, taking her on to his lap.

'Cup of tea, Lily?' asked Miriam, smiling at her.

'I think I'd better go,' Lily said, not looking at anyone. 'Gran will want me to help with the Vines.'

'Harry's just arrived and your pal Dora,' Dad said laughing. 'It's bedlam in there.'

''Bye everyone,' she said. 'See you all later.'

''Bye,' said Miriam, walking to the door with her.

Lily sat on the wall between the two houses, wanting a breathing-space before being swamped again by Mary, Blyth and the twins. Everything kept shifting about and changing places, and there wasn't an ounce of privacy anywhere.

'Lily, I been here ages. What's up with ya? Blimey, Lil, what's wrong?'

322

Dora's sharp little face was full of concern as Lily burst into tears. She sat beside her friend and put her arm around her shoulder.

'I've been horrible to Miriam and Gran and everyone,' she wailed. 'And now I don't know what to do.'

'Have a good beller,' said Dora. 'When you calms down it won't seem 'alf as bad.'

'Dora, what am I going to do?' she grizzled. 'Even Gran's fed up with me. And I don't even like myself any more.'

'Well, I do. You and me are pals. Trouble with you, Lil, you seen all this marrying with your Dad and the lady next-door from where you're standin'. You got to cross the street like and see it from where they are.'

'Miriam said hadn't I never thought my Dad might be lonely.'

'And hadn't you?'

'I just thought he was happy with me and Gran and didn't need anyone else.'

'We all gets puffed up with our own import-ance,' said Dora. 'Then when we finds we been foolin' ourselves, it's like they've stuck a pin in us and we shrivels up like a burst balloon. That how you feel?'

Lily nodded. 'You're a real pal, Dora. What would I do without you?'

'Blimey, you'd have blown away ages ago. We wouldn't have found a pin big enough.'

'What a cheek,' snorted Lily, punching Dora playfully on the arm.

'Why don't you blow yer snitch and I'll sneak us out a cup of tea and a bit of bread puddin'? Yer

323

Gran's just offered me some,' said Dora. 'Besides,' she winked at Lily. 'I wants another dekko at that Harry Vine. She says he's due home at any minute.'

Lily was astonished. 'Harry?' she gasped. 'When did you meet him?'

'Ages ago,' said her friend airily. 'He's a friend of me brother, Mark.'

'You can't like Harry, he's,' she shrugged helplessly, 'he's a Vine.'

'They ain't got the plague, you know. There's more to Harry than slimey old Bernard.' Lily snorted somewhere between a laugh and a sniffle.

'That's better,' said Dora. 'Now does modom want to dine indoors or shall I serve the confectionery on the terrace?'

Lily laughed. 'You're a real pal,' she said hugging her tightly. 'Tell Gran I'll be in in a minute to do the dishes.'

While Dora went back up the path to the kitchen Lily dried her eyes. After the temper and the tears with Miriam she felt hollow. The thought of going to work the next day seemed a blessed relief and distraction from the turmoil of life at home. She wasn't happy with things as she found them between Dad and Miriam, but there was a faint possibility that she would become so given time.

Chapter Twenty-Nine

One tea-party after another, thought Beattie. You'd think we were the Rothschilds. At least Monday's meal was happier than yesterday's fiasco. The Vines and Forrests wedged around the kitchen table full of bread pudding and chat. Almost a party, if you discounted Mary nursing an empty plate, her boot-brown eyes staring fixedly at the door. Beattie could have wept. 'Come on, love, let's you and me see if we can spot that brother of yours. It's gone half-past four. He should be here any minute,' she said.

Mary leapt to her feet. Faith and Mercy prepared to follow her down the passage to the front door. 'Stay there,' said Mary fiercely. 'I got to see him first.'

The twins were about to argue when Alec said coaxingly, 'Let's get that bag of toffees down from behind the Whale's Tooth. Didn't know my Dad caught a whale, did you?'

'You spinnin' us a yarn?' asked Mercy, spraying her sister with cake crumbs.

'Greedy guts, you took the last one,' shouted Faith, snatching the remains of the rock cake from her sister's plate. She turned to Alec. 'You being straight wiv' us about the whale?' she said, as he brought the tooth and the toffees to the table. He winked at Beattie as she hurried after Mary.

The girl and the elderly woman leant against the window waiting for Harry, Mary perched ready for flight the instant her brother appeared. Beattie watched the tensed figure beside her with concern, as she chewed her fingernails and tapped her right foot continuously on the pavement. Faith and Mercy were tough nuts and Blyth still had the charm of babyhood but beneath Mary's bravado was a frightened little girl. Then she was gone in a blur of arms and legs, tearing down the street, screaming, 'Harry, Harry, Harry,' and throwing herself into her brother's arms. They landed in a heap along with his cap and kit-bag.

Harry got slowly to his feet, setting his cap back on his head and shouldering his bag. ''Ello, Mrs Forrest,' he said. 'Good of you to have the nippers. They all right?'

'Right as rain.' Beattie smiled at the lanky nineteen-year-old. The navy had certainly spruced the lad up no end and mended his manners. Whether he was equal to the task ahead of him was another matter. 'D'you want to come indoors for a cuppa before we sort anything out?'

'No he don't,' snapped Mary. 'We got things to do. Come on home.' Shrugging helplessly, Harry followed his sister.

'Bring you something on a tray a bit later?' Beattie called after them.

'Ta,' said Harry closing the door behind him.

Keep your powder dry, Beattie counselled herself. Give them some time together before you weigh in with your five-pennyworth. As soon as she re-entered the kitchen the twins grabbed her attention. 'Where's Harry? We wants to see him,' they clamoured.

My godfathers, thought Beattie wearily, these kids would eat me alive and swallow the pips, if I let them. Alec, for once, rode to her rescue. 'This table has got to be cleared and the washing-up done first,' he said.

'We wants to get our rope and go skippin',' said Faith, undeterred by his mock severity.

'First things first,' Alec said firmly. 'No work, no play. We'll all pitch in and it won't take us five minutes. Faith, table clearing, Mercy, washing-up, Blyth and me drying-up and putting away. Quick smart and we can all be out skipping.'

'Son, you're a lifesaver.' Beattie sank into her armchair, took a cup of tea from him and drank thirstily.

Her granddaughter, Rosie, face flushed from sun and sleep was snoring softly in the other chair. Perching on the arm, Alec smiled down at his daughter. 'I'll take her back in to Mirry when we've squared away in here.'

Beattie nodded. 'Thanks, son. God knows what state the place is in next-door or how long I'll be there straightening things out.'

'Well, leave the other kids to Mirry and me,' he said.

Hastily making some fresh sandwiches and setting some cakes she'd reserved for Harry on a plate, Beattie assembled the promised tea-tray and set off down the yard.

The stink of their old dog caught at her breath as she stepped through the back door of the Vines' house with her loaded tray. Coming in

327

from the sunshine it took her a while to accustom herself to the gloom behind the dusty curtains. But there was light enough to see that the kitchen was a shambles of smashed plates, up-ended furniture, heaped-up clothes and torn paper. 'My godfathers,' she gasped. Finding a vacant space on the floor, she set down the tray. Where was that stench coming from? Her nose led her to the source of the stink: a sodden rag rug. Holding her breath she hauled it out into the yard and then with another gasp of fresh air, she tossed it over the wall into the back alley. Its final destination could be decided upon later.

One thing was certain, she thought, as she gave her hands a quick rinse under the tap, those kids couldn't eat their tea in that kitchen. Righting the four chairs, she set them out in the yard, using one of them to hold the tray.

She walked back into the house calling, 'Tea up.' The sound of voices led her up the stairs. 'Harry! Mary?' There was no answer. They were sitting on Dolly's bed with their backs to the door.

'She might never get better, then what'll 'appen to us?' Mary's voice wobbled uncertainly.

'God knows,' said Harry. 'Can't think about that, now. Got to get this place straight. It's gone to buggery. Tomorrow I'll go and see Ma and find how the land lies. Call at the barracks and see the welfare. You can stay home from school and make a start on the house.'

'No I bleedin' well won't,' Mary shouted. 'Trust you to pick the easy bit. I ain't staying off school. It's 'andwritin'. I'm getting a fountain pen off the 'eadmaster, 'cos I'm best in the school.'

Harry sighed. 'I'll get you a pen. Just give us a hand tomorrow, Mary, please. If we don't get straight you'll all end up in the orphanage.'

'Don't want your bleedin' pen. I don't care what happens after tomorrow. Mr Foster's givin' it me tomorrow in front of everyone. I want that pen.'

'Selfish cow!' Harry snapped. 'Here's the family fallin' apart and all you're moanin' about's a friggin' pen.'

'I waited and waited fer you,' screamed Mary, bursting into angry tears. 'Then all you wants to do is bugger off. I 'ate you.' She rushed out of the room into Beattie's arms. It took all Beattie's strength to hold the child and prevent them both from falling down the stairs. She looked at Harry, who'd sunk back onto the bed, his jaw clenched and eyes bright with unshed tears. Clutching the bannister with one hand she managed to ease herself and Mary down onto the top step. The child cried out all her pent-up grief as Beattie held her close and stroked her mousy brown hair. Mary's arms tightened around her. Slowly, slowly her sobbing came to a shuddering halt. The bib of Beattie's apron was wet with tears. 'Here, my pet, mop yourself up a bit,' she said pulling a hankie out of her sleeve. 'Ready to come downstairs now?' she asked gently.

Mary gave her nose a resounding blow then nodded. Harry stood staring out of the window, his back to both of them.

'There's tea in the yard for both of you,' said Beattie, tapping him gently on the shoulder.

Harry avoided her eyes. 'Ta, Mrs Forrest,' he

mumbled. Beattie followed them down the stairs out of the house. It must be nearly six, she thought, looking at the darkening sky. Still the oppressive heat of the day hung in the air. The weeds between the paving-stones were rusty with thirst.

Mary sat jiggling in her seat. Pale-faced, she nibbled around the edges of her cake.

'I don't know where to start,' mumbled Harry, staring into space. 'There's the house and the kids and Ma.'

'Falling out with your sister's not the best place,' said Beattie.

'Sorry,' he said, patting Mary on the knee.

Mary flung his hand away. 'We won't 'ave to go to the orphanage, will we?' she asked.

'Steady now, the pair of you. Nobody is going anywhere,' said Beattie. 'We must all pull together. There's a knack to tackling a job the size of this one. If you look at it all at once, it's like trying to cram a whole loaf of bread into your mouth in one go. You choke on the task. What you have to do is cut it into manageable slices. Then you decide which slice comes first and what can be left until tomorrow.'

Mary and Harry said nothing but Beattie could sense an easing of the tension between them. 'You look to see how you can share the slices out. There are things you can do, Harry, you too, Mary and the twins aren't helpless. Then there's Mrs Naylor, Alec and me. One thing's for certain, Mary is not staying away from school.' She looked Harry straight in the eye. 'She's barely thirteen. Half an education is no good to anyone.'

Harry dropped his gaze and scuffed his boot against the chair-leg.

Beattie handed him a plate of cheese and pickle sandwiches. 'Now,' she said firmly. 'While we pile into this food you need to come up with a few things we can do before it gets pitch-dark so's we'll have a better start in the morning.'

'We can't tackle any cleaning till we've unblocked the sink, it's full of spud peelings and tea leaves. There's the grate to clean out and re-lay before we can boil up any water,' said Mary.

'I could clear the sink, if you could sort out the grate,' said Harry tentatively, looking at his sister. Mary nodded.

Beattie smiled at this first faint sign of cooperation. 'Right, lad,' she said, 'nip over our wall and bring back two buckets of hot soapy water and a box of soda crystals. While you're over there, have a word with your brother and sister – they're dying to see you.'

As Harry disappeared into Beattie's kitchen she turned to Mary. 'What slice have we to cope with?' she asked.

'Well, after I've done the grate I could wrap up all the bits of broken plates and stick 'em in that,' she said, pointing with her toe to a tea-chest standing near the lavatory. 'Upstairs needs scrubbing and the mattress in the back bedroom needs chucking out, Blyth's peed all over it. After dark, me and Harry could sling it into the back garden of that empty house round the corner.'

Normally Beattie would have been horrified at the thought of dumping rubbish in someone else's garden but now was not the time for

331

another lecture. 'Good idea,' she said, brightly. 'You can take that mat I slung in the back alley too. Anything else we can do tonight?'

'We could scrub out both the bedrooms.' Mary scratched her head. 'Could you lend us some sheets, then me and the twins could pile in Mum's bed tonight?'

'Let's not go raving mad,' said Beattie. 'We'll keep the sleeping arrangements same as last night and Harry'll find a corner to tuck himself. We'll just ditch the mattress, do one floor and you can wrap the plates.'

Beattie was heartened by the young girl's resolve as Mary tied an old towel around her waist and began her tasks. She made herself and Beattie kneeling pads with folded newspapers and started shovelling the ashes out of the grate into a cardboard box.

'Right, lad,' Beattie said as Harry returned with the brimming buckets. 'I'll make my way upstairs with one of those and leave you to the sink.'

'I'll nip up first and shove the mattress out the back window into the yard,' said Harry, briskly. 'It'll give you a clear start.' Beattie followed him up the stairs. 'I bet the twins were pleased to see you,' she said, setting down her bucket in the corner of the room.

Harry beamed. 'They ain't half grown up,' he said, 'and Blyth is a proper little lad, now.'

'You got a family to be proud of,' she said, as Harry hauled up the window and shoved the smelly mattress through it.

'Ta, Mrs Forrest,' he said awkwardly. 'I'll leave you to it and get on with the chores downstairs.'

332

Beattie bundled up sheets from the back bedroom, wedged them into a pillowcase and stowed it on top of a rickety chest of drawers before plunging her scrubbing brush into the bucket of suds. She put down her kneeling pad and set to work.

From downstairs came the sounds of Harry whistling at his work and the rattle of Mary's shovel.

Beattie sent Harry over the wall for more water and a floorcloth. Her knees throbbed and her back ached by the time she'd finished. Satisfied that the room smelt sweeter she dried her hands on her apron and carried the bucket downstairs.

'I reckon we've done with the first slice of this loaf,' Beattie said looking around the kitchen. The floor was clear of broken china and papers, a kettle boiled on the range and Harry had left the sink scoured and the taps gleaming. Mary had bundled up the clothes into a bag and brought the chairs in from the garden.

Beattie smiled at the two of them. 'You've done wonders. I'm proud of the pair of you.' They grinned sheepishly.

'Ta, Mrs Forrest,' said Harry. 'We wouldn't have managed without you.'

Beattie put her hand on his shoulder. 'Might have taken you a bit longer,' she said, 'but you two would have pulled together in the end. Now, all you've got to do is take that stinky stuff off down the back alley,' she said with weary satisfaction. 'Don't forget when you get back to shut up all the windows or the cats will be back again.' After a lot of heaving and shoving, the

333

mattress and mat were tied into a manageable roll. Beattie held open the back door and waved Harry and Mary away down the alley.

I'm getting too old for all this, she thought, walking back into her own kitchen. The snap's going on my elastic, I'm getting overstretched. Taking a bottle of stout from the dresser cupboard she poured it into a glass then went out into the darkening street. She leant against the windowsill and looked about her.

She laughed to see the diminutive Chippy Dowell and the tall stately Mrs Rowan turning the skipping-rope while the twins jumped in and out. On the pavement in front of Albert's house, Rosie and Blyth were rolling marbles. Watching them from a pair of kitchen chairs were Miriam and Alec. Beattie waved a greeting and Alec gave her his chair before settling Miriam on the remaining one. 'Surprised to see Ethel Rowan out here,' said Beattie. 'She's usually seeing to poor Arthur.'

'They've carted him off to Netley Hospital, to give her a rest,' said Alec. 'He's been getting her down. I expect playing with the littlins cheers her up.'

Beattie nodded in Esther's direction and got a wave in return. Poor soul, she thought, fancy having her lad imprisoned in a wheelchair at his age. Thank God she had her other son to help her, even though, like Alec, Michael was rarely home. Perhaps she'd go and see her tomorrow.

Taking a mouthful of stout she savoured the bitter quenching liquid. In the still air she could count the eight chimes from the Town Hall clock.

It was almost too dark for those skipping to see what they were doing but everyone seemed reluctant to leave the cool sociability of the street. It prompted a thought. 'Here, Alec. Where's Lily and that pal of hers?'

Alec looked at Miriam before he spoke. Miriam shrugged. 'Sorry Ma,' he said. 'Told me to tell you, she's sleeping round at Dora's tonight. Promised to be home tomorrow to help with the sewing.'

'That's handy,' said Beattie, thoughtfully. 'I'll be able to bundle the three girls into her bed.'

Miriam shivered and got to her feet. 'We'll take the tots in now and settle them down,' she said looking at Alec. 'I'll send Blyth over to you in the morning.'

'Thank you,' said Beattie, noting that Miriam had avoided mentioning Lily. Had they had another dust-up? she wondered. 'I'm sorry to have involved you in all this but tomorrow night the Vines should all be back in their own home, barring poor Dolly, that is. If not, then Blyth can tuck in with us.' She smiled at Miriam, taking hold of her arm. 'I haven't had time to say this before but I think my son's a lucky man to have found you.'

'I won't let him forget it,' said Miriam, laughing up at Alec as he came towards her with Rosie in his arms.

As the door clicked behind them Beattie closed her eyes. It was all ebbs and flows, she thought. Alec's ship had at last come in whilst the Vines' craft was barely afloat. Soon Lily would be casting off and leaving her, like a battered old

335

jetty, with empty moorings. For a few fleeting moments she envied Alec and Miriam the absorption and intensity of their lives. She shook her head. It was their moment at the flood of things – she must content herself in the shallows.

'We're finished for the night,' said Harry, tapping Beattie on the shoulder. 'The governor wants to show you her list.' Mary glowed.

'What you got lined up for yourself?' asked Beattie, getting to her feet and holding the paper under the street lamp. The writing was impressively neat.

Find: Naval allotment book, key to front room. Girls can sleep in Ma's bed. Harry and Blyth back bedroom. Harry show Blyth how to use the lav. Write to Dad. Have we got any plates left???

'I think you've got things well under control, Mary. Bring those bundles of washing over and I'll go in and make you and the twins some cocoa.'

Mary took the list back and studied it. 'Ma said the key to the front room was lost but it's in the house somewhere. See, she took all the stuff out of it down to the pawnshop. That's why she got the curtains drawn in there. I knows that 'cos I looked through the gap in the middle. We just got to find her handbag. I got to think where she'd've stowed it.' She wound a strand of hair round her finger and then uncurled it. Looking up at Beattie she said, 'D'you think our Mum will get better?'

Beattie put her arm around Mary's narrow shoulders. 'I don't know, my duck,' she said. 'I reckon she needs lots of peace and quiet.'

'And a rest from the booze,' said Mary. 'Still,

we can get some money back from all her empties, the shed is full of them.' Beattie sighed. What a survivor this child had suddenly become. Mary put her fingers to her mouth and gave a piercing whistle. ''Ere Faith, Mercy, come over 'ere. We're 'aving our cocoa.'

'You'll do, Mary Vine,' laughed Beattie. 'You're going to be a bright young lady and don't let anyone tell you different.'

'Thanks for speakin' up for me about school,' said Mary shyly.

'Well,' said Beattie. 'Us women got to stick together.'

She was rewarded with one of Mary Vine's rare smiles.

Chapter Thirty

Miriam and Alec left Lemon Street with a whole Sunday stretching out before them.

'Make the most of the sunshine,' Mrs Rowan had said, standing at her door with Rosie and Blyth jigging about beside her. 'I've made them a tent in the yard. They'll be as happy as sandboys.'

Even Mr Pragnell had plans of his own. 'Mrs Forrest is accompanying me to the Labour Rally on the common,' he said. 'What with the brass bands and the speeches it promises to be a day to remember. Don't give me a thought, Mrs Naylor.'

'We're free,' laughed Miriam as they swung

337

along towards the sea-front. 'I can't believe we shall be on our own. I keep expecting one of the Vines to leap out at us.'

Alec laughed. 'I saw them earlier with Harry going to the beach. He says eating down there saves washing-up and the fresh air tires them out.'

They hurried to Clarence Pier and studied the blackboard at the entrance, detailing all the boat trips. 'We've got two minutes to catch the steamer to the Isle of Wight. What d'you think?'

'Yes, to everything today,' she said.

'Two second-class returns to Ryde will be three shillings and eight pence,' said the pier attendant turning the handle on the ticket machine.

The *Duchess of Fife*, a huge black-and-white steamer, awaited them at the end of the pier. They rushed up the gangway to the deafening blast of the ship's hooter and the hot-tar smell of the smoke belching from the funnel. The great paddle-wheel churned into action, frothing up the water and powering the ship away from land. They stood at the ship's rail watching Clarence Beach slipping into the distance.

'It's only a few days ago that we were on there looking out at the sea,' said Miriam, 'and now it's the other way around. I suppose this is how you see us when you go away. Little figures waving on the shore.'

'Not really,' said Alec. 'I'm always sweating down in the engine-room stoking the furnaces.'

'I shan't bother to wave you off next time,' she said sharply.

'I know Ma likes to wave to me from the jetty or the station because that's what she always did

338

with Dad.' Alec smiled at her, seeming to understand her disappointment. 'But when I go away again I'll want to see you and little Rosie waving from the doorstep in Lemon Street. My own private farewell party.'

She squeezed his hand. Watching the shore fading from sight Miriam felt her stomach lurch. 'We won't drown, will we?' she asked.

He shook his head. 'If we were in trouble they'd throw those seats over. See, they're made of slats of wood that float easily and those little rope handles are for catching hold of.' Her stomach eased.

'We'll see more on the upper deck,' said Alec. 'You go ahead, I'll follow behind you.'

She realised too late that her court shoes and hobble skirt were totally unsuitable for climbing up the metal steps and made awkward progress. 'You're a handsome woman,' said Alec, giving her a playful pat on the bottom.

Stumbling and blushing she stepped onto the upper deck. They looked at their fellow passengers. Sandwiched together between a portly vicar and a pale woman with wispy hair was a group of old ladies swathed in shawls and bonnets. 'Look at that one in the middle,' said Alec. A sharp-faced woman had pulled a small bottle out of the pocket of her skirt and was taking a stealthy swig. Catching Miriam's eye on her she gave a broad wink. Miriam winked back, approving the little act of rebellion.

Two boys in sailor suits sat together examining their model yacht beside a heavily pregnant woman. 'Oh thank you, Charles,' she gasped, as

339

her husband handed her a glass of lemonade.

'Would you like to have a drink in the bar?' Alec asked Miriam.

'You go,' she said. 'I'm enjoying the sunshine.' She looked out over the sea towards the Isle of Wight, still a tantalising blur in the distance, wanting to hold the moment. Sunday the seventh of September. One by one the days ahead passed through her mind like the beads on her necklace. Days of waving Alec away, welcoming him home. Nights of lying beside him, of loving him and waking in the morning to find him with her still.

'You were miles away,' said Alec as he tapped her on the shoulder.

'I was just being happy,' she said, taking the glass of lemonade from him. 'Thinking about us being a family.'

'How big is our family going to be?' he asked.

Miriam blushed at his scrutiny. 'It would be nice to have a boy to complete things.'

'Should we step ashore and get started?' he whispered. 'Have a little label on him, made in the Isle of Wight.' Miriam giggled.

'We could spend the afternoon hidden away. The warmth of the sun on our naked bodies.' He laced his fingers through hers and Miriam felt a surge of desire stirring between her thighs.

'Here, mister, how did they build that fort in the sea?' said one of the boys Miriam had spotted before.

'The Spit Bank Fort – the one we're just passing?' The boy and his brother nodded eagerly. Miriam sipped her lemonade and looked at the black-and-white structure rising out of the water

340

like a huge stone jelly mould, except for the wooden jetty and stone doorway. She shivered. Living out there you would shout in vain for a neighbour's help and be maddened by the constant pounding of the waves. Its isolation frightened her.

Alec, talking to the boys about 'watertight caissons' and 'air under pressure', had let go of her hand.

'Tom, Algy, stop pestering the sailor and come and help Mother with the luggage,' called their father.

Alec dipped his head under the brim of her straw hat and kissed her. 'Was I showing off a bit?' he asked smiling ruefully.

'Just a bit,' she said.

The steamer slowed her engines and the Isle of Wight seemed to swim out to greet them. Above its sandy hem rose the wooded cliffs of Ryde studded with white houses. 'Foreign lands,' laughed Miriam, as they waited at the pier head for the little train to take them to the shore.

'We don't need to be back here 'til five,' said Alec. 'Hours and hours away. What shall we do first?'

'Walk along slowly taking it all in, making it last,' said Miriam, looking about her at the tree-lined esplanade with its big hotels: The Ryde View and Royal Eagle. All the horse-drawn carriages and charabancs promising trips to every corner of the island.

'Let's go towards the boating lake,' said Alec. 'I know a little café called the Speedwell, not far from there.'

341

The lake was much bigger than Miriam expected with boats pulled up along the edge. She saw Algy and Tom from the steamer with their father rowing them away from the shore. She had almost given up hope of finding the café when she spotted a little brick building in the distance with a blue flag and the word Speedwell emblazoned on it.

'D'you fancy a cup of tea and a crab sandwich?' Alec asked, holding open the door.

'I could eat a horse,' laughed Miriam, settling herself in a wicker chair beside a glass-topped table. When they had both studied the hand-written menu card Alec rang the brass bell set on the counter between two glass-domed plates of cakes.

'I can smell baking,' said Miriam, as the door behind the counter opened and a large woman in a black dress and snowy apron appeared.

'Sorry to keep you waiting, sir,' she said, 'I was just getting another batch of scones out of the oven. What will you have?'

'Well,' said Alec consideringly, 'it was going to be crab sandwiches but now I don't know.'

'Why don't you start with the sandwiches and a pot of tea,' said the woman smiling at both of them. 'Then see what you can manage later.'

'We must start making plans,' said Alec, when their tray of tea had been brought to the table. 'The wedding's only four months away. Do you want to get married in church with a white dress and all?'

'I just want a quiet wedding,' said Miriam, biting into her sandwich. A memory of herself playing in her mother's shoes with curtain net on her head, clasping a bunch of wilting daisies, stabbed at her and she blinked away the sudden tears.

Alec touched her arm. 'I wish it was the first time for both of us.'

'Then there'd be no Lily or Andrew.'

'I couldn't wish them away,' he said quietly, brushing a strand of cress from his moustache.

Miriam took his hand and kissed it. 'I know you couldn't,' she said, 'they're part of you, like Rosie's part of me.'

'But you're my future, Mirry. You're the one I want to be with, the one I've chosen.' He smiled at her and she felt suddenly dazed with joy.

'I don't think we could get married in church. I wasn't ever christened. Dad wanted me brought up a Catholic and Mum was a Baptist, so it never happened. It's only by good luck that I've got my birth certificate. Aunt Florrie saw to that.'

'I'd love to see Florrie again,' laughed Alec. 'Will she make it from Devon?'

'I hope so,' said Miriam, nodding to the woman to bring over a plate of scones. 'Apart from Rosie she's my only relation. Oh, Daisy wrote to me just the other day. I'm sure she'd be thrilled to come.'

'Daisy sounds a real gem,' said Alec, spreading a scone liberally with jam.

Miriam poured him another cup of tea. 'Is it really going to happen? Will we really get married?'

He leant forward and kissed her cheek. 'All you've got to do is go down to the Registry Office and get their advice. Ma has got all the papers: my birth certificate, marriage lines and Mary's death certificate.'

'Poor woman,' said Miriam, tears threatening once more. 'We've got our happiness at her expense.'

Alec reached across the table and gripped her hands. 'We can't let the dead rule us. Our life's been given us and our part is to live it to the full.'

'I know, but I can't help feeling sad for her that Lily's grown up to be such a pretty girl and she isn't here to be proud of her. If I couldn't see my Rosie…'

'No tears today,' he said. 'Remember, we are going to find ourselves somewhere warm and secret.'

Hardly had he finished speaking than the door burst open and a noisy quartet of customers came in, laughing and talking. Miriam wondered where she and Alec would find their precious secrecy on such a crowded island.

Alec rubbed his stomach. 'We shall have to walk some miles to shake this lot down,' he said after settling their bill.

'Where shall we go?' she asked as she closed the café door behind her.

'We could go to Sea View, have a look at the chain pier and walk back through the woods.' She looked doubtfully at her shoes. 'You could go in the ladies' lavatory over there and take off your stockings then we could walk barefoot along the beach.'

Hastily Miriam bolted the cubicle door, slid down her stockings and garters, folding them into her handbag and wedging the shoes at either end. Alec was waiting for her with his boots tied together and slung over his shoulder. Hand-in-hand they threaded their way between bathing-tents, picnic parties and ice-cream stalls. The sand was warm under Miriam's feet and she felt a delicious sense of freedom. They walked down to the water's edge and the sea lapped icily between her toes. She felt as if she and Alec were cocooned in a world invisible to others. Impenetrable by swooping gulls, screaming children or the raucous cries of the Punch and Judy show.

They sat on the edge of the promenade at Sea View and looked at the pier with its chain links strung between twin towers striding out into the distance. Later they wandered from the beach and through the village. A signpost led them up a path to a field leading into some woods.

Alec sat on a stile and pulled her down beside him. She nestled her face against his neck feeling the sun warming her back. Slowly, languorously they began to kiss, their lips salty from the sea air.

Miriam looked about her at the hedgerows smothered with blackberries and here and there grey cobwebby sheets of old-man's-beard. 'Be nice to take some blackberries home, but I've only got my handbag.'

'We'll have to take them in our stomachs,' Alec said, stretching up and picking a large ripe berry and dropping it into her mouth. They dawdled over the fruit-picking and laughed at their purple lips.

'I don't think I'll be able to get over the stile in

this skirt,' she protested.

'You'll just have to haul it up above your knees,' he laughed. 'Nobody will see you.'

'Close your eyes,' she demanded.

Alec shook his head. She rolled up her skirt, her skin tingling under his watchful gaze. They crossed the field in silence and passed through a gate into the wood. It was cool and dark after the heat of the beach. Alec drew her into his arms. 'Let's just listen to the spirit of the wood,' he whispered against her neck. Miriam closed her eyes. There was the sound of water trickling somewhere, birds calling and the faint buzz of insects. 'It's all so beautiful,' he whispered.

'I know,' she breathed.

He took her hand and they crept away from the path and deeper into the wood. Beyond a circle of trees they came upon a thick stretch of ferns waving waist-high in the late summer breeze.

'Nobody will find us in here,' he murmured, drawing them into a green enchanted world of warm honey-scented bracken.

'Are you sure we won't be seen?' Miriam asked, anxiously.

They pushed their way deeper and deeper into the centre of the waving stalks. As they moved ahead the bracken sprang back into position, closing the path behind them. Alec bent over several tall fronds making a flat springy bed. Slowly he began to undress her, pausing between garments to kiss her neck and breasts. He folded her clothes and left them on another smaller bed of bracken.

Kneeling naked beside him Miriam abandoned

346

her fears. She saw that she was beautiful – his eyes told her so. Revelling in his admiration she began to take the pins from her hair to let it swirl around her shoulders in a golden banner. She bent to put the pins in her jacket pocket before Alec pulled her against him, slotting his fingers through her hair and tugging her head back. He kissed her lips, pushing them apart with his tongue, probing her mouth, leaving her breathless. They drew apart and Miriam began to help him out of his clothes, pulling his jersey over his head, untying his collar, unbuttoning his trousers.

The sunlight filtered through the trees dappling their faces with shadowy leaf patterns. They lay down together on the forest floor and rediscovered one another. Miriam smiled up at him as he kissed her breasts and then her belly. Tenderly he stroked her, his fingers moving over her skin, re-awakening her to the pleasures of her body.

'We're like Adam and Eve,' he whispered.

'Before the serpent,' she said, lightly stroking his penis.

Alec gasped and moved her hand away. 'It's impatient to visit your garden,' he whispered before climbing astride her body. Miriam giggled. She twined herself about him gripping him fiercely, shuddering as he entered her. They glided smoothly against each other climbing higher, deeper, faster until they were spent.

Drowsing afterwards in the heat of the afternoon they became gradually aware of the sounds of the forest, the breeze riffling through the trees, the sound of water in the distance and the buzzing of tiny insects.

'I've been eaten alive,' said Alec, standing up and slapping at himself. 'There's probably a little stream nearby where we can paddle and cool down a bit.' They picked up their clothes and shook them vigorously.

'We look a real couple of wrecks,' said Alec, pulling bits of leaves from Miriam's hair. 'I'll put on my trousers and find the water.'

Miriam gripped his arm, pushing him down below the top of the bracken, holding her finger to her mouth. 'I can hear voices, they're getting closer.'

'They'll be here any minute,' gasped Alec, spying through tall green stalks.

The murmur of voices grew louder. Gradually they began to distinguish the sounds.

'Pack up your troubles in your old kit-bag,' sang a group of young voices. Alec peered through the branches. It was a straggle of Boy Scouts lumbering towards them, complete with tent poles and cooking pots.

Miriam laughed softly. Here she was, a soon-to-be-married woman, hiding naked in the woods.

'What would Baden-Powell say?' whispered Alec. They hugged each other, giggling at the absurdity of their position.

'It won't be so funny if they decide to make camp here,' said Miriam. 'We could be trapped for hours.'

Alec slapped his arm. 'Bloody midges,' he said. Miriam sneezed.

At an excruciatingly slow pace and with much singing and clanking the Scouts moved off. Hot, itchy and helpless with giggles Miriam and Alec

348

dressed quickly and pushed their way back through the accommodating ferns.

Alec, still naked to the waist, went off in search of water. 'It's about ten paces in front of you and then fifteen to the left,' he called.

Miriam laughed. 'It's not much more than a puddle.' She knelt down and splashed her face. 'Gosh, you've been well and truly bitten,' she said, looking at the red blotches on Alec's back and arms.

'All in the service of love,' he said as she dabbed at him with her wet hankie.

She dried herself on her petticoat and reached into her bag for her stockings and garters before sitting on a tree stump to put them on.

Alec knelt in front of her and kissed each foot before sliding her stockings up over her toes. 'I've been in paradise,' he said. 'The two of us like one heart, one body.'

'It's been like a wonderful dream,' she whispered taking his face between her hands and kissing him on the lips. 'I don't want to wake up. Soon you'll go away again for months and months.'

'Only four,' he said, 'and those will soon pass in all the getting ready for Christmas and the wedding. You'll hardly have time to miss me.'

'Whatever I'm doing,' she said, 'there'll be a corner of my mind that will be counting every second and wanting and missing you.'

Chapter Thirty-One

Beattie wished she had gone Christmas shopping to Charlotte Market with Miriam, Alec and Rosie. Her task that afternoon was much more onerous, that of visiting Dolly at the asylum. But if she didn't go, there'd be no one to bring the poor soul a bit of Christmas cheer.

Dolly's own children shrank from the task. On that last visit their mother had sat empty-faced and silent while the girls fidgeted and gibbered like frightened monkeys. On the tram home Mary had turned to Beattie and said, 'We ain't never goin' again. Not 'til they puts her head to rights.'

Beattie pushed the Christmas parcel into her bag and nerved herself for the afternoon ahead. Half an hour later she walked through the iron gates of the Borough Asylum. As she walked up the long drive a crocodile of inmates, considered sane enough to enjoy a weekly visit to the local shops, passed her, shepherded by two nurses huddled in their black hospital cloaks. The large brick asylum with its clock-tower and steps leading up to a central revolving door could have been a stately mansion, she thought. And we could be members of the gentry arriving to take afternoon tea, if you discounted our lagging footsteps and the porter at the desk with his heavy bunch of keys and book to check us in.

The clock struck two as she reached the top of the steps. A babel of sounds engulfed her as she negotiated the revolving door into the long corridor. Female inmates, in grey institution dresses, sat on benches shouting, crying or laughing wildly. Dolly and another woman were pacing and singing, strands of tinsel caught in their hair.

Beattie paced with them. 'Fred's coming home from Hong Kong,' she said as Dolly drew breath. 'The girls will be excited to see their Dad.'

'Who's Fred?'

'Your husband, Dolly.'

'Bugger off, Fred,' Dolly snapped. 'Away in a manger.'

Beattie looked at Dolly's companion whose face was curtained by strands of long grey hair. She clutched a rag doll and had the shuffling gait of the long-stay patient.

'What's your baby's name?' Beattie whispered.

The woman turned suddenly, almost stepping onto Beattie's shoes. Her hair fell away from her face. 'Lily,' she said, her breath sweet and fetid.

Beattie gasped. The woman looked for all the world like an older tireder version of Mary Kenny. Trembling, she snatched her gaze away and stared at the floor. The diamonds, cubes and circles on the polished tiles merged and separated in a demented dance. Get a hold of yourself, she told herself.

'Here, Dolly, I brought you a little something for Christmas.' She rummaged in her bag and put the brown paper package into Dolly's hands.

'No crib for his head,' droned Dolly as she tore

351

at the paper.

'Christmas Day tomorrow,' Beattie said with forced cheerfulness. 'Your Harry is cooking dinner for Blyth and the girls. Good boy, your Harry.'

'Good boy, Harry,' repeated Dolly, pulling the paper apart and scattering the contents on the floor. She knelt down and scooped the sweets, the cards and the bar of soap towards her, encircling them with her arms like a wall. 'Mine, mine, mine,' she screamed when some of the other inmates tried to help themselves to her goodies.

Beattie waited while Dolly gathered everything into her pockets. She tried to calm herself. Perhaps she was overwrought with the wedding and all the Christmas preparations. It had been a trick of her imagination. Covertly she risked another look at the woman beside Dolly. Although grey-haired and stooped and nearly fifteen years older, there was something of the earlier Mary about her. And calling that rag doll Lily? There must be hundreds of Lilys about – that proved nothing.

Beattie tried to gather her wits. Now she'd paid her Christmas visit and given the children's gift to her, there was no need to stay longer. Dolly wasn't a relative after all.

So far she'd had two quick glances at this woman that she'd frightened herself into thinking was Mary, and there'd been a surface resemblance. Either she could take her leave and not visit again, just do what she could for the rest of the family, or she could pluck up her courage and try to find out for certain.

Dolly had stuffed all the toffees into her mouth at once and was scuffling the coloured papers along the floor in front of her. Beattie nerved herself for another look at the woman she feared was Mary. She was occupied with the rag doll.

'Mary?' she said softly. The woman turned to look at her. Beattie stared. There was the mole at the right-hand corner of her mouth and the cleft chin and thick straight eyebrows of Mary Kenny. Even the bitten fingernails as she brushed a strand of hair away from her dark eyes were familiar. Still Beattie wavered. 'What's your name?' she asked.

'Don't know,' the woman answered.

'What's her brother's name?' Beattie pointed to the lumpy grey doll. The question was said before she'd had time to think.

'Be a big boy for Mummy.'

Dolly suddenly swooped on Beattie, giving her a sticky kiss and whirling her round the corridor. This was madness. She must get away from the pair of them. There was too much to do for her to be stirring up things better left alone. 'No, Dolly,' she said firmly. 'I'm leaving now.' Roughly she pushed her away and straightened her hat and made for the entrance.

'Andrew Joseph for his Grandad,' shouted the woman. 'Andrew, Andrew, Andrew.' Beattie fled towards the entrance.

Dolly and Mary lumbered after her. ''Nother kiss,' insisted Dolly. 'And she wants a kiss, too.'

Beattie was caught between the two of them. Their sweaty bodies and that sweet unknown stink on their breath made her want to gag. Panic

353

lent her strength and she fought her way clear of them, shoving desperately to right and left.

'Ladies, ladies, calm down. Let go now or I'll take your dolly away.'

'Not dolly, Lily, it's Lily.'

'Are you all right, my dear?' said an elderly nurse, helping Beattie towards one of the benches. 'Here, let me set your hat straight.'

'I must go,' gasped Beattie, dry-mouthed and terrified.

'Well,' said the woman reassuringly, 'no harm done. You two, come back to the ward with me.'

No harm done! Christ, what did she know? 'I must leave,' Beattie said to the porter. 'So much to do.' He nodded briefly as he unlocked the side-door and let her out.

The cold air and the implications of her discovery hit her both at once. Beattie flinched. Mary Kenny was alive. She wasn't the drowned woman that Alec had identified all those years ago. She had sensed that all along, but refused to admit it even to herself. There was no joy in the discovery. It opened up a pit beneath her feet. She thought of Alec and Miriam earlier that afternoon, their faces alight with happiness. How could she go home and snatch that happiness away?

One thought held her together. She must talk to Joseph – she could not bear this knowledge on her own. Walking, that was it, walking till she was too tired to think. It was miles before she would reach Joseph but after talking with him she would know what to do. All she was conscious of was the cold and the effort of setting one foot in front

354

of the other. She trudged through Milton and into Fratton Road dodging past prams and jostling shoppers, her mind filled with thoughts of Mary Kenny.

Nineteen years ago that girl had knocked on Beattie's door. She'd been barely sixteen, put into service from the naval orphanage. There she'd stood in the front room, six months gone and bold as you like.

At least Alec had had the grace to blush when she and Joseph tackled him. There'd been terrible words. 'You're no son of mine,' Joseph had raged. 'To sully this girl and leave her to face the consequences.'

'How do I know it's mine?' Alec had blustered. 'I wasn't the first.' Joseph slapped him hard across the face. It had torn Beattie apart.

Alec had rushed from the house dragging Mary after him. They'd got married a few weeks later, with Beattie's grudging permission, and gone to live in cheap lodgings in Blossom Alley.

Yes, 1900; Beattie had reason to remember the start of the new century. Her son's hasty marriage had soured her last months with Joseph before he left for China. 1900, the year when Joseph had died of wounds at Tien-sin, and life had almost stopped for her. The same year Alec and Mary had moved in with her, bringing Andrew, her first grandchild. Andrew, who gave her a reason to go on living.

Mary, hungry for new things and new sensations, had been a disastrous wife for Alec. Always in debt and hating ever to be on her own. But what was it that had finally tipped her into madness? Was it the birth of Lily or the news of the lengthy foreign draft awaiting Alec?

Could he have saved her? Beattie shook her head. They were both very young and eager for experience. There was a dark earthy attractiveness to Mary that drew men to her, but life with two young children had to be more than coupling if it were to last.

Could she have been more helpful? The thought was painful to her. Mary reminded Beattie of one of the figures in a child's weatherhouse, sometimes sunny, sometimes stormy, never calm and never predictable. In her sunny phases she could be enchanting: dancing little Andrew around the room or singing nursery rhymes in a clear sweet soprano. But her storms could wreck the china and find her swearing like a fishwife. Had there been some clue to the impending tragedy that she might have spotted? Certainly she'd been flushed and hectic that last morning. She'd settled Lily in the chair by the fire with such tenderness, then hugged Andrew fiercely making him cry with fright. Even kissed Beattie and thanked her for looking after the children. Then suddenly she was full of tears, slamming the front door and running down the street as if the devil were after her.

Now she was bleached and hopeless.

Oh Christ, Joseph, what am I going to do? At last Beattie reached Victoria Park and stood in front of the Orlando Memorial trying to pick out the letters of his name in the wintry gloom. She waited, desperate to feel his familiar presence. Joseph, Joseph, Joseph, the word throbbed in her heart. Beattie shivered and stamped her feet. 'Please Joe, for God's sake help me.'

She knew he was dead, of course she did. No amount of wishful thinking would make it otherwise. But here she'd always had a glimmer of comfort like a flicker of the compass needle pointing her in the right direction. Now there was nothing but the sound of the wind sighing in the trees and the bitter acceptance that she had been talking to herself.

The Town Hall clock loomed white-faced over the park; it was half-past three. No point in staying here any more, no point in ever coming back. Never had she felt so abandoned. It would be so easy just to lie down and let the chill winter afternoon do its worst. To let go of everything, for without Joseph – what was there?

But she couldn't do it. Giving in was not her way. She breathed deeply and shook herself like an old dog, squared her shoulders and walked towards home. Who would be there? she wondered. Not Lily, she had gone to Dora's for the afternoon. Alec, Miriam and Rosie were coming to tea after going to the market. Would they be back yet? Could she face them if they were?

Suddenly she thought of Albert. Albert would sit and listen. She walked towards Lemon Street, trying to put her thoughts into some sort of order.

Both houses appeared in darkness but there was a light in Albert's studio. Beattie looked about her before hammering on his door.

'Beatrice, come inside. You look frozen, my dear.' He stood before her wiping his hands on a

357

paint-rag. 'Come into the kitchen. It's warm and I've just made some tea. My dear Beatrice, whatever has happened?'

'It's private,' she said not looking at him. 'Can we go upstairs?'

If he was startled at her request he gave no sign. 'You sit yourself down in the studio and I will bring us a tray.'

Beattie went upstairs and sank into a battered old dining-chair. The room smelt of linseed oil and turps. Although the walls were lined with paintings she could focus on none of them. She took off her gloves and warmed her fingers over the paraffin stove.

Albert smiled at her as he set the tray on a small card-table and poured the tea. 'Right, Beatrice,' he said, 'fire away.'

'I don't know where to start,' she said, cradling the cup between her frozen fingers.

'All seemed well with you when you set off to see Mrs Vine,' said Albert, seating himself on the other chair. 'Has she taken a turn for the worse?'

'No, she was more lively than she's been for weeks. Singing Christmas carols she was.'

'That sounds hopeful. But it's not Dolly – it's something else, isn't it?'

'She was with Mary Kenny. You know, Alec's first wife.'

'Dear Lord!' exclaimed Albert. 'What a dreadful shock. She was one of the patients?'

'Yes.' Beattie's voice shook. 'She looks terrible. I hardly recognised her she's got so thin and unkempt. Shuffling about. Oh Albert, it was terrible.' Beattie put her cup back on the table

358

and covered her face with her hand. It was all too much.

Albert knelt beside her chair taking her other hand into his. She cried for the vivid dark-haired girl that was lost. For Dolly and all the other husks of humanity gathered around her and for herself.

'My dear, dear friend,' he said, gathering her into his arms.

Beattie rested her head against his old wool jumper which he'd patched so neatly, and wept without restraint. When her crying ceased she sat with her eyes closed, feeling his heart beating steadily beneath her ear.

'Albert, what am I to do?' she asked. 'What's the right and honest course to take?'

He got up and drew the other chair up to face hers. 'They may be two different things, Beatrice. You've thrown this in my lap and I'll try to unravel it for you calmly and quietly before you do something you may regret.'

'I'm sorry, I shouldn't have burdened you with it.'

'Of course you should have. I'm your oldest friend.' He handed her a crumpled handkerchief before getting up and walking about the room. 'As far as you can tell Mary is a long-stay patient at the asylum? And yet you've not seen her before when you've visited Mrs Vine? And do you think Mary recognised you?'

'No, she's got that rubbed-out look that Dolly used to have. Carrying a tatty old rag doll around, calls it Lily.'

'Where has she been all these years, I wonder.'

359

'A lot of them were sent to places over the hill during the war when the Americans used the asylum. Now they're being sent back in dribs and drabs.' Beattie dried her eyes and put Albert's hankie in her pocket. 'What in God's name am I going to tell Alec?'

'Need you tell him anything?'

'Jesus, Albert!' Beattie exclaimed. 'He's getting married in a week's time. Mary's his first wife. It's only right if I'm to prevent him committing bigamy.'

'As I said, let's try and look at this calmly, strand by strand. Let's start with Lily.'

'She's a right to know, as well,' Beattie said. 'Mary's her mother.'

'What picture do you think Lily has of her mother?'

'The picture I gave her of a pretty dark-haired woman who laughed and sang.'

'Could Mary, on the evidence of today, be a mother to Lily again?' Beattie shook her head.

'It's almost fifteen years since she disappeared and yet from what you have said she still sees Lily as a baby. What will she make of the reality, of her daughter as a young woman? Is she capable of making a home for her? Is Lily capable of looking after her mother? What will you have achieved by bringing them together?' Beattie shook her head. 'Is it right, who will it benefit? Lily or Mary?'

'I don't think I could live with such a secret, Albert.'

'Do you remember how we talked on the beach, some months ago? You were very anxious. Hester, your sister-in-law, had said something about seeing Mary on a tram.'

'Oh yes,' said Beattie. 'She pulled the cork out of the bottle good and proper. I hadn't thought about Mary in years. Or I believed I hadn't.' Beattie shrugged. 'But you know, Albert, she was in the back of my mind all the time. Poor Hester, she'd no idea of the fright she gave me. To her it was just a casual remark. She'd be horrified if she knew the truth, worse still that I'd known all along.'

'When you think about it, Beatrice, you've kept this secret for years already.'

'It's strange, Albert,' said Beattie, beginning to feel calmer. 'When I first set eyes on her this afternoon, for a few seconds I felt relieved. It bore out what I'd known in my heart. It's what flows out of this knowing that concerns me.'

Albert nodded. 'Let's consider Alec. He's on the point of marrying again a young woman whom he loves deeply and as far as we can see she loves him in return. They can make a new life together and a home for little Rosie. What possible advantage will it be to them to do what is honest? Who could prove that he didn't identify the body in good faith? Besides, he has the death certificate.'

Beattie sighed.

'As for Miriam, you'll knock away the first bit of security she's ever had.'

'Poor girl, I've grown really fond of her in the last few months. Like the daughter I never had.'

'Who is going to have the care of this wretched soul, supposing the authorities think she's fit to leave the asylum? Miriam may well go down to

361

her Auntie in Devon. That leaves yourself and Lily.'

'You're right, Albert,' said Beattie, noticing for the first time the plate of biscuits on the tea tray and helping herself to one. 'At least I'm not keeping the secret on my own.'

Albert smiled. 'You have me to share it with you,' he said.

Beattie smiled at her old friend. 'Albert, I don't know what I'd do without you.'

'It's mutual, my dear,' he said, squeezing her hand. 'We're well weathered aren't we, you and I? The seasons have shaped us like pieces of driftwood in ways we would never have expected.'

'And they're not done with us yet,' she said, getting to her feet and making for the stairs. 'I must stir myself. There's the tea to get, a bird to pluck, stuffing to make and a hundred other things to see to.'

'And I must get to the station,' said Albert opening the front door.

'Where are you going?' asked Beattie, in alarm.

'Oh, only to Samuel's in Romsey. I'll be back on Sunday night.' He smiled down at her. 'Have a Happy Christmas and put this business to one side.'

Beattie smiled back, doubting that she could even for a moment forget the events of that afternoon.

Once indoors she busied herself stirring up the fire and setting the table. She'd got the plump chicken out of the wall safe and set the giblets to simmer when she heard a hammering on the door. That was odd. Alec or Lily would have

362

pulled the key through the letter-box. She hurried down the passage in no mood for visitors.

Chippy Dowell, his face pinched with cold, thrust two loaded shopping-bags into her hands. 'What this all about, Chippy? Why have you got my shopping?' she snapped.

'Chippy, cold, Chippy frightened,' he blubbered, knuckling his fingers into his eyes.

Beattie looked anxiously down the street. What in God's name had happened?

Chapter Thirty-Two

A real family, that's what we are, thought Miriam, as they made their way to Charlotte Market with Rosie jiggling along between them. It was all so different from the year before when she'd waited at the window, her heart thumping against her ribs, for the first sight of Alec. And then the sickening feeling of disappointment as he rushed from the house. Yes, Christmas 1919 was going to be utterly different in every way. She just wished his mother hadn't knocked on the door just at the moment when she was going to share her secret with him. Silly really, she should have written and told him weeks ago but she had wanted to see his face breaking into delighted disbelief. 'Yes, I am,' she'd say and he'd dance her round the room.

She smiled as the crowds swirled around the stalls and the air rang with the competing cries of the traders, selling paregoric cough-sweets, bags of oranges five a penny, hot chestnuts or crockery.

'For you love-birds I'll give them away,' said the man on the china stall, winking at Alec and Miriam, as he threw cups plates and saucers high in the air. Everyone cheered when he caught them and chuckled when he threw in a chamber-pot to accompany the tea-set.

Miriam squeezed Alec's hand. 'Don't you just love it down here,' she cried. 'The lamps hissing and all the shoving and joshing.'

He gave her hand an answering squeeze. 'We'd better wire in and get the bird for tomorrow and all the trimmings.'

'You get the meat and I'll get the veg,' said Miriam.

Alec swung Rosie up on his shoulders to avoid her being trampled by the eager shoppers. 'Fairy, get fairy,' she demanded.

'We won't forget,' he said. 'We'll go to Auntie Nellie's stall a bit later on.'

Standing in the vegetable queue Miriam thought about the last few frantic weeks packed with wedding and Christmas preparations. Mr Pragnell had asked her to stay on as his house-keeper and agreed to Alec sharing her rooms, provided he paid for their food and clothing. Fifteen shillings a week she'd have.

Already they'd made changes. Her bedroom was now divided in two by a heavy curtain and Rosie had a bed of her own made from a door and a couple of drawer fronts. Miriam had sewn a silver moon, a cow, and a cat and fiddle on to the curtain and Rosie had been entranced.

Hung in their wardrobe were their wedding clothes. Miriam had stood for hours in the queue outside Marshall's for Rosie's little silk dress. As for her own outfit, though she said it herself, she'd performed miracles of skill and economy. But, no, she mustn't tempt fate by thinking about that. She'd already taken a chance by hanging Daisy's picture when she'd vowed not to look at it even, before the ring was on her finger. But suddenly she couldn't wait. It was after all Christmas Eve, ten days before their marriage. The banns were called and the ring bought. They were so very nearly married.

Miriam had climbed on to the sideboard and lifted down the portrait of Mr Pragnell's parents and hung 'One of the Family' in its place. It was her talisman. There beneath the glass were the family of her dreams that she first glimpsed that afternoon at Daisy's house in Gosport. There was the farmhouse kitchen with the horse leaning over the door and the little girl reaching out to him with a piece of bread. Miriam smiled to herself – she was glad that she'd done it. It was like nailing her colours to the mast.

''Ere missis,' rasped the stallholder, 'you stood 'ere for the good of our 'ealth or you goin' to buy sommink?'

'Sorry,' gasped Miriam, blushing. 'Ten of spuds, two of carrots, onions and brussels, please.' She staggered under the weight of her vegetable bags and looked around for Alec.

'D'you know it's gone five,' he said drawing level with her. 'Let's go and get ourselves a cup of

365

tea. It'll set us up for the walk home.' He put Rosie down on the pavement and she clutched at her mother's hand.

'Fairy, fairy,' she demanded.

As they neared the stall, Miriam heard a drunken man shouting at a pale-faced youth. 'Move out of me way you clumsy bugger. Step on me again and I'll land yer one.' The voice struck terror. With trembling fingers Miriam pulled her scarf around her face and stepped off the kerb.

It was Taffy Jenkins.

Like a blinkered horse she looked straight ahead, clutching Rosie, whilst Alec took the lead. They were within a whisker of sliding past him. ''Ere Alec, me old mate.' Taffy grabbed him by the shoulder.

Still they could have passed unnoticed, what with the noise of the market traders and the press of people pushing and shoving. But Alec turned and faced him. Coldly, deliberately, he handed Miriam the shopping.

'No, don't please,' she begged but he pushed her aside. Weighed down with a young child and four loaded bags Miriam could not escape. Wedging herself against a lamppost she dragged the bags around her then lifted Rosie up into her arms.

'You bastard, I've got you now,' Alec roared. He turned Taffy around and punched him in the mouth. Rosie screamed.

The two men circled each other grunting and glaring. The crowd divided into those who wished to escape the fight and those interested to see the outcome. Taffy swung wildly, landing Alec a glancing blow on the jaw. The return punch sent him reeling.

Alec was animal in his rage. He hit Taffy again, sending him crashing against the lamppost and into a gutter. With his teeth bared and the flesh on his face stretched between the harsh ridges of his cheekbones he was unrecognisable to Miriam. She tried to shrink inside herself away from the terrifying new Alec and the loathsome Taffy panting and snuffling at her feet.

He pulled himself upright with the aid of her coat and swayed, bloody-faced, in front of her. From the gutter, he had acquired a veneer of rotting vegetables that one by one slid back onto the ground.

'It's Frosty Drawers,' he sneered at her his voice thick with blood. 'But I 'ad you in the end, didn't I darlin'?' His breath swirled up into her face, rank and rum-sodden, unlocking her nightmare. She screamed as his hand reached out to her. Alec snatched at his collar yanking Taffy away from her and punching him in the eye.

'Couldn't get enough of me,' Taffy blustered, before sinking to the ground.

Rosie clutched at her mother, her body trembling with fright. As Miriam tried to quieten her daughter's panic her own fear turned to anger. She vowed never to forgive Alec for exposing their child to such brutality. He could have walked away. Staying to fight was nothing to do with her protection. It was about being top dog.

'Jesus! He's got a bottle, send for the patrol,' shouted someone in the crowd.

Taffy had dragged a beer bottle from his coat

pocket and smashed it against the kerb. While Alec drew back his fist Taffy lunged forward and jabbed the neck of the bottle into Alec's upraised arm. Blood spurted everywhere. Women and children screamed and Alec gasped with pain.

Taffy lunged again but he was halted in his tracks by Big Arthur who sprang from behind the stall with a butcher's steel in his hand. Swiftly, he cracked Taffy on the back of the head with the handle of the steel, sending him sprawling. Arthur turned to Alec and clamped his hand on his arm. 'Come on, son,' he said, 'let's fix you up 'fore you bleeds all over me chickens.' With his other hand he beckoned to his apprentices. 'Jim, you and Bert drag this mad bugger off into the cold-room. This all got to be cleared up before the patrol gets here.'

Miriam looked at Alec's chalk-white face as he was helped past her then everything began to spin. She was falling, falling down and down. 'See to the child now quick or you'll drop her.'

'Tea ... will you ... get some, sweet and three sugars.' The words advanced and receded in a meaningless jumble.

Miriam came to herself on a box at the back of the toy stall. Rosie was trying to force her eyes open. 'Wake up, Mummy,' she sobbed.

Someone held a cup to Miriam's lips. It spilled down her coat. She couldn't stop shaking. Slowly she focused on Rosie's face. Seeing the fear in her daughter's eyes she tried to rally. 'Find Mummy's purse in her pocket and we'll get the fairy now.'

Nellie Foy, with a nutcracker jaw and a face like Punch, took Rosie around to the front of her stall and lifted her up to see the display. 'Put a smile on your kiddies' face, come on now. 'Ere, Mister, look at this jumping Jack.' Sliding Rosie onto one hip she held her with one hand while she handed out toys with the other, rummaging for change in her apron. 'What's your name, my babes?'

'Rosie.'

'Now ain't that pretty,' she rasped. 'Let's find you a fairy.'

''Ello, Mrs Naylor.' The wizened apple face of Chippy Dowell peered at Miriam. 'Hitting, don't like hitting.'

''Ere Chip's, stick this in yer gob and Happy Christmas.' Nellie pressed a lump of toffee into his mouth.

Miriam wondered how she would ever manage to drag her shopping home plus carry an exhausted child. 'Could you carry my bags back to Mrs Forrest?' she said. 'Tell her I'll not be long.' Chippy looked doubtful. 'I need someone strong. Mrs Forrest said she'd got a present for you.'

Still chewing on his toffee, Chippy slipped the handles through his fingers and lumbered away.

'Nellie Foys for all your toys.' Still holding Rosie on one hip, the stallholder fetched a youth a crack on the head, with a book of adventure stories. 'I'll give you a bleedin' adventure, you theivin' tyke.' She gave Rosie a gummy grin. 'Which is it goin' to be? The goldy fairy or the one with the scarlit slippers?'

'Goldy!' Rosie cried.

Nellie placed the doll in a bag and turned to another customer. 'Good choice, darlin'. That kaleidoscope, only sixpence, ever so pretty.'

Miriam dug her gloves out of her pockets. She must get Rosie home and into bed.

Across the blood-stained street Big Arthur was talking to the naval patrol man. 'Got a soldier's 'ad a skinful and slipped up on some veg. Fetched 'isself a crack 'gin the lamppost.'

'Always calls us when the show's half over,' muttered the patrolman, following Arthur behind his stall.

'Now then,' the butcher shouted, 'who's buying the last chicken?'

'Don't fret, babes,' said Nellie. ''E just nicked his arm. Arthur will 'ave walloped some iodine on it and bandaged it up, pronto. 'E's gettin' that other drunken bugger taken away in the paddy waggon. Rosie's chosen a lovely fairy, ain't ya babes?'

Rosie nodded and Miriam pressed a sixpence into Nellie's weathered hand. 'Thank you for everything,' she said, getting up and taking hold of her daughter's hand.

'You fit to walk home, gal?' said Nellie. 'Face on you the colour of alabaster.'

'I'll take it steady.'

'Who wants some soldiers? Not you madam, I'm talkin' to the lad 'ere,' Nellie snapped.

Rosie had made a remarkable recovery thanks to Nellie's fairy and trotted along full of talk about Granny Forrest's Christmas tree. Miriam willed herself to walk the few streets back to her home, to smile at the Salvation Army band as she passed by them.

Beattie was standing on the doorstep, talking to

370

Chippy as she approached. 'Thank you kindly,' she was saying. 'Here's a few bits of Christmas cheer I've parcelled up for you.'

'Much obliged,' he said, shuffling away.

Alec's mother's face was furrowed with anxiety, 'What in God's name's been going on, Miriam? Poor Chippy was scared witless. Is Alec badly hurt? Fighting in the street. I've never known him to...'

'Arthur the butcher has taken care of him. He's cut his arm but not badly. Look,' said Miriam swaying with tiredness, 'I must get indoors with Rosie. It's all been a shock.'

'Oh, my dear, of course. I'll bring you in a tray of tea. It's gone six, you must be famished. Mr Pragnell's not long gone. He left the fire banked up. You get inside. Big Arthur will have Alec home in two ticks.'

Miriam turned to pull the key through the letter-box next door. Mrs Forrest cried out: 'Your lovely coat, Miriam, there's blood all down the side. Let me take it from you and try and clean it.'

Miriam started up. It was Taffy's blood. She wrenched the buttons undone and flung it onto the pavement. 'No, no! I don't want it now,' she said fiercely. 'You can get rid of it. Just for God's sake leave me alone.'

'Show Nana Forrest my fairy,' pleaded Rosie, reaching out to Alec's mother.

Miriam slammed the door, leaving Rosie, the shopping and Mrs Forrest outside. She rushed out to the kitchen and banged the kettle down on the stove before racing to her bedroom to get her nightdress. She was soiled, infected by him.

371

Clean, she must be clean. Nothing could be done until she'd washed away every last trace of that afternoon. Alec's face, ugly and contorted with rage, swam before her. She'd never seen him like that before. Rosie had been terrified, just as she was about to tell her that Alec was her daddy. She waited for the kettle to boil in an agony of impatience. What would become of them all? What if Alec were badly hurt and couldn't work again?

She poured the water into a basin and dragged off her clothes, scattering them on the floor, then scoured herself with a flannel and soap. Savagely she rubbed at her skin with a towel, making it red and tingling before hauling her nightdress over her head. If only she could crawl into bed but there was Rosie to look after. Miriam sighed. She couldn't even look after herself. Left her daughter out in the street not even waiting to see if she was taken care of.

The fight had stirred up memories of the men who had visited her mother. The shouting and swearing and frightening shadows on the bedroom wall. Then she had hidden under the table dragging her coat with her for warmth. All she had wanted was for the noise to stop, to fall asleep and wake up with everything different.

The latch on the back door rattled and she went through to the scullery thinking it was Mrs Forrest with Rosie.

'Get away from me,' she screamed.

'Mirry, I'm sorry, Mirry.' Alec fended her away as she began to hit him.

She could not stop screaming and hitting. Fear and anger boiled together in a scalding tide of accusations. 'Why couldn't you ignore him? Why did you have to make a show of me? You frightened the life out of Rosie, you know that, don't you?' Words rained down on Alec along with the blows. 'You were no better than him. A couple of beasts that's what you were.'

They staggered around the room in weary deadlock, Miriam accusing and Alec pleading, until exhaustion overcame Miriam and she sank weeping into a chair.

'Mirry, please, please, don't look at me like that,' Alec begged. 'I just saw red. Didn't stop to think. I'm sorry, I'm so so sorry.'

'I'd never seen you like that,' said Miriam. 'All the shouting and fighting I grew up with. I never thought you could be ... I never thought I'd be frightened of you. And Rosie to see her new Daddy like a–' Miriam shrugged, 'well I don't know what.'

They both started up at the tap on the window. 'I've brought her in to go to bed,' said Mrs Forrest, carrying Rosie through the back door that Alec held open for her. 'I'll go straight back, I've a deal to do. Lily will give me a hand but if you could come back later, Alec, I would be grateful.'

Miriam blushed. 'I'm sorry about earlier. It was all too much.'

'I'm sorry too, Miriam,' his mother said quietly, 'but the least said soonest mended at this stage. I'll see you for dinner tomorrow. A good night's sleep is what we all need. It's been a very long day for all of us.'

Something in her voice made Miriam look up

at her. For the first time she saw uncertainty and weariness in the face of Alec's mother. 'Thank you for having Rosie,' was all she could think to say. Mrs Forrest nodded absently before going out again.

Rosie climbed on to Miriam's lap and looked steadily at Alec. 'I've been a very naughty man,' he said softly. 'I frightened you and I'm very sorry.' Still Rosie stared at him. 'Will you let me tuck you in and read you a story?'

Rosie studied Alec closely before sliding off her mother's lap. She touched his bandaged arm. 'Hurt hisself,' she said.

Alec winced. 'All better soon,' he said. 'What story are we going to have?'

'Billie Goats Gruff,' she said taking hold of his other arm.

'Good night, my angel,' said Miriam.

Rosie ran across the room to kiss her before walking off with Alec. Miriam envied the child her resilience. 'I'll make us some tea, when she's had her story,' he said. Miriam said nothing. There were so many tasks she'd set aside for the evening. Mostly finishing touches to gifts for everyone: embroidering the initials on some handkerchiefs for Alec's mother, putting the ribbons on the pigtails of Rosie's new doll, setting the pins in a cushion for Lily so that they spelled out her name. Little loving touches for her new family, that she hadn't the heart for now. Weariness stole over her and she sank into sleep.

It was the cold that woke her, to find the fire gone out and the blanket that had been draped around her in a heap on the floor. She looked at the clock on the mantelpiece. It was half-past seven on Thursday the twenty-fifth of December. Last year she had awoken to equal feelings of despair but by the end of the day, when Alec had come in with Rosie's blanket, she'd had reason to hope. Slowly over the year her hopes had been realised and she'd looked forward to this Christmas with quiet confidence. Not only were she and Alec about to be married, but she'd been accepted lovingly by Alec's mother and she and Lily were almost back to their old friendly footing. But it seemed, like all the other Christmases since her father had left her as a child, that this one was doomed to failure.

Always there was a want of something, be it food or warmth, kindness, security – always a spectre at the feast. No, that wasn't true. One year shone out from all the others. Her first Christmas with Rosie in that little house in Gosport. Going downstairs with her baby in the chill of the early morning, to be overwhelmed by the rich scent of early hyacinths that Daisy had potted up especially for the day. The little tree decorated with shiny toffee-papers and cotton-wool snow. Daisy, her chubby face alight with joy, hugging the pair of them. 'Don't a baby make a Christmas,' she'd said. 'They brings their own magic with them.'

Miriam wiped her eyes with the back of her hand. Whatever else, she must make a Christmas for Rosie. Picking up the blanket she realised that Alec must have covered her up sometime last night. Did she have anything to eat? She couldn't remember. Perhaps she'd make some toast, once she'd lit the lamp and got the fire going.

Glancing around the room she was startled to see Alec, asleep in the armchair opposite her. Looking at him revived an old nightmare in which she had run after him, touched his shoulder, only to have him turn around smiling out at her through Taffy Jenkins' face. Did she still want to marry him? Did she still love him? A few hours ago there would have been no question in her mind.

Miriam looked up at her picture, at the family secure behind the glass. In the chill light of early morning they seemed to mock her fake security. She shivered and drew the blanket around her shoulders. The question of what she would do if she did not marry Alec gnawed at her. Where would she go and what could she tell Rosie? Lemon Street had become her home. Besides, there was Alec's mother and Lily and Mr Pragnell to consider. In marrying Alec she became part of a family and in refusing she would deprive Rosie of a grandma, a father and a sister.

She looked again at Alec's sleeping figure slumped in the chair opposite, the dried blood on his bandaged arm. His face was chalk-white, his features smooth and defenceless. He could be so tender towards her, so loving to Rosie. But she had been terrified by the sudden change in him. What if he were ever to lose his temper with her?

But then a worm of conscience gnawed at her. What of her screaming at Alec last night, hitting and punching him? How had she been any better? She wrapped her arms protectively around her stomach. 'What shall we do?' she whispered.

Chapter Thirty-Three

Lily and Dora stood with their workmates outside the Theatre Royal. In a few minutes they would crowd inside to see the Boxing Night performance of *Sleeping Beauty*, the tickets a present from Mr Denby and Admiral Shanks.

Miss Markham teetered on high heels, her face ghostly pale under a generous layer of face-powder. 'Looks like she fell in the flour bin,' Dora hissed.

Mr Savours sported a white silk scarf and a black homburg hat. 'For you, Lavinia,' he said, presenting Miss Markham with a bag of sugared almonds. Dora and Lily giggled helplessly.

The wind whipped along the queue and Miss Pearson drew her fox stole, complete with head and paws, more closely around her shoulders. Its glass eyes stared balefully at the two girls. 'Wonder when she shot that,' whispered Lily, and once again they shook with laughter. She squeezed Dora's arm and said, 'I've been looking forward to this even more than Christmas Day.'

Dora smiled. 'So have I,' she said. 'Christmas is all right when you're small but when you get older you see all the snags.'

'What d'you mean?'

'It's like those snowstorm things in bottles what you get. It's all magic when you're a nipper, then when you grows up you knows it's just water and bits of paint. This year our mum was worked off her feet, Granny had hysterics and hit Mum with her stick and smashed her glasses. Mum reckons she's goin' mental. Keeps hiding bits of food in her handbag. When she dropped off to sleep, after Christmas dinner, we found a roast potato in there stuck to her powder-puff.'

Lily gave her arm a sympathetic squeeze. Christmas had been strange for her too. Of course it had been different from last year when she'd made that sickening discovery about Dad and Miriam and gone hurtling out of the house. The shock had taken months to come to terms with.

'You're just enjoying being a martyr,' Gran had snapped when she'd confided her unhappiness.

'No I'm not,' Lily had shouted.

'You've got these little seeds of resentment and you're watering them for all you're worth with jealousy and bitterness. If you're not careful that pity-plant will choke all the good things and turn you as sour as a bottle of vinegar.' Then she changed tack. 'Mind you, your father could have prepared us better, instead of going about it all arse-about-face.' She chuckled. 'I sometimes think men should be left on their own with their uniforms and tool-boxes. I'm sure us women couldn't make a worse fist of running the world.'

Lily smiled. Being called a woman had taken the sting out of Gran's rebuke. Now she was friendly again with Miriam and quite looking forward to the wedding. Or she had been until Christmas morning when she'd seen Dad sitting in the armchair, nursing his bandaged arm. From bits of overheard talk between him and Gran she understood that there had been a fight in the market. She couldn't believe it. But then, last year she'd not believed he could fall in love. His distress saddened her but she could think of nothing to do or say that would relieve matters. It wasn't just Dad who worried her. Even Gran had been distracted and far away, not entering into the spirit of things with her usual gusto. The only consolation had been Rosie. At nearly three she was ready for stories, recognising the pictures now and shrieking with delighted terror at the wolf in *Little Red Riding Hood* or the antics of naughty Goldilocks. Lily was convinced that she could now spell out her name with the alphabet bricks she'd bought her earlier, and felt a real affection for her little sister.

But even Lily felt strange. It seemed as if she were watching everything from a distance. The food and presents, the visit from Aunt Hester and Uncle George, having Dad at home. She felt none of the intense joy that Christmas used to hold. Somehow the centre of her life had shifted away from home, and towards what she didn't yet know.

It was almost a year since she'd started work and now she was as fast as Ivy on the sewing-machine. Of course, there was still a lot of tedious hand-sewing, such as basting the lining to jackets, and she was still having to make the tea and sweep up each night, but she enjoyed her work. The skills she'd learnt were put to good use making her own clothes. She and Dora had spent hours at Charlotte Market sifting through tired cast-offs. Dora had found a black brocade skirt

379

from which they cut a matching Dorothy bag, and under a mildewed corset was a satin blouse missing two buttons.

'I shall set this off with Gran's stimulated pearls,' Dora had said.

Lily had a mental picture of the 'stimulated pearls' escaping from Dora's neck and snaking their way around the auditorium. She was impatient to take off her coat in case it crushed her new outfit: the peach silk blouse with crystal buttons and the black barathea skirt which had had to be practically remade. What set off the whole outfit were her mother's gold earrings.

Across the street two buskers began singing and playing their accordions. 'I'm forever blowing bubbles,' she sang with the rest of the crowd. The windows of the theatre were ablaze with lights, framed by pillars linked with delicate wrought-iron tracery. 'It's like a wedding cake, from one of those posh bakers,' she said, linking arms with her friend.

Dora nodded. 'Reminds me of a painting of a galleon sailing out into the midnight sea,' she said. 'Wait till you see inside.'

Catching sight of Bernard approaching her, Ruby sneered, 'Cripes, it's Lord Rothschild.'

'Good evening, ladies,' Bernard drawled, sweeping off his top hat. He opened a box he was carrying and handed Lily a red carnation buttonhole. 'I'll pin it on your dress when we get inside,' he promised.

Lily blushed. She didn't know whether she was glad or sorry to see him. Talking with her friends she'd felt grown-up and excited to be part of the theatre crowd. Now, with Bernard, she felt like a small girl trying to walk in her mother's shoes.

'Where did you get that outfit,' Ruby called from behind him. 'Off the dummy in the side window?'

Bernard swung around in his black overcoat and glared at her.

The crowd suddenly surged forward. 'Ooh, they're going in, they're going in,' Miss Markham cried.

The foyer was a blaze of lights reflected in the huge gilt-framed mirrors. There was a heady mixture of pomade, cigar smoke and competing perfumes floating above rain-damp overcoats. Top-hatted gentlemen escorted women in furs up the scarlet-carpeted stairs to the dress circle. All the Denby and Shanks staff were seated along a high-backed red velvet bench up at the back of the pit.

'Let me help you off with your coat,' said Bernard. Lily blushed as he slid it from her shoulders.

'You shall go to the ball, Cinderella,' he said, pinning the buttonhole to her blouse. The flower set the seal on her evening. She bent her head expecting to smell the rich clove perfume of Aunt Hester's carnations, but it was totally without scent. Bernard placed himself with Lily on one side and Dora on the other. Ruby, sandwiched between Mr Savours and Miss Pearson, cast her a poisonous look. The stage was hidden by a vast scarlet curtain. One above the other on either side rose golden scallop-shaped boxes, filled with men smoking cigars and women laughing.

'Ooh Claude,' Miss Markham cried, 'look, in the middle box, it's Admiral Shanks. I made those epaulettes,' she said proudly. 'All my gold work on display.'

'He wants melting down,' said Bernard, out of the side of his mouth.

Lily looked at the large balding figure and wanted to laugh at his self-importance as he settled himself fussily in his gilt chair. Around her, in the pit, ordinary soldiers and sailors, women in big hats and girls all squeezed together. Expectation tightened like the strings on the orchestra's violins. The theatre darkened and the curtain rose.

The stage was like a shimmering flowerbed as troupes of fairies waved their gauzy wings. Presiding over the scene in their glittering crowns were the King and Queen of Arcadia while lurking in the background, oozing menace, was Siva the wicked witch. Lily reached behind Bernard and nudged Dora. 'Looks like Ruby,' she hissed. With her red hair and white face Siva was the image of their workmate.

At the christening of Princess Bonibelle, Siva held the stage as she predicted:

Your Daughter dies – nought will placate my
    rage
Your cherished child shall never come of age
A spindle sharp when eighteen years have
    passed
Shall pierce her hand and then she'll breathe
    her last

Amidst the clash of cymbals and rolling of drums of Siva's exit, Lily became aware of Bernard's arm resting on her shoulder. She turned to him but he seemed absorbed in the pantomime almost as if his arm had moved of its own accord. She was piqued to see that his other arm was resting on Dora's shoulder.

On the stage, the scene had shifted to the palace gardens. The audience began catcalling at the arrival of the Princess's suitors: Major General Dug-Out, the oily businessman; Isaac Moses, who had comfortably sat out the war; the effete Lord Fitzherbert Blue-Blood, and their favourite, Joe Basher the boxer. Howls of laughter greeted the advice of Bonibelle's faithful nurse: 'When you want a husband have one made of sweet stuff, then, when you're tired of him you can eat him.'

She was the travesty of the caring attendant, with huge bouncing breasts, an orange wig and vast frilly drawers hanging beneath her starched apron. The soldiers and sailors jeered and wolf-whistled.

There were groans of dismay as the Princess pricked her finger and fell into a fateful sleep. The stage darkened to a haunted forest with twisted trees and wicked goblins thwarting the path of the handsome prince.

Bernard took Lily's hand and squeezed it. She looked away from the stage and was relieved to see that his other arm was no longer around Dora. With the fate of the Princess now hanging in the balance the curtain fell and the lights came on in the auditorium. 'Let's go and get a drink,' said Bernard, thrusting his way through the crowd who were making their way to the basement bar. 'Port and lemon, ladies?' he asked as Dora joined them.

'Gin and tonic, please,' said Lily trying to sound sophisticated.

'You won't like it,' warned Dora. 'It's like drinking scent.'

'How d'you know what I'll like?' snapped Lily.

Dora looked puzzled. 'Why you being so uppity?'

'I'm not.'

'It's 'cos Bernard put his arm round me, isn't it? Blimey, Lil, surely you don't think he fancies me?'

'Course not,' muttered Lily, wishing she hadn't made a fuss.

'He can't bear to be ignored. I'm a challenge 'cos I won't put up with his nonsense. Oh ta ever so, Bernard,' Dora said, mockingly as he handed her a port and lemon.

'And one for you too, Lily.'

'I thought I asked for gin,' Lily protested.

'Gin's not a drink for a lady,' said Bernard smiling at her. 'Besides, it'll ruin your complexion.'

'Oooh, Ruby, you don't half look nice. Doesn't she, Claude?' Miss Markham said looking at Mr Savours.

Her curiosity aroused, Lily turned towards Ruby who had just taken off her coat to reveal a tea-gown of lemon georgette. The front panel had tiny orange and yellow flowers embroidered on it with glittering sequinned centres. She wore a matching tricorn hat with an orange tassel. 'Very fetching,' said Bernard.

Grudgingly Lily said, 'It's ever so pretty,' as she raised her glass to her lips. She's like a peacock strutting among us sparrows, she thought, wondering how Ruby could have afforded such an outfit. Her eyes smarted from the cigarette smoke that was soon thick in the air. Near the door she saw Harry Vine and Michael Rowan with a group of shipmates. Forgetting about the drink in her hand, Lily waved to them.

'You clumsy bitch! Look what you've done,' Ruby screamed at her. Lily turned around to see a deep brown stain seeping into the flowers on Ruby's dress. She looked in horror at her empty glass. 'Christ, I could kill you.' Ruby was spitting with rage.

'Ruby, honest it was an accident,' gasped Lily, horrified at what she'd done. Her face was hot with shame as people started looking at them. 'Let's go to the Ladies and I'll help you to sponge it clean.'

'I'll tell you what you can do,' Ruby shouted, 'you can go to Handleys tomorrow and pay them six guineas.'

'I can't do that,' whispered Lily. Ruby drew back her hand and slapped her face.

Lily put her hand to her flaming cheek and there was a gasp from the onlookers.

'It wasn't your fault. No, don't cry, she's not worth it,' said Dora taking her arm.

It wasn't the pain of the slap that caused her tears but the public humiliation. Not only had Ruby made a show of her in front of strangers but Bernard and Michael and Harry had seen it. Her usual response to anger or embarrassment was to take to her heels and put a distance between herself and the cause of her discomfort. In the packed bar she was forced to stay where she was.

'It's all right Lil, Miss Pearson's taken charge of her. Dragged her off to the cloakroom, most likely. If anyone can get that stain out it'll be Miss Pearson,' said Dora reassuringly.

A bell rang and a voice announced, 'Ladies and gentlemen, kindly take your seats. The curtain will rise in five minutes.' No, she couldn't go and sit back in the theatre as if nothing had happened.

'I'm going,' she hissed, pushing Dora away and giving in to her need to escape. 'I'm going on my own.'

'Lily, don't be so daft, all the best bits are to come, there's the flying ballet and all sorts. Oh Lily!'

The night air made her shiver as she rushed headlong past the Town Hall and square towards the familiar streets of Portsea. The windows of the town pubs lit up the December sky, exposing her to the curious glances of the passersby. By the time she had turned into Queen Street her teeth were chattering and her shoes had rubbed her heels raw. She had fled leaving her coat on her seat next to Bernard. Hopefully he or Dora would take it to work for her in the morning. But in the meantime she'd have to explain its absence to Gran and Dad. Lily bent down and unbuckled her shoes. The chill hard pavement under her feet completed her misery. She felt like Cinderella when the clock struck midnight. As she hobbled through the side streets she heard footsteps behind her. She hurried faster, so did they, and when she stopped the following footsteps slackened too. 'You want to give me a heart attack?' demanded Bernard, catching up with her.

'Go away,' Lily mumbled. 'I don't want to see anyone.'

'Well,' gasped Bernard, pulling her around to face him. 'I want to see *you* to make sure you're all right.' To her fury, Lily burst into tears, the last thing she wanted to do in front of him. 'Sh, sh Lily,' he whispered. 'Your troubles are over, Ruby's have just begun.'

'What d'you mean?' she asked.

Bernard laughed. 'You don't think she paid for that dress, do you?'

'You don't mean she stole it?' Lily was shocked.

'Got it at Handleys overnight on approval.'

'But how could she do that? You've got to be an account customer.'

'Pretended she was Admiral Shanks' niece.'

Lily could hardly believe it. 'Cripes! What a nerve! How did she get away with it? I mean, she doesn't look a bit like a lady, in her ordinary clothes, and she doesn't speak right.'

'You haven't seen our Ruby when she's putting on the pot,' snorted Bernard. 'She probably borrowed a coat and hat then swanned in there bold as you like.'

Lily couldn't help admiring Ruby's daring. 'If it hadn't been for me spilling that drink, she'd have got away with it.'

Bernard held her away from him and smiled quizzically. 'Don't tell me you're sorry for her?'

Lily blushed. 'What will happen to her now?'

Bernard shrugged. 'If Miss Pearson can get the stain out and make it look good as new, Ruby can take it back to Handleys, no questions asked. But if not...' He shrugged.

'Could she get the sack?'

'Probably. If Admiral Shanks finds out, she'll be finished and she'll have to pay for the dress.'

They walked along in silence. Lily thought of the portly Admiral she'd seen earlier that evening, and wondered what he would think of Ruby's antics. She realised that she knew nothing of Ruby's life or what losing her job would mean to her. At the corner of Lemon Street she hesitated.

'Is this where you live?' Bernard asked.

'You needn't see me to the door,' Lily said, anxious to avoid him being seen by Dad or Gran.

He drew her into a shop doorway. 'We'll say goodnight here then,' he said, bending to kiss her.

'Thank you for looking out for me,' Lily said shyly.

Bernard kissed her again, lingeringly on the mouth. 'We'll have to have a real night out just the two of us,' he said, pushing her further into the doorway and pressing his body against her. 'No longer the little girl,' he said, as he slid one hand down the front of her blouse and pinched her breast before attempting to undo the top button.

'Don't, Bernard. I don't like it,' Lily said, trying to push him away.

'Oh yes you do, Lily. You've been panting for me.'

'I haven't, I haven't,' she cried, stung by the truth of his words. For months she had wanted to be alone with Bernard, had imagined his kisses, but this grubby exchange was hateful.

He took her hand and held it against his leg. 'I've been wanting you too.' Lily snatched her hand away as if it were on fire.

'Little cock-teaser, that's what you are,' he sneered. 'Don't know why I bothered. Ruby would have – Jesus Christ! What the hell is it?' Bernard shrieked with fright then began prancing about, clawing at his hair. Lily couldn't believe it. She didn't know whether to laugh or cry. 'Get it off me,' he snarled, leaping about in a frantic effort to shake the creature loose.

There perched on his shoulder was Granny Dowell's monkey. Bernard's normally enigmatic features were twisted with fear. 'It's only a monkey,' Lily said witheringly. 'You two are well matched.'

Relief gave way to laughter as Lloyd took Bernard's hat and leapt away with it onto the top window of the shop. 'Serve you right,' she said. 'I just wish the others could see you now.'

'You silly little bitch,' he hissed. 'You tell anyone and you'll be very sorry. As for that piece of vermin,' Bernard made a sawing movement with his hand across his throat before turning away from her and stalking into the night.

Laughing softly to herself Lily walked down

Lemon Street towards home. She pulled the key out of the letter-box and turned it in the lock.

'That you, my duck?' called Gran, from the top of the stairs. 'I'm off to my bed, I've left you some cocoa in the pan. Tell me all about the panto tomorrow.'

'I will, Gran,' said Lily, grateful for the reprieve.

Chapter Thirty-Four

Beattie stared out into the morning darkness of the yard. Sunday the twenty-eighth of December, the fag end of the year, less than a week till the wedding. Today Albert would return from his stay in Romsey. Not since Joseph was alive had Beattie waited with such impatience for anyone. As she washed and dressed she was comforted by the thought of seeing Albert later in the day. Come hell or high water he'd promised to be there. Her dear, dear friend. What she would have done without him didn't bear thinking about.

The secret she'd shared with him was like a millstone weighing on her mind. Hardly had she digested the fact that Mary Kenny was still alive than she'd had Miriam abandoning her child on the pavement. Hot on her heels was Alec, chalk-faced and bandaged. At the sight of him Rosie had screamed the place down. It had taken all her resources of patience to calm the child. How she had managed to pluck the chicken, make the stuffing and all the other preparations for the Christmas dinner she couldn't now remember. For all the attention Alec and Miriam gave to her cooking she needn't have bothered. They could have been eating salt pork and weevily biscuits for all the pleasure they'd got out of it. Never once did their eyes meet and getting any sort of conversation going was like pulling teeth. Only Lily and Rosie enjoyed themselves, playing together as if they'd been sisters all their lives.

Alec's misery was painful to her. He had crept into the scullery on Christmas morning looking pale and wretched. What in God's name had he been thinking about, fighting in the market? A man in uniform brawling in public. He was lucky not to have been picked up by the Naval Patrol and be sitting in a cell this very minute. As for Miriam, the woman looked fit to drop. Beattie was relieved when she pleaded a headache and went home.

How had it all gone wrong? They'd all set out on Christmas Eve with smiling faces and now? There was the demented Mary Kenny casting her shadow and some mysterious other person wreaking equal damage.

If things were not resolved Miriam and Rosie would likely move away. The thought distressed her. Her grandchild had become a part of her life. In the last few weeks Rosie had taken to calling her Granny instead of Auntie Forrest. How she would miss her, that cheery smile, those plump little arms flung around her neck.

Miriam too. Beattie had grown to love her. There was a steadfastness and courage to the girl and no doubt about her feelings for Alec. Something had shaken that young woman's confidence but not her love – of that Beattie was certain. Oh, Albert, she pleaded, please, please hurry yourself.

'Morning Gran,' Lily drifted into the kitchen, yawning and stretching. 'What's for breakfast?'

'You'll have to forage for yourself. I've got some sewing to finish.'

'I think I'll have a piece of cake, some pickled onions and a bit of cheese.'

'God bless your innards,' laughed Beattie.

'When are we setting off for Auntie Hester's?'

Oh damn and blast! She no more wanted to go to Hester's than fly in the air. Seeing her sniping at poor George, having her interrogations about the wedding, the clothes, the food, all the whys and wherefores. Every visit left her frazzled and today she needed to be calm. Still, the preparations Hester would have made for the tea-party, the cakes baked and the serviettes starched! She would have to go regardless of how she felt.

'Dora's coming with me. We'll probably take Rosie if Miriam doesn't mind.'

'Does Auntie Hester know about this? You know what a fuss she makes if there's the slightest change to her plans.'

'Well, Uncle George would like it,' said Lily defensively. 'Besides Dad's so grumpy we'll need someone else to cheer us up.'

Beattie smiled. Lily's youthful normality was a tonic. 'Is he awake yet?' she asked.

'Don't think so,' Lily said, hacking herself a slice of Christmas cake and tidying up the crumbs on the board before finding herself a plate. 'There was no sound when I passed the door.'

'We'll let him wake up when he's ready. Could you give us a hand with the collars? I'm all out of sequence what with Christmas and the wedding,' Beattie said. 'I'll machine if you can press and do some hemming. There's just six left to make up three dozen.'

'I'll get washed and dressed,' said Lily, taking her plate out to the sink.

'How was the pantomime?'

There was a pause and then the girl said, 'It's a bit of a long story. I'll tell you later, Gran, after I've got dressed.'

She's hiding something, thought Beattie, taking an empty bobbin out of its shuttle. But it will have to wait; I'm overloaded as it is. Detaching the wheel from the needle, she clicked the bobbin into place and treadled gently, watching it fill with thread. The steady whirr of the machine soothed her and the routine tasks anchored her body while her mind busied itself thinking how best to help her son.

Perhaps they could send the girls on ahead to Hester's this afternoon. Later she and Alec could maybe walk along the seafront, chew things over. With Rosie and Lily out of the way poor Miriam might recover her senses. She had acted out of panic and exhaustion on Christmas Day, saying she must be alone to think. Beattie knew that the rumpus in Charlotte Market had been far more than a storm in a teacup. But given time they might yet pull through. They would have to – if she wasn't much mistaken, the poor girl was carrying again. It was struggle enough to bring up one child without any support but two! It didn't bear thinking about. Had Alec been told?

'Hello, Mrs Forrest, is Lily about?'

'My stars, you made me jump, Dora,' said Beattie. 'Who let you in?'

'I did, Ma,' said Alec, standing in the doorway in his vest and trousers. Beattie glanced quickly at him, noting the shadows under his eyes and his general air of defeat. She wanted to gather him in her arms.

Instead she said, 'You get out into the scullery and put yourself to rights. There's a full kettle of hot water on the range.'

Turning to Dora she smiled. 'Run up and fetch Lily, my dear, she's in her bedroom.' As the girl turned back into the passage Beattie asked, 'Whatever are you doing with her coat?'

'Lily left it behind at the panto. Went off like a penny rocket.'

'You girls,' sighed Beattie, smiling at the youngster. 'I wish I had your energy.' She rested her hand on Dora's shoulder. 'She'll tell me about it when she's ready, I suppose. Now chivvy her up, there's a dear.'

'Right ho, Mrs Forrest.'

There was the sound of water being poured out in the scullery. 'D'you want me to look at that arm?' she called.

'Least of my worries,' he answered morosely.

Beattie shrugged. The direct approach always set up resistance. She would have to, as Albert would put it, draw nigh obliquely. When he came

394

out of the scullery she had her head bent over her sewing.

He stood by the window, staring across the yard. 'You're in my light, son,' she said. He continued to stare out of the window. 'You go and get into the rig of the day, Alec, then we'll have a cup of tea. How will that suit you?'

Abruptly he went out into the passage and up the stairs.

Just as she had poured the tea he came down again and slammed out of the house.

'Oh bugger you,' she snapped. 'Bugger, bugger,' she shouted, then drained her tea, almost scalding herself. The next couple of hours passed in finishing the collars while Dora regaled them with highlights from the pantomime. She was a natural mimic and Beattie was glad of the diversion. What a long weary day to get through before Albert arrived.

'We'll have a bit of a scratch dinner, girls,' she said at midday. 'You can make up at tea-time with Auntie Hester. There's chicken soup and bread and mince-pies to follow.'

'I think we can pass on the pies,' laughed Lily. 'I've eaten so many of them over the last few days I shall begin to look like one.'

'Sweet, fat and round,' teased Dora. They all laughed.

'Shall I go and get Rosie?' asked Lily when they had eaten their fill.

'Why not, my duck, I could do with seeing her cheery face.'

It seemed an age before Lily returned with Rosie dressed in her coat and hat and clutching her sister's hand. 'Hello my pet,' said Beattie, leaning down to kiss the child, 'how's your Mummy?'

'Gone bye-byes,' said Rosie. 'Where Uncle Forrest?'

'I don't know where he's gone,' said Beattie.

'Rosie find him.'

'Miriam looks awful,' whispered Lily. 'I think she's been crying. I had to dress Rosie, she was still in her nightie.'

Beattie sighed. 'Well, an afternoon's rest on her own might help matters.' She ached to go and see her, but feared to intrude, in case an ill-judged word made things worse between the unhappy couple.

As the clock struck two Lily said, 'We might as well be off then,' and gave her grandmother a kiss. 'See you at Auntie's, later.'

Resignedly, Beattie went upstairs. She was setting her hat straight when she heard the front door slam and Alec's footsteps down the passage. Biting her lip she stood indecisively at the top of the stairs. Should she leave him alone or snatch this moment to – what? She didn't know.

'I've forgotten that thread I promised Hester,' she said, as she opened the kitchen door and went past him to rummage in her sewing. 'See you later, son.' Beattie was halfway along the passage when he called to her.

'Don't go, Ma.'

Oh God, she thought as she hung up her coat, let me find the right words. Albert, please, give me some of your wisdom.

'Tea, I'll make us a cup of tea.' He stood clutching the kettle. He ran his hand distractedly through his hair, a gesture familiar to his mother since early childhood and a sure sign of his distress. 'It's all falling apart, Ma. And I can't mend it. I try and try but I just make things worse.'

Beattie spooned some rum into the cups and added a heaped teaspoonful of sugar and set them on a tray.

'She said she'd never, never forgive me,' said Alec, staring into the fire. 'Oh, Christ! Why did he have to come back? Why couldn't he have died?'

Perched on the old piano stool, in front of him, Beattie said, 'Alec, I'm sat here trying to do a jigsaw with only half the pieces. If I'm to be of any use you'll have to give me more to go on.'

'I don't know where to start.'

Beattie sipped her tea. 'Let me ask you a question,' she said. 'When you first told me about Miriam you said everything had been set fair for you to marry. Then, around the time Andrew died, Miriam was badly hurt. Now, this man in the market, was he the one who…?'

'Evil, evil bastard,' Alec shouted, jabbing the poker at the fire and sending a shower of sparks flying up the chimney. 'I wanted to kill him.'

Beattie was startled by Alec's sudden outburst, but anger she could deal with. It was despair that rattled her. Choosing her words carefully, she said, 'So until you met on Christmas Eve neither of you had set eyes on him?'

Her son nodded.

'That must have been a hell of a shock.'

'It was, I leapt straight at him.'

'Alec, Alec.' She leant forward, taking the poker from him and laying it down by the grate. 'I'm not thinking about you. It's Miriam, I'm seeing it from her side. There she is Christmas Eve with the man she's going to marry, with her little girl, everything before her. Suddenly out of the crowd steps the last person she ever wanted to see again and what happens?'

'I hit him. What else could I do?'

'In your shoes, son, I'd've done the same. But, if you're ever to make things right between you and Miriam you've got to see it through her eyes. See how the mere sight of him must have plunged her back in the past, making her feel, again, helpless and terrified.'

'I can see that I frightened her and little Rosie. Ma, I've said I'm sorry over and over.'

'When this man raped her, let's not beat about the bush, that's what all this is about?' Alec nodded. 'You weren't there to protect her. The next time she sees him, what do you do? Abandon her in the crowd and be as violent to this man as he was to her. Then you're carted away covered in blood and she's left to stagger home as best she can with Rosie and all the shopping. Not knowing whether you're dead or alive.'

'What can I do? I know I frightened her, I know that. I'd give anything...'

Beattie leaned forward and put her hand lightly on his bandaged arm. 'You can do nothing, son. You must let her rest and recover, let the shock of it begin to fade.'

398

He rubbed his eyes. 'I don't think I can just wait and do nothing.'

'That's what she had to do all those months when she thought you were lost to her. A young woman, seemingly abandoned, she kept faith with you. All that time she was here, a stranger to us, she waited for you to tell us in your own good time.'

'Christ, Ma,' he said, his voice breaking, 'what if she never forgives me.'

Beattie put her arms around him, 'Sh, son. Come on now, never's a word said in haste and shock. Sh, sh, you're weary. Just cry it all out. It's just you and your old Mum.' Old was what she felt. Old and sad and desperately sorry.

Gasping as if in pain Alec pressed his face against her shoulder and the tears came. The fire hissed and crackled, the clock ticked away and still she held him. Her back ached and her legs felt as if they would scorch from the heat of the fire. She was at the point of shifting her position when Alec shuddered and drew away from her, sinking back into the armchair. He looked at her, smiling shamefacedly, not ready yet to talk.

Beattie looked at her son. As always his sharp features were transformed by his smile. What a face of contrasts. The soft brown eyes with their thick lashes, his pale skin stretched tight over his cheekbones, the full sensual lips set in the black beard. How beautiful he is, she thought, and how different from his father.

For the first time, since standing desolate at the memorial, she was able to think of Joseph without anguish. Perhaps he had not gone from her.

Perhaps it was she who had set him free to be at rest. Perhaps her life was, now, set on a new course.

'Let's just see to that arm of yours and then you can go up and have a sleep,' she said, getting out her box of bandages from the dresser cupboard. The water was still warm in the kettle. She poured some into a basin and spooned in some salt. She set a fresh bandage, some lint and cottonwool on a tray along with the basin and put it down on the table. Gently she unwound the bandage. Alec winced as she took off the lint dressing which was stuck with dried blood. Looking at the deep arrow shape cut into his arm, Beattie felt a fierce anger towards the man who had committed such an outrage. It scored through the centre of his butterfly tattoo, appearing to sever the wings. Although obviously still painful, especially as she swabbed away the dried blood, the edges of the wound were a healthy pink and the arm was not unduly swollen. 'We must keep an eye on this,' she said, 'we don't want it to fester.'

'Thanks, Ma,' said Alec getting to his feet. 'You and Dr Sleep,' he said. 'What would I do without you?'

'Get along with you,' she said with mock impatience.

The clock struck four. That's put paid to my trip to Hester's, Beattie thought wryly. She probably thinks I've been run over by a tram. When I've been down the yard I'll drop her a line and get one of the nippers down the street to drop it in the post.

As she hurried back from the lavatory Beattie saw the light from between the kitchen curtains in the house next-door. What was Miriam doing? she wondered. Was she as heartbroken as her son?

She wrote Hester the briefest of notes pleading a sick headache, pushed it into an envelope and stuck on a stamp. She stood at the front door looking down the street. Michael Rowan was standing at his door opposite, about to take his bicycle into the passage.

'Could you do me a kindness, Michael?' she said. 'Drop this letter into the post-box, would you? I should have been up at my sister-in-law's in Cromwell Road, but time's got away from me.'

'Over at Eastney, isn't it?' he asked, pushing his bike over towards her.

Beattie nodded. 'Opposite the Marine Barracks.'

'I'll nip it up there, if you like. Ma is up at Netley visiting Arthur and I'm at a loose end.'

'Well, if you're sure, Michael. That's most neighbourly. You'll likely catch Lily and Dora up there.'

'I might walk home with them,' he said, grinning at her. 'That would be a bright end to a dull day.'

Poor lad, she thought. Not much of a Christmas for him with his brother crippled and broken in spirit and his mother grieving over him. Watching him cycle down the road Beattie wondered what age Michael was now. Of course, he was two years older than Andrew, making him twenty-two. Beattie sighed. Had he survived

Jutland, her grandson could have been married now with a baby on his knee. No, she would not dwell on that – she had had sadness enough today.

Turning to go indoors she saw Albert walking down the street towards her. Watching him draw closer she felt an immediate lifting of her spirits.

'Beatrice,' he said, his smile full of concern. 'How have you been faring?'

She took his hand and kissed it. 'Oh, Albert, you don't know how much I've missed you.'

If it hadn't been for the uncertain light in the passage, she would have sworn that Albert Pragnell was blushing.

Chapter Thirty-Five

The nightmares had returned to Miriam with an alarming new twist. It was not Taffy's face that woke her, sweating and terrified, but Alec's, his features distorted by rage.

It was now Friday morning, Friday the first of January, the day before her wedding. Miriam stood at the kitchen window, nursing a cup of water, her mind in a ferment of indecision. If only there was a way of being certain, a sign like in the Bible, a voice from the burning bush or a pillar of cloud. Her heart lurched in alarm. Someone was rapping on the back door. The tapping continued. It was Lily. 'Let me in,' she demanded.

'It's only seven o'clock, what's wrong? Is it your Gran or Dad...?' Miriam asked as the girl strode into the kitchen.

'Would you care if he was?' Lily challenged her.

'Of course I would care.' Miriam was stung by the anger in Lily's voice. How dare she come in here, presuming she knew things that were none of her business?

'Dad's ill.'

'Is it his arm?' she said in alarm. 'I saw the bandage on the line yesterday.' Why had she given so little thought to him? It had been all her own wants and wounds. Now she was stricken with guilt.

'You made him feel so bad,' Lily burst out, 'just 'cos he stuck up for you.'

'We were terrified. He could have been killed,' Miriam cried. 'Rose was hysterical. You've no idea what it was like, and yet you come in here as if–' Miriam shrugged, at a loss for words.

'I think Dad wishes he had been killed,' said Lily quietly.

'You're making it up,' Miriam blustered, beginning to feel frightened.

'You haven't seen how unhappy he is. Scared you're going to call off the wedding.'

'Well,' shrugged Miriam defensively, 'that should answer your prayers at any rate.'

For the first time since her bold entry into the kitchen Lily looked uncertain. 'I know I was horrible to you and Dad,' she said, avoiding Miriam's eyes, 'but I'm older now.'

'Sit down,' Miriam said, looking at her with new respect. 'I'll make you a cup of tea.' She began to think of Alec and how he must be feeling. Her fears had been so consuming she'd not given a thought to his anxieties. She set a cup on the table.

'Aren't you having one?'

'No,' said Miriam, 'water's as much as I can swallow at the moment.'

She saw the speculative look in Lily's eyes but chose to ignore it. Fidgeting with a loose strand of cotton on the sleeve of her nightdress, she said, 'I love your Dad and I want to marry him, of course I do, but what happened in the market...' she swallowed hard. 'It terrified me.'

'Why?' Lily demanded. 'I don't understand.'

'It brought everything back.'

'What d'you mean?'

'How helpless I was as a child,' said Miriam, digging her nails into the palms of her other hand. 'The drunken men hitting my mother, then being helpless again that night when that man...'

'But my Dad would never be like that!' Lily was incredulous.

'But he was,' Miriam insisted. 'I saw him with Taffy in the market. Rosie saw him.'

'But he was so angry, that man had been cruel to you. What would you have done if someone hurt Dad or Rosie, really hurt them?'

'I don't know,' said Miriam, her hand shaking as she poured the water into the teapot. 'I would hope somehow...'

'Dad was there face-to-face with the man before he had time to think.' Lily was almost pleading. 'Try to see it from his side.'

404

'It brought it all back. Seeing Taffy again has ruined everything.'

'Only if you let him, Miriam. I know I was a silly, jealous kid but now I understand more. You make Dad happy and that's what I want more than anything. You and Dad and me and my little sister to be a proper family.'

Miriam looked at Lily in her white blouse and black business skirt, her hair pinned up. How changed she was from the wilful child she'd met last year. 'I just need to be sure,' she said.

'Gran always says certainty's for cowards,' said Lily. Miriam blushed. 'I never thought you were cowardly,' Lily went on, helping herself to sugar, 'even when I hated you the strongest.'

'I certainly felt hated. Some of your looks could have turned me to stone.'

Lily smiled shamefacedly and Miriam was reminded of Alec. It had been a weary week of uncertainty. She'd glimpsed him in the yard and in the street but only through the window, never face-to-face. Now she ached to see him.

'You won't let him go to the Registry Office and leave him standing, will you?' Lily asked, breaking into her thoughts.

Miriam shook her head.

'Well I'll be off, now,' Lily said, standing up.

Miriam kissed her cheek. 'It was brave of you to come,' she said.

When she had gone, Miriam sank down into a chair and drank another cup of water. The thought of Alec's deep regret and unhappiness, of his patient waiting for her decision and his daughter's stout defence of him softened her heart, already biased in his favour. Somehow Lily had given her courage. She was still uncertain but the panic had passed.

Taking some notepaper and an envelope from Mr Pragnell's desk she dipped a pen into the inkwell and began to write.

Dearest Alec,

I am sorry to have kept you waiting so long for an answer. What happened at the market brought back terrible memories. But I am trying to put them behind me and look to our future.

Of course I forgive you. The fault lies with Taffy.

Come and see me this morning as there is something I want to tell you.

All my love, Mirry.

PS. I hope your arm is better.

She blotted the paper and slid it into the envelope, before slipping her coat over her nightdress and posting the letter through the Forrest family's letter-box.

The morning dragged by with Mr Pragnell seated immovably at his desk and Rosie settling to nothing. 'Go and feed the birdies,' said Miriam, giving her a bag of crumbs, knowing that she would step over the wall and need someone to bring her back.

Eleven o'clock chimed and still Rosie had not been returned to her, and Mr Pragnell seemed even more firmly rooted to his seat. When she was at the point of screaming, slowly, un-hurriedly he stood up.

'I have several errands,' he said. 'Perhaps lunch

could be delayed until one o'clock?'

The front door shut behind him and Miriam folded up the ironing-blanket and set the clothes-horse around the fire. She ought to go and fetch Rosie.

There were footsteps coming from the passage. 'Mr Pragnell, what have you forgotten?' she asked.

Alec stood there with his arms outstretched. She ran to him, nestling her face against his chest, feeling the steady beating of his heart.

'Just say yes,' he whispered. 'Let's start again from now.'

'Yes,' she breathed.

He kissed her and they walked into the kitchen together. Settling himself in an armchair he drew her onto his lap. 'Thank you for your letter,' he said. 'I was so relieved when I read it. But what's all this about having something to tell me?'

'Where's Rosie, first?' Miriam asked. 'Is she all right with your mother?'

'They're out shopping.'

'But she didn't have her coat.'

Alec chuckled. 'When Albert came out the front door I pinched her hat and coat from the hook in the passage and gave them to Ma before sneaking back in. So, what have you to say for yourself?'

'Do you remember our day on the Isle of Wight?'

He smiled at her. 'Just the two of us, the kissing and loving and the Boy Scouts, and being bitten alive...'

'Shh! Do you remember saying something

407

about a label? "Made in the Isle of Wight"?'

Miriam looked at his face as she spoke, watching his expression change from amusement to startled delight as he took in what she was saying. 'You're having our child?' he gasped.

She nodded.

'Mirry, Mirry,' he said, laughing then covering her face with kisses. 'That's wonderful news. Why didn't you write and tell me? When will he be born?' He became suddenly serious. 'Are you feeling all right?'

'I'm fine,' she said, smiling reassuringly at him. 'Baby should be here in early June.'

'Stand up and let me look at you,' he said.

Miriam laughed as he knelt down in front of her and kissed her belly. 'We've so much to look forward to,' he said.

It was ten-thirty on her wedding morning. Miriam was surprised at her own calmness. In two more hours she and Alec would be married. The bogus Mrs Naylor with her pawnshop wedding-ring would be no more. She would be a proper naval wife, going to the post office each week with her allotment book. Mrs Miriam Forrest with her daughter Rosemary Forrest and later young Joseph or Daisy.

The only disappointment was the letter from Aunt Florrie reporting a fall she'd had on an icy pavement. Enclosed with it was a crisp white five-pound note and a hand-embroidered handkerchief with the initial 'V' clumsily stitched to the corner.

Your mother sewed this hankie when she was about eleven. I thought it might do for the something old on your outfit. That way she could still play a part in your day.
Will be up to see you in the spring,
Regards to Alec,
Love and good fortune, Aunt Florrie.

Miriam ran her fingers over the faded, lumpy stitches and wondered fleetingly what her mother had been feeling on her wedding-day. She sighed and tucked it into her pocket.

'According to the weather forecast in here, you'll have to tie your bonnet very tight. It's going to be cold with an easterly wind,' said Mr Pragnell, standing in the kitchen doorway with the paper in his hand.

Rosie bounced out of her chair and ran to him.

'When you're properly dressed, young lady,' he said, 'your Grandma wants to see you. I must take some chairs next-door or she'll read me the Riot Act.'

'Come on pet, let's get you into your new frock,' said Miriam, prising Rosie's arms from around Mr Pragnell's legs.

She dressed her in the green silk frock she'd bought weeks ago, combed her tawny curls and put on her matching green bonnet. Rosie looked enchanting. She stuck out her chest and ran her fingers down the bodice of her dress. 'It's all slippy, Mummy. You feel.' Miriam touched the silky folds then hugged her daughter tightly.

'Go see Granny,' Rosie said, struggling out of Miriam's arms.

'Please, can Mrs Forrest send her to me again just before twelve to give us time to walk to the Registry Office?' she asked a breathless Mr Pragnell, resting after hauling six dining-chairs down from upstairs. He nodded before taking Rosie by the hand.

Almost a bride. Miriam stared at her reflection in the living room mirror. The sky-blue collar of her blouse softened the stark navy of her costume jacket. She twisted her hair into a knot at the nape of her neck before taking hold of her soft-brimmed velour hat. The matching blouse and hat intensified the deep blue of her eyes. Smoothing her skirt over her gently swelling belly she whispered, 'We're going to be happy, all of us.'

'Quite, quite beautiful,' Mr Pragnell said, standing in the doorway.

Miriam blushed with pleasure. 'You look very elegant, too, Mr Pragnell.'

'Not bad for an old buzzard,' he mocked, tucking his Paisley scarf inside his collar before putting on his homburg hat. He coughed uncertainly. 'Miriam,' he said, using her Christian name for the first time. 'There's a little matter I would like to discuss with you.'

Miriam twisted a button on her jacket, unable to guess what the matter could be.

'Who will be accompanying you and Rosemary to the Registry Office?'

'Well, nobody, Mr Pragnell,' she said.

'Mrs Forrest will be escorted by her son and the best man. I would like to accompany you, if that meets with your approval?'

'That would be lovely, Mr Pragnell,' Miriam

said, touched by his kindness. 'It would be like you were my father, so to speak.'

Mr Pragnell shook his head. 'I would not presume to suggest such a thing. But I wanted to render that small service.'

Miriam smiled. 'Thank you very much, Mr Pragnell,' she said, startling the old man by kissing him on the cheek. 'You're a real gentleman.'

'I try to be,' he said quietly.

There was a tap on the kitchen window and Alec's mother came into the kitchen with Rosie. Dressed in her best black gabardine coat and a purple cloche hat, she had the dignity of a duchess. 'You go and show Uncle Paggle your lucky horseshoe,' she instructed her granddaughter.

Miriam blushed. It was the first time she had seen her since leaving early on Christmas Day. 'I'm so sorry about last week,' she mumbled.

Mrs Forrest brushed her words aside with an impatient sweep of the hand. 'You look lovely, Miriam,' she said, her voice warm with affection. 'I must be off now. Alec and young Michael Rowan are waiting for me next-door.' She kissed Miriam on the cheek. 'Bye Albert,' she called.

'Are you sure as sure can be?' asked Mr Pragnell, proffering his arm.

Miriam smiled and nodded. After giving the bridegroom's party a ten minute start they set off. Rosie trotted down the street in front of them, chatting and waving her horseshoe. It was bitingly cold, making them quicken their steps.

'Forrest-Slattery wedding?' asked an usher

411

outside the turreted brick Registry Office.

'Yes, Chief,' said Mr Pragnell, acknowledging the old sailor's uniform.

'The Marriage Room upstairs, if you please,' he said.

Panic-stricken at the sea of faces in front of her, Miriam gripped Mr Pragnell's arm.

She stared down at the faded green carpet, gradually becoming aware of two polished black shoes approaching her. She looked up into Alec's eyes and everyone else ceased to matter. Mr Pragnell released his arm and sat down behind her.

'Good afternoon, Mr Forrest and Miss Slattery,' said the Registrar. 'We'll just check the accuracy of the details I shall enter on your certificate, with our register.'

Miriam was conscious of the warmth transferring from Alec's fingers to her own as they were shown to a pair of faded leather chairs in front of the Registrar's table. From a door behind the table came the Superintendent, pencil-thin, in a pin-stripe suit. 'This room has been solemnised by law for the celebration of marriage,' he announced, 'and you are all here today to witness the joining together in matrimony of Alec Joseph Forrest and Miriam Violet Slattery. If anyone here knows of any lawful impediment why these two should not be joined in matrimony they should declare it now.'

The silence throbbed with awful possibilities, then there was the sound of a chair being overturned.

Miriam stared straight ahead, her heart pounding.

'Beatrice, Beatrice, are you all right?' Mr Pragnell's voice was sharp with anxiety.

'Ma's fainted,' Alec whispered to her, 'but Albert's looking after her.

'Smelling-salts, quickly,' Mr Pragnell rapped out.

Please, please let her be all right, Miriam prayed. Nothing must spoil it now, I'm so close to being married. There was a lot of shuffling behind her and murmured thanks from Mr Pragnell.

'May we proceed?' the Superintendent asked, and she heard Beattie give a faltering 'Yes.' Alec turned to her and made his declaration.

Miriam made hers, hesitating over the familiar words. 'I know not of any lawful impediment why I, Miriam Violet Slattery, may not be joined in matrimony to Alec Joseph Forrest.' The Superintendent nodded and Michael Rowan handed Alec the ring.

'I call upon these persons here present to witness that I, Alec Joseph Forrest, do take thee, Miriam Violet Slattery, to be my lawful wedded wife.'

She could feel Alec's hand tremble as he slid the ring on her finger. All her fears dropped away from her. They were really truly married. Happiness welled up inside her and she could see her joy mirrored in his face.

'I give you this ring as a symbol of my fidelity and love,' he said, holding her hand and looking into her eyes. 'May it seal our partnership now and forever.'

'I accept your ring with joy and in the loving

413

spirit in which it was given to me,' Miriam replied, in the words agreed between them, 'and will wear it faithfully all my life.' She wanted the moment to be fixed forever between them as they stood together, hand-in-hand.

The Registrar cleared his throat and shuffled his feet and the moment was gone. He handed a gold-nibbed fountain pen to Alec to sign his name. When it was her turn, Miriam found the pen slippery and cumbersome. After signing she gave her husband a tentative smile.

'Hello, Mrs Forrest,' Alec whispered.

Then it was the turn of the witnesses, Alec's mother and Michael Rowan.

The Registrar blotted everyone's signatures. Alec paid the fee and handed the certificate to Miriam. 'D'you want to keep the Marriage Lines in your handbag, Mrs Forrest?' he asked.

Laughing, she tucked them away, and they walked out of the room and down the stairs to a flurry of confetti.

'Congratulations!'

'Daisy, oh, Daisy, I'm so glad you could come.' Miriam's heart soared at the sight of her friend. 'I was worried you'd not got my letter,' she said, hugging her tightly.

'You know me. I was never one for writing much.'

'This is my husband, Alec,' she said proudly. 'Alec, meet my dearest friend.'

Daisy's round weather-beaten face shone with joy. She dragged her brown beret off her head and shoved it into the pocket of her shapeless tweed coat before thrusting her hand at Alec.

'Ooh! This is a real happy ending,' she cried. 'Ever so pleased to meet you Alec.'

'I hope you'll come back with us for a bite to eat,' said Alec, 'and Henry, wherever he is.'

'He's too busy,' said Daisy proudly. 'Market gardens don't run themselves. But I'll come and gladly.' She looked eagerly around. 'Where's Rosie? I'm famished for the sight of her.'

'Look,' said Miriam, 'she's with Lily, that pretty girl in the fur hat.'

Daisy darted away and Miriam was swallowed up by well-wishers.

'Welcome to the family,' said Alec's mother, detaching herself from Mr Pragnell's protective arm. She gave Miriam an affectionate hug. 'I think a new daughter is a fair exchange for a troublesome son.'

'Get on with you,' laughed Alec, squeezing her hand. 'What were you up to back there, falling off the chair? You sure you're all right now, Ma?'

'Right as rain, son,' said his mother, her face paler than usual but her eyes bright with excitement. 'Albert took charge of me. I think it was missing my breakfast that did it.'

They were all milling about on the pavement laughing and talking together.

'Smile please,' said Michael Rowan, flourishing his box camera.

'Lily, Rosie don't dash off, join the picture,' said Alec, beckoning them forward.

'Come on, Mother, we want a picture with you,' said Miriam, squeezing Beattie's hand.

'Well, it'll have to be quick,' she said, 'I've left Mrs Rowan holding the fort. I want to be back home to see to the punch and welcome every-one.'

Lily was beaming, especially when Michael passed the camera to his mother and stood beside her.

'Happy?' asked Alec, taking her hand.

'Yes, yes, yes,' breathed Miriam. 'I can't believe it's true. We're really married.' She touched his injured right arm. 'Is it healing all right?' she asked.

'Sore still,' he said. 'You'll have to be gentle with me, Mrs Forrest. I shall need breakfast in bed and no undue excitement.'

Miriam giggled.

Laughing and chatting the wedding party made its way back to Lemon Street.

As they passed the Vines' house, Blyth and the twins rushed out flinging confetti at everyone. 'You havin' a party?' Blyth asked.

'Get your sisters to come over the back in an hour and we'll find you something,' said Alec.

'How long's an hour?' Blyth asked Mercy.

'Bleedin' ages,' she muttered.

Beattie was standing at the front door beaming at everyone. 'Where's the happy pair? Let's get you seated first.'

A rich blend of lavender polish, mothballs, sherry punch and pickled onions wafted towards them. Miriam and Alec perched themselves almost on the windowsill behind the greatly extended table. All Beattie's best china had been pressed into service. There were plates of cheese sandwiches, dishes of pickles, slices of pressed tongue, bowls of trifle and a large fruit cake

416

encircled with a gold satin ribbon.

Beattie handed round brimming glasses of sherry punch. 'Toast the Bride and Groom,' she commanded.

Warmed by sherry and good wishes, Miriam smiled her thanks to everyone. They all looked so splendid in their best clothes. Uncle George's collar was starched to suffocation and his Boer War medals clinked as he reached across the table for a slice of pork pie. Beattie was resplendent in her purple satin blouse and Lily glowed in a red velvet jacket. Michael Rowan looked immaculate in his uniform with its white satin wedding ribbon, threaded through the lanyard. Nervously he tapped the table with a fork.

'I would like to welcome everyone to this wedding party for Alec and Miriam.'

There were loud cheers.

'Most of you will be expecting Alec's friend Jim Stenson to be here. Unfortunately, at the last minute, he was drafted to the Mediterranean. Although not the first choice, I feel, as Andrew's friend, that I am his representative on this happy day.'

There was a short pause and everyone looked solemn.

'Thank you Michael,' said Alec quietly.

'Hurry up lad or the beer'll go flat,' called out George.

'Leave him alone,' everyone protested.

Undeterred Michael said, 'I would like to read you out the telegram received from the stokers' mess in HMS *Manchester* lying at Scapa Flow.

Dear Shipmate,

As you tie the knot be grateful for the bride you've got,

She'll keep you warm when you're ashore and when you've gone she'll semaphore,

Please Jack come home the nights are cold and I love you more than gold.

Report your position at midnight we hope your line will get a bite.

Ever yours, Chippy, Spud, Knocker and Dusty.'

Michael sat down, scarlet-faced, amid cheers and laughter.

Alec got to his feet. 'May I propose a toast to the four beautiful women in my life: my dear wife, Miriam, my mother Beatrice, and my two daughters, Lily and Rosie. To the four beauties!'

'The four beauties,' everyone chorused.

'The cake,' said Beattie, handing the knife to Alec.

He and Miriam cut the first slice together and then Aunt Hester took over. She was about to take a bite from her cake when Alec stood up again.

'Friends,' he said, 'this is not only her wedding-day but it's almost my wife's twenty-first birthday. I think we should all raise our glasses to the new Mrs Forrest on her special day.'

Miriam laughed. 'What with all the excitement, I'd forgotten all about my birthday,' she said.

'We hadn't,' said Lily, 'had we, Rosie?'

The little girl had relinquished her horseshoe and thrust a large silver cardboard key into

Miriam's lap. 'Birthday, birthday!' she shouted.

'Thank you,' said Miriam, kissing both of them. 'You especially, Lily,' she whispered. 'I couldn't have done it without you.'

'Yes, you could,' said Lily, smiling at her. 'You just needed a friendly nudge.'

Everyone joined in singing Happy Birthday to You. Miriam looked around her at all the smiling faces, touched by the warmth of their affection. She rested her hand on her belly where, as if in response to all the good wishes, her child made its first fluttering movement.

Chapter Thirty-Six

The wedding party in the Forrest household was almost at an end. Toasts had been drunk, speeches made, ham sliced, pickles speared, songs sung and cheeks kissed. Lily was enjoying every moment. Wedged between Michael and Dora she sipped her sherry punch relishing its rich raisiny flavour. Today she felt herself to be an attractive young woman, one whose wise words had secured the success of the day. Even Miriam had acknowledged it.

Beneath all the feasting, toasting and general good wishes another appetite was at work. It was apparent in the laughter and nudging and winks aimed at her father and Miriam. It was crackling in the looks exchanged between Harry and Dora and it urged Uncle George to the raucous singing of 'A little of what you fancy does you good.'

Lily was alternately embarrassed and excited. Later in the evening she and Gran would be looking after Rosie so that Dad could have the night alone with his new wife. She remembered how aroused she had been glimpsing the stranger in Miriam's kitchen, all that time ago, and how acutely uncomfortable she'd been to discover it was her own father.

And then there was Michael. She had known him all her life and yet, today, they seemed no longer childhood friends, but on the verge of something more. Every so often she would catch him looking at her with a question in his eyes. And then he would catch her looking at him and drop his gaze. Michael's eyes were a light brown with green glints in them and fringed by long black lashes. Lily was fascinated: why had she never noticed them before? There was a cleft in his chin that she wanted to kiss. Then there were his long fingers presently twisting an elastic band between them as he spoke with Dad. As he turned towards her she pretended interest in her plate.

'There was something I wanted to ask you. That argie-bargie at the panto. What was it all about? That girl in the yellow frock looked ready to scratch your eyes out.'

'Well,' said Lily unwillingly, 'I spilled wine on her frock. It was all an accident, of course, but I couldn't blame Ruby for being angry. I felt a real fool in front of everyone.'

'I should think most people were on your side, Lily. I was, anyway.'

Lily blushed. 'Our head of the workroom, Miss

Pearson, tried all sorts to get the stain out. Soda water, salt, everything, but it was hopeless. So in the end she lent Ruby the six guineas the dress cost and she's taking it out of her wages.'

'What's the six guineas about?'

'The dress wasn't hers. She had got it out on approval from Handleys and thought she could wear it for the evening and take it back no questions asked. But I spoilt it for her.' Lily shrugged. 'So, I've been giving her a shilling a week because I feel partly responsible.'

'I suppose it's the excitement of dressing better than you can afford and having the life of a lady, if only for an evening,' said Michael thoughtfully.

'She'd have got away with it, if it hadn't been for me.'

'Well, you played fair with her,' he said smiling at her.

Gran touched her arm. 'Chippy wants you. He won't come in. Go and see to him, there's a love.'

Reluctantly Lily wedged past everyone and made her way to the front door.

'I'll come with you,' said Michael, 'I could do with some air.'

As usual Chippy was dancing about from one foot to the other. 'What is it?' said Lily, stepping out into the dark street. He thrust a string shopping-bag into her arms. Inside was a small newspaper parcel tied tightly with string.

'It's for you. This bloke gave it me.'

'What was he like?' laughed Lily, her curiosity aroused.

'Yellowy hair and posh voice.' Chippy's face was creased in puzzlement. 'What d'you reckon it is?'

421

Lily wanted to be sick. She flung the bag away from her. 'Chippy, I'll tell you tomorrow. Just go away. You mustn't,' she shouted as Michael went to pick it up. 'It's horrible, horrible.'

'You don't know what it is yet, Lily.'

'I do, I do,' she sobbed. 'How could he do it? It's so wicked.'

Michael held her firmly by the shoulders. 'Let's go in our house and you can tell me about it.' He led her across the street, carrying the bag in his other hand. After lighting the lamp in the kitchen, and stirring up the fire, he placed the bag on the table and drew out a chair for her.

Lily sat on the edge of it, chewing her hand. 'Put it on the floor,' she cried.

'Shall I open it for you?' Michael asked.

'Take it away.'

'Why don't I throw it out in the dust-bin?'

'You can't, you can't,' she sobbed. 'It's Lloyd, I know it is.'

'That little monkey of Granny Dowell's? You don't think he's in there?' Michael looked at her astounded. Lily nodded.

'We'd better open him up quickly,' he said, reaching for the bag, 'or he'll be...'

'He's dead. I know it.'

Carefully Michael picked up the bag. 'Lily,' he said quietly, 'we must find out for certain. It may be a nasty joke. It could just be a bag of earth or wood-shavings. If it is Lloyd we must tell Granny Dowell.'

'I can't look at him,' Lily said. 'I'm not that brave.'

'I'll take him down to the lav and light the

candle and cut open the string, see for certain.'

Lily nodded and Michael went outside closing the door behind him. She paced about the kitchen thinking about Bernard snatching at her, in the doorway, after the pantomime. His breath hot in her face, his voice no longer polished but rough and impatient. He'd never cared for her, she was just another silly little shop-girl. She shivered at the memory of his furious face when she'd laughed at him, at the slow throat-cutting gesture he'd made as the monkey capered off into the darkness. It was her laughing that had killed Lloyd.

The back door opened again. Before saying anything, Michael went to the sink. He washed his hands then rinsed his mouth with a cup of water. Lily knew what he had found.

'What a low cowardly thing to do,' he said, shaking his head disbelievingly. 'Poor little wretch.'

Lily began to tremble. 'He said he'd cut his throat. Tell me he didn't.'

'Just looked as if he'd gone to sleep. Some sort of powder round his mouth. Probably poisoned his food. Let's hope it didn't cause him any pain.' He shook his head. 'What a bad, bad business.'

'I just wish, I just wish,' said Lily, her voice trembling, 'that I could go and really hurt him like he's hurt Lloyd.'

'That would make you as bad as he is, Lily,' said Michael.

'What can we do with him?' she sobbed. 'We can't throw him away like rubbish.'

'Take him to Granny Dowell's.'

'We can't tell her he's been poisoned, that would be too horrible. Couldn't you bury him in your garden? We could just say nothing and after a while she'll give up looking for him.'

'Lily,' Michael took both her hands in his, 'you can't really believe that's the right thing to do.'

'No,' she said looking away from him, 'just the easiest.'

Michael put his arms around her and she sobbed against his shoulder. He held her close and she felt warmed and comforted. 'Poor little monkey,' she gasped.

'Poor Lily,' said Michael. 'You sit there and we'll think what's best to do. What's behind all this? Do you want to tell me? It's up to you.'

'It's my fault really,' she said, taking her hankie out of her pocket and drying her eyes.

'That can't be true.'

'I was silly, Michael, I just rushed home from the panto and he followed me. I thought he was being nice to me and then–' Lily faltered. 'Well it all got nasty, and poor Lloyd got mixed up in it all. He jumped off a windowledge onto Bernard's head and ran off with his hat. And I laughed at him. Oh, I wish, I wish I hadn't. It made him so angry.'

'It was that fellow that bought you and Dora the drinks at the panto. A proper lounge lizard. It's all right, Lily.' He held up his hand. 'I shan't go and hit him. Someone else will do that eventually.'

'I've been so stupid,' she said, 'and Lloyd has paid for it.'

'I think we should take him to Granny. Face up

424

to it and get it over. You don't want to have it hanging over you all night. But first, if you like, we could have a cup of cocoa to warm ourselves up.'

'Let's get it all over with in one big lump,' said Lily, getting to her feet. 'I'll be all right, just as long as I don't have to look at him.'

'We'll see it through together,' said Michael, squeezing her hand.

Lily paced about while he went out into the yard and collected the string-bag.

The two of them stood shivering in the darkness outside number nine waiting for the door to be opened.

'Havin' our supper,' said Chippy, fork in hand. 'You come to tell me about that bag I give you?'

'Who is it, Chips?' Granny's voice quavered from behind him.

'That Lily girl and Mrs Rowan's boy.'

Granny Dowell, frying-pan in hand, peered out at them. 'You're Beattie's young maid and Esther's boy,' she said. 'What you be wantin' this time of night?'

'It's private, Mrs Dowell,' said Michael. 'Can we come in?'

'You best had,' she said, turning her back on them, her silvery plaits swinging behind her. 'Our chitterlings will be getting cold.' Lily and Michael followed the ample figure inside her house. Chippy had gone ahead with the candle.

'Sit you down on the sofa,' she instructed. 'Cast those clothes to one side.'

Lily felt sick. The room stank of stale lard, unwashed clothes and urine. Granny Dowell,

425

barefoot and in a voluminous nightie, turned her back on her guests and spooned the blackened contents of the frying-pan into tin plates. She and her son began to eat. 'What's your purpose?' asked Granny, after spearing the last of the chitterlings into her mouth.

'Someone found your monkey, Granny,' said Michael.

'Where'd they find him? Where? Where?' demanded the old woman. 'Chippy's been scourin' the streets all day.'

'They gave it to Chippy to give to Lily. It was in this bag he brought her.'

'They couldn't get 'im in no bag,' Granny cried. 'My Lloyd's way too lively fer no bag.' She glared at Michael. 'What you meaning, young man?'

'When they found him he was dead.'

'Let me see him,' she said hoarsely, snatching the bag. Michael had re-wrapped and re-tied the bundle. Granny weighed it in her arms. She peeled back a corner of the paper and then sank back into her chair. Cradling the bundle in her arms she began to rock back and forth, tears running down her seamed brown face. 'My little pal,' she sobbed, 'my dear, dear little pal.'

Lily wanted to run away. It was all too smelly and muddly and awful. Chippy sat pulling his fingers until the knuckles cracked making her want to scream.

'Would you like me to come and dig a hole in the yard and bury him for you?' Michael asked. 'It would have to be tomorrow morning. It's too dark now.'

Lily stared at Granny Dowell's large bare feet, at the swollen joints making her big toes point away from each other at a quarter to three. She forced herself to focus on the feet and not on the limp parcel in the old woman's arms.

'I'd be obliged, young man,' said Granny, after a long pause when Lily began to think she hadn't heard what Michael had said. 'That would be fitting. And you must come,' she said turning to Lily, 'and those little maids over yonder, and the little shaver and Miriam's babe. All must see my little Lloyd off to the kingdom. For He has hidden things from the wise and revealed them to the simple hearts of children.'

Lily looked up into Granny Dowell's face and saw wisdom in her dark eyes. 'I'll get them all together,' she said.

'I'll come along about half-past nine and get the ground ready,' said Michael, getting to his feet, 'and Lily could bring everyone about ten.' Granny nodded and Chippy shuffled to the door behind them.

Lily and Michael stood together under the lamplight after Chippy had shut the door.

'It wasn't as bad as I thought it was going to be,' she said.

'But not something I'd want to do again,' said Michael, shivering.

'D'you want to come back to the party?'

'I'm not in the mood, now,' he said. 'Besides the lights are on at home so Ma will be there. I'll see you tomorrow.'

'Thank you, Michael, for everything. I would have panicked without you.'

He put his hand on her shoulder. 'We're friends, Lily,' he smiled down at her. 'Tomorrow won't be half as bad.'

Reluctantly she turned away. When she walked into the kitchen she found Gran sitting in the armchair with Rosie asleep on her lap. 'Hello Lily, you sorted out Chippy?' asked Gran, looking questioningly at her.

'Yes, Gran,' she said. 'Can I tell you all about it tomorrow, only it's a bit involved?'

Gran nodded. 'Tell you what you can do. Take Rosie up to your bed. My leg's gone to sleep and I'm anxious to follow it. Ethel and Albert cleared up for me so we can have a good pow-wow in the morning.'

Lily slid Rosie into her arms and struggled up the stairs with her. Gran followed behind her and opened the bedroom door and turned down the bedclothes. Lily was comforted by the warmth of Rosie beside her, as she lay in the darkness. It had been a peculiar day, starting out so joyfully and ending in such a muddle of different feelings. The only certainty was that she was cured of her passion for Bernard and held him in the greatest contempt. She was still trying to decide exactly what she felt for Michael when she fell asleep.

'Poor Mrs Dowell,' said Gran the next morning, when Lily gave her an edited account of the events of the night before. 'That little monkey was like a child to her. Let me see what flowers we can give you to take along. There's these two or three chrysanthemums Hester brought yesterday.' Gran looked about her. 'Or there's this pot of daffs that Daisy brought. I suppose by rights they belong to Miriam but I'm sure she'll see it's a good cause.'

'I'll take the daffs,' said Lily. 'What d'you think about taking Rosie with me?'

'You go and gather the Vines together and I'll get little Missie here dressed and ready.'

'A funeral,' said Mary, standing in her doorway arms crossed, like a woman of forty or more. 'We only just had a wedding. 'Ere you lot, Granny's monkey's died.' Faith and Mercy burst into tears and after watching them Blyth joined in.

'Poor little bugger,' sighed Mary. 'What time d'you want us?'

'About half an hour. I'll go and get Rosie. See you at Granny's.'

The door to number nine was open and the funeral party trooped in, shepherded by Chippy looking scrubbed to within an inch of his life and wearing a tweed jacket several sizes too big. Granny, with a black scarf wound around her head and a coat of indeterminate colour, was in the yard holding a small cardboard box.

Michael stood leaning on a spade. In the centre of a patch of withered grass under the kitchen window he had prepared Lloyd's grave. It was such a small yard there was barely room for everyone to stand around it. For some reason they held hands and looked to Granny for a signal.

'All you young people knew and loved little Lloyd,' she said. Everyone looked at the little box. 'Before we return him to the earth I want all of you to say something to mark his passing.' She

429

looked around her. 'You being the oldest maid shall begin.'

Lily coughed nervously. 'Lloyd brought us the news of the Armistice. He came and tapped on our window with a flag in his hand.'

'He was a real little character,' said Michael. 'I remember seeing him on a summer evening, dressed as a sailor, sat on Granny's shoulder while she drank her ale.'

''E pinched birdseed out of Drake's cage, and Grandad Onslow called him a bleedin' little varmit.' Granny Dowell laughed. 'That he did, young Mary,' she said.

'All things bright and beautiful,
All creatures great and small,
All things wise and wonderful
The Lord God made them all,'

sang the twins in high true voices.

'I got you a 'nana,' said Blyth, handing a blackened speckled banana to Granny Dowell.

'Food for the journey,' she said, smiling at him.

'Monkey gone bye-byes,' said Rosie solemnly.

Chippy stood, the picture of dejection, sobbing quietly and rubbing his nose with the sleeve of his jacket. 'Family, 'e was family,' he managed to gasp.

Granny knelt with some difficulty and put the box into the earth and covered it with a woollen blanket, placing Blyth's banana on the top. 'Not a sparrow falls to the earth but Our Heavenly Father knows of it,' she said. 'We shall remember this, one of God's creatures, who brought us laughter and joy in all the days of his short life.'

Everyone sprinkled earth on the little coffin and Michael had soon covered it over. He took the daffodil out of the pot and planted it over the grave.

'Nana all dirty,' said Rosie looking mystified.

Granny Dowell stood for some moments in silence. 'Thank you for coming,' she said. 'I'm an old foolish woman but you have done me a great kindness.' She reached into the pocket of her coat and took out a bag of sweets. Handing them around she said, 'With my Lloyd's good wishes.'

Mary and the children trooped back through the house. Granny turned to Lily and Michael. 'I want you two to join Chippy and me for a drink,' she said, 'just to round things off.

'To Lloyd,' said Granny, raising her cup of ale.

'Lloyd,' said Lily, swallowing the bitter liquid with some difficulty.

'To friendship,' said Michael, smiling at her.

Chapter Thirty-Seven

She could not have survived the last couple of weeks without him, of that Beattie was certain. She had clung to Albert as if he were a lifebelt.

He had stayed with her, after the wedding, until the last plate was dried and put away. Sensing her deflation he'd said, 'It's your birthday next Saturday. I think we should have a celebration. Why don't I take you out to lunch? Tell Douglas

Fairbanks and the Prince of Wales that you're otherwise engaged.'

It was now Saturday the tenth of January, her sixty-fifth birthday, and Beattie was impatient for her treat. Sitting at her dressing-table she took a small jewellery-box from the bottom drawer and opened it. Inside was the forget-me-not brooch that Albert had given her for her eighteenth birthday. He had pinned it to her dress and kissed her. She had not worn it since.

Why wear it today?

All her energy and will had been focused on the wedding, getting Alec and Miriam safely married. Once that had been achieved she began to examine her own changed position. Her son had now gone from her and in the next few years her granddaughter would follow suit. She would be alone. Joseph had now been dead almost as many years as they had been husband and wife. Beattie sighed. What a poor substitute memory was for the physical presence of her husband. How shadowy and insubstantial he had become. She realised that her grieving was over now, and she would have to seek her consolation among the living.

She pinned the brooch to the cream blouse Lily had helped her to make. Wearing Albert's brooch signalled her awareness of a change in their relationship. There was a tension between them, a way of looking at one another as if each were making a new discovery. As she smoothed a grey wisp of hair into place Beattie said to herself, 'That's more than enough soul-searching for one day, my girl. Life goes on and you with it.'

Promptly at twelve Albert knocked at her front door. He was immaculate in grey pinstripe suit and maroon silk tie. 'Happy Birthday, Beatrice,' he said, kissing her on the cheek.

'Thank you,' she said, startled at this new formality between them. Their normal greeting was a hug, especially on birthdays. 'I'll get my gloves. Do you think we'll need to take the umbrella?'

'The weather won't matter today. I've ordered a taxi for us.'

'My stars, Albert, you are pushing the boat out,' gasped Beattie. 'I've never ridden in a motor car in my life.'

'I want this to be a day to remember,' he said, shyly.

'Did Alec get off all...'

'Miriam told me to tell...'

'No, you first, Albert.'

'Beatrice, what were you going to say?'

This was ridiculous. Why were they suddenly so awkward with each other? They leapt nervously at the loud rapping on the front door.

'Taxi for Mr Pragnell,' said a man in a black coat and peaked cap. Behind him, parked outside her house, was a large black car.

'Yes, thank you,' said Albert, taking her arm as the driver held open the door. 'Your carriage awaits, my dear.'

Beattie smiled, too flustered to speak. Half the street were on the pavement gawping at her as she seated herself beside Albert on the soft leather upholstery. There was a smell of polish and cigars. Her mouth dried and she clutched the looped handle at the side of the window as the driver started up the engine and the car juddered into life. She gave a serene smile to the vinegary Mrs Perks scowling at her from her front window and then burst out laughing. 'I can just imagine what she's thinking. "Look at Beattie Forrest, putting on the swank. Who does she think she is, bleedin' Mary Pickford?"' They both laughed and became comfortable with each other.

'The Continental Café, Commercial Road, please driver,' said Albert.

'This is a novelty,' said Beattie, still clutching the handle, 'sweeping past everyone like royalty. I feel like waving.'

'And why not, my dear,' smiled Albert. 'This is your day.'

The car sped up Queen Street and along The Hard, past admirals taking pink gins at the Keppel's Head, ratings knocking back their ale at the Ship Anson and nippers sharing bread pudding at Driver's Café.

'We're going the wrong way,' said Beattie, 'but never mind. Let's swan through Southsea past all the posh shops.'

'Driver,' said Albert, 'please loop around Southsea and then down through Elm Grove.'

'Right you are, Sir.'

'I shan't forget this in a hurry, Albert. I am enjoying myself.'

They glided past the elegant shops in Southsea and eventually arrived outside the large bowed windows of the Continental Café, its name cut out in coloured glass. Beattie studied the display of chocolate in one window, and the roast turkey in a silver tureen offset by fans of crisp white serviettes. Albert paid for the taxi and the driver opened the door for her and she walked the few steps across the pavement to the Café entrance.

'Good morning Madam, Sir,' said a waiter in bow-tie and tails. 'Have you made a reservation?'

'Table for two in the name of Pragnell,' said Albert.

'Your coat, Madam.'

Beattie swallowed hard as the waiter stood beside her, hands outstretched. This was going to take a bit of getting used to. Her feet sank into the thick carpet and she was dazzled by the snow-white tablecloths topped by stiff mitred napkins seeming to stretch to infinity. The walls were hung with mirrors interspersed by brass hat-stands, and towering green ferns in brass pots. On each table was a cut-glass vase containing fresh white carnations.

The waiter took her coat. 'Ah, yes, Sir, Madam. James will show you to your table.'

They passed through the lobster bar with its marble-topped tables to the dining-room. The distance from the front door to their table seemed enormous. Beattie felt exposed to the eyes of the other diners, as she followed the waiter to a corner table. He drew back the swirly bentwood chair and she sank into it gratefully. Her handbag, what should she do with it? There was no room on the immaculate table and she could hardly sit with it on her lap. Covertly she looked about her while Albert ordered two dry sherries.

435

'Underneath, by your feet,' he whispered. She shot him a grateful glance before setting it down on the floor.

He took her hand and gave it a reassuring squeeze. 'I hope you're going to enjoy yourself, Beatrice. You look splendid. Some of the people eating here are a bit puffed up and showy but I thought it would make you laugh, seeing all of them taking themselves so seriously.'

Beattie sighed. It was going to be all right. She looked around her. A hard-faced woman with a peacock feather in her hat sat smoking a cigarette in a long black holder. A jowly old matron peered at her menu through a lorgnette.

'Looks a bit like a bloodhound,' murmured Albert as the waiter brought the sherry. Beattie giggled.

'To you, Beatrice, a Happy Birthday, my dear.'

She sipped the sherry, unprepared for its dry medicinal taste. 'Thank you, Albert,' she said, trying not to wince. 'To Alec and Miriam and the New Year.'

'We seem to have forgotten that in all our busyness. I wonder what 1920 will bring us.'

'Well,' said Beattie, resolutely drinking her sherry, 'the Peace has been a bit of a disappointment so far. Everything seems so unsettled. Dockyard maties being laid off in their hundreds or on short time, poor sailors still out in the Baltic, waiting to come home, troops off to Ireland and people without homes or work or food.'

'The Peace was seen as a magic wand,' said Albert. 'It was supposed to cure everything. It's

436

just lifted the lid and shown us what a mountain of work there is to be done to right everything.'

'I wish there was a mountain of work. I suppose that was one thing about the war, it kept everyone busy.'

Albert passed her the menu. 'I declare this table a neutral zone. We can only talk about your birthday.'

'Why don't you choose for me, Albert? I fancy playing the helpless, rich widow today.'

Albert chuckled. 'That will be a novelty for you.' He beckoned the waiter. 'The lady and I will have Pâté d'Italie. He raised his eyebrows questioningly. 'Fillet of whiting and sauce with boiled potatoes and peas, I think. Have you a chilled Sauterne available?'

'Oh yes, sir. Château La Flora Blanche.'

Beattie studied Albert as he conferred with the waiter. She looked at him appraisingly as if she were, indeed, the rich helpless widow. His white hair, curling behind his ears, gave him a slightly dandyish air but that was countered by his quiet dignity and sober tailoring. He was, now, after having sported a beard for many years, clean-shaven and his face was lean and ruddy from his being out painting in all weathers. But as he looked down over the menu his best features were hidden, his grey eyes with their long black lashes. Beattie smiled to herself. At sixty-seven Albert had worn well and grown in confidence over the years. In fact he was quite a catch.

'Does that suit you, Beatrice?' he asked, taking his serviette and shaking out the creases before smoothing it over his lap.

The gesture reminded her of her days as parlour-maid in the Pragnell household, spending ages, under Mrs Frostick's supervision, starching and ironing the table linen, folding the serviettes into bishop's mitres only to have Samuel and Albert shake them free in seconds from their meticulous folds. If Aggie Frostick could see her now dining out with the young master, she'd turn in her grave.

'Madam,' said the waiter, uncorking the wine and pouring her half a glass.

Beattie sipped appreciatively – this was far more to her taste. 'Very nice,' she murmured. 'This pâté doesn't amount to much more than posh dripping on toast,' she said when the waiter was well out of earshot.

Albert laughed. 'I'm glad it meets with your approval. Oh, I forgot to tell you. Miriam says to wish you a Happy Birthday and she'll see you later.'

'Poor girl,' said Beattie, taking another mouthful of the cold sweet wine. 'She's bound to feel a bit downhearted with Alec off to Scotland today. Only a week married and then parted. Still, he's only got a couple more years to serve and he'll be under her feet for good.'

'She did look a bit crestfallen, this morning, and I think Rosie will miss her Daddy.'

'I'm just thankful it all went so smoothly in the end. My God, Albert, it was a close-run thing, wasn't it?'

'It was a question of everyone keeping their nerve,' he said as he refilled her glass.

'Strange, I was thinking when I said goodbye to

438

him last night, I shall be glad to get back into the old routine. Then I realised that it will have to be a new routine altogether. He won't be coming home to me any more. In a few years Lily will likely fly the coop and then, I don't know,' Beattie shrugged.

'You'll be busying yourself with Miriam's children.'

The conversation lapsed while the waiter set down their fish and served their vegetables. The juggling with the two silver tablespoons seemed an elaborate waste of time and an intrusion on their privacy, but she nodded graciously and he left them to their meal.

'Do you regret being a bachelor all your life?' she asked.

Albert smiled. 'I miss not having children certainly, having their affection, watching them grow. But I have been blessed with good health, a chance to see something of the world, good friends, and of course my painting.'

'But has it been enough?' she persisted.

Albert shrugged. 'Who knows, Beatrice? I wonder sometimes when I see all the young men crippled by war and the poor women bringing up families on their own why I should still be here. It would have made more sense to have snatched me up and left some father to see his children grow.'

'Oh, Albert,' she touched his hand. 'Don't say that. I would miss you so much.'

He got to his feet. 'Will you excuse me a moment?' he said, before walking off to the back of the restaurant.

Beattie finished her whiting, wishing she could dip her bread roll into the sauce, it seemed such a waste. Dear, dear Albert, she was so fond of him. He'd been so patient with her over the years. Proposing to her every so often and taking her refusals with resigned good-humour. She gasped as a daring thought occurred to her.

Albert came back and Beattie could barely contain herself. She was about to put her plan into execution when the waiter returned with the dessert menu. 'Banana and apple fritters, please,' she said briskly, anxious to be rid of him.

'Yes, for me too,' said Albert. He smiled at her. 'Beatrice, you look full of mischief, what are you plotting?'

A small voice in her head murmured, 'Fools rush in,' but she stifled its cautionary words. 'Albert,' she said, 'I know what I'm going to do with the rest of my life. I'm going to look after you. It's Leap Year and I'm asking you to marry me.'

The waiter arrived with the fritters making Beattie seethe with impatience.

Albert smiled at her as if he hadn't heard. 'They look delicious, don't they?'

'Oh bugger the fritters,' she snapped. 'Didn't you hear what I said?'

He folded his serviette and put down his spoon. The waiter approached again from behind Beatrice and Albert waved him away impatiently. He looked at her steadily for a long disconcerting moment. 'You are ready to marry me, Beatrice,' he said quietly. 'Has it never occurred to you that I might have grown tired of waiting?'

Chapter Thirty-Eight

'I can't do it,' said Miriam, standing at the doorstep, her face crumpling.

'Just one last hug,' said Alec, holding her tightly to him.

'I promised myself I wouldn't cry,' she sniffed, drying her eyes with her fingers.

'Come on, my love, it won't be long. I'll try and get down at Easter.'

'Daddy, kiss,' insisted Rosie, holding out her arms.

'An Eskimo kiss or a piggy kiss?'

'Piggy, piggy,' squealed Rosie.

Alec swept her up into his arms and snuffled and snorted into her neck. 'And what has my little girl to do?'

'Kiss Daddy picture every night?' she shouted triumphantly.

He put his daughter down and held Miriam, kissing her tear-stained face. 'Take care of yourself and Rosie and the little nipper. You've got Ma and Lily and old Albert around you.' Reluctantly he drew away from her. 'I must go my love, or I'll miss my train. Bye-bye.'

Miriam clutched Rosie's hand and they stood waving until he turned the corner. It wasn't fair, only a week married and he was snatched away from her. She'd got used to the warmth of his body next to hers, his face smiling at her across the table, the two of them squeezed into the armchair by the fire. Even the struggles to get Rosie to stay in her own bed had been a source of amusement between them as they resisted her determined wiles.

'Rosie bed cold, Rosie bed wet, Teddy want to sleep with Daddy,' all had gained her no reprieve.

Miriam knew it would be all too tempting to succumb to her pleading when Alec was gone and she was lonely.

'Please don't give in to her, Mirry,' Alec had said. 'It'll only cause trouble when I come home again. She'll see me as the bad man. I've taken a lot of care in explaining that I'm her Daddy and she's come to love me. We don't want all that undone especially with the little one coming along.'

It was making decisions together that gave her a strong sense of being a family. If only they could be completely on their own away from Mr Pragnell, tactful and discreet though he was, and Lily and Alec's mother. She knew she was being selfish considering the number of families who had to make do with one room. Miriam sighed. A few years ago she'd been lonely, pregnant and desperately afraid. Now she had a real ring on her finger, a husband who loved her, a little daughter and a baby waiting to be born.

'What we do?' asked Rosie, tugging at her skirt.

From across the street, Mrs Rowan called to her. 'I was just going to knock on your door, Mrs Forrest,' she said. 'Michael has gone back, too. I thought you might like a cup of tea before settling to anything?' Miriam nodded, too tearful to speak.

'Rowan,' cried Rosie, rushing towards her.

Mrs Rowan held open the door. 'You know where the toy box is, don't you, Miss?' she said, smiling at the little girl's eagerness.

A rich smell of baking wafted up the passage as Miriam stepped inside. 'Sit yourself down, I won't be a minute. I must just get the biscuits out of the oven.'

Miriam had only ever handed Rosie over the doorstep on the odd occasion that Mrs Rowan had cared for her; now she had the opportunity to look around. The furniture was old and solid and well polished, the walls hung with photographs and paintings. She realised she knew little about her neighbour, beyond the fact that her husband had drowned at sea and that her eldest son, Arthur, was terribly damaged by the war. 'I love this room, Mrs Rowan. It's so light and full of colours,' she said.

The woman smiled, as she poured the tea and handed a cup of milk to Rosie. 'I hate the first day, don't you? I always wander around in a daze. It takes me a while to settle to the away routine.'

'What do you mean?' asked Miriam.

'Getting used to writing to Michael again instead of talking to him, scanning the paper for things to tell him. Getting my plans started.'

'I don't understand.'

'Oh, just little things,' she said. 'I make some new thing for the house, I rearrange things in the yard or buy a few seeds.'

'My friend, Daisy,' said Miriam, shyly, 'she used to send her husband planting designs and all sorts.'

'I try to learn something new.' She laughed. 'One year we made semaphore flags and the boys used to signal to each other between the garden and the bedroom window.'

Miriam stirred her tea. 'I just want the baby to arrive safe and all of us to be well.'

'Of course you do,' said Ethel, leaning forward and patting her arm. 'I can see you've got lots of things to fill your time.'

'Biscuit, Rowan?' asked Rosie, hopefully.

Ethel laughed. 'I invited you in for biscuits and then forgot all about them. Come on, Rosie, let's see what we can find while your Mummy takes a look at things.'

Miriam gazed up at the photographs and pictures. There was one of a man in sailor's uniform with a little boy on either knee, a snapshot taken on the beach of Ethel seated in a deckchair next to the same sailor. She looked so different from the quietly-spoken, rather serious woman that Miriam was accustomed to. Her head was thrown back and she was laughing as Michael knelt in front of her waving a thick rubbery strip of seaweed. The paintings were bold, vivid depictions of scarlet poppies in a cornfield, marigolds in a bright blue vase, sunflowers against a garden wall. Here spread before her were all the bright memories of her neighbour's life.

'You must miss your husband,' said Miriam, as Ethel came back into the room with Rosie and the biscuits.

Ethel nodded. 'All the little loving moments with the children, seeing him carrying them up to bed on his back, the quiet times when we were alone together, the wonderful letters he used to write.' She sighed. 'Having him at all was a miracle. Me, the plain one of the family and five years older than him. Sometimes I can be grateful for the time we had and others I feel a rage at all the years he missed of the boys growing into manhood.' There was a long silence while Ethel stared at the pictures and then she said, 'One thing – I'm grateful he never saw Arthur and what the war has done to him.'

'Do you ever wish that Arthur had not come back?' Miriam put her hand to her mouth in dismay. 'I'm ever so sorry, Ethel,' she said. 'I could bite my tongue really. I–'

'Please, Miriam, I am grateful that you have been honest enough to ask me. Yes, yes, many times. When I walk down the drive at Netley Hospital and see all those poor men, pale shadows of the laughing boys they were, I want to hurl a shell at them and have the whole place obliterated.' She looked at Miriam and smiled. 'But sometimes there will be just a remnant of the old Arthur. He'll remember something we did together or when I take him out into the grounds he'll point out a tree or a plant.' She put her hand to her face and tears welled in her eyes. 'Living on remnants,' she whispered, as if to herself.

'How about Michael?'

'Ah, Michael,' she said. 'He's precious to me but I must be so careful not to cling to him. He'll want a family of his own and I mustn't hold him back.'

Rosie looked up from her biscuit, her mouth coated with crumbs. When Ethel had passed one to Miriam and settled herself back in her chair the child climbed onto her lap. She hugged the little girl, smiling down at her. 'I expect you'd like another one,' she said.

'Please, please, please,' Rosie cried, taking one from the proffered plate.

'When is your little one due?' asked Ethel.

'I'm not quite sure, but I think the beginning of June.'

'Have you been to book your midwife?'

Miriam shook her head and smiled. 'I suppose that's my first plan, next week. Today is Alec's Mum's birthday, so I must think about a present.'

'Well, I mustn't keep you. Only, Miriam, there was just one thing I wanted to say.' Ethel grasped Miriam's arm and stared fiercely at her. 'Don't just see the time that your Alec is away from you as time to be got through. Live every minute. Life is so precious and so uncertain.' Impulsively Miriam turned and hugged her neighbour.

She was standing at her front door with the key in her hand when the Vine children erupted onto the pavement. Further down the street was a sailor with his kit-bag on his shoulder. 'Dad! Dad!' they screamed, rushing pellmell towards the skinny figure lurching towards them. The combined enthusiasm of Mary, Faith and Mercy brought Fred Vine to his knees. Blyth hung back, fingers in his mouth watching them all.

Miriam laughed. It seemed a good omen having arrivals in Lemon Street as well as departures. In a few months Rosie would be running towards Alec and she herself might be standing in the doorway holding their new baby in her arms. Greatly cheered she took her daughter inside and set about her housework. She was glad that Mr Pragnell was out for the day – it meant that she could pretend the house was her own, if only for a while.

Rosie sat on a stool by the fire with her sweets in a little dish and shared them with her dollies. Miriam lingered with her duster over the framed photograph of her wedding, so new it hardly needed cleaning. Alec looked so happy and so did Rosie and Lily and Mother as she was beginning to call Beatrice. She looked up at her picture 'One of the Family'. How near she had come to smashing it to pieces in those anxious days before the wedding. A family, she smiled to herself. Alec had knelt in front of her on their wedding night and covered her belly with kisses. She had held his hands and they had both felt a faint flicker of movement beneath their fingers. Going to sleep in each other's arms, waking with Alec still beside her, kissing his sleeping face into wakefulness, those were the moments she would treasure always.

'Miriam, Miriam. I've been calling for ages.' Lily startled her out of her daydreams. 'Rosie let me in. Have you got anything to eat? I'd forgotten that Gran was out with Uncle Albert.'

Miriam blushed as if Lily had read her thoughts. 'I've hardly done a thing this morning. I'm all in a muddle.'

'I'm family,' said Lily, 'you don't have to try and impress me. Besides it's food I'm after, not inspecting the ironing.'

Between them they got together a plate heaped with toast and dripping. 'Monkey in garden,' said Rosie, looking questioningly at her sister.

'What is she on about?' asked Miriam, making her daughter some toast fingers.

Lily swore her to secrecy, before telling her about going to the pantomime, some forward fellow called Bernard, what she thought he'd done to Granny Dowell's monkey and the subsequent funeral in the garden.

'Poor little scrap,' said Miriam. 'Still he had a decent burial and he'd been so well loved by old Granny. Besides it's given you a sort of bond with Michael.'

'D'you think so?' asked Lily, hopefully.

Miriam nodded. 'As to Bernard, he's done you a good turn. You've seen him in his true colours before you got in too deep with him.'

Lily laughed. 'He got his come-uppance, this morning. I took the jackets round to the shop and when he opened the door, I told him that I'd heard a monkey had been found and the police thought it had been poisoned. Told him I'd seen Constable Wilkes and given him his name and address.'

'What did he say?'

'Well,' said Lily, taking another slice of toast, 'he called me a stupid bitch and slammed the door so hard the glass fell out and smashed to smithereens.'

'Bitch, bitch,' shouted Rosie.

Lily blushed, 'Oh, sorry.'

'Pretend you didn't hear,' whispered Miriam. 'Less fuss we make, more likely she is to forget.'

'Anyway, the best bit was that the shop manager had come up behind me and he was furious. Made Bernard apologise to me for using insulting language and gave him an official warning. I left him sweeping up.'

'I've got a secret for you, too,' said Miriam before turning to speak to Rosie. 'Go and get Sailor Doll that your Daddy made you.' The little girl trotted eagerly away.

'You're going to have a new brother or sister, Daisy or Joseph,' said Miriam, watching carefully for Lily's response.

'Oh, that's really, really good news. Oh, I'm so excited.' She leapt from her chair and hugged Miriam. 'Does Gran know?'

'Not yet,' said Miriam, delighted at Lily's warm response to her news. 'I thought I'd tell her at tea-time – it can be an extra birthday present.'

'Oh, yes, that would be just right.' There were footsteps running down the passage and Rosie rushed in with the doll that Alec had made. 'That is just the best sailor dolly in the world,' said Lily.

Watching the two girls Miriam smiled to herself. It was all so different to her last preg-nancy when she'd crept around shame-faced and fearful. Alec was right, the months of absence would soon pass, if she kept herself busy.

'Look,' said Lily. 'I've hidden away the cake and the birthday card and I've laid the table. It's only half-past one, why don't I give you a hand to get straight in here and then we'll all go in next door about three and see Gran all together?'

'Lily, you're a gem,' said Miriam. 'You sure you haven't got any plans of your own? It is Saturday after all.'

'Only Gran's birthday. Dora is going out with Harry tonight, so I'm at a loose end.'

'Well, if you could keep Rosie occupied in the bedroom, I'll have this room to rights in no time.' By three o'clock Miriam had swept and polished, damped down a heap of ironing for later, and generally left the room spotless. Taking off her apron, she wrapped up the navy woollen scarf she'd knitted and tied it around with a piece of scarlet ribbon. Giving her hair a quick comb she hurried along to the bedroom.

Lily and Rosie were looking out of the window at the black motor car that had returned Beattie and Mr Pragnell to the street. As they stepped out of the car Constable Wilkes came out of Ethel Rowan's house and went to speak to him. Looking grim-faced, Beattie went to her own house and slammed the front door.

Mr Pragnell said something to the driver and then crossed the street to Ethel's house.

Miriam felt her stomach lurch in fear. It must be something to do with Arthur. Oh, poor, poor Ethel, she thought.

'I'll go in and get the kettle on,' said Lily. 'I expect Uncle Albert will want to speak to you. I'll see you later.'

Miriam nodded, watching events across the street. Should she go over and offer to help? She went to the front door and stood anxiously on the step. Mr Pragnell came back across the street accompanied by Ethel Rowan, carrying a small case. Seeing Miriam, he said, 'I'm off to Netley with Mrs Rowan. I may not be back until to-morrow. I'll just step inside and put a few things together.' Miriam nodded and went up to Ethel as she was about to step into the car. She touched her shoulder.

Ethel turned towards her. 'It's my Arthur,' she said, her eyes shining with tears. 'He's free at last. Free of all that anguish and despair.'

Miriam kissed her cheek. 'I will come and see you when you get back,' she said.

Mr Pragnell nodded to her and got into the car beside Ethel Rowan. Miriam stood at the kerbside until it drew away. She lifted Rosie up into her arms and hugged her fiercely.

She was about to knock on Beattie's door when Lily opened it to her. 'Gran's in a very funny mood,' she whispered. 'Says she's been a very foolish woman and wants to be left alone.'

Miriam went indoors. What a lot she had to write to her new husband that evening.

Chapter Thirty-Nine

Dear Lily,

Thank you for writing and telling me all about poor Arthur's funeral. I felt desperate at not being able to be at Ma's side to support her.

She was so brave to stand up to the army in refusing to have a military funeral or shots fired over his grave. Arthur was such a gentle chap who hated all the noise and carry-on of service life. We used to walk along the beach and skim pebbles into the water or talk about the mystery of tides and currents. I thought I'd have my brother for the rest of my life. Of course we had fallings out, like you must have done with your Andrew, but there is such a gap now.

I will be home at Easter and hope to see you then.
Very best wishes, Your affectionate friend Michael.

Lily read and re-read Michael's letter. Each time, her eyes lingered over the word affectionate. What did he mean? Affectionate was somewhere between love and liking, wasn't it? But which of the two feelings was it closest to? It was now Easter Monday and she had barely seen him. Of course Michael needed to spend time with his mother but surely he wanted to see her, too, didn't he?

Sighing she put the letter back in her pocket and waved to Harry and Dora who were running down the road to meet her at the tram stop.

'I love the Easter Fair, don't you?' laughed Dora. 'There's so much to see and do. All the crowds and the noise and liveliness!'

Lily smiled. Dora had become a swan. Her little pinched face glowed with happiness and her brown eyes sought out Harry's at every opportunity. He too seemed taller and more assured. To Lily he had always been just Harry, one of the Vine tribe, but now he had become almost handsome.

'How did you break free of the nippers?' she asked him.

'Dad's made them go up with him to see Ma, then they'll come up later. With a bit of luck I'll be free of them all day.'

Lily was going to ask him how his mother was but he looked so carefree that she decided against it. After the wild behaviour resulting in her admission to the asylum Dolly Vine had become blank-faced and unresponsive. Instead she said. 'What are you going to try first? I love the gallopers and the swing-boats.'

'I reckon I'll have a go at the shooting gallery.'

'Oh, Harry! Reckon yourself to be Buffalo Bill, do you?'

'It's here,' cried Lily and the three of them clattered upstairs. They went to Cosham on the open-topped tram, laughing all the way. The fair was set out on the lower slopes of Portsdown Hill below the grounds of the military hospital. As the crowds made their way up the muddy track their ears and noses were assaulted by the sounds and stinks of the Easter Fair. The 'William Tell Overture' blared from the steam organ urging them forward, drowning out their excited voices. A brew of competing smells filled the air, from the stench of beer and engine-oil to the reek of cockles and the scent of hot sugar.

'I'm torn between the hoop-la and the coconut shies,' shouted Lily, looking about her.

'Ooh don't them brandy snaps look good,' yelled Dora. 'Let's have one each and walk about a bit, see what there is to see before we makes up our minds.'

Lily crunched into the golden lattice and her mouth was flooded with gingery sugar. Dora licked her fingers and dried them on her hankie. 'Right, Harry,' she said, pointing to the shooting gallery. 'You ready to win me a tea-set?' She turned and yelled to Lily. 'You comin' too?'

'I'll see you at the gallopers when you've won your plate,' said Lily, not wanting to spoil their time together. Besides she had the faint hope that Michael might be somewhere on the teeming, smoky hillside. She pushed her way through the crowds wondering if he was one of the sailors at the beer tent or the boxing booth. An old bearded man in a straw hat presided over a circular metal tank filled with water. 'Let my little people dive under the water and bring to you a message from the future,' he roared.

Lily was intrigued. She stood in the queue of young girls with pennies at the ready. In the tank little figures such as Neptune, a mermaid, a king and a queen, an Indian chief and a pirate all bobbed up and down. At a signal from the old man the little people would dip down under the bubbling blue water and come up again with a tiny package wrapped in waterproof material which would be delivered to the purchaser on the end of a striped fishing-rod.

'What a swizz!' snorted one of the girls in front of Lily, as she unwrapped her message and then threw it on the ground.

Lily bent to pick it up. '"Life is half spent before we know what it is."' She laughed as she tossed it away, wondering idly who would pick it up again.

'Who shall be your messenger?' asked the old man.

454

'I'll try the mermaid,' Lily said, handing over her penny.

After several taps on the side of the tank the stallholder persuaded the metal mermaid to dive under the water and to return with a green oilcloth package the size of a postage stamp. Eagerly Lily took the package from the end of the fishing-rod and unwrapped it. 'Desires are nourished by delays,' was her cryptic message. Blushing, she put the paper in her pocket and threaded her way through the crowd towards the sound of the merry-go-round.

'Lady, lady, stop a minute.' Two young girls tugged at her sleeves. 'Could you sit here with our grandad for five minutes? We want to look at the animals in the menagerie. He's blind and if we leave him alone someone might pinch his money or he'll get himself lost. Please, we'll only be ten minutes and our mother will be here soon.'

'Don't be long,' said Lily, settling herself on a little grassy hillock with a bewhiskered man in the blue suit of a hospital patient.

'Much obliged,' he said, grasping her arm tightly. 'Tell me what you can see. Be my eyes for five minutes. Tell me where the girls have gone?'

Lily peered through the shifting crowd. 'It's a bit striped tent,' she shouted, 'with a placard outside saying that it's Wombwell's Menagerie of Rare and Exotic Animals. A penny a look.'

'Sounds like the Pobble who had no toes or the Quangle Wangle.' He laughed.

'There's something about a Nilghau from Egypt, whatever that is,' said Lily, squinting at

455

the last line of the zoo placard. She looked down the hill at the rifle range where Dora and Harry were waiting in the queue. They were standing with their arms about each other not seeming to care when their turn came to shoot.

'What is it, what is it, why are you laughing?' her companion demanded.

'It's just a family from my street,' she yelled. 'I can see them at the coconut shy. The Dad, Fred Vine, is holding three coconuts and the man in charge is pushing him away and his children are jumping up and down with excitement.'

The steam organ blared out 'The Red Red Robin' and the old man beat time with his walking-stick. 'Keep a sharp look-out for Marigold and Daisy May,' he said, 'or they'll slide off somewhere.'

Lily was impatient to be up and away but felt obliged to stay where she was until the two girls returned. She was startled to see Bernard and Ruby. They walked past, within a few feet of her, looking sour and discontented. As Bernard waved to a pretty girl at the hoop-la stall, Ruby put her arm through his. She darted the girl a poisonous look and gave Bernard a fake smile. Lily felt as if she were seeing them for the first time, stripped of their glamour. Ruby, for all her bright ribbon floating from her hat, her rouged cheeks and jacket strained over her ample bosom, appeared anxious and unhappy. Bernard in his straw boater and linen jacket looked somehow counterfeit. A lounge lizard, thought Lily, remembering Michael's words. Bernard had been her puppet-master and she had danced to his tune, eagerly, desperately wanting him to return her devotion. And now she was free.

Having lost sight of Ruby and Bernard, she spotted the Vines.

'Dad, let's 'ave some cockles.'

'No, I want a brandy-snap.'

'How about a toffee-apple?'

'Ice-cream, ice-cream,' pleaded Blyth, jumping up and down.

''Ere you four, there's threepence each. Get what you like – I'm off for a beer.'

They caught sight of Lily. 'Look after the coconuts will ya?' they pleaded.

'Give them to me, my dear,' said the blind man. 'You search out those girls. It's time you had some fun.'

'Marigold, Daisy,' shouted Lily, catching sight of them sauntering off to the fortune-telling tent.

'We only been gone five minutes,' they muttered sulkily.

'That's as may be,' said Lily, firmly. 'It's my turn now.'

She was surrounded by people eating, laughing and shouting as they clambered up the steps of the roundabouts, staggered out of the boxing-booth or beer-tents or hoisted themselves high in the air on the swing-boats. Babies screamed, dogs barked and stallholders yelled their competing attractions. The excitement was infectious.

Lily re-read her message from the mermaid. 'Desires are nourished by delays.' It was like the saying 'absence makes the heart grow fonder'. Was it the absence of Michael over the last few weeks that had changed her feelings for him, made her wish for something more than friendship? Or was it the day of the wedding when he'd calmed and supported her over the business of Lloyd? A few months ago she'd been besotted by Bernard. Was she becoming flighty? But with Bernard there had been very little liking and certainly no respect. With Michael there was liking and respect, and something else, something as fragile as the wings on Dad's butterfly tattoo.

Threading her way through the crowds she made straight for the merry-go-round with its barley-sugar poles and prancing horses.

Waiting in the queue were Dora and Harry. They ran up to her swinging her round between them. 'Lil, Lil, we got somethink to tell you,' they shouted, faces shining.

'You won the plate?' she asked.

'No, you silly date,' laughed Dora, 'can't you guess?'

'I've popped the question,' said Harry, 'and Dora said yes.'

'What?' gasped Lily, not knowing whether to laugh or cry. 'When's the happy day?'

'Oh ages yet,' bellowed Dora, over the fairground music. 'Harry's off to the Far East in June on HMS *Lister*, for three years. It'll give us time to save up.'

'I'm ever so glad,' said Lily, kissing her friend warmly.

'Let's get back in the queue,' shouted Harry. 'I can see our Dad weavin' 'is way over here. Quick, look the other way.'

The three of them mounted the steps of the merry-go-round and Harry swung Dora up onto one of the gallopers and settled himself behind her. Lily climbed up onto Monarch, a grey horse with a white mane. She clung onto the barley-sugar pole and the merry-go-round swung into action. It was getting dark and the naphtha flare lanterns on the different stalls were a fuzzy orange blur as Monarch swung past them to the 'Blue Danube' waltz. Up and down, round and round they went. Lily clenched her knees against the galloper's wooden sides. Faster and faster they went. Lily began to feel giddy. Slowly, slowly the ride came to an end.

'Let's have another go,' said Harry, 'all of us.'

Lily shook her head, wanting to get down, but it was too late. As the gallopers began to move a sailor ran up the steps and slid onto the back of Monarch. Lily turned to protest but the words were lost, drowned out by the swell of the music. 'It's me, Lily. It's Michael,' he shouted.

Up above the crowd they rode, round and round in a glorious whirling world of their own. Lily gripped the barley-sugar pole and Michael slipped his arms around her waist. Affectionate friend, affectionate friend, the words sang in her heart.

The music had stopped for some little while before they realised the ride was over. Michael got off Monarch's back and held out his hand to help her down. They stood at a distance from the merry-go-round, suddenly shy with each other. 'Hello, Lily,' he said, smiling down at her.

'Michael,' was all she could say.

'I must have just missed you this afternoon,' he said. 'When we got back from the cemetery, your Gran said you'd be up here.' He squeezed her hand. 'Do you want to wait for Harry and Dora or shall we go and get some chips?'

'Chips, please,' yelled Lily. Hand-in-hand they shoved their way across the fairground, guided to the chip stall by the smell of hot vinegar. Standing in the queue laughing and talking, their words were tripping over themselves in their eagerness to share thoughts with each other.

'How long are you home for?'

'Just a week. I'll be back the beginning of June to join HMS *Lister*.'

'That's the ship Harry's going to. You know he and Dora are getting engaged? What do you think of...'

'I wish I wasn't going now.'

'Goodness knows what the kids will think. I mean, Mary and the twins and Blyth. Why don't you want to go?'

'Dora must like a challenge. Why do you think I don't want to go, Lily?'

'You'll miss your mother?'

'No, someone else.'

'Who?'

'You.'

'Oh.' Lily blushed.

'Two ones with salt and vinegar,' said Michael, handing over the money. They sat on the step of a disused ride and set about eating their chips.

'Your letter was lovely,' Michael said. 'It helped me so much. I felt so bad not being able to get home, not being with Ma.'

460

'It felt important to tell you everything.'

'Why do you think that was?' he asked, throwing the chip paper into the darkness.

'Because I wanted to be your witness,' Lily said. 'If Andrew had been able to have a funeral I know you would have done the same for me.'

'I felt your voice in the letter,' he said. 'It underlined the words.'

'What did you mean by writing that you were my affectionate friend?'

For a long heart-stopping moment Michael said nothing. Lily sat beside him afraid to do anything and then he turned to her. He held her face between his hands and kissed her with great care, slowly, tenderly, as if she were precious to him. Lily closed her eyes. His lips were soft and tasted of salt.

'I was afraid to say loving friend,' he murmured. 'I thought you would be able to read between the lines.'

'So affectionate was a sort of code between us?' she said.

'Yes,' he whispered. 'I thought you would put it somewhere between loving and liking. Then when I saw you again I wanted to chuck it out and not be so feeble.'

'Yes,' said Lily, kissing him until they were both breathless. 'I think we can chuck out affectionate.'

Chapter Forty

Beattie supposed she could be described as a woman scorned after Albert had refused her proposal. But scorn had never been a part of Albert's character. However much she sieved and weighed his words that day, scorn was absent from them. His tone had been more one of exasperation.

'You are ready to marry me, Beatrice. Has it never occurred to you that I might have grown tired of waiting?'

No, she had not felt scorned but somehow ridiculous. While she sat avoiding his eyes, waiting for her coat, she realised that she had acted purely and simply out of panic. That, and two glasses of chilled Sauterne. If only she had taken his refusal lightly, turned it into a joke. 'I shall have to cast my net more widely,' or, 'I was just practising on you, Albert, while I wait for my rich admiral to appear.' Failing that she could have simply apologised. 'I'm sorry, Albert. That must have been the wine talking. Let's get back to our old comfortable friendship.'

But on their return to Lemon Street, there was Constable Wilkes and Ethel Rowan and all the grief over poor Arthur.

Directly the funeral was over Albert had come to her and said, 'Beatrice, we were at cross-purposes, on your birthday. I feel I was very brusque with you. Please let us be friends once more.'

'It was a joke, Albert,' she had replied, her face stiff with injured pride. 'Now, if you've nothing else to say, I really must be getting on.'

If the breach was ever to be healed it was for her to make the first move. She grieved for the loss of his friendship but could not take the necessary step to repair it. It was now over four months since her birthday and still the breach had not been healed. Albert had spent two weeks in Romsey over Easter and now at the beginning of May they were still not reconciled.

Unexpectedly, Alec had managed a week's leave. Today she and Lily had been invited next-door to Sunday dinner with the happy couple before he returned to his ship the following day. Ordinarily she would have been delighted to have a family meal that she'd not laboured over herself, but the inevitable presence of Albert cast a cloud. She greeted him stiffly and stood by her chair talking with Rosie.

'Sit down Ma, for goodness sake,' said Alec. 'You're the guest today.' Grudgingly she took her place.

Albert was his usual self. Wearing a blue smock and red neckerchief he looked like the amiable, artist-grandfather presiding over the family meal. 'This is a new chapter,' he said, smiling at her, 'being a guest at your son and daughter's table.' Beattie nodded. She felt resentful that he should be so much at ease while she felt awkward and out of place.

'It all smells wonderful, doesn't it, Gran?'

appealed Lily.

'Very nice,' she answered, staring at the table-cloth.

'Are you all right, Mother?' asked Miriam, fluttering about between the stove and the table.

'Perfectly,' she said, shortly. Miriam blushed. I'm like the bad fairy at the Christening, Beattie thought. I'm almost as bad as Lily was when we had that tea-party for Miriam.

'Ooh,' everyone but Beattie chorused as Alec carried the steak-and-kidney pie to the table. Rosie banged her spoon in anticipation.

'Will you tie this tea-towel around her neck please, Mother?' Getting no response Miriam repeated herself: 'Mother, will you tie—'

'Give me a chance,' she snapped.

As Miriam went back to the stove for the potatoes, Lily leant across the table and whispered fiercely, 'Don't be such a crosspatch.'

'Very tasty,' she muttered, after managing to swallow a scalding mouthful of meat and pastry.

'It's your recipe,' said Miriam smiling at her. If only everyone would ignore her, she might be able to calm down and settle to the meal.

'Did Mirry tell you the names we've agreed on?' Alec asked. Beattie shook her head.

'Daisy Beatrice or Joseph Andrew.'

They were all looking at her with such anxious, loving faces, waiting for her approval. The names were just what she wanted, giving a sense of continuity to the family. They were a great compliment to her and she should have responded with gratitude and affection. She sat staring down at her plate.

'Ma, please, say something. We chose them especially for you.'

If she opened her mouth, Beattie knew that she would cry. Instead she blinked and nodded, trying to convey enthusiasm.

'I think they're lovely,' said Lily. 'What do you want Rosie, a brother or a sister?'

'Bunny rabbit,' the little girl cried, delighting in the laughing response to her words. She banged her spoon into her dish and splashed Beattie with the gravy.

'Rosie, naughty girl,' said Miriam reaching behind her for a cloth.

'It's all right,' said Beattie, more sharply than she intended, pushing Miriam's hand away. 'I need some air,' she gasped, pulling her chair from the table and opening the door into the passage.

Miriam followed her into the passage. 'What's wrong?' she asked.

'Please, leave me,' Beattie cried, slamming out of the house.

It took her three attempts to get the key to work. Once indoors she flung herself in her armchair and burst out crying. Not since she'd got the news of Joseph's death had she felt so alone and friendless. What a proud stupid old woman she was. And worse than anything else she had ruined Miriam's Sunday dinner. She had looked so pretty in the full sail of late pregnancy, glowing with happiness, her hair all fluffy from recent washing. And little Rosie excited at all the company. When she thought about how furious she had been with Lily at her sulks when Miriam had first come to tea, she squirmed with shame.

Oh, Albert, no wonder you've done with me. What a poor reward it's been for all your constancy.

The back door rattled. Someone was coming in. Beattie leapt to her feet and tried to get out of the kitchen and into the passage. But her visitor was too quick for her.

He stood in front of the kitchen door and blocked her escape.

'I'm too old a bear to play round and round the garden, Beatrice. Whatever the misunderstanding is between us it's making you very unhappy and everyone around you.' Albert caught hold of her arm and propelled her back to her chair. 'Now talk to me. I'm not going to leave until you do.'

'I can't explain,' she shrugged her shoulders. 'I just can't.'

'Beatrice, you can and you must.'

'It's painful and I don't want to.'

'Beatrice, I know you have the courage of a lion,' he said, 'I know it. It's something else.' She couldn't look at him.

'It's pride, isn't it?'

'Well, if you know, why ask?' she snapped.

'I've not come in here to humiliate you or drag a confession from you. I love you, Beatrice.'

'You made me look ridiculous.'

'How did I do that?'

'Saying all that about growing tired of waiting. Making me feel a fool.'

'Yes, I can see that I hurt you. But didn't you take into account when you asked me that I might say no?'

'No, I didn't.'

'Wasn't that rather taking me for granted?'

Beattie looked at Albert in surprise. 'I supp
so,' she said.

'Beatrice, I am deeply sorry that I made you feel foolish and I have tried to tell you the reason, so many times. But don't you think you had a hand in it yourself?'

'What d'you mean?'

'You asked me to marry you on a whim, on the spur of the moment. No,' he raised his hand to stop her saying anything, 'let me finish. You did not ask me because you genuinely loved me and wanted to make a life for us. Alec has left home and Lily will be going soon. You asked me as a crutch to shore up your loneliness. If you felt ridiculous, Beatrice, what do you think I was feeling?'

Her cheeks burned and she couldn't meet his eyes. 'I didn't think. I acted out of panic.' She put her head in her hands. 'Albert, I'm sorry.'

He leant forward and took her hand. 'Beatrice, you have said to me often and often how hard it has been for you to spend half your life waiting. You and all the women who marry sailors.'

He paused and Beattie looked at him. His grey eyes were bright with unshed tears. 'I have waited for you all my life. You must take me for myself or not at all.'

'Oh Albert,' she cried, 'I wouldn't have hurt you for the world.'

'But you have, Beatrice, and we can't go forward together until you see that and understand it.'

'Yes, you're quite right. I've been selfish and

467

I'm truly, truly sorry. And Albert,' she could hardly speak for crying, 'I have missed you.' He gathered her into his arms.

They sat together in silence save for the ticking of the clock. Beattie thought back through the years from her first tentative knocking on Doctor Pragnell's door, as the new scullery-maid, to the young Albert helping her with her reading, protecting her from Mrs Frostick's temper; Albert giving her the forget-me-not brooch and his forgiving letter when she told him about Joseph. He was her well and she had drawn deeply on his friendship and counsel over the years.

'I do truly love you, Albert,' she said. 'It's only in these last lonely weeks that I've come to appreciate how much.'

Albert began to laugh. Beattie was infuriated. Here she was making a fool of herself again and he had the cheek to laugh. 'Oh, oh, Beatrice, I'm so, so sorry. I've been very cruel to you. But you see at the very moment that you were making your proposal to me, I had planned to make mine to you. The waiter was coming up behind you with the champagne in the ice-bucket. I was just so furious at being pipped at the post that I decided to teach you a lesson.' She didn't know whether to laugh or cry, it was all so ridiculous.

'Beatrice, my darling. I beg of you, don't be cross.' He looked so contrite that she hadn't the heart to scold him. And it *was* very funny when you thought about it.

'We should know better at our age,' she laughed.

'I know that you love me,' he said, 'but it is

468

good for an old fellow to hear the words said from time to time.' He kissed her on the cheek. 'Now, I shall make us a cup of tea and then I think you have business to attend to next-door.'

'Ah, yes, Miriam,' Beattie sighed. 'It seems to be my day to eat humble-pie.'

'If you do it gracefully enough,' smiled Albert, spooning the tea into the pot, 'you might be able to follow it with Miriam's steak-and-kidney.'

She got up and walked over to him as she stood by the range waiting for the kettle to boil and put her arms around him. 'It's so good to be back on the old footing,' she said.

He turned and kissed her. 'Life goes forward, my darling. We shall have to make new footings.'

How she had misjudged him. Beattie shivered at the thought of how near she had come to losing Albert. They sat at the table and drank their tea together, delighting in the comfort of friendship restored.

'Before we return next-door,' said Albert, reaching into his jacket pocket, 'I want to give you your birthday present. Somehow I haven't had a chance to do it yet. But I've carried it around with me until the right moment.' He placed a maroon leather ring-box on the table between them.

Beattie opened it, and recognised immediately the garnet engagement ring that had belonged to his mother. 'Albert,' she gasped, 'what a gift. Your mother treasured this.'

'I hope that you will, too,' he said.

She took the ring and held it in her hand watching the stones sparkle a rich winey red

469

under the lamplight's gleam. 'What does this mean?' she asked.

He gave her a smile of great sweetness. 'That's for you to decide,' he said.

Beatrice took off Joseph's ring for the first time in forty years and put it on her right hand. Taking Albert's ring she put it on her wedding-finger. Albert raised the hand to his lips and kissed it. 'I think it's time that we went in to see the family,' he said.

Chapter Forty-One

'Miriam, will you sit down,' said Alec, pulling her towards the armchair. 'You've been on the go all day.'

'I know, love. I just feel restless, that and heart-burn after the dinner. Mother was so ratty, I kept filling my mouth with food to stop myself from screaming at her.'

Alec laughed. 'I fancied emptying the trifle over her head. Old Albert doesn't know what he's taken on.'

'I think he does,' said Miriam, sinking into the chair and holding out her feet for Alec to take off her shoes. 'He knows her through and through.' She leaned forward and ruffled her husband's hair. 'It's so romantic, better than any book. Loving and waiting all that time.'

'All in a good cause. Albert was like a dog with two tails. I've never seen him so excited.'

'Poor Mother,' laughed Miriam, 'she's not very good at saying sorry, is she? But didn't she tuck into the pie, once we'd all calmed down?'

'This puts me in a funny position with Albert, when he and Ma get spliced. I'll have to call him Daddy.'

'I don't think so,' snorted Miriam. 'And what about me? My employer will be my father-in-law.'

'It was kind of Ma to take Rosie back with her. Give us our last night together.'

'Not that we'll be able to do much with it,' laughed Miriam, 'with me the size of a mountain.'

'It'll be good to sit up in bed with the lamp on and not talk in whispers all the time, with Rosie off the scene.'

'Funny,' said Miriam, kissing his neck, 'what we think marriage is going to be like and what it turns out to be.'

'Are you disappointed?'

'No, oh no. What I meant was you think of making love and sleeping together and having children but you can't know beforehand of all the tiny little things that make it up.'

'Tell, tell me,' he said, kneeling in front of her holding her feet in his hands.

'Well, I didn't realise that every couple do things differently and that between you, you invent your life together. Like, for instance, you said we must get Rosie to sleep in her own bed. Our bed belongs to us. We sort out the money and you have your bit set aside for smokes and I have my few coppers that are mine alone, having our own teacup and lots of things.'

'Me reading the paper first and you having a lay-in on Sundays.'

She nodded. 'It's like we weave a cloth between us made up of different threads, workaday wool and Sunday silk, sadness, disappointment, peacefulness and passion. And it armours us and gives us courage.'

'What a wise little bird you are,' he said. 'Let me take you off to bed and cuddle you.' He pulled her to her feet and stood with his arms about her nuzzling his face into her neck.

'This might be my last few months away,' he said. 'With a bit of luck I should get drafted in September and serve my last eighteen months in my home port.'

'What – in the dockyard just down the street?'

'I hope so. They're bringing in courses, now, for men leaving the service, things like bricklaying and even driving and vehicle maintenance.'

'So you could end up driving a taxi, like the one that took Mother out the other day?'

'No. I was thinking of truck-driving, delivering beer for Brickwood's Brewery or something like that.'

Miriam chuckled. 'As long as you're not paid in booze. I wouldn't care what it was as long as you were home every evening.'

Alec nodded. 'With Ma and Albert getting married I shan't have to help her with money any more and I might even make Petty Officer before I finish. That would mean an extra few bob and then there's the half-a-crown a week the navy will allow you for the baby. The happy couple will probably move in here and we can go next-door to live.'

'What about Lily?'

'She's a young woman. I think she'll go with Ma until some likely lad takes her fancy.'

'They already have,' said Miriam. 'Didn't you see the way Michael was looking at her the other day?'

'My little girl, growing up before my eyes,' Alec said. Miriam yawned. 'You go along to bed and I'll make the cocoa.'

'I'll have a cup of hot water and bicarb. I'm still suffering from being a pig at dinner-time.'

Once in bed, Miriam tossed and turned, unable to find a comfortable position. She would be glad when the pregnancy was over and she could have her body to herself. Not that she had felt any movements in the last few hours. How long had it been, now? She began to feel anxious. Why had it stopped moving? She tried to cast her mind back to when she was having Rosie. What had Nurse Boyden said? 'They quieten down in the last twenty-four hours or so. The head is in position and they're getting ready for the off.'

Tomorrow would be May the third, over two weeks before her expected date, although even then Nurse Clifford had said that May the twentieth was only a rough guide. 'It could be two weeks either side, Mrs Forrest. There's still a lot of mystery attached to childbirth. Nature will decide, regardless of our calculations.' It would be lovely for Alec to see his new son or daughter before he went back to Scotland but it wasn't very likely.

It was no good, she would have to get up and go to the lavatory. Carefully she slid off the side of the bed and searched with her toes in the dark for her shoes. Alec was sound asleep and he had a tiring journey ahead of him tomorrow.

Coming back from the yard she felt some vague niggling pains, but put them down to the busyness of her day. She decided to heat some milk and sit in the armchair for a while. The clock struck midnight. If she was lucky the warm drink might settle her off to sleep again.

Although it would be a relief to have the baby early it would be better to hang on for a few weeks until Auntie Florrie managed to get down from Devon. She had promised to stay for a month and Ethel Rowan had offered her a bed in her house. It seemed a lifetime since Miriam had last seen her aunt. So much had happened in the time between. She could remember standing on the ferry going to Gosport waving to Florrie through her tears. How lonely and frightened she had been, and how ignorant.

As her first pregnancy had drawn to an end she had been terrified of what lay before her. She had stood in the little kitchen in Frobisher Row her teeth chattering with fright, praying for Nurse Boyden to appear.

Now she was healthy, strong and happy, surrounded by her family with nothing to fear. Joseph or Daisy would appear in their own good time after a lot of hard work on her part and some assistance, she hoped, from Nurse Clifford.

She drowsed uneasily in the armchair, startled into wakefulness by a cat yowling in the yard.

When she had struggled to her feet she became aware of a nagging pain in her back. She felt along the mantelpiece for the matches and lit one, holding it in front of the face of the clock. Two a.m. This could be the baby or simply the awkward position in which she'd fallen asleep. She felt excited. Putting the kettle on the range she pondered whether to wake him yet. She'd been hours having Rosie, but everyone said the second one would be quicker. The pain in her back was no imagination. Perhaps a cup of tea and a stroll about for a bit.

'Alec, I think the baby's started.'

'Jesus! Are you sure?'

Miriam clenched her teeth as her belly was gripped in a spasm of pain. 'Yes, yes, Alec. This is it.'

'Right, right, right.' Rubbing his eyes, Alec got out of bed and began dragging on his trousers.

'Where's the midwife live? Shall I get Gran in here?'

'Fourteen Bishop Street. No, don't fetch Mother, that'll wake up Rosie as well. Can you get Lily? She'll be able to stay with me till you return. Love, you've got your boots on the wrong feet.'

'I'll just get Lily, then I'll be on my way.'

Mirry stood rubbing her back, her mind racing. There was a timid tap on the bedroom door. 'Miriam, are you all right?'

'Come in,' she called.

Fully dressed, Lily popped her head around the door. 'If you could heave that cardboard box out from under the bed, we can begin to get things

475

ready,' Miriam told her calmly.

'You sure it's me you want and not Gran?' Lily's dark eyes were wide with alarm.

'Listen to me,' said Miriam firmly, 'I'm having a baby. I'm a healthy woman and it's on its way whether we're ready or not. There's every chance that Nurse Clifford will be here any minute.' She gripped Lily's arm as another wave of pain broke over her. 'Just do as I say and we'll be fine.' The confidence in Miriam's voice seemed to calm Lily.

'While I walk about a bit, you cover the mattress with the mackintosh and put that old patched sheet over the top. Now, go and fill the kettle and while it's boiling bring in some soap and a nailbrush, oh and a towel, for when the nurse gets here.'

Miriam lay panting on the bed. She wondered whether to have Lily bring in the clock so that they could time the contractions, but decided against it. Timing wouldn't make any difference – Joseph Andrew was on his way.

'That's it Lily, put it all on the dressing-table.' She took hold of her stepdaughter's hand. 'Listen, love, you're going to be the first one to see your new brother or sister. The first person Joseph or Daisy sets eyes on.'

'Are you frightened?' Lily asked.

'No,' gasped Miriam as another contraction followed quickly on the last one. 'Just help me to sit up and rub my back. Wh, wh, wh,' she panted. The next pain brought a rush of warm fluid. 'Huhhh, the waters have broken.'

'What does that mean?' asked Lily, nervously.

'The baby floats in a bag of water and when it's time for the birth the water flows out to leave room for him to push his way out.'

'D'you want me to change the bed?'

'Lily, quickly wash your hands and scrub the nails. Get a dry towel and put it down between my legs. Can you wipe my face over with the flannel?' Miriam grunted as she was overtaken by an overpowering desire to push. 'No, bed's no good.' She clambered onto the floor and squatted on the mat by the empty fireplace. 'Quick, quick, in front of me.' Miriam looked into Lily's anxious eyes, trying to encourage her. 'Babies are hard work,' she gasped. 'Put the towel on the mat. Ah, ah, aaah, it's coming. Can you see him?'

'Yes, oh, yes. I've got its head and shoulders. It's stopped coming. No, yes I've got all of him. Oh, Mirry, it's a boy.' The baby gave an outraged wail.

Miriam lay down on the floor and signalled Lily to put the baby on her stomach. 'There's a little sheet in the box, cover him over.' She leant up on her elbow and looked at her baby son. 'Hello, little Joseph,' she crooned. 'What a surprise you are, coming so early.'

Lily was crying as she covered him in the sheet. 'He's wonderful, Mirry. Oh, I'm so excited. What do we do next? He's still joined to you. What do I do about the cord?'

'We'll worry about that in a minute. I thought I heard someone in the street, it's probably the nurse. Come here,' she said. 'Give me a kiss. Lily, you were wonderful.' Then they were both crying so hard they didn't hear the footsteps in the hall.

It was Nurse Clifford and a distraught Alec. 'It looks as if you've started without me,' she said, smiling at Miriam and Lily. 'Mr Forrest, make sure the kettle is on and send it in to me when it's boiled. Young lady, you had better find something for your brother to sleep in.'

'Mirry, love, Oh Mirry are you all right?' said Alec kneeling beside her and kissing her damp forehead. 'And the little one? I tore around to Bishop Street but...'

'Alec, just go and get the water for Nurse. I'll see you when we're both prettied up. Lily,' she said drowsily, 'there's blankets and baby clothes in a case by the hallstand. He'll have to go in a drawer for the moment.'

'Rather taken you by surprise,' said Nurse Clifford, rolling up her sleeves.

'Joseph Andrew, eight pounds five ounces. Arrived at five o'clock on Monday the third of May 1920,' said Alec much later on in the morning when Nurse Clifford had set mother and son to rights, and an exhausted but elated Lily had gone back home for a sleep. He turned to Beattie and Albert standing beaming in the doorway. 'You two old-timers missed all the fun.'

'And so did you by the sound of it,' laughed Beattie. 'Chasing around from one street to the next.'

'Poor Nurse Clifford – she had four babies last night,' laughed Miriam, holding out her arms for her son. 'But Lily did wonders.'

'She's tucked up with Rosie, says she'll be over later. Now let's have a look at Master Forrest. Long fingers like his dad,' Beattie pronounced, 'and neat little ears. But I think he's going to have your blond hair by the little thatch I can see so far. There's something of Andrew but I don't know yet what it is. It'll come to me.'

'I'll go and get the port,' said Albert. 'This calls for a celebration.'

'I'll fetch the glasses,' said Beattie, following Albert out of the door.

Miriam lay back on her pillows in a haze of happiness. Joseph Andrew gazed at his mother out of milky blue eyes.

Alec lay on the top of the bed beside her. He stroked his son's downy head. 'I'd give anything to stay at home,' he said. 'I shall miss you both so much. He'll be so changed by the summer.'

'So will I,' laughed Miriam.

'To Joseph Andrew,' all four of them said, raising their glasses.

'I'll cook you a good breakfast,' said Beattie to Alec. 'Set you up for the journey.'

'Can I have one, too, Mother?' said Miriam. 'I'm starving.'

Beattie laughed. 'What's a trip in a train compared to all your hard work?'

'Come in!' they called at the impatient tap on the door.

Rosie bounded in with Lily close behind. 'What's in that blanket?'

'It's your baby brother,' said Alec, sweeping her up into his arms and carrying her across to Miriam.

Rosie stared at Joseph Andrew for some minutes without speaking. 'Put him in my dolly pram?' she asked.

'We'll put him in the drawer,' said Miriam, handing him to Lily. 'Now who's going to give her Mummy a cuddle?'

After they had breakfasted royally on bacon, eggs and fried bread Alec chased all the visitors from the room. 'I want a few minutes with my wife and son before I have to leave,' he insisted. 'I'm in a daze,' he said, 'I'm so happy.'

'Come and lie beside me on top of the bed,' Miriam said, holding out her arms to him.

Before joining her he knelt beside the dressing-table drawer and kissed his small son.

Miriam leant into the shelter of Alec's arms. 'I think I shall sleep for a week,' she said, drowsily.

Alec kissed her. 'Doesn't it seem a lifetime ago? When I walked into the Captain Hardy and you smiled at me?'

Miriam turned and kissed her husband. 'Another world,' she said.

Chapter Forty-Two

Since their meeting at the Easter Fair life had galloped apace for Lily and Michael. He had returned to his ship and they had showered each other with letters, exchanging news about the birth of Joseph Andrew, the tedium of life in Scapa Flow and the amazing change in their feelings for one another.

'It's strange and wonderful how I have come to love you more and more,' wrote Michael. 'I remember you as Andrew's sister, as someone in the background as he and I nattered together of this and that. And then when we met up just after Jutland I just knew how bitter your disappointment was at losing out on your scholarship.

'Afterwards I thought how at ease I had felt talking with you. But I think it was Granny Dowell's monkey that really brought us closer. Then at the fair you looked so bright and beautiful I fell in love there and then.'

Seeing her reading the letter for the umpteenth time Gran laughed and said, 'You'll wear the words off the page with looking, my girl.'

Laughing too, Lily ran up the stairs into her bedroom. She pulled out her box of notepaper and envelopes from under the bed and began another letter.

Time seemed to have slowed to a crawl and Lily began to feel that May the twenty-ninth would never come. She envied Dora with Harry at home all the time.

'It's not all paradise, I can tell you,' Dora said. 'Got to share him with his dad and his brothers and sisters. Then when I gets home my Dad starts on me.

'"How you going to cope with all them kids?" he says. "That father of theirs ought to show more responsibility".'

'How *are* you going to cope, though?'

'I don't know, Lily and that's the honest truth. Still, it'll be three years or so before I'll have to try, won't it? By that time Mary could be away in service, their Mum might 'ave got her head seen to, the twins will be twelve and Blyth'll be a schoolboy.'

Lily tried to sound encouraging. 'All sorts of things could happen and you'll have Harry to help you.'

'They're good-hearted kids, you know, and I am getting fond of them.' She shrugged. 'If I want Harry, Fred and the kids come too. And I want Harry more than anything.'

Another slow week passed and then it was Saturday. Lily sat after breakfast willing the hands of the clock to hurry themselves. 'I hate waiting,' she moaned.

'Well you'll have to change your tune if you've fallen for a sailor,' said Gran, taking the dishes to the sink.

'But Michael's so kind and writes such lovely letters and Gran–'

'What time does his train get in?'

'Three o'clock, hours away.'

'Right,' said Gran, 'you can clear away the dishes, wash over the kitchen floor, take my collars to Goldstein's and bring us back some corned beef from Liptons. When you get back you can peel some spuds and lay the table.'

'Didn't you hate waiting?' Lily asked, as she put the bread back in the bin and folded up the tablecloth.

'Yes, I always have,' said Gran as she swished some soda into the sink. 'When I first met your Grandad I felt as if every nerve and muscle and fibre in me came alive. When he was away from me I just existed, counting the hours and days till I saw him again. When I knew he was coming

482

back,' she laughed softly, 'my whole body was expectant. I was like a clock and it was your Grandad that set me ticking.'

'But how could you bear him being away so long?'

'It's wonderful what you acclimatise yourself to when there's no alternative,' she said. 'Paper lives, we called it. We poured out our hearts to each other in our letters as well as putting down the little day-to-day bits of living.' She looked at Lily as if she wanted her to mark what she was about to say. 'That's what makes us survivors, us women. Having to overcome things that you can't change. Like you having to accept you weren't Daddy's princess any more. Making friends with Miriam and not panicking when the midwife was late. You're growing up, my duck, and I'm proud of you.'

Lily flung her arms around her grandmother and hugged her tightly. 'Oh, Gran I do love you.'

'We're blessed to have each other,' said Gran kissing her cheek. 'Now you get cracking and I'll go and see my grandchildren.'

Imperceptibly the time passed and she was at the station with the hissing, steaming engine slowing to a stop. At first, there was just a mass of sailors pouring out of the train and families sweeping them up and away.

Then she saw him closing a carriage door before dragging his kit-bag onto the platform. She picked him out by his cap-ribbon: HMS *Lister*. From a distance he was an anonymous young sailor. But standing there smiling at her, holding out his arms, he was her Michael, tall and skinny with the loving face. She ran towards him. They held each other closely, wordlessly, for several moments then he swung her round and round. 'Good to see you, Lily. I feel as if I've been in that train for ever.'

'Let's walk back through the park. I want you to myself before anyone else can claim you.' She took his arm. 'It's been such a long time since I've looked at you.'

'Have I changed?' he asked.

Lily studied him carefully. The same tall grace and curious greeny-brown eyes but his skin looked more tanned than she remembered. 'I think you must have been lying out in the sun,' she teased.

He gave a shout of laughter 'What! In Scapa?'

'Let's go over to the little pagoda,' she said. 'I want to introduce you to my Grandad.' She guided his fingers over the raised letters of the name: 'PO J. Forrest.' They stood together with her hand partially covering his, then she laced their fingers together bending hers over and pressing them into his palm, looking at the engine-oil under his nails. 'I want to know your hands,' she said, 'every detail, all the lines and veins and tendons, all the little patches of roughened skin, so I can picture them when you're away from me.'

'Your letters bring you close,' he said. 'I read them over and over especially the one about the baby. How is he?'

'He's just wonderful. Blond and blue-eyed and every day there's another tiny, tiny change. My Dad wrote to me saying how proud he was of me

484

and how birth is like a miracle.' She released his fingers and held her arms around herself as if hugging a secret. 'It is, you know, Michael. Even though I knew Miriam was carrying a baby, that it was alive, all folded neatly inside, it wasn't real to me. And then when he appeared, all pink and wailing, I was just speechless at the wonder of it.'

'You're full of wonder,' Michael said, bending towards her and kissing her eager upraised face. 'That's why I love you.'

Regardless of all the children milling about, the old men reading their papers, the harassed mothers, they stood and kissed each other, again and again. 'I missed you so much,' Lily said as they finally drew apart.

Michael hitched his kit-bag on to his shoulder and they walked out of the park. 'I must go and see Mother and be with her for a while,' said Michael, almost apologetically. 'When I go off to the Far East she'll have no one. I'll call for you tomorrow about three.'

'But I–' she bit back her disappointment. 'Of course,' she said. 'I'll see you then.'

'Lily,' he said, 'I'm sorry, I want to be with you, too.'

She gave him a tepid smile and went indoors. It was a strange week. Instead of willing time forward she tried to hold it back, resenting every moment spent apart. They walked and talked, in the street, in the park and along the beach. One dinner-time he met her from work and they sat in Driver's Café eating bread pudding. 'Remember ages ago, when we had tea in here?' asked Michael.

'When I was in a rage with Gran because she couldn't afford to send me to Secondary School.' Lily nodded. 'It was so important to me but now?' she shrugged. 'It doesn't seem to matter.'

'You could say that was our first outing together,' Michael laughed as he cut the bread pudding into squares.

'What did you think of me then?' she asked, watching him closely as he replied.

'I admired your fierceness and wanted to hold you close and kiss you.'

She blushed with pleasure. 'I thought, I've never really noticed him before. Perhaps we're going to be friends. So much has happened since then, I feel as if I'm a different person.'

'What were the most important bits?' he asked.

'Oh, the war ending, starting work, meeting lots of new people.' She thought of Bernard, how desperately she had wanted him to notice her and how that attraction had turned to disgust. 'Falling out with Dad and Miriam and slowly, slowly getting over all the jealousy. Poor Lloyd dying, how he brought us together. And helping Joseph Andrew into the world.'

'It's a lot, isn't it?' he said. 'I've grown up too. Losing Dad and losing Arthur. I never wanted to join the navy. I'd wanted the dockyard appren-ticeship so much. But now, I'm on my way to being a leading hand. I enjoy being a torpedo man, there's lots of mathematics and mechanics and I enjoy that.' He looked at her apologetically, 'And, of course, seeing foreign places – Hong Kong, Singapore, China and Malaya. I wish I could take you with me.'

486

'You'll have to write and tell me everything about them and take lots of photographs.'

'We'll have three years to tell each other what we think and feel about everything under the sun.'

All at once it was the night before he sailed. Gran had gone out with Uncle Albert and they were sitting together in the kitchen.

'I've got you an early present,' he said, handing her a ribboned package. 'Happy Birthday for tomorrow, Lily.'

In all the passion and anxiety of the week her sixteenth birthday on Sunday had faded to the back of her mind. Eagerly she tore away the paper. Inside was a black Waterman's fountain-pen with a gold nib.

'So there'll be no excuse for not writing,' he said.

'It's a lovely, lovely present,' she said. 'I shall only use it for writing to you.'

Michael held her face between his hands and kissed her. 'Happy Birthday, Lily.'

'It's all running away from us,' she said angrily. 'After tonight it'll be ages and ages till we're together again. Writing's not touching, Michael.'

He drew her onto his lap and she clung to him, covering his face with kisses.

'I've got to go,' he said, trying to get up from the chair. 'Please, Lily, don't make it so hard for me.' They were almost fighting. 'No, don't cry, Lily, I can't.' He stared unhappily at the floor. 'Look, tomorrow, you could come into the dock-yard with my mother and wave from Farewell

487

Jetty with all the other families.'

'I don't want to share you with all those people.'

'Well, don't spoil these last minutes on our own, then,' he pleaded. 'I want to carry your smile with me.' Lily swallowed hard and blinked the tears away.

'I must go,' he said, still holding her hand. At the front door he turned and kissed her lingeringly before opening it and walking away.

'Come home safe,' she cried. He nodded but did not turn to look at her.

Lily closed the door and rushed up the stairs, flinging herself on to the bed in a storm of weeping. Their last night and she'd spoilt it. His last memory would be of her being bad-tempered and clinging. She got herself ready for bed unable to face Gran again that night. After hours of tossing and turning in the darkness she awoke the next morning, weary and tearful.

'Happy Birthday, my duck,' said Gran as she trailed into the kitchen. 'There's your cards and presents on the table. Miriam and the children will be in soon to see you.'

'I can't face them,' she said, flinging herself into Gran's arms.

'You go out to the sink and have yourself a good hot wash and you'll feel brighter. Come on, now Lily, you can't spend your whole birthday in tears.'

'I spoilt it,' she wailed. 'Michael's last night and I was all scratchy and bad-tempered.'

'Well, you'll be able to write and tell him you're sorry, won't you.'

'He asked me to go to Farewell Jetty with his mother and wave goodbye but I said I didn't want to share him with all the other people.'

'You've robbed yourself of another chance to see him and now you're sorry?'

Lily nodded.

'You could still get dressed and run down there but it's after nine now, they'll all have gone aboard.'

'No, I'll leave it now.'

'Go and brighten yourself up, Lily. It'll all come right in the end.' Lily pressed the hot flannel to her face and tried to calm herself. Why, why had she spoilt it all?

'What would you like for breakfast? There's a couple of rashers or how about some gypsy toast?'

'Gypsy toast,' she said, leaving Gran to dip the bread in the beaten egg and fry it, while she went upstairs to dress.

'Birthday, birthday,' said Rosie, leaping at her from the back door. Lily hugged her little sister, kissed the top of the baby's head, and Miriam's cheek before sitting at the table. Gran set the plate of toast in front of her. 'Rosie like toast,' said the little girl wistfully. Laughing, Gran set up a place for her at the table.

I can't believe I'm eating and talking and smiling, Lily thought. I want to scream and shout. I want to have last night back and be warm and loving and say goodbye to Michael with a smile.

'Open present,' demanded Rosie.

Lily unfolded the tissue-paper and found a soft

489

green triangular scarf with a long silky fringe. 'That's lovely, oh, thank you,' she said getting up and kissing them both, before draping it around her shoulders.

'What plans have you got for the day?' said Gran to Miriam as she took Joseph into her arms and stood cooing at him.

'Thought we might spend the day up on the beach by Sally Port,' Miriam said. 'I'll take some sandwiches. We don't have to rush back. Uncle Albert's in Romsey. We can wave to the ships as they go out.'

'Lily coming?' asked Rosie. The question hung in the air as Lily held out her arms and Gran handed the baby to her. She held him close and kissed his cheek. Joseph put out a tiny pink tongue and licked his lips.

'Why don't we all go,' said Gran, 'and make it a birthday picnic?' She turned to Lily. 'You could wave your new scarf as Michael goes by.'

'But I won't know which one he is,' she said doubtfully. 'They'll all be up on deck together. He won't know I'm there.'

'But you'll know,' said Gran, putting her hand on her shoulder, 'and you can write and tell him. Besides, what else are you going to do all day but moon about feeling sorry for yourself.'

Lily hugged Joseph, drawing in his scent of milk and newness. 'All right,' she said, forcing a smile.

'Right, action stations, everyone,' said Gran. 'Lily, you wash up and clear away. I'll knock up some sandwiches and you get your things, Miriam. We'll set off in about an hour.'

Reluctantly Lily handed Joseph to Miriam and

set about her tasks. 'I'll open the rest of the presents when we get back and the cards.'

'Good idea,' said Gran, 'and we'll save the cake for then. I can't see us lighting candles on the beach. They'd be blown out in no time.'

By eleven o'clock, they had loaded the pram and set off for Old Portsmouth. Lily had a twinge of unease as they passed Michael's house but she swallowed it down. Taking Rosie's hand they swung along with Gran and Beattie following with the pram.

'If these stones could talk,' said Gran as they walked up the High Street towards the beach. 'There's the house where the Duke of Buckingham was killed, the George Hotel, where Nelson had his last breakfast.'

'Bet it wasn't gypsy toast,' laughed Lily, beginning to feel almost happy.

'What crowds of people have passed down this street to the sea,' Gran continued. 'Admirals, trollops, pickpockets, poor sailors' wives waiting for the glimpse of a sail and the hopes of some money, let alone a husband.'

They passed the square tower and walked through the Sally Port archway and down the wooden steps to the beach. Lily helped Miriam lift the pram onto the shingle.

'I wonder if Emma Hamilton was waving from her carriage,' said Gran, 'as old Horatio was getting into his boat and being rowed out to the *Victory?*'

Scattered along the beach were groups of day trippers with parasols and binoculars, soldiers from the nearby Point Barracks, and little knots of women and children constantly turning their gaze towards the harbour.

'Wish we could climb up inside the Round Tower and stand up on top and wave,' said Lily, looking at the stout building around which HMS *Lister* would hopefully soon pass.

'I think our Commanding Officer would have something to say about that,' said one of the soldiers. Lily blushed.

As Gran and Miriam spread out an old blanket and settled themselves on it, a shout went up as a grey cruiser came into view. Families rushed to the water's edge, waving and shouting.

'Is that the *Lister?*' asked Miriam, shading her eyes.

'No,' said Gran, squinting into the sun. 'That's a cruiser, it's much too big.'

'Who you looking for?' asked a man with binoculars.

'HMS *Lister,*' said Lily, looking towards the harbour.

'She'll be here in a few minutes.'

'Rosie, come down to the water with me,' said Lily, holding out her hand. The little girl ran to her. Before going down the beach Lily took her green scarf out of her bag. Together they crunched over the shingle to the edge of the sea. Rosie giggled as the water lapped at her boots then threw in handfuls of stones.

'Here she comes,' cried the man with the binoculars.

HMS *Lister* rounded the tower, its upper deck lined with sailors standing at ease. People rushed down the beach.

'Michael,' called Lily, waving the shawl back and forth, her eyes straining to distinguish one sailor from another. 'Michael! Michael!' she cried, a great surge of grief washing over her. Michael, she prayed, please, please, be safe.

'Michael,' cried Rosie, tugging at her hand.

And then – so quickly she could never be sure afterwards that it had really happened – one of the sailors took off his cap and then replaced it quickly on his head. Please, please, let it be Michael signalling that he had seen her. 'Michael, Michael!' she shouted.

As the ship moved past the beach and out into the Solent it created a wash which swept up the stones, covering Lily's shoes. Still she waved until it disappeared. Holding Rosie's hand she walked back up the beach to Beattie and Miriam.

June the fifth 1920. I'll never forget this day, she thought. Four years ago Andrew's telegram stole my twelfth birthday. Now on my sixteenth I'm waving goodbye to Michael. Much had happened in the years between. Laughter, tears and oceans of waiting. She looked down the beach at the women waiting to wave to the next ship rounding the tower. What will have happened to all of us, she wondered, by the time our ships return?

The publishers hope that this book has given you enjoyable reading. Large Print Books are especially designed to be as easy to see and hold as possible. If you wish a complete list of our books please ask at your local library or write directly to:

Magna Large Print Books
Magna House, Long Preston,
Skipton, North Yorkshire.
BD23 4ND